ANGEL IN TOBAGO

By the same author

Writing as Timothy Edward
Lessons in Humiliation

The Slave to Beauty Trilogy
Body Language
Love Knot
Casting Couch

Bartholomew expertly weaves themes of faith, morality, and redemption into this engaging narrative. Gabriel's struggle to come to terms with his identity and purpose is mirrored in his interactions with those around him revealing the thrills of family dynamics and the power of forgiveness. Bartholomew's writing is descriptive and evocative, conjuring vivid images and the cultural settings of post-colonial Tobago. The plot is engaging and unpredictable, a gorgeous novel spiced with humor, a page-turner with lovable characters, and a setting that absorbs readers. It is an intelligently accomplished literary fiction with an unforgettable hero and writing that feels like music to the ears. The perfect escape into the sun-kissed shores of Tobago.

– *The Book Commentary*

A witty, thought-provoking thriller that brings the sights and sounds of Tobago stunningly to life – from the island's dazzling bird life and beautiful coastline to its ecological and political dilemmas.

– *Emma Lee-Potter*

ANGEL IN TOBAGO

TIM BARTHOLOMEW

Published in 2024 by Lidham Press

Copyright © Tim Bartholomew 2024

Tim Bartholomew has asserted his right to be identified as the author of this Work in accordance with the Copyright, Designs and Patents Act 1988

*ISBN Paperback: 978-1-0685358-0-2
Ebook: 978-1-0685358-1-9*

All rights reserved. No part of this publication may be reproduced, stored in a retrieval system, or transmitted in any form or by any means, electronic, mechanical, photocopying, recording or otherwise, without the prior permission of the copyright owner.

All characters and events in this publication, other than those clearly in the public domain, are fictitious and any resemblance to real persons, living or dead, is purely coincidental.

A CIP catalogue copy of this book can be found in the British Library.

*Front cover photograph - Julie ffrench - Dawn over Bloody Bay, Tobago
Back Cover photograph - Tim Bartholomew - a Trinidad Motmot*

For background and inspirational material, and photos of people and real-life locations, please go to angelintobago.com

*Published with the help of Indie Authors World
www.indieauthorsworld.com*

IndieAuthors
World

For Julie

Foreword by Faraaz Abdool

I first met Tim on the verandah of the Asa Wright Nature Centre in Trinidad in 2019, after conversing for months over Instagram on our shared passion for bird photography. A naturalist at heart with a genuine desire to not only learn more about the environment but also to save it from destruction, Tim and I immediately connected on a deeply personal level. Since then, we have spent countless hours together in the sweltering heat of tropical rainforests, patiently waiting for manakins and motmots to hop onto a desired branch. When apart, we never cease corresponding, his effusive personality doubtlessly essential in bridging the gap across oceans.

It must be said that Tim has fallen in love with the Caribbean twin-island nation of Trinidad & Tobago, and it is this love that has been a motivational force behind the penning of *Angel in Tobago* which has come perhaps at the most pertinent time possible. As if conjured by some prophetic wind, the novel expertly and precisely describes the goings-on leading up to scenes of a fictional planned hotel development on an unspoilt patch of Tobago's coastline. Eerily similar plans of which have since been frighteningly realized by the current administration.

Tim's ardent observation of every facet of Tobagonian life is most apparent throughout this book. Those familiar with the island will surely recognize both place and personality. Unknown to the author at the time of writing, *Angel in Tobago* is now destined to play a leading activist role for the very real situation of ecological murder currently unfolding at Rocky Point; indeed both for this and future iterations of hare-brained ideas of bulldozing pristine areas to replace trees with concrete on an idyllic tropical island.

Faraaz is a wildlife photographer, conservationist and writer in Trinidad and Tobago.
His website is faraazabdool.com

Prologue

'Ladies and gentlemen,' came the Captain's announcement, his delivery smooth and confident, 'welcome to Tobago where the local time is five thirty-three and the temperature a balmy twenty-nine degrees.'

My neighbour in the window seat was a pallid young man wearing a khaki vest, camouflage shorts and a green canvas belt with 'Riley B' inked onto it. He had spent the entire nine-hour journey from London cocooned in headphones beside me. As the plane came to a halt at the terminal building, he gave his tightly cropped scalp a good canine scratch, struggled to his feet and, using the seat backs as leverage, vaulted right over me long before the seatbelt sign was even extinguished. I watched him wrestle down his rucksack and merge with the throng of groggy passengers shuffling towards the exit. I tried smiling goodbye, but he was still avoiding eye-contact and so didn't notice.

I remembered my father lecturing me about being on the receiving end of this brand of entitled and evasive disdain. 'You might as well get used to it,' had been his advice. 'People can sometimes be frightened of what they're not used to: those whose difference they regard as a threat. But when push comes to shove – and I hope it never does – remember St. Luke Chapter 6: *And unto him that smiteth thee on the one cheek, offer also the other.*'

I slid into the vacated window seat and peered out. The rusting and engineless shell of some antediluvian airliner with square portholes lay abandoned in long grasses behind a helicopter, its rotors drooping sulkily in the heat. To the left, beyond a row of swaying palms near the end of the runway, the sun was sinking over a strip of sea which glittered like a tray of cut diamonds. The Caribbean. I was transfixed by the contrast between the Gatwick Grey I had left behind and this natural beauty rendered in so dazzling a palette of colours and light.

My phone had mysteriously adjusted itself to the new time zone, but my own body clock was completely out of sync. Could it still only be Friday, a mere four days after all this had kicked off? My heart thumping with anticipation, I rose from my seat, lifted my hand-luggage from the overhead locker and made my way stiffly towards the phalanx of weary flight attendants lined up at the forward door of the aircraft.

'Last but not least, sir,' said one, his face contorted into a rictus of a smile.

'Yes. Sorry.'

'Did you enjoy the flight with us today, sir?'

'Absolutely. Thanks so much.'

'Visiting relatives?'

'Er, no. Business, actually.'

'Have a nice day, sir.'

'And you.'

Shielding my eyes against the dazzling light, I stepped out into a blast of furnace-like heat, breaking into a sweat before I was even halfway down the staircase. Once on the baking concrete, I stopped to shed some layers. There was shouting a few yards ahead; Riley B was involved in an altercation with a tall, no-nonsense lady in a hi-vis jacket and a black suit with the slogan "Reset Expectations" embroidered on the sleeve. Bizarrely, she seemed to be requiring him to remove his shorts. Crouching to stuff my jacket into the top of my bag, I couldn't help but overhear: 'Camouflage clothin' any kind ban by law!' Riley B's face was a picture. 'Empty de pockets, fella, remove de belt an' give me de shorts or I have you arrested for impersonation of de military.' Cowed by the official, the poor lad hopped about first on one leg then the other until he was free of the offending garment. 'Now, keep movin'! Stay to de left of de cones an' no walkin' under de wing.' The woman swept an imperious arm upwards towards the mighty and still slowly rotating blades of the Rolls Royce engine.

I stood up, wiped my brow and braced myself to meet the fierce lady's glare. But her face had broken into a beatific smile. 'Take yuh time, bro,' she said, looking at me as she might an old friend. 'Life, he short, but de line, he long.' Winking at me, she rolled up Riley B's shorts and tucked them under her arm. I wondered who was to be the beneficiary of the garment. 'No problem.'

'Oh. Right.' Relaxing, I returned her smile. 'Thanks so much.'

Since there was now no rush, I took a moment to refold my jacket and zip it securely into my bag. Ahead squatted the A.N.R. Robinson Airport building painted the colour of pistachio icecream. Over the glass door to Arrivals hung an unfamiliar red flag with a black and white diagonal stripe, and from somewhere beyond came the steady *douf-douf-douf* of what sounded to my classically-educated ears like a blend of rap and pop music with a dollop of reggae thrown in. Before entering the building, I closed my eyes and inhaled a deep breath of the warm, salty breeze, the low sun scorching the back of my head. I was going to need a hat.

'You okay, bro?' My hi-vis friend had rematerialised beside me. She was eyeing me over her shades, enormous brown eyes dancing.

'Mm? Oh, absolutely.' I could become used to such cordiality.

'You here for Carnival?'

'Er, well—'

She handed me a crumpled flyer depicting a beautiful and vibrant female dancer costumed in feathers like some gorgeous fantasy butterfly. The model would have given Joseph (he of the Coat of Many Colours) a run for his money. I scanned the paper: *Fog Angels Welcome You to Sunny Tobago. For Best Jouvert, Book Online Today!*

I asked, 'What are *Fog Angels*?'

'We de best Carnival band on de island. Just head for de ChillOut Bar, ask for my brother Roots and say Maisha send you. He go give you best ticket price.'

'That's kind. When is Carnival, though?'

'Eh-ehh.' She peeled off her shades and looked me up and down. She could only have been a few years younger than me. 'Twenty-four February, bro. Eleven days. Everyone know dat.'

'Of course,' I muttered. 'I remember now. But unfortunately, I'll be back in England by then, God willing.'

'What you say? You come five thousand mile and you not stayin' for Carnival?'

'It's just a short visit. Family business, you know.'

She laughed aloud at this, a great bellow of infectious energy and joie-de-vivre which made me feel all warm inside. 'Have yourself a wonderful evenin', bro.' She was holding open the door for me. 'But what yuh name, so I tell my brother to expect yuh.'

Under the intensity of her smile I found myself momentarily at a loss. 'Gabriel,' I stammered. 'Gabriel Cassidy.'

'Good to meet you, Gabriel.'

'You too, er—' She had mentioned her name only a minute ago.

'Maisha.'

'Maisha, of course. Thanks so much.'

'Welcome to Paradise, Gabriel.' She chained the doors behind me.

1

It had been one of those cold, dank and grey Monday mornings when by ten fifteen I had achieved nothing but set off the washing machine, wave to the bin men and torpedo the uneasy truce that served as stony topsoil to my thirty-year marriage.

To give my wife her due, Sarah was a woman who devoted all her winter energies to the Whitsun Camp Steering Committee at our Church. Her frustration with me over breakfast had culminated in one of her habitual and melodramatic exits which had shaken the house to its Edwardian foundations and cracked a pane of stained glass adjacent to the front door. Today's infringement of our fragile domesticity had hinged upon my failure the night before to prepare her sandwiches. 'I gave you one job,' she'd snapped, banging the fridge door shut. '*You* might have the luxury of early retirement and mooching about the house all day, but me? —not so much!' And with the efficiency of a hangman, she'd looped a red woolly scarf round her neck, seized her handbag and jammed on her tortoiseshell driving glasses. 'I suppose I'll just have to stop at BP and pick up a meal-deal, won't I?'

'Look, darling, I'm sorry, but—'

'You really are the *limit*, Gabriel Cassidy. I'll see you tonight, God willing.'

I remember listening half-heartedly to the end of the *Today Programme* and then, having stowed my muesli bowl and coffee cup in the dishwasher, took a defiantly indolent mid-morning shower to the strains of my favourite Hans Zimmer played at full volume. Afterwards, revelling in my solitude, I wandered naked over to my bedroom window and peered in time-honoured suburban fashion between the net curtains.

Beyond the rectangular patch left in the driveway by Sarah's car, the bare and pollarded limes of south-east London raised lumpen fists skywards in impotent rebellion. Opposite, at Number 56, workmen in reflective jackets and hard-hats were emptying bags of rubble into a skip. A crisp packet blew in off the pavement and lodged itself in one of the leggy and leafless fuchsia bushes which Sarah said I was supposed to have pruned by now.

Out of habit, I picked up my phone and with sinking heart read "Missed call: Uncle Neville." 'What on earth can he want?' I muttered aloud, placing the gadget on a polished mahogany chest of drawers above which hung a faded sampler, a wedding present from Sarah's late Auntie Marianne. *Christ is the Head of this house*, it stated in dark green wool and without a shred of irony, *the Unseen Guest at every meal, the Silent Listener to every conversation.*

I permitted myself a wry smile and padded downstairs in dressing-gown, slippers and freshly laundered shirt in pastel blue. Uncle Neville could wait: I needed to start composing the exhortation I was booked to deliver at the Meeting on Sunday. As a Christadelphian of some three decades' standing, my duties as a Speaker were, if not exactly arduous, demanding enough to warrant my devoting considerable time each week to Bible study.

It must have been about minus fifty in the lounge that doubled as my office: I could see my own breath. Sarah had long ago primed the central heating system to turn itself off at eight-fifteen on weekdays, and reprogramming the digital touch-screen panel was quite beyond me without a YouTube seminar. I tugged the dressing-gown more tightly about me, grabbed the camera I always left by the bay window and took a couple of photos of a disconsolate blue tit at the feeder. Deleting them immediately as being altogether too drab and blotchy, I plonked myself down at my father's old desk and opened the Bible at John Chapter 1. I tried to marshal my thoughts. *In the beginning was the Word, and the Word was with God, and...* I shivered: surely it was coffee-time.

A loud iPhone jingle from my pocket made me jump: Neville again. My thumb hovered over the Dismiss button because for some reason I had a bad feeling about answering. I shut my eyes for a second: *Father, I pray you give me the strength to do what is right.* 'Hello, uncle.'

'Ha! So you deign to answer this time, do you, you blasted waste of space?' My elderly relative could be relied upon to give immediate offence to all who strayed within his orbit.

'And a very good morning to you too. To what do I owe this unexpected—?'

'Why didn't you bloody well call me back?'

'I was just—'

'I know, I know! You didn't dare defy wifey by communing with your Uncle Beelzebub!' Horrid laughter crackled across the ether. Surely he couldn't have been at the sauce already? 'How is the scrawny old bag, by the way? Still hard at it minding everyone else's business?'

'Uncle, I'd be grateful if you could moderate your—'

'Shut up with your mealy-mouthed bollocks, and listen.'

Sighing, I capitulated. 'I'm all ears.'

'Finally. Gabriel, I need you here pronto. Important matters of State to discuss.'

'Well, I'm rather tied up at the moment but maybe I could pop down at the end of the week. And of course, I'd have to discuss it with... check my diary.'

'Four o'clock suit you?'

'What? When?'

'Today, tosser! No time like the present.'

'But—'

'For Christ's sake, Gabriel, don't pretend you're busy. My spies have informed me about the sale of your sodding business for an absolute bloody fortune so you'll have time and money on your hands.'

'Uncle—'

'Don't want you sitting around on your arse all day twiddling your thumbs, do we? Time to rally round and make yourself useful for once!'

The line from Corinthians popped into my head: *But the greatest of these is Charity.* I capitulated for a second time. 'Well, I suppose so, if I must.'

'That's the ticket. There'll be a solicitor in attendance, so don't be late.'

Three hours later, I was – ever the dutiful nephew – heading south towards the quaint Wealden village of Ticehurst in East Sussex. I loved my new Toyota Hybrid and was soothed by the hum of its eco-friendly motor and the swish of its windscreen wipers making light work of the pouring rain. I had never dreamt of being able to afford such a space-age-looking car, but after the sale of Hillcrest Insurance Brokers even Sarah had agreed we might break the habit of a lifetime and allow ourselves this one extravagance.

How pleased I'd been when the suits from Homewise.com turned up at my offices to gauge the financial potential of the business. They consumed vast quantities of coffee and biscuits, scanned my hard-won client list and then swallowed me up like some vast tropical snake devouring a be-ribboned kitten. This admittedly lucrative transaction allowed Sarah to throw in the towel as a veterinary assistant, but when I suggested a celebratory world cruise she shouted me down with a 'Don't be ridiculous, Gabriel: you know I hate the heat!' and instead redoubled her efforts with good works various for our Church. For a while I wallowed in my new-found earthly freedom, pottering in the garden, dithering about whether I should employ someone to repaint the stairwell in matt "Misty Mushroom" or "Freshly Morning" and avoiding speaking to anyone unfortunate enough to have twelve or fifteen more years before them chained to a desk.

But the honeymoon period had lasted only a few weeks and, with irritating accuracy, my irascible old uncle had in one short phone-call that morning put his finger on the nub of the matter: that after a lifetime of daily routine, diligence and responsibility, sitting around at home avoiding mundane tasks and stroking an invisible, intangible nest-egg was proving no substitute for having some actual purpose in life.

It had long been a source of ironic amusement to me that it was badly behaved Uncle Neville who had been cast as the black sheep of the Cassidy family. Despite this, though, in my role as dutiful nephew, I had in the old days persuaded Sarah to accompany me on the occasional visit to check up on the cantankerous old boy. She had however drawn the line under this arrangement after an incident at Neville's seventieth birthday party eleven years ago when he had – somewhat the worse for wear even then – slapped the behind of one of the female catering staff. Outraged, the poor girl had ditched a tray-load of fondant fancies into my uncle's lap and it had been as much as I could do to persuade her not to press charges. Sarah made it clear to me that she wished never to set eyes on Neville again and so, in deference to her, I had reduced any contact with him to a Christmas card and the occasional phone call.

In a downpour at Flimwell I turned right and crept the last three miles to Ticehurst behind a tractor hauling a dripping trailer full of manure. With three minutes to spare, I crunched to a halt on the potholed driveway of the wisteria-clad Georgian pile, formerly *The Old Vicarage* and then renamed by my smutty-minded uncle *Badger's End* when he inherited the place from my grandparents in the 'eighties. Putting up my umbrella and dodging puddles, I ran for the steps. The door was opened by a dumpy and cross-looking nurse labelled "Mabel". She wore thick spectacles, a white Care Company uniform and, although the Covid pandemic was now but a distant memory, a double-layered disposable blue face mask and latex gloves. 'Yes? How can I help you?' she enquired. I couldn't tell whether or not she was smiling, but her oddly conspiratorial manner unnerved me.

'Hi, sorry. I think my uncle's expecting me.'

'Oh, you is Mr. Gabriel? I didn't know you was...' she hesitated just a moment too long, '...goin' to be here so soon. Not in dis weather.' I couldn't place her accent. Not Jamaican, but definitely West Indian. 'Please come in.'

'Thanks so much.'

She handed me a fresh mask from a packet on the sideboard and, ever compliant in the presence of a member of the nursing profession, I looped it round my ears. At least, I thought, wearing a mask would limit inhalation of the musty aroma of moth-eaten upholstery, dyspeptic uncle and antiseptic.

'Is everything okay with him?' I asked, instinctively straightening a trio of brightly coloured prints of Caribbean scenes hanging by the kitchen door. 'He seemed pretty agitated on the phone.'

Mabel lowered her voice to a tone befitting a crematorium chapel. 'Oh, he doin' fine, bless him. He a bit up and dong today, so I give him sometin' to cool his herbs.'

'Oh, rightoh.'

Standing on the threshold of the drawing room I saw the vast and sagging Chesterfield sofa had been heaved against the wall to make space for an ugly metal-framed wheelchair. This contained the shockingly diminished form of my uncle. He was hunched before the fire with his back to me, shoulders bony and narrow and that once cruel-sea mop of hair reduced to a few wayward wisps combed over a yellowish, liver-spotted scalp.

Mabel moved aside a Zimmer frame and beckoned me in. 'We pretty well today, not so, Mr. Neville?' she enunciated. 'We bin lookin' forward to seein' our nephew.' There was a lengthy pause during which the old man did not stir. He seemed particularly comatose considering how venomous he had been only a few hours ago. Mabel gently shook his shoulder. 'Mr. Neville, you sleepin'?'

With a sudden whistling intake of breath, my uncle jolted upright. He spun round and slammed an almost translucent hand down on an adjustable Formica side-table. Orange squash slopped over the untouched *Daily Telegraph* crossword. 'Christ's sakes, woman,' he screeched, 'stop bloody patronising me!' His profanities struck me an almost physical blow. 'I'm not a complete gibbering idiot! Not yet! Just make with that tea, can't you? – Earl bloody Grey and not that builders' muck you served up yesterday!'

I was horrified at his tone and, above the mask, Mabel widened her eyes for my benefit. 'Sure ting, Mr. Neville.' She walked slowly to the door and closed it behind her.

I shuffled off my Parker, the heat being tropical. Sarah would have had views. 'Uncle. Hello.'

With a snarl of impatience, Neville ferreted out a silver hip-flask from the inner pocket of his smoking-jacket, unscrewed the top and put it to his lips. 'Don't lurk in the shadows, boy. Come here where I can see you!' He seemed perfectly lucid once more.

I reached for his hand and squeezed it. His skin was warm and papery to the touch, almost translucent; dark purple stains of bruising mottled his wrist. 'You're looking well,' I lied, offering up a silent prayer both for forgiveness and protection.

'You mean I'm looking ready for the blasted pickle jar, you serpent-tongued hypocrite!' Although it was a matter of some regret for Sarah that Neville was leaving his body to a London teaching hospital, I hoped that someone would maybe discover and eradicate the strain of DNA at the root of the man's unseemly behaviour and bad language. 'And take that bloody mask off so I can see your ugly mug.' I peeled the thing from my face and used it to wipe away the film of moisture that had gathered on my upper lip. Neville reached out and prodded me in the midriff. 'Good God, boy, you're all skin and bones. That harpy not feeding you?'

'We try to eat sensibly.'

Neville winced, shifting in his seat. 'Christ alive, my bastard back hurts.'

'Please, uncle!'

He wagged a finger at me, blue eyes alive with mischief. I braced myself. 'Listen, you smug and judgmental little sod,' he began, 'don't take that tone with me. You may be a big cheese in Philadelphian circles, but this my house – so my rules apply.'

'As you are aware, uncle, I am a Christadelphian, and as much as it might irk you, we aspire to live cleanly whilst eschewing bad language, immorality and blasphemy. We are nothing to do with either Pennsylvania or soft cream cheese.'

Ignoring me, he tinkled a small brass bell used in the old days for summoning servants. A door to my right opened. 'Gabriel, behold our family solicitor!' The newcomer beamed at me. 'D'you recognise the bugger?'

'Goodness!' I stared at this vision from the past. 'Max Gibson! I've not set eyes on you since university.'

'The Angel Gabriel as I live and breathe!' Max stepped forward, hand extended. He seemed taller, or maybe I'd shrunk. Freckled and ruddy-complexioned in a tight grey suit and pink tie, he looked pretty much the same muscular lad-about-town I remembered.

'I should watch out, Gibson,' cackled Neville, his bushy white eyebrows arched, 'for the Lord permitteth not his loyal adherents to be addressed in terms of such flippancy. Biblical satire is orff-limits.'

I mustered a smile. 'It's true, Max, no one's called me Angel for years. But you look like you've done pretty well for yourself.'

'Absolutely, Ange.' He handed me a card. 'Gibson, Gibson and Mitchell, Solicitors to the Great and the Good. Just taken over from the old man.'

Neville piped up, 'Gibson *Père* looked after my affairs for nearly forty years.'

I glanced up at my old friend. 'Listen, maybe we can talk later?'

'Defo, Ange. You can stand me a drink or three. It'll be good to catch up.' The abbreviation of my university nickname had ignited a flash of nostalgia: the two of us swilling pints of subsidised lager in the smoky, beer-sticky surrounds of the student union bar. Happy days.

Neville coughed with impatience. 'Right, let's get on with it.' He jerked a thumb over his shoulder. 'Gabriel, see that photo on the corner cabinet?'

'Yup.'

'Bung it over to Gibson.'

I was familiar with the sepia picture. It showed a large white Caribbean house with tall windows, corrugated roofing and a louvred central tower. Luxuriant vegetation hemmed it in on all sides. At the foot of a double staircase from the first-floor balcony were posed twenty or so members of the estate's work-force in their Sunday best. Above them, leaning over the balustrade, a young white couple in matching colonial suits. I passed the photo to Max.

Neville tutted. 'Sit down, lads, for God's sake. You're making the place look untidy.' I sank into a dilapidated armchair adorned with a stained anti-Macassar. Max perched on a carved wooden stool near the fire. 'Gibson, this is Shurland, the jewel of my estate in Tobago. A thriving cocoa plantation in its time – and my home for decades.'

Max let out a low whistle. 'It looks beautiful, Mr. Cassidy.'

Neville reached for the frame. 'This snap was taken in 1963 just a few weeks before the hurricane. October the seventh, to be precise: the day I lost Beryl.' He stroked the image of her with his forefinger. 'My wife.' His eyes were welling up at the memory. 'We'd been married only a matter of weeks.' Something seemed to switch off again and he slumped into silence, his eyes expressionless.

I touched his arm. 'Uncle?'

'Mm?'

'Are you all right?'

With a snort, he sat up again. 'Christ's sake, why must everyone constantly ask me if I'm all right?'

'It's just that you seemed to, well, disappear for a moment.'

Max added, 'We were worried, Mr. Cassidy.'

'Oh, piss off the both of you. I'm fine, I tell you. Just feeling a bit woozy today.'

'Okay, okay,' said Max, glancing at me in some consternation, 'but what happened after your wife died?'

'I've told you 'til I'm blue in the face!' The old man was without doubt losing his grip on reality. 'No one ever listens to me! After the funeral, I set the workforce to clearing up the worst of the fallen timber and then sacked the bastards. All except a young couple I kept on as caretaker and cook.' He scratched at the back of his neck. 'For a year or so we ran Shurland as a guesthouse and bird sanctuary.'

I looked at Max. 'The poor birds would have lost much of their habitat in the storm.'

Neville gave me a withering look. 'Unlike my nephew here who *loves* his bird photography, I don't give a toss about our little feathered friends. Ahaa!' He shot out an arm to point above my head, starting eyes fixed upon the light fitting. 'There's one of the little Scheisters now!'

I swiveled to follow his gaze. 'Uncle—'

'A pink and yellow hummingbird in East Sussex: who'd have bloody thought it?' He seized his newspaper and flapped it at the imaginary intruder. 'Listen to the little bastard: it's hissing at me!'

I grabbed his arm. 'Uncle, there's no such thing as a pink and yellow hummingbird! And certainly not in East Sussex! There's... there's no bird in here!'

'You suggesting I'm hallucinating, boy?'

'I—I don't know, uncle.'

'Well, be quiet, then!' He grinned suddenly at Max. 'What was I saying, Gibson?'

'You were talking about running Shurland as a guesthouse, Mr. Cassidy, but perhaps we could move on to the point of this—'

'Oh yes, bloody disaster area that was.' He ran a trembling finger across his lower lip. 'Being forced to make small-talk with squadrons of boring-arsehole birdwatchers—'

'Uncle!'

'Twitchers! Give me strength! The dreariest bunch of tossers who ever roamed the planet.' Neville reached out and slapped my leg. 'Gabriel's parents might have given him his first camera, but they never brought him out to Shurland to see real birds.'

'Why was that, Mr. Cassidy?'

'Because, Gibson, I'd fallen out with my brother. Religious differences, you know. Didn't speak to the po-faced dick for years. Families, eh?' Max opened his mouth and closed it again. 'So I sodded orff and taught British History at an oil refinery school over in Trinidad until, like Gabriel here, I took early retirement and slung me hook back to Blighty. I left the house in the care of that dullard couple – I forget their names now but they'd had a daughter by that time. Sweet little thing.' He paused and stared into the middle-distance again, his fingers fiddling with the frayed hem of his jacket.

I gave this latest lapse a few seconds, long enough to exchange another look with Max. 'Uncle?'

'Mm, what now?'

'You were saying? About this couple?'

He gesticulated towards the rain-spattered window. 'Don't see many coconut palms in Ticehurst, do you? Blasted jungle's encroaching. Need to speak to the council about it.'

'Uncle, it's a privet hedge!'

'Stop shouting me down, Gabriel! How many times?' He jabbed a finger at Max. 'Tobagonians are a race apart, though. They subsist on breadfruit, mangoes and rum – and above all, on the good opinion of the local Obeah woman – a supposedly wise woman a bit like a witch doctor, I suppose. They rely on her as much as they rely on God, as does my Philistadelphian nephew here. But if you ask me, Gibson, they're a lazy, uneducated and superstitious people, and good for not a lot – apart from the women, of course. Good-looking, some of 'em: not to be sniffed at, if you take my meaning.' Embarrassed and ashamed, neither Max nor I responded to his predictably naughty-schoolboy leer. I took a breath to bring this excruciating soliloquy to a close, but he wasn't finished: 'Know much history, Gibson?'

Max looked at his watch and sighed. 'A certain amount, Mr. Cassidy.'

'Well then, you'll be aware that the Caribbean plantation owners absolutely relied upon slaves in the old days. African imports, mostly, many of 'em from Ghana.' He winked at Max and I knew what was coming. He'd always loved goading me on this topic.

'Max,' I said, 'my uncle is about to embark upon a favourite quasi-historical fantasy of his. I suggest you ignore him.'

'Pah!' Neville took another slurp from his flask. 'You telling me Gabriel never bored you with the tragic tale of his origins in Johnny Foreigner-land and how he came to be brought up in England?'

'Mister Cassidy—'

'How as a wee mite he was rescued from the smouldering wreckage of his family's mud-hut by a pair of passing do-gooders? – I refer of course to my brother and sister-in-law, Christian missionaries of note.'

'Er—'

'Never mentioned being dragged wailing from the fly-blown corpse of his murdered daddy, Chief Mbongobongo, or whatever his bloody name was?' Max had the look of a man wishing to peel off his own face. 'Nor of Mummykins and her myriad virginal sisters being hauled away by savage militiamen?'

'Uncle, this is beyond objectionable.'

But the crazy old boy was not to be put off. 'It was quite the scandal, Gibson, even by African standards. Made the local papers.'

I cleared my throat. 'And entirely fictitious, uncle, as well you know. You've been trying to frighten me with this nonsense for as long as I can remember. Luckily, mum and dad made a point of assuring me when I queried the tale that you were just being "wicked and silly".'

Neville guffawed. 'Oh, I can hear your lacklustre mater saying just that.'

'Although, Max,' I said, 'it's true they did adopt me from an orphanage in Accra.'

Neville snorted. 'What a lucky escape to have been shipped back to Western civilisation.'

'Uncle—'

'Shush, boy.' Neville held up a hand. 'Thing is, Gibson, you were Gabriel's best friend at that posh public school in Kent – where was it?'

'Sevenoaks.'

'And as soon as the lad declared he was going to the same university as you, my brother took fright!'

'Mr. Cassidy, you can't be suggesting I—'

'Of course! He so feared the secular and liberating influence of friends like you he decided to *save* Gabriel by forcing him to abandon his English degree – plus a potentially successful career in writing more than likely – and have him baptised as a sodding Philadelphian instead.'

'Uncle, Max doesn't need to know all this.'

'Swapping the pitfalls of an authentic worldly existence for the security of a marriage to simpering Sarah, beloved daughter of a family friend and girl of their dreams. The proud parents between them then set up the newly-weds in a cosy little house in suburbia, a cushy job with prospects for Gabriel in the insurance lark and *voilà*! – their cup overfloweth! Three bloody cheers for blinkered, unambitious and manipulating parenting!'

'Please, uncle, I—'

'In Gabriel's defence, Gibson, he'd always been ridiculously shy, awkward and unworldly.' He managed to pinch my arm. 'No doubt he'd been led to believe that if he was a really good boy and worked hard at his religious beliefs, true love and – heaven forfend! – carnal desire for his prim little wifeling would one day overcome the couple's self-evident lack of affinity.' He swung round. 'Can you deny it, boy?'

Having long regarded this family elder as a challenge placed in my path by God it was my policy to try not to lose my temper with him, but a frankly Old Testament urge to smite him with the poker was becoming irresistible.

'All the same, Gibson,' Neville ploughed on, now prodding at my shoulder with a biro, 'my brother was always irritatingly smug about how well his little rescue-dog Gabriel had turned out – especially considering how he'd only been showered with *every* bloody privilege money could buy.' He leant over to slap my knee again, but I crossed my legs out of reach. 'And how smoothly did Goody-two-shoes Gabriel choose to pay back my brother's munificence?'

Max was looking at his watch again. 'Mr. Cassidy, might we—?'

'By becoming twice as unimaginative and compliant a bloody Philadelphian as his dad ever was!'

Neville had folded his arms and was staring at me, willing me to rise to the fight. What was that verse in the Book of Proverbs?

A soft answer turneth away wrath, but grievous words stir up anger. 'Uncle,' I said, 'with respect, I must ask you—'

'Or perhaps deep down you yearn to rejoin your forebears swinging about in the trees?'

Since Brexit, casual xenophobia had been in the ascendant in the U.K., but having to deal with this intoxicated racist was beyond the call of even family duty. Time to draw this to a close. 'Listen, uncle,' I said, through gritted teeth, 'if you've dragged us here simply to air your revolting and outmoded views, then we'll be making tracks.' Max was already on his feet, cheeks flushed, but like Jonah in the jaws of his whale, I was failing to extricate myself from the confines of that moth-eaten armchair.

With a bark of fake laughter, the old curmudgeon grabbed my arm. 'Christ alive, lads, loosen up, fuck's sake. What do you want me to do, apologise?'

Before I could formulate a reasoned response there was a tap on the door. Neville stuffed the flask between his thighs as Mabel rattled in with the wooden tea trolley I remember my grandmother using. Max and I made grateful noises.

'Here, Mr. Neville,' said the carer, handing him a cardboard beaker of something. 'Drink dis for me.'

'What is it?'

'Vitamins.'

Neville knocked it back with a grimace. 'Right, now clear orff, girl. We're talking business.' He sat back and made much of inspecting his fingernails.

I mouthed 'Sorry' at Mabel as she withdrew.

'I don't trust her one inch,' whispered my uncle. 'She's only been here two weeks but there's something shifty about her.' I couldn't bring myself to respond. 'Be that as it may, lads,' he went on, pushing a hand over his balding pate, 'I did ask you here for a reason. Thing is – tidings of great joy and all that – but some bloody sucker's crawled out of the woodwork wanting to take Shurland orff me 'ands. Which is good news because old age is an absolute bugger and full-time care is costing me a fortune. Selling the Tobago estate is the obvious answer.' Neville leant towards the solicitor. 'Gibson, as I'm pretty much brassic, I'm hoping your chaps will do the conveyancing at mates' rates, yes?'

'Well, we—'

'Excellent.' Neville flapped a hand at me. 'Also, I'll be needing someone out there to oversee the arrangements. The last thing we want is anybody or anything screwing up this opportunity.'

I stared. 'Meaning what, precisely?'

'Meaning it's high time you made yourself useful. You can't spend the rest of your life rattling about in that pebble-dashed shithole of yours reading Bible stories and doing odd jobs for the missus. I want you on the spot in Tobago eftsoons and right speedily.'

'Me?'

'Who else? It's a simple enough task: sweep the aforementioned squatters orff my land, hose the place down and put fresh coffee on to brew for when the agent brings the buyer round. In short, I need you to expedite the sale.' He peered at me. 'Well? Don't just sit there gawping like a bloody mahi-mahi!'

'A what?'

'Like a fish, man!'

'Well, I'd need to consult Sarah.'

'Bollocks! Listen, you're exactly the man for the job. You'll blend in with the scenery.' Catching me unawares, my insufferable uncle managed to tweak my ear. 'You've bags of money, time on your hands and a crotchety little Hausfrau who'll be only too glad to see the back of you for a week or so.'

'But I can't just up and leave!'

'Gibson, back me up here, for God's sake.'

But Max was on his feet again, tapping at his phone. 'I do apologise, Mr. Cassidy, but I really must dash.' He gathered up an expensive-looking coat. 'I'll leave you two gents to settle on a way forward and await your instructions. I'll be happy to help in

any way I can. Good to see you looking so perky, Mr. Cassidy.'
The old man did not reply; he had slumped to one side again and was staring into the dying embers of the fire. Max looked awkwardly at me. 'Sorry to leave you in the lurch, Ange, but let's keep in touch this time, eh? Don't leave it another thirty years. You've got my number.'

As Max took his leave, Mabel materialised again – how could anyone walk that slowly? – this time bearing a menacing assortment of rubberised paraphernalia, pads and pill-pots.

'I'm afraid he's having one of his funny turns again,' I said. 'I don't know what's the matter.'

Mabel raised her voice. 'Mr. Neville, what happenin' wid you?'

With a grunt, my uncle rolled his face towards her, his mouth open. He seemed to be having difficulty focusing. 'Eh?'

'Mr. Neville, is time for yuh medication.'

Once again, he flung himself to the upright, this time uttering a cry of joy. 'Marie, my own darling! Look at you! You came back! It's a miracle!' Inexplicably, he was waving both arms in the air. 'Come here, girl! Where've you been all this time?'

Hands on hips, Mabel made a strange sucking noise through her teeth. 'Eh-ehh, Mr. Neville! Since when I name Marie?'

'No, no, no...' Neville's mouth clamped shut, his face ashen and distraught. He turned abruptly to the fire, hands quivering. He seemed as frightened as a little boy caught stealing a sixpence from nanny's purse.

Mabel went on, 'But say goodbye to yuh nephew before we do we procedures.' She left the room again, not quite closing the door behind her.

I reached for my anorak. 'Well, uncle, I'll be off.'

Slowly this time, Neville turned his head. I was amazed to see tears in his eyes again. 'Sorry about that, boy. Bastard brain seems sort of scrambled today. Must've mistaken her – Maud, or whatever her name is – for someone else.'

'I shouldn't worry about it, uncle. It's probably the drugs.'

He managed the ghost of a grin, the hallucination over. 'Thank you in advance, boy, for agreeing to this little trip.'

'I've agreed to nothing of the sort – as yet. You've been eye-wateringly rude to me today and I need time to think – and talk it over with Sarah. I'll ring you tomorrow.' I opened the door and almost knocked over the nurse in the act of balancing a pile of folded towels and pyjamas on a chair. Had she been listening? 'Mabel,' I whispered, 'might I have a word?'

'Sure ting.' She followed me across the hall to the front door and, ripping open a bale of sanitary pads, met my gaze with what my uncle I'm sure would have regarded as impertinence. 'Yes?'

I took a deep breath. 'I'd like to apologise to you for my uncle's appalling treatment. He's always had difficulties with his social filter.'

'No problem, Mr. Gabriel. Is what we expect from de older generation.'

'Why do you think he called you Marie?'

'Maybe it because I a Trini.' This time I knew she was smiling.

'Say again?'

'I come from de Caribbean, Mr. Gabriel: Trinidad and Tobago. Maybe I remindin' him of someone he knew one time.'

'Surely even he can't still think we all look alike?'

'Not for me to comment, Mr. Gabriel,' she mumbled, adjusting her mask. 'Doh forget yuh umbrella.'

'No. Right. Thanks.'

'You're welcome.'

I opened the door. A flurry of icy wind flicked three or four wet leaves across the threshold. 'Cheerio.'

'Have a bless day.'

As I turned the car, I spotted the nurse on her phone at the hall window. Seeing me staring, she gave a little wave before closing the curtains. I suppressed the absurd notion that she was talking to someone about me. Edging the Toyota through the potholes and puddles of the driveway, I turned left and headed back towards London.

2

Inside Tobago's terminal building it was cool. Not quite the claggy, toothsome chill I had left behind but a relief nonetheless. I mopped the back of my neck with a spotted handkerchief of my late father's and opened my passport at the right page. It's always good to be at the back of a queue, I find; you can look around you without being shoved, judged and hassled.

Although the bulk of today's human cargo had grabbed their wailing offspring and piled out at Antigua two hours earlier, there were still sixty or seventy passengers ahead of me corralled within a snaking corridor of black ropes. Immigration being in no apparent rush to process us, I pulled out my phone and joined airport Wi-fi. A single message from my wife Sarah pinged onto the screen.

'You rly left? Half expecting you to come back, esp after what you left behind. [Bulgy-eyed emoji] Roaming charges horrendous. No reply rqd.'

'No phone use!' barked a barrel of male officialdom squeezed into a beige uniform and orange singlet. He was grinning widely whilst fondling the butt of his pistol.

'Oh. Sorry,' I muttered, and pocketed the device.

Twenty minutes later I was one person away from the passport booths but no nearer to working out what it was Sarah had found. I rolled my shoulders and neck and stared out through the plate glass. Gaggles of ground staff stood around. I saw Maisha, arms akimbo, rocking backwards with laughter, her hi-vis jacket flapping in the evening breeze. Such energy and charm, so very un-English, I thought. Baggage handlers sweated and heaved. I spotted my own suitcase being tossed from a trolley. Thank goodness I'd carried my laptop and camera equipment with me as hand luggage.

'Good day, sir, and welcome home.'?

'Oh, actually, this is my first—'

'Passport and landing card.'

The official studied my documentation. She was another good-looking woman with tinted tortoiseshell spectacles perched on the end of her nose. 'Oh–kay. So, you is British?' She glanced at me then back at my mugshot. 'Where you stayin'?' The passport was pushed into a scanner.

'At Shurland.'

She paused and looked up at me again.

I added, 'Near Black Rock.'

'I knows Shurland, sir. Stonehaven Bay.' She rattled at her keyboard then hit the return button five or six times with the undue force of a seasoned bureaucrat poised to clock off for the day. 'How long you stayin'?'

'I'm not sure,' I replied. 'About ten days, I expect.' But something on the screen had caught her attention and she wasn't listening. My heart jumped a beat. *Please, Lord, let there not be a problem with my paperwork.*

'One moment. Dis need verification.' The lady took my passport, rose unhurriedly to her feet and shambled over to the same security man who had told me to put my phone away. I caught myself looking apologetically behind me, loath to be the cause of any delay despite knowing full well that I was the last passenger in the Immigration hall.

While I pondered this instinctively British behaviour of mine, my lady engaged her colleague in whispered conversation.

I watched with increasing concern as, looking over occasionally at me, they checked and double-checked that my details matched something on a clipboard. After a minute's debate, the man pulled out his phone, dialled a number and disappeared through a door marked "Private". My official, all smiles now, wafted back and squeezed herself once more into her chair. Making a little too much of her power over me, I thought, she proceeded to rubber-stamp pretty much any virgin space she could find on my paperwork. 'All in order, Mr. Cassidy.'

'Was there a problem?'

'No, no, mere formality. New regulation comin' in all de time. We oblige to be vigilant.'

'Ah.'

She handed me my passport, her smile perhaps a touch less warm than it had been. 'When you see Lily at Shurland, tell her Keisha say Hi. We ol' friends.'

'Oh, really? I will. But how do you know her, if I may ask?'

'Tobago a small island, Mr. Cassidy,' she responded with now not the slightest hint of a smile. 'Have a nice stay.'

'Thanks so much.' As I bent to pick up my bag, I saw the door to backstage opening again. The security man poked his head out, glanced at me and nodded to Keisha. What could have been so problematic about my arrival, I wondered? Given how chatty everyone had been since "doors to manual", I'd been naively expecting these immigration officers to have been more forthcoming. This in itself was doubly unnerving because I wasn't used to being engaged in conversation: at home I was accustomed to being ignored.

I walked in as composed a manner as possible through to Baggage Collection. There I was reunited with my suitcase, whirling round and round, lonely and abandoned on the otherwise empty carousel. Through yet another double door I rejoined my fellow passengers, this time for a wearisome wait at Customs. I was nuzzled by a sniffer-dog, quizzed by two more officials and then finally released. (Sarah would have denounced the situation with "what a palaver," one of her stock phrases.) Declining offers of a lift somewhere from a welcoming committee of smartly dressed taxi drivers, I emerged finally into a steamy blast of hot, kerosene-laden night air and stood for a moment watching the comings and goings of fellow travellers and marvelling at how so relatively painless a journey could land me in so alien and exciting an environment. Within seconds I was sticky with sweat, a new experience for me, but not unpleasant. I glanced at my phone: UK time, I calculated, it was nearly midnight.

As arranged, I was scooped up by an ebullient gentleman called Marlon from Island Car Hire who drove me the short distance across the car park to his depot. There, after much good-humoured form-filling and the presentation of what he termed my "drivin' licen'" and credit card, I was given a tourist map, a tired old Honda automatic smelling of cheap perfume and sent on my way.

I was as excited about my first foray into the tropics as any ten-year old at the gates of Disneyland. Inwardly I was overjoyed at the excuse to escape even for just a short while not only Sarah's disdainful attitude towards me but also the monotony of suburban life in the depths of an English winter. In three decades of summer holidays, Sarah and I had never once ventured further than the foothills of the Pyrenees, so to experience the untold delights of the Caribbean had sounded too good a chance to pass up. I assumed I'd be able to complete my business in time to spend a few days alone, soaking up the atmosphere and photo-graphing some birds without the weight of my wife's constant negativity and her knack of sucking the joy out of any situation.

At eight o'clock it was already dark. Following Marlon's scrawled indications on the map, I nudged tentatively north-east-wards up the island. Past brightly lit stalls selling pineapples, yams and coconuts, I drove onwards past thumping rum shops, buzzing pizza joints and clothing stores displaying their wares on flamboyantly dressed mannequins. The main thoroughfare was heaving with people both on and off the pavements so that driving here put me in mind of fairground dodgem-car rides of my youth. Even then I knew I was a natural target and I remember going to any lengths to avoid collisions with fellow revellers; equally, it was not in my plan tonight to add to the Honda's all too visible history of dents, scratches and scrapes. I could only flap a hand in contrition as irate local road-users in towering Hilux pick-ups honked and bellowed at me as they swerved past in clouds of exhaust fumes. At least, I thought, they drive on the left in Tobago.

I missed my turning owing to the presence in the road of a flock of goats. Baptised into the Truth, I had long ago been taught to scoff at the concept of the Devil, but seeing so many pairs of yellow eyes reflected in my headlights nonetheless sent a tremor through me. I jammed the car into reverse and, taking care to avoid a deep concrete storm drain, swung the car up a steep track to the right. Through dense forest the Honda wheezed and rattled as I negotiated ruts, rocks, fallen branches and, oddly, a number of red-eyed little birds apparently snoozing on the ground in the middle of the track. I passed a pock-marked sign reading "Welcome to Shurland", swung to the left and emerged into a clearing.

Security lights flashed on to reveal, dead ahead, the sideview of a white mansion. I bumped to a halt on a mat of twisted roots and silenced the motor, my arrival sparking a furious snarling and yapping from a cage alive with guard-dogs. I don't as a rule mind the attentions of what my dad used to term "our canine chums" but the ferocity of this pack made the hairs on the back of my neck stand on end.

A ground-floor door partially hidden by bushes opened and an old man in shorts, T-shirt and Wellington boots appeared in silhouette. A piercing whistle and the dogs fell silent. I clambered out of the car as he lifted a hand in what I took to be a salutation.

'Goodnight,' he rumbled.

I was mystified that in his view our encounter was already concluded but I surmised it was a Caribbean thing. 'Good evening,' I replied. 'Is Lily Pitt here? She's expecting me.'

'Ah,' explained the man, indicating the steps to the first-floor balcony. Evidently the main living quarters were upstairs. Anything else he might have added was swallowed up in a crescendo of buzzing cicadas.

I said, 'Right. Thanks so much.' This would have been a good time for the man to come over and introduce himself but, customer service perhaps not being his forte, he remained steadfast in his doorway batting away insect life. Sighing, I heaved my luggage out, slammed the car door and squeezed the key-fob to lock it. Nothing happened so I was obliged to scrabble about in the inky black to locate the keyhole. Something brushed against my neck and made me jump. I hoped it was only foliage or a liana dangling from the enormous tree above; I had no clue as to what Tobago might offer in the way of airborne creepy-crawlies or spiders.

Without the benefit of the Honda's air-conditioning, sweat was again dribbling down my chest. I'd been unaware that night air anywhere on the planet could be so hot and humid. I dragged my case across an area of spiky grass masquerading as lawn and bumped it up the righthand staircase, pausing at the top to mop my brow again. I leant my luggage against the white-painted wooden balustrade, turned my back on the velvety blackness of the night and crossed the polished floorboards to a window. Every light inside was blazing and something was flitting and crashing about between brass lamp fittings. It was about the size of a bat but bore more of a resemblance to one of those miniature drones you see demonstrated in toyshops than to anything living. I watched for a moment before stepping to the doorway and uttering a polite 'hullo'. There being no response, I ventured inside.

The room was spacious and airy with wooden lattice-work at the eaves allowing the breeze and assorted wildlife to waft through. It was furnished with dark wooden furniture: mirrored sideboards, two dining tables, capacious wicker armchairs with green cushions, and display cases containing faded paperbacks, corals and seashells. A gentle snuffling drew my attention to the left. On one of a pair of identical sofas, partially out of view behind a pillar, I spotted a recumbent figure, a substantial-looking lady dressed in enough red, purple and yellow fabric to fashion, I thought, an entire Carnival costume. She was asleep with the pale soles of her feet towards me. An open magazine rose and fell with her gentle snoring and beyond the generous dome of her tummy, an array of chins creased into the benign smile of contented slumber. A pair of gold-rimmed spectacles had been placed out of harm's way on a low table nearby.

Not wishing either to startle or embarrass her, I withdrew, took a breath and tapped loudly on the door frame.

'Who dat?' came the husky reply after a few seconds.

'Hi. Only me. Gabriel Cassidy.' In the ensuing pause I heard the magazine plop to the floor. 'From England,' I added.

'Ooooh, sorry! Hold on!'

When she hove into view a few moments later, Lily Pitt's billowing and colourful progress between the sofas put me in mind of a yacht sailing under full spinnaker during Cowes Week. Glasses askew, this five-foot nothing lady rolled towards me tucking a wayward hank of greying hair into a copper-coloured headscarf. 'Oh, Mr. Cassidy,' she puffed, 'I so sorry, I must be...'

She looked up.

For a moment she remained rooted to the spot, hands on hips, her lips forming a perfect pink circle. 'Lord bless us all, Mr. Cassidy,' she whispered. 'You is black!'

3

There was a pause pregnant with tropical possibilities after Lily's most astute observation on the topic of my personal melanin quota. Back home, where colour- and gender-blindness was becoming a fact of life, I might have at least feigned offence at such a comment, but here such considerations seemed both irrelevant and prosaic. Also, I thought, rooted to the spot in a state of unaccustomed awkwardness, who could have predicted that the demands of an obnoxious and racist old uncle could have so swiftly uprooted me from my home and four days later dropped me into this alien land and the presence of such a lady?

Lily, continuing to appraise me with both hands clamped over her mouth, all of a sudden broke the spell with an explosion of laughter. Intoxicating and exotic, her energy and ebullience entwined me in its magic and I found myself laughing with her. Here was a woman, I realised with a jolt of disloyalty, whose spellbinding vivacity and *joie de vivre* had in mere seconds established her as the polar opposite to my wife under whose pious and disapproving strictures I had laboured so long.

Still unsure how to proceed, and grateful that Sarah wasn't there to curb such untoward levity between strangers, I managed to regain some formality by holding out a tentative hand. With a shout of 'Come to Lily, fella!' she tugged me into an embrace which in its fervour almost caused me to lose my balance and land us both on the shiny dark floorboards. I resisted an instinct to wriggle free; never before had I been hugged with such overwhelming enthusiasm; rarely had I laughed like this. I suppose the lady's incredulity had tickled me.

I managed to respond with a couple of pats on the back. How warm and soft was Lily's body against mine, so unlike the hard exoskeleton of my own dear, oh-so-English wife.

'Oh, Mr. Cassidy,' she cried, beaming up at me, an almost spherical figure quaking with a delight. 'You have me surprise tonight! You is certainly nothing at all like your uncle.' She had grasped my hands again.

'Ah, that'll be because he and I share no DNA.'

'You doh say?' My companion shrieked again, bright blue eyes round with merriment. Letting go of my hands, she made that strange sucking noise in her teeth, just like Mabel had done. 'Where you family from?'

'London.'

'No, fella: originally!'

At home, the incipient racist undertone of such an enquiry (most famously from the lips of a future King of England) always made my hackles rise; coming from Lily, though, it was entirely inoffensive. 'Oh, I see what you mean,' I replied. 'Africa.'

'Like all ah we!' She lifted an eyebrow, waiting for me to elaborate. I had never seen so expressive a face. 'But which part?'

'Long story.' Time to change the subject. I turned to collect my luggage.

For a moment she looked crestfallen. Had I offended her? 'I show you your room, Mr. Cassidy.'

'Please call me Gabriel,' I said, trying to make amends.

'Tank you, Mr. Gabriel.' She was all smiles again. 'So please to meet you at last. I'm Lily.' We shook hands.

I said, 'Oh, I almost forgot: Keisha at the airport says Hi.'

'Keisha? Oh, she an ol' client of mine.' Lily exploded into laughter once more. 'Say, Mr. Gabriel, you is really nothin' like your uncle! Follow me.'

I wheeled my luggage in her wake through the living room, veering left out onto an internal balcony leading to the bedrooms. At the end of the passageway, Lily pushed open a door to a cosy cabin of a room painted in pale blues and yellows. Cocooned in a mosquito net stood a double bed and above us, the rusting blades of a ceiling fan rattled and creaked. 'This is very nice,' I said. 'Really lovely.'

'Bathroom through there, Mr. Gabriel.' She clicked a remote and a modern air-conditioning unit whirred into life. 'So, I guessin' yuh need a drink. I got beer or tea or jus' plain bottle water. Doh drink from de taps: water from de tank is bad.'

'A cold drink would be most welcome,' I said, closing the bedroom door behind me and following her slowly back along the balcony. 'I don't remember being so hot in all my life. What are the local beers?'

'I got Carib and Stag, Mr. Gabriel.'

'Which do you recommend?'

'Well, as dey say, "A beer is a Carib but Stag is a man's beer."'

'Oh, go on, then: I'll have a Stag. Thanks so much.'

The kitchen faced my bedroom on the opposite wing of the building. It was a pretty spartan affair compared to our own recently installed shrine to the Sunday roast at home. Sarah had argued that if I were to be allowed a new Toyota then she must have the top-of-the-range kitchen of her dreams with gleaming black marble surfaces, knife block, and Nespresso machine; as she put it, 'all the bells and whistles'. She would have been horrified at Shurland's primitive facilities: sagging Formica shelves laden with pans, a crooked aluminium sink unit and a rusting five-burner stove attached to a gas-cannister; in the corner, a vast white refrigerator, its door and sides also blistered with rust. The window shutters had been hooked back allowing free access to airborne intruders the like of which I had not imagined possible outside the Insect House at London Zoo. Decades of defenestrating unwanted six- or eight-legged intruders for my wife had inured me to any U.K.-sized moths, wasps, spiders and beetles but my forbearance was put to the test when something landed with a clang on a roasting tin only a few inches from my ear. Slowly swiveling my eyes, I recognised the new arrival to be the flying beast I had seen ten minutes before, a colossal green- and copper-coloured cricket the size of a langoustine. Waving a pair of three-inch antennae at me, it bristled with tiny claws and spines. I was mightily glad it hadn't elected to land on me.

Lily flung open the 'fridge door and passed me an ice-cold bottle of beer. 'You starvin', Mr. Gabriel? I make you chicken pelau wid pigeon peas an' ochro.' She was dragging out a large frying pan of something covered in cling-film.

'Thanks so much.'

'And while you dinin', let we talk 'bout why you here. Plenty phone calls for you already tonight.'

'Phone calls for me? That's odd. I've not been in contact with anyone.'

'You uncle, he email me,' she went on, her voice cracking. 'He say he wishin' to… to sell Shurland. I doh know what we goin' to do, Mr. Gabriel.'

I realised with a jolt that this was a situation I had not considered; depriving people of their livelihood might be more complicated than I'd imagined. 'Lily, can we talk business tomorrow?' I asked. 'There's no great hurry, is there?'

'No hurry at all. Best you take your cool time, Mr. Cassid—Gabriel.' A sudden thought seemed to restore her spirits. 'An' if you like, I make you a cup of my special herbal tea before bed.'

'Sounds lovely.'

Lily lit the gas and banged the saucepan down onto the ring. 'Now tell me dis time, fella, which part in Africa you family from? Nigeria? Senegal? Côte d'Ivoire?'

I spotted a bottle-opener on a nail and ripped the top off my Stag. With a beer in my hand, I felt more ready for this conversation now. 'Close,' I said. 'I was born in Ghana.' The beer was delicious. Strong too.

Lily looked up from stirring the food. 'Go on.'

I leant against the counter. 'Well, my father John – Mr. Neville's brother – married my mother Rachel in 1970. Instead of a honeymoon, though, they left almost immediately for Ghana to do missionary work for our Church.' How many times had I recited these exact words? For decades the neat mantra had sounded plausible when justifying my existence to British Caucasian society, but here, talking to a fellow person of colour – especially one with a sceptically arched eyebrow like Lily's – the words rang smug and hollow. 'I had been orphaned and so Rachel and John adopted me. I was brought up in the U.K. and, well, wanted for nothing really: the best schooling money could buy, then a stint at university... decent job prospects.' I drained my beer. I usually skated over the details of the next bit. 'So, I'm married to Sarah and – until only a few weeks ago, when I sold my company and retired – was blessed with a reasonably successful career as an insurance broker.' Listening to my complacent droning was making even me feel queasy.

Lily set her jaw and made that sucking noise again. 'What does that mean, Lily?'

She cocked her head. 'You never "steups" in England?'

'Well, I—'

'Mr. Gabriel, a Caribbean steups imply either you is way outta line or I not sure you tellin' de truth.' She pronounced it 'troot.'

'And which one applies to me right now?'

'Eh-ehh, Mr. Gabriel, you decide.' A gobbet of rice plopped out of the pan and onto the floor. Lily ignored it. 'So, what you doin' in retirement?'

'Just pottering about at home. The first few weeks of relaxation were all well and good but now, with Sarah out most of the time, I'm at a bit of a loose end. Mr. Neville's call last Monday changed all that, though, and so here I am.'

'Here you is.' Lily was scrutinising me, waggling the wooden spoon distractedly.

A sudden pressure between my shoulder-blades as if I'd been hit with a ping-pong ball. 'Lily,' I hissed, turning my back towards her. 'Tell me it's not that turbo-cricket thing again.'

Lily yanked the pan off the gas. 'Stand still,' she said. I felt her warm hand on my shoulder. When had I last been touched so gently? 'Is a scarab beetle,' came a whisper. I turned. On her finger was perched a shiny little monster about two inches long; it flashed gold, copper and green as she turned it about for my inspection. 'One land on you bring you luck, Mr. Gabriel.' The beautiful creature spread its wings and buzzed away. Peering into my eyes, Lily went on, 'But I see you no believe in luck, good or bad. You know is Friday thirteenth today?'

A well-rehearsed comment about worldly superstition was on the tip of my tongue, but I swallowed it back. 'Lucky for some,' I remarked instead. 'I'm having a lovely day.'

She sniffed and fired off the question I dreaded: 'So, your parents: what missionary work we talkin' 'bout?'

'We're Christadelphians.'

'Oh, we got plenty ah dem here. Is a local ting. It have a meetin' hall in Scarborough.' She steupsed again. 'Misguided but harmless.'

I gave her the neutral smile we 'in The Truth' are trained to use in order to discourage further questioning. 'May I help myself to another beer? Will you join me this time or are you driving home?'

I saw her shoulders relax as she continued to stir. 'Tank you, Mr. Gabriel. I will. And no, I doh own no *vee-hickle*. I livin' my whole life downstairs wid Churchill.'

I blushed at the dreadful realisation that I had been sent on a mission not only to make two people redundant but also to throw them out their home. I turned to the fridge, found two bottles of Carib and fumbled with the opener. 'Ah, yes, Churchill,' I said. 'I saw him. Is he your husband?'

She whooped with incredulous laughter at this. 'No, he my daddy. He doh say much, praise be. He talk mostly to he dogs.'

'Oh, I see. Well, cheers, Lily. And thank you for your hospitality.'

'You're welcome. You enjoy your stay.'

A tiny, scratching sound above my head. I looked up and locked eyes with a greeny-brown lizard poised head-downwards on the wall, our wriggling scarab beetle clamped in its jaws. The creature cocked its head at me and scuttled off into the rafters. 'Well, I'll be...' I murmured, 'a baby dragon.'

'Woodslave,' Lily squeezed my arm, 'he welcome you to Shurland.'

A few minutes later I was seated in solitary state in the dining area. Lily arrived bearing aloft a tray laden with a third beer, a little pot of something mysterious and a plate of chicken pelau piled as high as a molehill. Sarah would have insisted we eke out such a portion for both of us over two dinners. 'Lily,' I declared, seizing a fork, 'you are a woman I can do business with.'

She laughed, unscrewing the lid of the little pot. 'As soon as I sees you I knows you a man need feedin' up. Wife starvin' you?'

'No, just health conscious. And what, pray, is this?' I took the pot from her and sniffed. It had the innocence of Tesco's-own pesto but smelt altogether more potent.

'Homemade hot pepper sauce, Mr. Gabriel. But take only slight pepper. If you like it, you upgrade to plenty pepper in a day or so.' Her hip pushed against my elbow, warmth radiating from her. 'You is a soft Brit and yuh palate need acclimatisation.'

Despite my repeated objections, Lily waited upon me as I gorged myself, never once complaining about my table manners as Sarah was prone to do. Indeed I only realised halfway through my second helping that I had omitted to give thanks to God at the beginning of my meal. I felt a momentary spasm of guilt about this but in my defence, I was a long way from home and the Trinidad-brewed beer was exceedingly potent. As is the Christadelphian custom in public places or amongst strangers, I closed my eyes and gave silent if tardy thanks.

While Lily was busying herself with a tub of coconut ice-cream, I thought what a pity it was to be selling Shurland when it was so obviously brimming with possibilities as an Airbnb or restaurant. If I could pluck up sufficient courage to defy Neville, I might raise the matter with him in the morning.

Lily seemed particularly gratified with my appreciation of her herbal tea. It tasted of nutmeg, lime and something I couldn't for the life of me place. 'What do you put in this,' I asked her, comatose on a sofa. 'It's delicious.'

'Eh-ehh, Mr. Gabriel, if I tell you, I go have to kill you.'

'And then what would my wife say?' The thought of Sarah taking delivery of a bulging body-bag made me laugh until I got the hiccups.

'You tell me about her tomorrow,' said Lily, pouring me a second cup. 'Two cup is all you permitted. Otherwise you nuh sleep.'

'Yes, m-ma'am, w-wha'...whatever you—ss—say.' My lips and tongue had become unresponsive and sluggish. 'You—you've done enough for me, Miss Lily. More'n'enough.'

'Mr. Gabriel, I jus' finish up here. If you wan' keep me company...'

Next thing I was perched on a stool by the fridge, its vibrations soothing and soporific, the rusty metal cool against my temples.

'You know anythin' at all about Shurland, Mr. Gabriel?'

'Only wha' Neville's tol' me.' Was I being taken ill or was it the beer?

'Well, Shurland plantation, it famous for Tobago first slave rebellion in 1770.' I was in no state for a history lesson. 'Slave call

Sandy, he up an' kill his British master an' dey all hole up here. What happen was dey escape to Trinidad from near where de airport is now. Some folk say dat why it name Sandy Point.' She flapped a dish-cloth towards the black square of one of the windows. 'Shurland still have ruined slave quarters in de bush. If you hearin' screamin' in de night, is only de ghost of slaves. Sometime dey walk.' She put a finger to the side of her nose. 'An' sometime, ol' Mrs. Cassidy, she join dem.'

What was she talking about? 'I don' believe in g-ghosts.'

Lily steupsed. 'All in God good time, Mr. Gabriel.' She gave a laugh. 'Oooh, is nine-thirty and you fallin' asleep.' Was that her hand feeling my brow? 'You not accustom to beer? You is no Trini.'

I remember leaning on my hostess and stumbling towards bed. In the shadows, a lump of rock used perhaps for propping open doors lolloped away across the floorboards and vanished behind a large pot plant. 'Lily, wha' was that?'

'What you sayin'?' She opened my bedroom door.

'Something amph-amphiribbean.' Either the room or the ceiling fan was revolving.

'He Kenny de crapaud, Mr. Gabriel.' Lily switched on a lamp. 'He livin' dongstairs where de shower water come out. He up here evenin' time to catch insect. Tonight he inspectin' you.'

Then I was flat on the bed, stripped to my boxers and a mosquito net draped around me. 'I hope you enjoy your first night in Tobago, Mr. Gabriel,' said a distant voice. 'Maybe tomorrow you go decide you not sellin' Shurland after all. Sleep well, fella.'

The door closed.

4

An hour and a half later I was awake again and feeling dreadful, my head pulsing. Fearful of disgracing myself on Lily's starched bedlinen, I fought my way out of the mosquito net, drank a whole bottle of water in the bathroom then brushed my teeth. Retrieving my camera-and-laptop bag and specs, I prepared myself for what I should have done earlier: improve my frame of mind and calm myself with the daily Bible reading. Even in my nauseous state I knew today was Exodus Three, the chapter about Moses and the burning bush. Like Christadelphians the world over, it was our routine – Sarah's and mine – to sit up in bed before lights-out to read and discuss the prescribed biblical text. Indeed, this had been our practice since our wedding night in 1992.

Ignoring something long and low scuttling across the floorboards by the bathroom door, I propped myself against the headboard and unzipped my bag to retrieve my Bible. I was assailed by a thought at once so unexpected, so disloyal and blasphemous that I broke into a sweat: if, as I suspected, it was the lack of children that had undermined whatever happiness Sarah and I might have enjoyed, was it not within the bounds of possibility that these decades of bedtime biblical analysis had worked as an actual prophylactic? 'Such thoughts are unworthy of you, Gabriel,' I chastised myself aloud, slapping at a mosquito. 'This is what comes of being so far from home. Get a grip.'

I reached into the usual compartment of my bag but my fingers encountered nothing more than the charger cable, plug adaptor and my external hard-drive. My heart pounding, I rummaged in disbelief, finally removing the laptop altogether and shaking the bag out onto the bed. Impossible: there was no Bible. My thumping brain was now buzzing with self-recriminations: how – *where* indeed could I have left it? I considered going downstairs to ask Lily if she had a Bible I could borrow. I dismissed the idea, though, given how late it was – and what beasts I might encounter en route. Imagine treading on Kenny the house toad...

The haughty tone of Sarah's last text to me now explained, I reloaded the bag, clicked off the light and closed my eyes. Sleep, however, eluded me because I was obsessing about where precisely my wife had discovered my escapee Bible. The thought of tomorrow's conversation with Neville wasn't helping either, so as a penance more fitting I felt than counting sheep, I began to recite John Chapter One. At midnight perhaps (four a.m. U.K. time) I became bogged down around Verse Twenty-three, *I am the voice of one crying in the wilderness,* and must finally have dozed off to jumbled images of the slave Sandy slitting his master's throat and, drunk on Carib, holing up in this very bedroom.

I was jolted awake by an unearthly scream from deep in Shurland's forest. At first I thought I must have dreamt it but then it came twice more, distant yet real enough to send a shiver through me – which was weird since the bed-sheets were soaked with sweat. The aircon was off and the light wouldn't work but according to my phone, it was four thirty-eight. My headache less acute now, I shuffled over onto a dry patch and gazed into the blackness. A soft breeze moved the dim grey outline of the mosquito net. All was silent. Even the cicadas had called it a night. Peace at last.

What seemed like moments later, I was bolt upright again. A cacophony of demonic squawks and chatterings outside had me clawing my way through the mosquito net, stumbling across the room and out onto the balcony. My heart thumping, I stood peering into the forest until the mysterious sources of the din seemed to retreat and the night sky took on the subtlest of purple hues. At which point, something I took to be outsized and hairy scuttled over my bare foot and I beat a hasty retreat back to bed.

At five-eleven a.m. – Sarah would be boiling the kettle for her morning coffee – the power and air-conditioning came on again and in the cool breeze I fell asleep. At six-fifteen, however, heavy footsteps and the clicking of switches outside my door – I assumed it was the taciturn Churchill turning off security lights – brought this mare of a night to its unnatural conclusion. I sighed and rolled onto my back, the signal for the bites I'd sustained despite the mosquito net to make their presence felt.

I forced myself to stop scratching, showered and thought about how, after breakfast, I must brace myself to phone my uncle.

Outside my room it was deliciously cool and so, in only my shorts, I crept along the corridor with my camera, over the creaking floorboards of the living room and out onto the main balcony. The panorama before me exceeded my wildest expectations. It was so still and beautiful it made my spine tingle. I leant against the white wooden balustrade mesmerised by the subtle changes in the light and colour of my first Caribbean dawn. Centre-stage, an enormous tree hung with creeper and bright orange flowers rose from a sloping lawn; beyond it, framed by dense, dark forest broken by two stands of impossibly tall palm trees, glimmered a misty strip of ocean. Vast, plumed towers of pink-tinged cumulus clouds floated above the soft grey line of the horizon and, even as I watched, spellbound, the sun broke through from the right to paint the sea in glittering silvers and blues, and the forest canopy in every green imaginable.

No one could accuse me of being prone to hyperbole, but I was stunned by Shurland that first morning. It was love at first sight. How long I stood there gaping I have no idea, but I was brought back to earth by a fluttering sound at the far end of the balcony. The new arrival was by far the most beautiful bird I had ever seen. About the size of our British magpie (which as you'll know is black and white with a hint of blue on the wings), this tropical extravaganza boasted an iridescent blue head, copper-coloured chest and olive-green back; its tail – about as long as my telephoto lens – ended in a pair of spade-shaped fans like lollies on sticks. The creature was surveying me with a bright red eye, its head on one side. I lifted my camera with infinite care, but the bird seemed unconcerned by my presence and offered me any number of lovely poses as it feasted upon a piece of fruit left in a dish. My obliging subject was presently joined by others, all equally colourful and exotic. I was in a birders' heaven. I took photograph after photograph, my lens trembling with an excitement I'd never known when snapping tomtits, sparrows or even yellowhammers at home.

'Good day, Mr. Gabriel,' came a voice from below. 'You admirin' our wildlife?'

I leant over the balustrade to see Lily, carrying something under a blue cloth, making heavy weather of the staircase.

'I make you coconut bake,' she announced as soon as she had breath to speak, holding it up for me to sniff.

'Mmmm, wonderful,' I sighed. 'Thank you. And I've fallen in love with this view, Miss Lily. It's magical – as are the birds. Do you know what they all are?'

'Well, de blue head is a motmot. Grey an' white ones, dem is mockingbird, and de little yellow and black ones, bananaquit.' She pointed to a feeder hanging from the eaves as something tiny buzzed past my ear. 'And him, jus' arrive, he a copper-rumped hummingbird. Dey feed on sugar water.'

'Amazing. And that green one?'

'Palm tanager. Blue tanager we is callin' blue-jeans. But if you want breakfast today, Mr. Gabriel, doh ax me no more question!'

I dragged myself away to help Lily in the kitchen. She had prepared me a cup of her excellent herbal tea and while I was singing its praises she volunteered that she was the mother of two grown-up children. 'My boy, he a business-man,' she said, setting my breakfast on a tray. 'Forty-two year ol' nex' August.'

'Er, you cannot be old enough to have a child in his forties!'

'Eh-ehh, Mr. Gabriel, you flirtin' wid me?'

'No indeed.' Nobody had ever accused me of that before. 'I'm just saying you look so young. You can't be more than...' Sarah's disapproving face rose in my mind's eye. 'Well, it's not for me to say.'

'Black doh crack, Mr. Gabriel!' Lily gave one of her operatic whoops. 'Maybe I has a Caribbean complexion but I is fifty-eight! My daughter, she thirty-three June twenty-fifth. She my good girl,' she added, leaving me in little doubt that her son's conduct left something to be desired.

I asked, 'Did you lose your husband, then?'

Lily emitted another shriek of mirth. 'Oh lors, Mr. Gabriel, I never marry!'

'Ah.'

'My babies from two father! I try sayin' "No ring no ting" each time but, Mr. Gabriel, we talkin' wotless badjohn an'...' she paused, biting her lip. 'Long story. But to make ting simple I tell my children dey have de same father.'

Outside the movies, I had never before encountered what my fellow believers would describe as a "fallen woman". Although having more than once delivered my Sunday exhortation on the topic of King David murdering Uriah the Hittite in order to steal his wife Bathsheba, I felt in no position to be judgmental about the circumstances of the youthful Lily.

After an excellent breakfast, she asked how I'd slept. 'I'm not sure I did,' I replied. 'I don't usually suffer from nightmares, but I was woken up by someone screaming.'

'Eh-heh, you already hear Shurland ghost?'

I suppressed an urge to make some comment that might sound patronising. 'Not sure about that,' I said, looking out to sea. 'But there was also a horrible racket in the forest at about five o'clock. Did you hear it?'

'Chachalacas, Mr. Gabriel: cocrico. He start up when he feelin' de dawn comin'. Look.' She pointed at a pair of dull brown birds with red beaks scrabbling about in the bushes outside. They were unremarkable to look at, a cross between a female pheasant and a partridge. And then, bang on cue, one started up its infernal *coc-oric-o, coc-oric-o, coc-oric-o* and at least a million others joined in at different pitches until my ears rang with the racket.

'I should have thought to pack a twelve-bore', I muttered.

'Doh *dis-re-spek* Tobago national bird!'

'Really? Why didn't they choose something beautiful and quiet like a motmot?'

'Mr. Gabriel, you make me laugh. But what you doin' today?'

'I need to touch base with the buyers or their agent then speak to my uncle. Tell him I've arrived safely at least.'

Lily's face darkened for a second. 'No use rushin' ting. Offices ent open yet. Better idea is you go dong an' take a swim at Stonehaven Bay before it too hot.'

'Well, I—'

'You do as I say, Mr. Gabriel!' She threw a towel at me. 'You back in forty minutes in time to make a call at nine!'

'Oh, rightoh.'

5

A five-minute walk down the drive and across the main road brought me through some low, scrabby trees and out onto a deserted picture-postcard beach of staggering beauty. To my left was a rocky outcrop hung with greenery; to my right, half a mile of platinum-coloured sand curved away past a couple of empty-looking hotels to a distant promontory with what looked incongruously like a bandstand on it. For the second time that day I could only stand and stare at the exquisite palette: the blues of the sea and sky, the bright greens of overhanging forest, the black of the rocks and the stunning white of foam of the breakers smashing over them.

I threw off my T-shirt and sandals and walked down the sand. As soon as the waves permitted, I threw myself into the water. Once again I was that seven-year-old on holiday at Bournemouth, the only difference being the absence of slot-machines, a pier, the Winter Gardens Theatre, electric yellow trolley-buses, cold grey sea and thousands of holidaymakers with handkerchiefs knotted on their heads... and, that the Caribbean was warmer than anything I could ever have imagined. I dived through a breaker and emerged in calmer waters way out of my depth. I was so intoxicated by the wonder of it all that an extraordinary thought occurred to me: why not take off my swimming shorts? With nobody on the beach – and nothing between me and Grenada to the north – my trunks were soon looped over my shoulder and I was off, naked in salt water for the first time in my life. What, I wondered, would Sarah have to say about this lack of comportment on my part? Nothing, because she would never know.

An hour later I was trudging back up the hill to Shurland trying not to raise too much of a sweat. I told myself I'd be ready to make my phone calls as soon as I had showered; more than ready, actually, because in the calming silky expanses of the Caribbean I had been rehearsing a few choice and persuasive turns of phrase about turning this paradise into an upmarket ecolodge and delaying – even abandoning – the sale. The more I thought about it, the more optimistic and excited I became at the prospect. It would be no skin off Neville's nose to hold off for a month or so to allow me time to do my research properly. After all, I thought, I could stump up some money myself to support my old relative if he really was as brassic as he'd made out. I liked the idea of this most worthwhile project.

Making those phone calls was not on God's timetable for me that morning. As I rounded the corner of the house I saw at the bottom of the staircase a monstrous black SUV with tinted windows and vast tyres. Leaning against it like some computer-generated King Kong, his back half turned to me, was what I took to be a chauffeur. Instinctively, I edged behind a stand of tall heliconia leaves and observed for a second how the burnished bronzed dome of his head shone in the sunlight, matched in lustre only by almost iridescent acreages of tight grey suit. A thick fold of bristly neck bulged over his white shirt collar. Something about the scene was causing a rush of adrenalin which made my heart thump. In the blazing heat of the sun, the irrational thought occurred to me that I'd stumbled onto the set of some long-running Netflix production.

Sensing my presence, the chauffeur turned, took six simian strides in my direction and stood towering over me with folded arms. The fat knot of his yellow tie was held in check by a gold chain hung between diamond studs. 'Meestah Cassidy? Señora Assistant Secretary is upstairs. She no like be kept waiting.' His accent was Hispanic. I had seen from Google Maps that we were only about twenty miles from mainland Venezuela.

'Assistant Secretary? Which Assistant Secretary? I wasn't aware I—'

A whoop of female laughter from above, the voice deeper than Lily's. 'Can that really be Mr. Cassidy?'

Even shielding my eyes against the sun, I could not make out the woman's face in the shadows. 'I am Gabriel Cassidy, yes.'

'Oh, this I do not believe!' The Assistant Secretary laughed again. Was I destined to be greeted with such incredulity by every female in this part of the world? 'Pablo,' she called, making a visible effort to come to terms with my skin colour, 'don't keep Mr. Cassidy talking in the heat of the day; he might melt! He's a Brit after all!'

The chauffeur inclined his head a fraction. 'Dees way, Meestah Cassidy,' he rumbled, revealing to my disappointment not a single caricature gold tooth visible through his obsequious grin. The giant was impertinent enough to indicate the way up to what I already regarded as home.

Trying to collect my thoughts, I dropped my swimming bag into a chair and turned to face a sturdy little lady in a brown gaberdine suit and scraped back hair powering towards me across the floorboards, her feet splayed like a duck's. My impulse was to run. 'You have me at a disadvantage, er, madam,' I stammered.

'Janice Cordner. A pleasure to meet you at last.' She handed me a card from which I learnt she was "Assistant Secretary for the Division of Food Security, Natural Resources, the Environment and Sustainable Development: Tobago House of Assembly."

Her accent seemed educated, westernised, if a little nasal. 'But call me Janice. How's your uncle?'

'Eh? Oh. Ah, he's fine, although much diminished, I'm afraid.'

'Neville and I go back thirty-five years. Did you know he was once my History teacher.'

'Indeed?'

'He didn't mention my involvement with the house sale?'

'No.'

'It's a long story.' She was peering up at me through narrow gold-rimmed spectacles. 'Neville didn't mention you were, ehh— one of us.'

'Black, you mean?'

'Of course.' She rocked with laughter again and squeezed my arm. I made certain not to flinch. 'I would naturally have expected his nephew to be Caucasian!'

'Another long story.'

'*Touché*, Mr. Cassidy.' She turned to pick up a gift-wrapped box from the coffee table. 'But listen – may I call you Gabriel? – I've brought you this with the compliments of my client. Trinidad rum.'

'Oh, thank you so much. I look forward to sampling it.'

Janice glanced over at the chauffeur, his colossal bulk blocking the light behind me. 'Wait by the car, Pablo,' she said. 'Mr. Cassidy and I have business to attend to.'

'*Sí*, boss.'

The man trotted with commendable nimbleness down the stairs as Lily materialised bearing a tray of coffee. The cold stares exchanged by these two formidable ladies left me in little doubt that, were it not for my presence, hostilities might have broken out.

'So,' smirked Janice, clearing her tubes with a snort that made my eyes water, 'your housekeeper has been most welcoming, Gabriel. She's a positive mine of information about the flora and fauna of the estate. I shall be certain mention her knowledge and enthusiasm to the client.'

'Actually, she's not a housekeeper,' I said, 'she is the manager here.' Out of the corner of my eye, I saw Lily flash me a smile.

'Leave the coffee there,' snapped the visitor, 'and close the door behind you.' Lily steupsed but did as she was told and when we had the balcony to ourselves, Janice laid hold of my arm again and lowered her voice to a theatrical whisper. 'I assume your petulant *manager* is making you as welcome here as she can, given how today is Valentine's.'

I cottoned on to her revolting insinuation. As my father used to say, "I'm not as green as I am cabbage-looking." 'Certainly not, Ms. Cordner! How dare you suggest I'd even contemplate such an immoral arrangement. I'm a happily married Englishman and a practising Christian.'

The woman had the decency not to laugh. 'My apologies, Gabriel. I didn't mean to offend.'

'Apology accepted. But regarding the topic of the sale, I ought to say I've had a few ideas.'

Janice was pouring coffee. 'Shoot.'

'I thought what a splendid idea it might be to turn the house and grounds into an ecolodge for birders and naturalists. Rather than selling it, you understand – or at least all of it, given I have as yet no idea of the extent of the estate. The place is so beautiful and it would be a shame to... thank you.' I accepted a cup; my speech wasn't coming out quite as I'd planned. 'I was, um, going to mention the idea to Neville this morning, but then you arrived unannounced and, well... I'm sure to be phoning him later.'

Janice eyed me and snorted over her coffee. 'I don't think the Neville I knew would embrace such an unambitious little plan, charming and worthy as it may seem.' She leant against the balustrade and snorted again. Did she have a cold or hay fever? 'The thing is, Gabriel, the client has authorised me to offer a generous sum of money in order to render any such objections or counter-proposals null and void.' A steely look from the woman sent another unpleasant surge of adrenalin though me. 'My client is not a man to be trifled with.'

'Am I allowed to know his identity? I've been vouchsafed no information.'

'Is that so?'

'None whatever.' Two hummingbirds had opened hostilities at the sugar-water feeder. I took a breath. 'The thing is, I wouldn't like you to think me a complete pushover, Assistant Secretary.'

'Call me Janice.' She reached out her hand again, but I avoided her bejeweled fingers by lifting my coffee cup.

'I'd like to be able to do some homework about this client of yours.'

Janice grinned at last. 'His name is Bill McClung – people call him Buck – a hotelier with decades of experience behind him.'

'I can't say I've—'

'He specialises in releasing potential.' She managed to grab my wrist this time. 'And he is determined to see this through without delay. Which is why you and I are going to reconvene tomorrow midday to sign the contract.'

'What? On a Sunday?'

'Buck thinks it would be appropriate for me to unfold his vision to you actually in situ, so we'll be meeting on the look-out above Back Bay. I'll bring the documentation. Your only task today is to agree the price.'

I was momentarily at a loss. Neville hadn't said it would be down to me to sign the deal. 'Right, how much are we talking about?'

'That's more like it, Gabriel.' She pulled out an iPad, flicked open a page and squeezed out a detail of what I presumed was a draft sales contract.

I peered at it and blinked. 'But this is an absolutely colossal sum. We're talking Trinidad dollars, I assume.'

'U.S.'

'What? Buck must be...'

'Out of his mind? Yes, I agree, but he's always been generous to a fault.'

'I don't know what to say.' Over Janice's shoulder, I was aware of movement at an open window along the balcony.

She sniffed and went on, 'Call your uncle and tell him the good news. And if you have a favourite pen, bring it to the meeting.'

I forced a smile to conceal a spasm of panic. 'It's just that I'm not used to being rushed like this, and we certainly don't seem to be going through the correct channels. We'd need time for the conveyancing solicitors to go through it all. And Buck's people will want to be carrying out searches and so forth.'

'Don't be so British, Gabriel.'

'This sort of transaction would take three to six months in the U.K.. Maybe even a year to iron out snags.'

'Snags?' Another peel of laughter. 'This is the Caribbean: we do things differently here.'

'So I'm beginning to understand.'

Janice leaned over the balustrade and called down. 'Pablo, start her up and make sure the AC's on full. I'll be done here in two minutes.' She placed her cup on the tray. 'A final word of warning, Gabriel: any delay on your part will incur a five percent daily drop in the offer price. Buck was clear on this point.'

'What? You can't just—'

She snorted and swallowed. 'As I see it, your job here is simply to expedite the sale as your uncle has instructed. Don't muddy the waters.' Her words passed through me like cold steel. Or so I imagined, having never been stabbed. 'Now, your *manager* will be able to direct you to the meeting place tomorrow. Park at the blue Private Property sign on the Mount Irvine road.' The woman actually squeezed my hip as she swept past, dazzling me with a politician's smile. 'Enjoy the rum, Mr. Cassidy.'

A moment later, the rotund *tour de force* was swallowed up by the SUV and swept away in a cloud of fumes. I remained motionless at the top of the stairs, my heart banging.

Lily was at my side. 'She really sometin',' she whispered.

'You heard all that, I take it?'

'Most, Mr. Gabriel.' She leant against me for second. 'I make you a cup of my special tea. Make ting not seem so bad.'

'Thank you.'

'She have reputation, Mr. Gabriel, for racy dealin' in business – an' with men. She recently divorce again. She likely keepin' an eye out for a rich Brit husband.'

'I tell you, I've never had such an unnerving conversation. Dreadful woman.'

'What you goin' to do?'

'Speak to my uncle and the family lawyer. Try and put the brakes on.' I flopped into a sofa. The interview had left me drained, especially after so little sleep. 'Max will know what to do.'

'Churchill an' me gettin' put out?'

'Not if I can help it, Lily. God willing.' She smiled and headed for the kitchen. I called after her, 'Why was she so hostile towards you?'

'Oh, you know, she jealous 'bout my callin' an' all.'

'Which involves...?'

'Well, Mr. Gabriel, I do plenty work for my own particular church an' so. Maybe I has a reputation for assistin' people in their daily lives.'

'So, you're as involved in your church as my wife is in ours?'

'We women always find a way of keepin' weself busy.'

6

To give me the strength necessary for the phone call to Neville, I made short work of two more slices of coconut bake washed down with Lily's wonderful tea and then, tempted by how good the morning light was, went down to a shady part of the garden with my long lens. With each photo I took I became more determined of the need to persuade my uncle not to sell. Shurland was a haven to nature and should remain so.

When Lily brought me another cup of her tea I showed her a few choice shots. Clapping me on the back, she announced that I'd already quadrupled my collection of hummingbirds: 'Not only you have Copper-rumps, Mr. Gabriel, but you also captured a White-necked Jacobin – see it blue head, white front and green back? – and dis one wid de bright red head and flashin' gold throat, he a Ruby Topaz.'

Exhilarated at these triumphs, I was nonetheless overwhelmed by a sudden imperative to lie down. Perhaps it was the effect of too much sun and salt water – or lack of sleep – or maybe I'd picked up some bug on the plane. A second or two later, or so it seemed, I was indoors flat on a sofa with Lily seated at the table nearby halving limes and squeezing juice into a jug.

The hummingbird print on her voluminous dress was sliding in and out of focus.

'You is tired, Mr. Gabriel,' she was saying, her voice a long way off. 'You overdoin' ting. You need sleep.'

'Mm. Don't feel well. Wake me soon, though. Must call Neville.'

'What de hurry?'

I could barely formulate my words. 'Six o'clock U.K.... sun over yard-arm... Neville too sozzled to deal with.'

'He still drinkin'?'

'I'd say. He's an old wassaname—a toper.'

Lily's eyes seemed to widen to the size of car headlights. 'Certain you doh talk like any black man I know, Mr. Gabriel.'

'No?' I was trying to lever myself out of the sofa. 'Where's my phone? Goodness, I'm feeling utterly sozzled myself. Did you lace my tea with Janice's rum?'

'No, Mr. Gabriel. De bottle right here.' Lily wiped her hands on a cloth and came to tower over me. 'Doh move,' she said, 'I fetch you phone.'

I obeyed her, mesmerised by a swarm of bananaquits bickering over the bowl of sugar Lily had left by the lime skins. The motmot landed on the wall and winked at me. Do birds wink?

Unaware that I'd even tapped in a number, I heard a familiar voice in my right ear: 'Eight-six-oh three-three-five.'

'What? Oh, hello, uncle, it's—'

'Gabriel, you little shit! About bloody time!' I'd forgotten about his coarse language, but it didn't seem to matter so much today. 'Have you contacted the agent?'

I grunted something in the affirmative, trying to concentrate. The now elongated motmot had put its head on backwards and was grinning at me, a thin green tongue slithering over sharp teeth. 'Uncle, I've... um, had an idea to exclude the house itself from the sale.'

'What are you babbling about, man?'

A hummingbird dive-bombed me, the wind from its tiny wing-beats cool on my cheek. 'Under attack here, uncle. Hold on.' I flapped the phone at the bird. 'Thing is, Lily and me... I... we thought we—'

'Who the hell is Lily? You're raving, Gabriel. How much are they offering?'

'Who?'

'The blasted buyers, of course!' The motmot had been joined by three monster mockingbirds holding wing-tips and waltzing around the plate of sliced fruit. 'For God's sake, Gabriel!'

'Mm? What was I saying?' A sudden break in the clouds: the birds evaporated and my head had cleared. 'Oh yes, Lily and I thought, let's turn Shurland into... into an ecolodge nature-centre thingy. For rich American birders. Good idea of mine, eh?'

'Gabriel, you're bloody pissed!'

'Mm?' I saw Lily had resumed her work with the limes.

'And pack it in talking about my business with this Lily woman!'

'She sends her love.' I paused: the floorboards had begun to undulate like reeds on a river bed. 'Lovely woman, Lily.'

'Gabriel, I'm going to ask you very nicely one more time: how much are they offering?'

I glanced up at Lily and belched. Someone was holding my hand. 'Seven point five million.'

'Are you deliberately trying to aggravate me, boy?'

I so wanted to sleep. 'No, no, uncle, I mean it. Seven point five million dollars U.S.'

Neville was breathless when at last he responded. 'Gabriel, Gabriel, I am well pleased with you. I knew you were the right man for the job. I'll drink to that!' I heard him take a slug of liquor. 'You said Yes, I hope?'

'Wanted to check first about my idea of an eco—'

'Shut it with your pansy ecolodge idea. Did you or did you not agree the price?'

A wave of nausea coursed through me. ''Nother meeting tomorrow.'

'Mother of God.'

Someone was dabbing at my temples with a cool wet cloth. 'Uncle,' I heard a clarion voice proclaim, 'will you *not* use this language!'

'Damn and blast you to hell, Gabriel! I'm asking you – imploring you – to say yes, yes, fucking *Yes* tomorrow! Just sign the papers on my behalf!'

'Mm?'

He was still screeching my name as the phone clattered to the floor. Then I was on my back, strong hands arranging my limbs on the sofa, the ceiling spinning, a vast pink gecko rotating on the light fitting. Lily's voice, deliciously warm and gentle: 'You okay now, Mr. Gabriel. Phone on de table.'

'Thanks so m—'

'Sshh. Sleep now. You not well. I wake you for lunch.'

7

When Lily woke me for a chicken sandwich a couple of hours – or days – later, I knew I'd spoken to Neville but was pretty hazy about what exactly had been said. To clear my head, I determined to set off on what Lily called an estate walk while I was feeling a bit better and before I lost the light.

Like so many Londoners after a hefty Sunday roast, Sarah and I tended to drive over to Greenwich Park and exert ourselves by plodding up the steep footpath to the Observatory. Even if the company might not be effervescent, the view north towards the monoliths of capitalism at Canary Wharf held a certain aesthetic interest. This afternoon's lone expedition up the hill behind Shurland was, though, in a different league of exertion altogether. Carrying my camera and supplies from Lily – including a flask of her iced tea and a bottle of mozzie spray – I was obliged to scramble over and under fallen trees, leap rivulets of muddy water and fight my way through a novelty jungle assault course almost too challenging for an out-of-condition suburbanite suffering from what I'd decided was a touch of the 'flu.

Leaning to catch my breath at one point against a tree-trunk, I was intrigued to glance up to observe what looked precisely like a loaf of Waitrose sourdough bread glued to a tree-trunk above me. Wiping the sweat from my eyes, I saw it was in fact a nest teeming with evil-looking black wasps. Edging sideways to avoid it, I almost trod on a snake in alarming pink and black livery. I held my breath as it slithered up the bank not six feet away.

I toiled uphill for twenty minutes, misty and slanting sunbeams painting a pageant of colour on the dense foliage in an ever-changing vista of shadow and light. Vast leaves came at me in all shapes and sizes: fan-shaped ones five foot across, smooth and shiny ones and, worst of all, spiky sabre-like horrors determined to lacerate my delicate Londoner's flesh. Bunches of tiny green bananas and grapefruit the size of Lewisham market watermelons dangled from ancient bushes like Christmas baubles. Lumpish orange cocoa-pods, remnants of the old plantation, hung against gnarled tree trunks like the eggs of alien invaders. As to the extraordinarily exotic flowers I encountered, there were ginger lilies in the brightest maroon, dazzling orange and yellow ones like bottle-brushes, dangling red heliconia like nothing I'd ever seen, and brugmansia or Angel Trumpet, with quivering white dangling blossoms like ballet dancers shimmying along their boughs. And when I looked up, the orange blooms of an immortelle tree positively sang against the deep blue of the sky, hummingbirds and tanagers darting between the flowers like bees.

As I emerged into an abandoned quarry on top of the world my head was once again pounding. I made one last effort and clambered onto a rock in search of the panorama I felt I deserved. Once reasonably comfortable, I pushed back the old Tilley hat Lily had found for me and looked about me. Close at hand was a savannah of tall and shimmering grasses punctuated with low, spiky-barked bushes. A stand of palm exploded skywards nearby, its rattling leaves ripped to tatters by warm sea-breezes. On the summit of the hill beside a clump of mahogany trees stood an imposing and, to me, utterly Caribbean-looking house with a wrap-around balcony. It had been painted in yellow-ochre, this splash of manmade colour only enhancing the exotic and refreshing nature of the scene. Ahead of me, over the shoulder of my ridge and two or three miles below, was the relatively urban sprawl of what I took to be Tobago's capital, Scarborough. Looking through my camera, I focused on pinkish-brown swathes of sargassum floating in the bay.

Swinging to the east again I spotted a man in a red T-shirt and white shorts sitting amongst a flock of goats. Beyond this pastoral scene – one of biblical antiquity, and eminently worth preserving, I knew – the wooded hills were disappointingly alive with the thump of modern music. To the south was the sea, and on its misty horizon the grey-blue forms of mountains I took to be Trinidad's Northern Range. To the west, the dull roar of a plane taking off. I watched it bank left and peel away over my head to vanish over green-topped mountains. The possibility that it might be heading for London fired off in my aching head an extraordinary question: if I could choose between the drear, cold and grey existence I had so recently left behind and the colours, beauty and warmth of Tobago, where would I put down roots? I was already feeling at home here with Lily and Churchill. Maybe it was time to prioritise my ecolodge plan, demand a one-to-one meeting with this 'Buck' McClung and persuade him to invest in such a venture.

I took a long swig of water and polished off half a pack of choc0late-chip cookies imported from Germany, I noted. I saved the best of my picnic until last: two cups of Lily's delicious iced herbal tea.

I was about to head for home when a flock of noisy green parrots settled in a dead tree behind me. In the late-afternoon light these cackling, comedy birds were irresistible and I settled myself to photograph them; but before very long I found myself unable to focus through my viewfinder. Not only did the parrots begin to change colour, but they also took it upon themselves to swell, deflate, swell again and then explode like popcorn in a pan. I was having another attack. What had I picked up on that plane to cause such vivid hallucinations? To make matters worse, while I was loading my backpack again, I dropped the lens cap into a low bush beside me. Reaching down to extract it, I scratched the back of my hand on nasty and almost invisible prickles protruding from the plant's stems. More alarming still was that, wherever I touched them, its miniature fern-like leaves clamped shut like a Venus flytrap. I wasn't imagining things because once on my feet, I brushed my boot across the infernal plant and the whole lot curled up. It occurred to me that even the ground seemed intent upon swallowing me alive if I didn't step up – stand up – to my uncle. I was glad Lily had made me wear full-length trousers and walking boots. 'You do as I tellin' you,' she had insisted. 'You doh wan' get chiggers burrowin' in you ankle.'

I had been expecting to struggle back though a thick screen of lianas which had posed a five-minute problem on the way up, but when I tried to push through from this direction, I was propelled backwards with such force that I lost my footing, slithered down a bank and came to rest in running water with the forest spinning overhead. I fought to disentangle myself from vines coiling snake-like about my ankles and, in a moment of clarity brought about by cooling waters seeping through the seat of my trousers, returned to the fray. Taking a deep breath, I selected two thick strands of dangling creeper and tried to prise them apart. Once again, I could make no headway through the mass of vegetation. I took it into my head that I was up against an invisible marshmallow of gigantic proportions.

It was out of the question that I should spend the night outside and at the mercy of this increasingly dark jungle. I braced myself one last time to make some progress downhill, but the force behind the liana screen remained immovable. I wondered whether I had fallen into some parallel universe where thin air could convert itself into matter. A rhythmic booming – my heart perhaps – resonated around the forest. It occurred to me – late in the day, I know – to offer up a prayer. *Father*, I murmured, *I come before thee to implore thee to rescue me from this nightmare. If it is thy wish for me at this time to*—

Something landed on my shoulder, scuttled across my chest and down my arm. Immobile, I stared as a spider – large enough to have enclosed the business end of my camera lens – paused for thought on my wrist. I felt it was weighing up the pros and cons of inflicting a terminal bite on the back of my hand.

And then it made up its mind.

I saw it crouch, could *feel* its furry body press against my skin. And then it jumped into the lianas and vanished.

With a yell, I leapt up the bank to my left and flung myself into the undergrowth. My one idea was to flee that place. In the panic of my own exodus I rather think I took the Lord's name in vain, berating Him for ignoring my plight and levelling accusations at Him for not wearing His *damnable* hearing aid. With twigs and leaves whipping at my face, and roots determined to bring me low amidst the wildest of imaginings, I crashed on downhill.

Tiring now, hot and breathless, I lumbered on through this awful labyrinth until the ground suddenly gave way beneath me and I was flung forwards into a void. I fell through utter darkness until my forehead smashed into something so unyielding that for an agonizing second all I could see was an explosion of yellow-white dots which faded to black.

How long I was out I have no idea but when I came to what I might loosely term "my senses", I was lying in dry leaves (and who knows what insect life) at the foot of what appeared to be, when I reached out to investigate, a brick wall. Feeling the lump on my head, I tasted blood on my fingers. Beyond my own heartbeat I could hear nothing but the buzz of cicadas, the sigh of the wind in the tree-tops and the scuttle of tiny feet somewhere to my right. Although my head ached horribly, I was struck by the thought that this infernal and sphynx-like forest – like those prickly plants that had tried to grab my lens cap earlier – was doing precious little to endear itself to someone intent upon saving it from the chainsaws of progress. But then, as I lay there in the claggy darkness, it occurred to me that this extraordinary variety of flora and fauna was all part of God's infinite creativity or – and here I forced myself to break with Christian jargon and be pragmatic – biodiversity in the raw. Should I survive, should I ever get over this damnable 'flu virus and its hallucinations, and should I ever be able to persuade my uncle and the Assistant Secretary Janice of the merits of my idea, my earthly work must henceforth involve straining every sinew to preserve the beauty, wildlife and mysteries of Shurland's forest for the future enjoyment and education of hikers, birders and naturalists the world over.

I drained the rest of Lily's tea and, dragging my bag behind me, crawled a few feet into the gloom, soon bumping against what seemed to be an iron pot or cauldron slung between twin metal posts above a pile of soggy ash.

And then the hallucinations started up again.

We Christadelphians don't believe in ghosts, but I found myself nevertheless closing my eyes and gripping my temples to banish an imaginary posse of amorphous phantom figures hunched on the floor and chained against the wall ahead. Beside them, silhouetted in a doorway, a seemingly female somebody stood clasping a small dog to her breast. It was their expectant silence that terrified me most.

From somewhere in the inky blackness came the unmistakable sound of a gun being cocked. I'd heard such a thing often enough in the movies and was pretty sure I was no longer imagining things. Humming tunelessly, this latest manifestation struck a match and lit a cigarette. In the brief orange glow I saw a man cradling a rifle, what looked like a pirate's cutlass hanging at his side.

I rose gingerly to my feet and leant against the brickwork. 'Who is this?' I enquired in as confident voice as I could muster. 'Please don't shoot. My name's Gabriel Cassidy. I'm staying at Shurland.'

A low rumble of merriment. 'Eh-ehh, what you doin' out here, Mr. Gabriel? Lily, she hollerin' for you.'

'Churchill?'

'Eh-ehh,' he repeated. 'I huntin' wild meat. I taught you was an agouti.' He considered me for a second. 'But you too big to go in my pot, Englishman!'

'Listen, Churchill,' I said, quelling an urge to hug him to my breast. 'I can't tell you how glad I am to see you. I've been up to the top of the track—'

'De trace?'

'Yes, the trace, if you like. Anyway, I stayed too long admiring the view and... well, it sounds stupid, but my way down was blocked by something and—'

'You meet de Phantom.'

'Say again.'

'De Phantom, Mr. Gabriel. You ent have no lighter?'

'Er, I don't smoke.'

'Den you ha' no fire to break through. Dat demon, de Phantom, he doh like fire.'

'Okay.' The man was insane. 'But then, right here, I saw—'

'Lily tell you 'bout de slave?'

'Actually she did mention something...' I gripped my temples again. 'Churchill, I'm not feeling too good.'

'You is fine, Mr. Gabriel. An' now de slave know you, you safe. We in Shurland slave quarters.' He gripped my shoulder. 'I guess you see Mrs. Beryl an' she lil' dog too?'

I grabbed a tree trunk to stop myself falling over. 'How on earth did you know?'

Churchill laughed so hard I feared he would drop his gun and shoot us both. 'Come back to de house wid me.'

Mystified and utterly disorientated, I followed him through dense undergrowth to the main path. I'd never have found it by myself. At one point Churchill stopped, pulled out a torch and shone it at another building I'd missed on my way up to the viewpoint.

'What's that place?' I asked.

'De ol' cocoa-house, Mr. Gabriel,' he said, shambling over to a new-looking door and giving a tug on the handle. It was secured with a Yale lock, which was odd since the main house itself was always left wide open. 'For lockin' up meh whacker an' so. For other gardenin', I have meh cutlash.' In the torchlight I saw the flash of steel as he whipped out a machete – he was calling it a cutlass – and slashed at encroaching bushes.

A minute later I saw through the trees the blessed lights of the house I was on a mission to preserve. Churchill gave a shrill whistle as we rounded the corner. Lily appeared on the balcony. 'Oh, Mr. Gabriel!' she whooped. She had been crying. 'Where you been? I worried sick!'

8

It was pitch black outside when I awoke fully dressed on the sofa. My back was in spasm and someone seemed to be pummeling my head with one of those fat green coconuts I'd seen on roadside stalls. I rolled to a seated position and groaned. I had a dim recollection of Lily feeding me spoonfuls of curry and pressing cups of her tea upon me whilst tending to my cuts and grazes. There was a plaster on my temple. I assumed it was she who had covered me with a light blanket. The woman was a true guardian angel.

I lurched dizzily out onto the balcony, slapping at the security light switch to spare my aching eyes. Sinking into a chair, I tried to relax and appreciate the tropical night. What were these hallucinations all about? That rubbery presence behind the lianas, for instance, the demonic entity Churchill had called the Phantom. Could such a thing have existed outside my imagination? Surely not. Basic physics told me that such an occurrence was impossible, and yet I had done battle with it and been thrown to the ground for my pains. I had the bruises to prove it. Perhaps that spider had bitten me. Or maybe I'd inhaled some super-COVID variant on the plane. These random collapses into incapacity were doing me no favours; I needed all my energy and inspiration to think of a way of spiking the enemies' guns and stopping the Shurland sale.

I managed to doze off but needless to say was soon wide awake once more and buzzing with adrenalin. An unearthly whooshing in the forest to the left had blotted out all other night sounds. The noise grew louder and, seconds later, what looked like a fireball came whizzing and crackling into view high in the trees bordering the garden. I shielded my eyes as leaves and branches glowed bright white as the thing hissed and fizzed about. Surely no one would be stupid enough to let off a firework in a forest? The thing roared twice around the samaan tree before hanging in mid-air over the lawn. It had spotted me. An easy target, I threw up my arms to protect my face. A flash of heat on my skin before whatever it was sheered away over my head. A loud bang– and I saw it burn through the corrugated iron roof above me and vanish into the blackness.

My heart banging, I stumbled over to flick the light back on. Squinting up, I made out a hole the size of a cricket ball in the galvanised roofing, its rough edges oozing some dark reddish gunk. I collapsed back into my chair and closed my eyes to banish this latest folly. 'Don't even go there, Gabriel,' I muttered aloud. 'You're not seeing blood. It's just a rust hole you haven't noticed before.'

It was almost daylight when Lily woke me with tea. 'Ooh, Mr. Gabriel,' she was saying, a catch in her voice, 'you lookin' like you been battlin' de Devil himself. Why you out here?'

'Lily, that hole up there in the corrugated iron: has it always been there? I've not noticed it before.'

She craned her neck. 'Sure ting. Rust comin' through. Churchill soon replacin' dat sheet of galvanise. It have a leak when de rain fallin'. It always bad since—' She stopped and scratched her nose.

'Go on.'

'Nuh my place to say. Mr. Neville, he wouldn' like it.'

'Oh, come on, Lily. I've had a bad enough night as it is.'

She paused, a hand to her head. 'Well, Mr. Gabriel, what happen, a piece of galvanise from de roof right there, it come off an'...' She stopped again, lips pursed.

'Lily!'

'An' kill yuh aunt.'

'Er, I never had an aunt.'

She steupsed at me. 'Your auntie Beryl! Mr. Neville marry her in sixty-tree. And den Hurricane Flora, she come and blow off dat galvanise. Beryl, she dead. Right dong here.' Lily was pointing to the base of the samaan tree.

'You mean—'

'Yes, Mr. Gabriel. I sorry.'

A series of gory images rushed me: Beryl partially decapitated; Neville, in the white suit I knew from that photo screaming for help as he rushed down the steps, carrying her back upstairs to lie her lifeless body right here where I was sitting. Meanwhile, the wind continued to lash the trees and bushes as it blazed its trail of destruction across the island. Events horrific enough to turn Neville away from God, seek sanctuary in the bottle instead and divest himself of any attachment to Shurland.

'Did Churchill tell you about the ghosts I imagined last night in the slave quarters?' Lily nodded. 'I was only hallucinating, of course, but there was a lady with them, holding a small dog.'

Lily seemed unfazed by my revelation. 'She Mrs. Beryl. She try to save dat lil' dog from de hurricane, but he dead too. Now Mrs. Beryl, she always walk wid de slave, holdin' she dog tight-tight.' It says much about my frame of mind that I failed to stop this surreal conversation in its tracks. 'Poor gyal,' went on Lily, 'she just twenty-one, Lord rest her soul. She and Mr. Neville only wed a short time. Daughter of British High Commissioner.' She glanced upwards. 'Mr. Neville, he make my father climb up and fix dat roof good. But now it need replacin' again.'

'Hang on, Lily, are you telling me Churchill was working here that long ago?'

'Sure. He come here when he had fourteen years. Den my mother Marie, she arrive in 'sixty-two and dey marry three month before de hurricane.'

And my uncle was asking me to chuck these people out of a place they'd lived for pretty much the whole of their lives? I paused to absorb this information before ploughing on as cheerfully as I could. 'Please don't think me mad, Lily, but earlier tonight I saw some sort of fireball thing shoot straight through the roof. It made that hole we were talking about. Maybe I was hallucinating again, but I'm pretty sure there was blood dripping out of it.'

Lily's eyes opened wider than I'd ever seen them. She blinked twice then crossed herself. 'Oh lors, Mr. Gabriel.' She laid a hand on my shoulder. 'You see a soucouyant.'

'Say again.'

Her mouth formed a perfect O as she exhaled. 'Mr. Gabriel, yesterday you seen de Phantom and ghost of slave. Now a soucouyant. You is *susceptible.*'

'That's the charitable explanation. What did you say it was called?'

'She a soucouyant. Some people say soucounya.'

'It's a she?'

'A ol' woman who live up de hill. Evenin' she come down to suck blood: cow blood.'

'Right,' I said. Lily crossed her arms in defiance of my raised eyebrow.

Lily gasped as if struck by an appalling revelation. 'Lors, Mr. Gabriel! Show me your chest.'

'What?'

'Take off your shirt. Quick, fella! Soucouyant, if she eh find cow, she go suck human blood.'

Against my better judgement I obeyed. 'I really don't think—'

Seeing my torso, Lily let out a shriek which set off the cocricos. 'Ooh, Mr. Gabriel, you get bite! Look at de mark!'

I peered down at two red-raw welts above my left nipple. 'They're just bites I picked up in the forest, Lily. I've not been sucked by some... I don't know... vampire! This is Tobago, not Transylvania!'

Lily glared at me. 'Mr. Gabriel, I nuh expeck such talk from you. I know what I seein'! What happen is when it time to fly out, ol' woman, she slip off she skin an' leave it behind in she house.'

'To facilitate morphing into a fireball. I get it.' I glanced up into the branches where the apparition had briefly roosted. 'To be honest, she sounds a bit of a liability, this old woman of yours.'

'Dat is why people wan' kill her.'

I sighed. 'And what's the approved method for slaying a blood-sucking fireball?'

'When you see she gone, you break in she house, find dat skin an' fill it with salt an' pepper.'

'Right.' I bit my cheek to discourage a knowing smile.

Lily picked up my jacket and shook it. 'Den, you shake it dong good.'

'Okay.'

'An' when she come back—'

'After she's sucked the cow—'

'She try puttin' de skin back on but de salt an' pepper hurtin', hurtin' her so much, she rush out again hollerin' an' screamin'. There popped into my head what Lily would have termed a *disrespeckful* question about whether there was a Royal Society for the Protection of Soucouyants I could contact about these outrages. I suppressed it. Lily pressed on: 'Havin' no skin, an' de sun risin', she dead!'

'Like a vampire.'

'Truth!'

'You're having me on, Lily.'

'No, Mr. Gabriel! I seen it wid dese eyes! One mornin' when I was a child, my mother, she show me a soucouyant lyin' curl up in a drain. No skin on, an' dead as dead. An' she an ol' woman neighbour.'

'Lily, you must have been mistaken.' I downed the rest of my tea. 'It was probably a dead monkey or something. I'm sorry, but I find it hard to believe in these old wives' tales of yours.'

'Mr. Gabriel, I know what I know.' With some energy, she folded up my jacket and set to work plumping up cushions.

'Are you cross with me?'

Lily came right up to my chair and gripped the back of my neck, her eyes blazing with a fervour I'd not seen in her before. 'I vex, Mr. Gabriel, because you is a ass!'

'Eh?'

'You is a African who should know better!'

I gawped at her. Had this been a Disney animation, my jaw would have dropped to the floor with a clang. 'And what has that to do with the price of eggs?'

'What you say?'

'I mean, what does my country of origin have to do with such folklore hocus-pocus?' I had escaped her grip and was on my feet now, pacing the balcony. 'Just because I was born in Ghana, you expect me to sign up for these naive superstitions?'

'Superstition which originate in Africa! Dey brought here by slaves, your own ancestor!'

'Oh, I see what you mean, but—' I stopped: after a lifetime of trying to convince other people of The Truth, I could appreciate Lily's frustration at such dogmatic incredulity on my part. 'Well, there it is,' was my lame-duck conclusion.

'Eh-ehh.' Lily folded her arms. She was quivering with emotion. 'Mr. Gabriel, when you reach here, you tellin' me you is a Christadelphian.'

I paused – a second too long to be truly convincing. 'Indeed.'

'Google say it have only fifty-thousand Christadelphian on planet Earth. You is a minority religion, a *cult*, Mr. Gabriel. You believin' God create de world in six days four thousand year ago, yes, boy? I read you ent believe dinosaur even existin'!'

This wasn't the time to engage with Lily about how God placed dinosaur fossils deep in the earth precisely in order to test our Faith. Besides, the very thought of voicing these admittedly simplistic-sounding beliefs made me nauseous. The floorboards becoming fluid once more, I leant against the balustrade. Kenny the crapaud, now bright yellow, lollopped across the floor and disappeared through the wall.

But Lily wasn't finished with me: 'Mr. Gabriel, what difference it have between what you believe about dinosaur-an'-dem an' what I tellin' you 'bout soucouyant?' Lily was smiling in that superior, sardonic way we are taught to ignore.

'I am talking about The Truth while you – and I say this with respect, Lily – you're talking about fairytales.'

'No, Mr. Gabriel, you is also believin' in fairytales. Jus' different ones to mines.' She was beside me, stroking my arm, her hand warm and soothing. Sarah never touched me these days. 'Listen, fella, I got plenty o' what you call superstitions to tell you about: de douen wid feet facin' de wrong way, a chile who die before he baptize. He lure other children into de forest to kill dem—'

'I really don't think—'

'An' de la diablesse who—'

'Lily! Enough!'

'All of we need fairytales, Mr. Gabriel. Without dem, reality drive us crazy.'

I forced a patient smile. 'I have my Faith to keep me sane, Lily. I look at the madness of the world and I know it is all *meant*. Meant by God our Father.' As if to mock my oft-repeated beliefs, the floor lurched beneath my feet. Looking round in panic, I threw up my arms to fend off a plant pot hurtling at my head. 'What's happening to me?'

'Mr. Gabriel! You okay?'

I could barely formulate my words. 'N-no... not feeling too good. Could we not have this argument now?' The staircase was curling and twisting of its own accord and, in the garden below the trees and bushes were being lashed by a sudden storm.

'Lors, whassup?' Lily was at my side, gripping my arm, supporting me against the ferocity of the gale.

'Down there, Lily! Can't you see her?' I pointed. 'Under the samaan tree.'

'Who?'

'Beryl! She's still alive! I must go to her.' But before I could take a step, the manifestation of my long-dead aunt had rolled over, a bloodstained hand raised, an accusatory finger pointing straight at me. I knew in that second that she would never let me rest until I had saved Shurland.

Lily had me by the waist and was dragging me away from the abyss. 'Mr. Gabriel! Stop! You hallucinatin' again!' She grabbed my face and looked into my eyes but I wrenched myself away to scan the garden for my relative. Nothing. Not even a motmot. Beryl's apparition had gone and the garden was peaceful once more.

'Mr. Gabriel?' Without Lily's supporting arm, I should have fallen.

'I'm sorry, Lily. I must be going mad. If only I could focus, but I feel so ill...keep seeing things.' I held up a trembling hand. There was filth under the nails. 'Ah! I remember now!'

'In that slave prison place, there was a pot...' I squeezed my throbbing temples '...a witch's cauldron, hanging over a fire-pit.'

Lily was guiding – almost lifting me – along the creaking corridor towards the homely safety of the kitchen. 'Is where I do my work, Mr. Gabriel. I invite you nex' time.'

'But what work can you possibly do in a forest?' My head was beginning to clear again, as seemed to be the pattern with these horrible episodes of mine.

'I perform exorcism, Mr. Gabriel. Maybe you hear one your firs' night.' Lily gave an odd little laugh as she sat me down on my stool by the fridge. 'Dat gyal, she a screamer, but she better now. Her mummy say she back workin' at de tax office.'

I peered up at the kindly round face. Her eyes were sparkling, forehead shining in the early morning light,. 'Lily, don't expect me to believe you're involved in... what do they call it?—Voodoo? Black magic?'

'Eh-ehh, guess again.'

My mouth was dry. A muscle over my left eye was quivering. 'You're not a witchdoctor?'

'No, my poor Mr. Gabriel.' Warm hands passed across my face, powerful thumbs pushing outwards over my temples, releasing unspeakable tensions. I may have been sobbing – or perhaps I dreamt it – but I clung to her for a minute or an hour, long enough anyway for the tempest of emotions to subside. Lily was still stroking the back of my head, soothing me like a little boy lost and whispering, 'I do what some people might call magic, Mr. Londoner-Black-White-Man who forget who he is. But it originate in Africa, same as you.' She lifted my face, bent and kissed me, just below the hairline. 'Gabriel,' she said, 'I is no witch doctor, no, no, no. I is a Obeah woman. Maybe I is helpin' you too.'

9

I ate breakfast and felt somewhat restored, but when I asked Lily for more of her tea she brought me a pot of strong coffee instead. 'I give you a flask of my tea for later,' she said, with a consoling pat on my shoulder. 'I sendin' you out explorin'.'

'But I've got this meeting—'

'How long?'

I glanced at my phone. 'About three hours.'

'So, I suggestin' you take a walk at Back Bay near where you is meetin' her. Clear yuh head, Mr. Gabriel.' She was loading a tray with my breakfast things. 'It have a beautiful beach at de far end of Shurland estate. Nobody know about it.'

'Alright, if you're sure I've enough time.'

'Sure as sure.'

I was having difficulty getting my head round how everything seemed to have reverted to normal despite my recent cratering and my hostess's unsettling revelations about being an Obeah woman. Heading for my room, I determined not to encourage Lily by broaching the subject again right now but would decide later whether or not to accept her invitation to witness her "work" – whatever that might entail. At the moment, other things were troubling me; yesterday's manifestation of my dead aunt Beryl in particular had shaken me. I tried telling myself it had been nothing more than a hallucination, yet I was still reeling from a sense of foreboding and guilt which bordered on panic. How was I to rationalise the thrust of this ghostly challenge? Rejecting the possibility that I'd soon wake up in bed to find it had all been a bad dream, I ignored my headache, loaded a bag and set off.

Cocooned in the cool of the Honda's cranky air-conditioning, I used the short drive to fix the tone I should take with Janice. I needed to be as calm and savvy as possible if I was to negotiate a way between the absurdly rushed demands of Neville and Janice, and what I had chosen to regard as my duty to safeguard Shurland. 'Be firm but flexible, Gabriel,' I lectured myself under my breath. 'Take no nonsense from her: no one's going to brow-beat you today.'

As instructed, I parked in the shade by the Private Property sign. I left a set of more formal meeting clothes on the back seat, skirted some raised corrugated-iron vegetable patches and walked downhill towards the sound of the sea. I was wearing the Tilley hat, a pink shirt and bathing shorts and carrying a macramé bag of Lily's containing snorkel, towel, flask of special tea, car keys and my phone. It occurred to me too late that I might as well have been carrying a fluorescent green banner with *TOURIST! PLEASE HELP YOURSELF!* painted on it. I entered some woods and began a treacherous descent down a rough breeze-block staircase pegged unevenly amongst a chaos of twisted roots. Half way down the escarpment, I perched myself on a log and took a long and welcome draught of Lily's tea. I tried to banish from my mind Beryl's phantom entreaties, Lily's nocturnal activities, her descriptions of the fireball soucouyant things, douens, the la diablesse and my humiliating early-morning breakdown – something my wife would have called "a collapse of stout party".

Sarah.

I hadn't thought of her for what seemed like years. She seemed to belong to another life already, but the thought of her reminded me that maybe I should be praying for strength. I tried closing my eyes but felt immediately so sick I abandoned the plan. 'Delete everything else,' I muttered aloud, 'and concentrate on the job in hand.'

Seen through the black silhouettes of almond and sea-grape trees, the Caribbean looked calm, benign and blue with innocent little wavelets lapping at the sand. A pair of mockingbirds fluttered and fussed in the leaves above me and a small blueish heron paddled in a brackish pond to my right. I rose unsteadily and, holding onto one tree then another to counteract my nausea, descended to the sandy woodland floor and headed unsteadily for the beach. Before I was clear of the woods, though, there was a pounding of feet and a muscular youth materialised at a run from between the trees. With a strangulated yell of outrage, he careered into me, the impact of the collision sending us both sprawling amongst sandy roots. I recognised him in an instant: it was Riley B, my taciturn neighbour from the flight over, he who had lost his camouflage shorts to Maisha at the airport. I lay for a moment on my back, foliage spinning overhead.

Riley B's face darkened my view. 'Dinnae fucking tell anyone you saw me here, right? This never happened, d'y'understand?' Glaswegian accent: curious, I'd had him down as a Londoner.

I hitched myself onto an elbow. 'Look, Riley,' I snapped, 'I didn't—'

'Christ! How d'you know muh bloody name?'

'It's written on your belt.'

He scowled. 'Just remember, arsehole, you didnae see me.'

'Got it.'

With a final sneer, the lad jammed a small jam-jar of green leafy stuff into his pocket and bounded away towards the staircase.

I scrambled to my feet only to realise I was yet again under scrutiny, this time from an old scarecrow of a man leering at me from behind a tree trunk. The latest arrival opened a toothless chasm of a mouth, belched twice and collapsed into inane fits of giggling, his popping yellow eyes evidence I assumed of long-term substance abuse. Tangled ropes of grey hair burst from a grubby blue cloth on the back of his head. He reminded me of Ben Gunn from *Treasure Island* – or one of those improbable CGI submariner zombies from *Pirates of the Caribbean*. The bearded loon was hopping from foot to foot as if the sand were too hot – despite our being in the shade. He was brandishing a partially plucked chicken.

Ben Gunn ceased cavorting for a second and shoved his awful face close into mine. A nauseating odour of farmyard excrement assailed my nostrils and set the trees around us waving like kelp on the seabed. I was beginning to formulate how best to address the poor creature when my wrist was grabbed from behind. I was flung about and pinioned against a tree-trunk. My hat arced to the sand where it grew crab-like legs and scuttled away.

Perhaps because of my size and colour I had survived unmugged and unmolested in south London for forty-odd years, but here the rules were different. Any temptation to laugh off the situation gave way to icy fear. I focused on my latest attacker. This was a younger Rasta in T-shirt and shorts, his hair also stashed away in a grey cloth like a turban that flopped about each time he moved his head. Sinewy and muscular, he had a long, foxy face with flecks of white like fake snow in his stubble. Although he was an inch or two shorter than me, there was a crazed look in his eye that brooked no argument. Besides, he had positioned a two-foot cutlass like Churchill's across my collar-bones.

The man spoke: 'Aye, asshole!'

It was evidently my turn today to be the recipient of verbal abuse. I dared not move for fear of being eviscerated. 'Mm?' I grunted. My assailant, however, was not talking to me.

Ben Gunn stopped leaping. 'Yeah, boss?'

'Lester, you ol' bastard, go fornicate wid your fuckin' chicken somewhere else! I got business to talk wid dis gentleman.' The blade twitched against my windpipe.

'No problem, boss.' The old boy scampered off down to the shallows where he proceeded with squawks of triumph to belabour the water with the dead fowl.

The "Boss" gently slapped at my face with the fingertips of his spare hand. Despite the proximity of steel to my jugular, I felt I should try and bond with the enemy like they do in kidnap movies. I drew in a careful breath and swiveled my eyes towards this Lester. I tried to say something but my voice failed me and I emitted only a half-hearted croak.

'Yah man, you addressin' me?' I made apologetic eyebrow movements in the negative. 'Cool,' he nodded, taking a drag on his roll-up and blowing smoke in my face. That sickly sweet smell again. (Not that I had ever mixed with smokers, but this was no off-the-shelf tobacco.) He peered at the plaster on my forehead. 'Been fightin', man?'

'Er, nope.'

He indicated my bag. 'What you have?' A rhetorical question since he had simultaneously tugged it from my grip and shaken it out on the sand. Extending his arm but keeping the point of his blade against my neck, he bent to pick up my phone. 'Ni-ice. Latest model.' He pocketed it. 'Where de cash? No cash, no purchase.'

'Actually, I don't need to buy anything today. And there's no point in stealing my phone; you'll need my thumbprint to open it.' Lame, but worth a try.

The man's eyes opened wide. 'You for real, man?' He burst out laughing, a baroque array of gold molars glinting in the dappled sunlight. He raised his voice. 'Eh, fellas, come look what de blue Caribbean trow up on de beach!' Five or six shady figures materialised from what I now saw was less a stegosaurus and

89

more a make-shift shelter of palm leaves and bamboo slung between branches. 'Black man talkin' like a white man.' He pointed at one of his comrades, a rotund young lad sporting golden ear studs and Chelsea football shorts. 'Eh, fat boy, check he pockets.'

The lad frisked me. 'Nuttin', boss.'

The cutlass was lowered. 'I tinkin',' the Boss went on, leaning the blade against the tree, 'He Royal Highness too tight-arse to hide cash… anywhere else.' He patted my bottom and the gang laughed.

'Listen,' I said, quivering all over, 'I was just off to do some snorkeling along the beach. I'm staying up the hill and—'

The Boss made a face. 'Where you stayin'?'

'Well, at Shurland actually and I—'

'Shurland?' His expression had changed even before he exploded with mirth again, thumping my shoulder. 'Why you ain't say so?'

'Well, I—'

'You stayin' by Lily?'

'Absolutely.' My headache took a turn for the worse.

'You is Gabriel?'

'How did you—?'

'Neville nephew?'

'Indeed.'

'Ehhh.' The Boss gestured to his companions. 'We expectin' a white fella!'

I tried to smile, but my facial muscles were not functioning. 'Easy mistake to make. But fancy you knowing Lily.'

A bandy-legged lad with the merest suspicion of a goatee beard sidled up and punched me on the other shoulder. I'd never in my whole life been so pummeled. 'Everybody know Lily, bro.' His voice rang with true reverence. The sand beneath my feet began to undulate again.

The Boss put his arm round me and squeezed. 'Right so, Gabriel, want me tell you how I know Lily?' He leaned in close, pupils dilated and his breath reeking.

'You must.'

'She my mudder.'

'Oh! You must be Trevor!'

'Yah man.' We performed one of those slow-motion to-me-to-you hand pumps before Trevor handed back my phone. 'But doh tell mudder I borrow dis, right? A lil' misunderstandin'. Lily, she... emotional sometime.'

'I can imagine.'

'You got parents, Gabriel?'

'No, both passed on, I'm afraid.'

'Bad.' He pulled the cigarette out of the corner of his mouth and offered me its soggy tip.

'No, really I'm fine.' This time I mustered what I hoped was an actual smile rather than a mocking leer; despite this new bonhomie, there was something unhinged and dangerous about Trevor, like dealing with a urinating drunk on the last train out of London Bridge; except this one was armed, powerful and backed up by a mob of stoned henchmen. The last thing I wanted to do was upset him.

Trevor regarded his spliff. 'Dis quality shit, Gabriel. As you is family, I do best price. Respec', man, no problem.'

'Oh, I'm only a house guest but that's very kind. I'll bear it in mind if ever I change my...' The ground gave a lurch and I almost fell.

Trevor was holding me up. 'You okay?'

'Absolutely. Just one of my dizzy spells. The heat probably. Not used to it. If you could just pass me that flask...'

Still holding my elbow, Trevor watched as I took a long draught. 'Dat Lily special tea?'

'Yup. It's delicious.'

He glanced at his mates. Did someone giggle? 'Tasty an' refreshin'?'

'Absolutely. But look, Trevor, I'd better get on. Things to do: fish to see.' I was laughing, my headache gone. That moment of clarity at last. 'In fact, I've a meeting later. Don't want to be late.'

'Understan'.' He let go of my elbow and peered into my eyes. 'Better now?'

'Yup, thanks so much.'

'Eh, fat boy,' Trevor commanded one of his colleagues, 'what you waitin' for? Collec' up we friend ting!' He gave me a wily look which implied that despite threatening me with death earlier and stealing my phone we were henceforth, if not exactly blood brothers, then best of friends. (Sarah would have opined at this point that 'the Lord moveth in mysterious ways'; I'd have countered that it was more my association with Lily that had saved the day.) 'We good, man?'

'Oh yes, absolutely: a pleasure meeting you.' I took my bag from Trevor's portly subordinate. 'Well, gentlemen, I'll see you around. Shall I give Lily your love?'

'No problem, man. Don' swim out too far. Big fish waitin'.'

'Ah.'

'Drink plenty o' Lily tea. Sun in sweet T&T hot-hot.'

'Unlike in the U.K.' I turned to leave, nodding to Lester as I passed. He was lying on his back in the shallows clasping the soggy chicken to his breast.

Trevor called after me. 'Aye, Gabriel!'

Something hit me in the back. 'Ah, my hat!' I cried. 'Of course. Thanks so much.' I saw Trevor raise a fist and grin.

Sensible of laughter and at least six pairs of eyes boring into my back, I made efforts to walk tall without weaving. With great deliberation, I clambered over a spur of dark stone and, once out of sight of what Sarah would call the 'druggies', collapsed onto the warm, damp sand and leant back against the salt-silvered trunk of a fallen tree. I tried to focus on the vista of jagged rocky outcrops jutting from the sea below the wooded escarpment, but even when I closed my eyes, everything continued to spin. I really hoped a swim might do me good because, with only two and a bit hours before my meeting, I needed to sort out my head – preferably without bumping into any more of Lily's family members or local nutters.

10

There was movement in the wet sand to my right as I opened my eyes: a crab the colour of spun gold was inspecting me through poky little black eyes on stalks, its reproving expression seeming to imply that this unpredictable illness of mine was somehow God's little joke, punishment for leaving my Bible behind in London. I began to fear that my belief system was in danger of being eroded in Tobago. I closed my eyes to pray for help but once more, my attempts culminated only in a surge of nausea so strong that it caused me to twist to one side and retch onto a pile of curly pink seaweed. Through screwed-up eyes, I saw the crab hastily burying itself in the sand.

My headache was receding, but any sliver of hope that I might be on the road to recovery was replaced by the absolute conviction that I was being watched. With forced nonchalance, I craned my neck to peep over the rock behind me, scanning the towering foliage to my left. Nothing. 'First you hallucinate,' I muttered aloud, 'then you throw up, and finally you become paranoid. To cap it all, you're talking to yourself. Perhaps it's time to see a doctor.'

I took a swig of Lily's life-saving elixir and, ignoring Sarah's voice in my head whingeing on about the dangers of snorkelling alone, hid my phone high on a rocky ledge and waded into the sea. The water was glorious. I ducked my head, tugged on my mask and dived through a low breaker to share the domain of the most beautiful and exotic fish I had ever seen outside a David Attenborough documentary. They came in all shapes, sizes and colours: bright blue ones with yellow eyes, shoals of tiny silver ones, fat tiger-striped specimens, miniature eel-like ones and even what I took to be a squid scurrying along near the bottom. The rocks I floated over were bristling with black, spiny sea-urchins; those above the water-line skittered with nervous black crabs.

I emerged at one point to rinse my steamed-up mask and found myself being eyeballed by a pterodactyl-type creature perched on a white-excrement spattered rock ten feet away. Treading water, I blinked at the alarming apparition until it morphed into a dirty grey pelican and flew off.

Swimming warily down shadowy channels and gulleys between sharp and glistening volcanic rocks, I soon convinced myself that unseen predators out to sea – the big fish Trevor mentioned – had me in their sights. The unseen presence amongst the trees just now had been bad enough, but out here it was far worse. With my nearly naked body vulnerable to anything lurking out there in that blank blue wall of ocean, I started to imagine the appalling pain of any one of my limbs being summarily ripped off and devoured. I'd read the news stories from Bondi Beach, hadn't I? – seen each of the *Jaws* movies multiple times. I'd no idea whether man-eating sharks were even resident in the Caribbean, but one thing was for sure: if they were, they'd be unlikely to be made of metal and rubber like the one at Universal Studios. And then, what about killer whales, giant squid or that thing called the kraken in *Pirates of the Caribbean*? I weighed up the possibility of climbing out and scrambling back over the rocks, but at what cost to my bare feet? For the second time in an hour, I feared for my life. There was nothing for it but to grit my teeth against my imagination and the unknown and swim back round to the beach.

When at last I felt the merciful sand between my toes, I retrieved my phone and bag and made my way through a sheltered gorge between a towering lump of obsidian and the wooded cliffside. To my left, a path wound away upwards, an alternative route back to my car, I surmised, which would allow me to avoid meeting Trevor and Co. again. The beach either side stretched empty as far as I could see so I strode out along an open spit and laid my towel down at a point where, with my back to the water, I could keep an eye out for unwanted company. For a while I felt reasonably secure, able to relax at last, worn out after my exertions. I drank the rest of Lily's tea and once again offered up thanks that I had her on my side. I felt in those minutes almost contented; so much so that I took a series of panoramic shots with my phone, the vivid combination of blue sea and sky through the gap in the cliff, the greens of the forest and the ever-changing black and white of foam against rock being too much to ignore.

Above the high water mark nearby stood a grove of weather-beaten trees growing in a curling chaos of twisted grey trunks dusted on their sunny side with bright orange lichen. Whilst admiring this cacophony of shapes and colour I was startled to see a man, using neither hands nor arms – and in open defiance of the laws of gravity – corkscrewing head-first down a tree. As I stared, appalled, his dark face appeared round the trunk, red eyes gleaming out of a serpent's head and a toothless mouth widening into a leer. A forked tongue flicked out. I had been spotted.

I didn't hang about waiting for it to slither over and introduce itself. I grabbed my stuff and legged it like a wild man up the cliff path, fear and adrenalin once more coursing through me. Behind, I sensed the thing snapping at my ankles, its hungry guttural cries amplified by the rocks. My only thought was escape, to avoid being seized, dragged back down the cliff and having my skull split open on a rock. Even the sea seemed angry with me now, an immense surge of foaming breakers smashing themselves against the beach with a roar that echoed in my head. Panic gave me the strength to grab at saplings and swing myself like a chimpanzee up the final steep steps to the top of the escarpment. Gasping for breath, I hauled myself through foliage and emerged trembling into the relative peace of baking sunlit grasslands. And then, percolating through the thumping white noise in my head, came very human cries of distress from somewhere beyond a stunted old tree. I dropped to the ground amongst long grasses. 'Please God,' I wheezed, 'what now? Let me not be going insane.'

I pushed forward through the barricade of grass and collapsed into a nest of dry leaves beneath the tree. For half a minute I lay on my back with my eyes shut, holding my hurting head. Someone had nailed a wooden sign to one of the branches spinning above me but from my angle I couldn't read what it said. I assumed it was something about this being private land. Well, my uncle was the owner, so what did I care?

The voices meanwhile were becoming more strident. I rolled onto my front and edged forward until I could peer under a banana leaf on the far side of the tree. Six people were gathered about fifty yards away near one of the tall coconut palms that punctuated this desolate spot. Before them was the burnt-out shell of car, one of those low-slung Japanese vehicles so favoured by the young males of Tobago. It had been abandoned to the conflagration at the end of a track, the grasses around singed and blackened. The anguished wailing was coming from three women – a mother and two grown-up daughters maybe – holding each other and staring tearfully at the still smoking wreck. Their menfolk remained silent, hovering in the background and looking half-heartedly round for some obvious explanation. In England I would have felt it my civic duty to approach them and ask if I could call a policeman. Here, though, after the day I'd had, my instinct was to suppress any sense of guilt and leave well alone. I thought about ringing Lily. She'd know what to do. I pulled out my phone but there was of course no signal. An hour and ten before my meeting. Maybe I'd feel better after forty winks. That seemed to be the pattern. I shoved my bag under my head and tried to relax, hoping that under this gnarled old tree I was concealed sufficiently from intruders. Why had Janice insisted upon this unsavoury location to conduct business, I wondered?

Thankfully, the sounds of human misery retreated and I drifted off to the dull roar of the waves below. In my dream, I was dead. I saw Janice and Pablo floating above the grasses, pointing this way and that as if attempting to locate my corpse. yet quite unconcerned at the news of my demise. I made as if to wave or call out but my defunct body declined to respond to any signals from my aching brain. I wanted to text and say I was sorry for having missed them, and had they thought any further about turning Shurland into a... and then I couldn't remember my plan.

After what seemed like minutes but must have been hours later, it felt as if somebody was sprinkling holy water on my body – not something we practised in The Truth – and I awoke in near darkness with rain pattering on the leaves above. I was soaked through and the skin above my left ankle was blotched and stinging. How stupid to have allowed myself to be sunburnt. Also, I'd been bitten all over again.

It was a while before it dawned on me that I'd missed the appointment: I could imagine only too well how Janice would react to being stood up.

I struggled out from under my tree and scrambled to my feet. Peering cautiously about me, I saw no sign of the grieving family. The sky however was an ominous grey and in the leaden-hot humid air of the dusk the sea boomed moodily below the escarpment.

On my way back to the road, something made me stop and glance inside the skeleton of the destroyed car. It was a horrible still-life in charred metalwork, a contorted and blackened mass of engineering perched like a sacrificial pyre at the centre of a pile of rain-pocked and darkened ash. I pulled off my hat, a sudden sense of loss and misery washing over me. Death had recently stalked this desolate corner of Tobago.

I trudged away as quickly as I could manage down the track. Soon, I reckoned, I must strike the main road. And with luck – a few hundred yards along to the left – I would come across my own car, intact and homely, my means of escape back to Lily and sanctuary. I pulled out my phone to see if I was back in signal yet but the battery was dead. I would just have to deal with the fall-out from Janice in the morning.

'Gabriel,' I chastised myself aloud as I unlocked the Honda a few minutes later, 'you're going to have to beat this virus and up your game if you're serious about saving Shurland.'

11

'Where you bin dis time, Mr. Gabriel?' Lily clasped my right hand in a state of panic as I entered the house. 'I so worried 'bout you again! I taught you was dead!'

'Not quite, although I've not been feeling too good – and my phone died so I couldn't call you. And I missed Janice.'

'Mr. Gabriel, she vex, plenty vex! She round here wonderin' where you was. And dat giant, he say dey find your car but no Gabriel. He tell me you drown for sure.'

'Drowning was the least of my worries. But listen, have you got some after-sun cream?' I propped my foot up on the balustrade and she gasped at the red, blistering skin on my shin.

'But what happen, Mr. Gabriel? Dat no sunburn.'

'No clue. I must have fallen asleep under an old tree on the clifftop and when I woke up it was raining and... now it really stings.'

'Lors, boy, you sleep under a manchineel tree! You ain't read de sign? It poisonous! If sap go in yuh eye, yuh blind. If you eat de fruit, yuh could o' dead by now. You lucky I know de remedy. Come an' sit down by me in de kitchen.'

I sat obediently while Lily dabbed at the affected areas with a cloth smelling of vinegar. 'I met someone this morning,' I said, wincing as whatever it was seeped into my raw skin. 'He claimed he was your son.'

Lily looked up. 'My Trevor? On de beach?'

'In the woods, yes. With a few, er, associates.' I omitted details of Trevor's spaced-out drug-dealer demeanour, his use of a cutlass as an offensive weapon and his seizure of my phone. If Lily wanted to share maternal confidences about her son with me, it was up to her. 'But anyway, after my swim, I began to feel really bad again—'

'You hallucinatin' like yesterday?'

'How did you know?'

'You got de virus bad. But I got sometin' make you feel better.' She opened the fridge door and pulled out a cellophane bag of brownish shards of something squished into bite-sized blocks. 'Sugar-cake: speciality of Tobago.' She produced another small bag. 'Also tamarind balls. Good for headache. Try.'

I picked up a sugar-coated, brown pellet the size of an old-fashioned gobstopper. 'Should I trust you, Lily?'

'Eh-ehh! Jus' mind de seed.'

Like an idiot, I bit into it, my taste-buds instantly assaulted by an explosion of garlicky sweetness and a diabolical sting-in-the-tail of hot chilli pepper. 'Woah!' I huffed and hawked, beads of sweat bursting out on my upper lip.

Lily was shrieking with laughter, her mouth cavernous and pink, teeth gleaming. 'Oh-ho! You is no Trini, boy!'

I spat out a shiny black stone like a coffee bean. 'Gordon Bennett, Lily, you might have warned me. For that, I demand a pot of your special tea.'

'You drink enough tea today, you understan'? I make you coffee instead. Very nice wid sugar-cake.'

'If you say so.' A pang of disappointment. 'But thanks for doing my leg. It's feeling better already.'

'You're welcome.'

'I'll plug in my phone and send a grovelling text to Janice. I suppose I'd better sort out a meeting for next week.'

I slipped down from the stool while Lily busied herself with coffee. Attending to domestic chores seemed to be her stock response to any mention of the sale of Shurland. 'I bring coffee on de balcony, Mr. Gabriel,' she said without looking up.

There were four messages from Janice delivered in a veritable crescendo of outrage and frustration. She must also have already whined to Neville because there was an absolute humdinger from him too deriding me as 'a wastrel son-of-a-bitch and a dullard. As my business representative,' he fulminated, 'you're about half as much *fucking* use as the proverbial chocolate teapot! Tosser!'

Lily was listening. Her hand came to rest on my shoulder. 'Dese people bad, Mr. Gabriel. You take care.'

'This is no way of doing business: no one shouts at me. And as for my uncle, he—'

'Mr. Neville, he racial. Always was. I remember how he use to treat us.'

My phone rang. "Caller ID Unknown". 'Sorry, Lily, I'd better take this.'

'Meestah Cassidy?' The familiar Hispanic voice was steeped in menace.

'Speaking.'

'Pablo here. Personal Assistant to Señora Assistant Secretary Janice Cordner.'

'I remember you.'

'Our meeting today—'

'I'm really sorry, I was—'

'Señora Assistant Secretary, she has a full schedule.'

'Yes, obviously, and as I said I'm—'

'However,' he paused, and I imagined him cracking his knuckles, 'she give you one more chance to meet. One. As soon as, *sí?*'

'Quite. Absolutely.' Lily was looking at me wide-eyed, shaking her head. I went on, 'What about nine a.m. on Monday?'

'More convenient to Señora Assistant Secretary is nine p.m.'

'All right, I'm sure I can—'

'Today.'

'What?' I glanced at the clock. 'But that's in five minutes! Listen, I'm still feeling pretty ropey and I—'

But the line was dead. Lily was peering out into the night, her expression nothing short of appalled. My heart thumping again, I stood and followed her gaze. In the trees below the end of the garden was the unmistakable flash of headlights. The government SUV was already creeping up the driveway. Lily gripped my hand. 'I nearby if you need anyting, Mr. Gabriel.'

I just had time to change my shirt and put on some long trousers before a heavy footfall on the stairs announced the presence of the Assistant Secretary. She was wearing another gaberdine suit, but this time in a dark purple to match her mood. My stomach turned over.

'Good night, Mr. Cassidy,' she snarled, her face barely distinguishable in the darkness.

'Janice, good – er – evening.' My mouth was dry. 'Listen, I'm so sorry about this afternoon. I came over all peculiar and passed out under a—'

'Spare me the excuses. Your absence was noted – and reported to your uncle – who shares my disappointment.'

'Yes, he has already phoned me to, er, express his feelings on the matter.' I slathered on an amiable grin.

But Janice was in no mood for smiles this evening. 'Shame you couldn't make it to the look-out I was planning on introducing you what is projected to be the hub of the site.'

'What site? What are we talking about?'

'I can't believe you ask such questions of me, Mr. Cassidy.' She gave one of her guttural snorts, slid her glasses off her nose and polished them with a tissue, all the while peering at me with contempt and malice. 'I advise you not to play games.'

Behind me, Pablo belched. I turned and, to my consternation, saw he had assumed a bouncer-like pose at the top of the stairs.

In his yellow blazer with arms folded, he reminded me of one of those colossal bulldozers you see relandscaping vast tranches of the planet to accommodate a motorway sliproad. Although I was trapped, Lily's shadow framed in a darkened window gave me strength enough to face him down: 'Something you wanted to contribute, Pablo?' The situation brought to mind a time forty years ago when two older boys cornered and beat me up in the school changing rooms before pushing an overripe banana into my mouth. 'Let that be a lesson to you, Monkey Boy,' they'd jeered. And since I lived with that blasted nickname until the end of my school career I wasn't now going to allow myself to be bullied by this Venezuelan mobster.

The Assistant Secretary flashed a sudden grin to break the tension. 'Now then, Mr. Cassidy, it's simple: the sooner we can get things signed, the better.' She reached into a leather folder. 'This document is a preliminary draft contract of sale. Signing it would be a gesture of goodwill on your part.' She slapped it down on the table, pointed a pudgy index finger at the price offered. 'You'll note that Buck is a man of his word and has reduced the sum mentioned yesterday by five percent in response to your delaying tactics this afternoon.'

'He can't—'

'Leaving an offer which in my view is still beyond generous.' She pulled out a pen. 'If you'd just sign here, Mr. Cassidy, Pablo I'm sure will witness.'

I took a deep breath. 'Janice, I can't and indeed won't sign.'

It was as if someone had opened the door to the abattoir coldstore. After a long silence broken only by the buzzings and chirrupings of the night, Janice put the pen down and looked into my soul. 'And why not, precisely?'

'Well, I should've thought it was obvious.'

'Enlighten me.'

'First, because I haven't discussed the deal with our solicitor, and second, I haven't read the small-print. It's usual practice in the U.K. that before contracts are exchanged, the conveyancing solicitor goes through the details. These things can't be rushed. We're not selling a... flippin' billy-goat.'

Janice exchanged a look with her henchman. I heard him move closer. 'Here in the Caribbean,' she said, forehead gleaming, 'we are not hampered by such bureaucratic niceties. If we want something done, we pay someone and it's done. The fact is, I have a deadline.'

'I'm sure we—'

'It is my responsibility to see this deal through my Planning Department within ten days: by Ash Wednesday, in fact, when Buck arrives in Tobago. It's what was agreed with your uncle.' Janice rooted amongst her papers and flashed at me the print-out of an email.

'I know nothing about such arrangements,' I said, sweat trickling down my back. 'But I'll be speaking to Neville tomorrow. I'll ask him to update me then.'

Unsmiling, Janice held the pen out again for me. 'Tomorrow will be too late, Mr. Cassidy. Isn't that right, Pablo?' The meatloaf shifted his weight behind me. I heard his shiny brown shoes creaking.

What I said next felt akin to placing my head on an executioner's block. I moistened my lips. 'The other problem, Ms. Cordner, is that I'm not actually *permitted* to sign.'

'What you say?'

'I have no Power of Attorney.'

Janice pursed her lips and breathed out through her nose. Did she nod to Pablo? For the look of it, I made a show of flicking through the paperwork but saw out of the corner of my eye Pablo step indoors. 'You a photographer, Meestah Cassidy?' came his sneer.

I spun round to see the brute handling my camera. He switched it on and peered at its display. 'Nice bird. What is it? A seagull?'

'Put that down, you great lummox.'

Ignoring me, he lifted it to his eye and pointed the long lens out into the night towards the twinkling lights of Plymouth. He was muttering appreciative noises for his mistress's benefit. And then, with a grunt he pretended to drop it.

I roared, 'Bloody put that down!' This was my first use of a profanity and I half expected the Lord to strike me dead. 'No one touches my camera!'

His eye to the viewfinder, Pablo continued to smirk. 'Uh-huh?'

'I said, put it down!' I leapt at him, smacking the heavy lens sharply upwards and grinding the camera body into the bridge of his nose. He screeched with rage. I seized the camera with both hands and ripped it from his grasp. 'Thank you,' I added.

Pablo pressed an enormous hand to his face and snarled '*Vete a la mierda!*' I have no Spanish but had a pretty good idea he wasn't inviting me home to meet the wife and kids. What I did know was that as a lifelong pacifist, my recent and unprecedented loss of temper might well have landed me in serious trouble. Pablo had triggered something deep inside me and yet I felt no remorse. Quite the opposite, in fact. And the fact that I had not yet been struck down proved once and for all that God moves in mysterious ways.

Ignoring Janice, I braced myself and waited for the colossus to make his move. Eyes aflame, Pablo closed his right fist. With his other hand, he squeezed the bridge of his nose to stem a trickle of blood that had materialised on his upper lip. He took two steps towards me and I darted behind the coffee table to place my camera out of harm's way on a chair cushion. Edging down the balcony, I prepared myself for fisticuffs.

'Eh! Enough!' Janice advanced between us and put a hand on Pablo's heaving barrel of a chest. She turned to me, her voice icy. 'Mr. Cassidy, today you seem determined to try my patience. Such displays of British prevarication will not go unnoticed by our client.' She indicated to Pablo to collect up the papers. 'However, now you are fully aware of our requirements, I suppose I must give you one more chance – in deference to the many fond memories I have of my former teacher. Such a handsome man he was in his youth, your uncle. Such charisma.' She looked into my eyes and I suppressed a shudder. '"Neville de Devil" we girls used to call him.'

'I'll be sure to tease him about this nonsense when I get home.'

Janice snorted again and tugged down on her jacket, emphasising her surplus pounds. 'I have decided to allow you time to sort out Power of Attorney, Mr. Cassidy. To be honest, I am disappointed you did not have the foresight to arrange one beforehand.'

'I've already told you, my uncle merely instructed me to—'

Pablo snapped, 'Shut it, asshole.' I was gratified to see three droplets of blood on the yellow lapel of his blazer.

Janice snapped. 'Thank you, Pablo. I'm dealing with this. Mr. Cassidy, to focus your mind, I shall email Neville a progress report momentarily. In the meantime, we meet again midday Tuesday to sign this off. I would have suggested tomorrow, Monday, but I have an important election committee to chair. Oh, and obviously there'll be a further five percent reduction in the offer price.'

'But you can't do that!'

'We'll see what I can and can't do.' She squinted up at Pablo and dropped her educated accent. 'For de love of God, fella, wipe your nose. You bleedin' like a pig.' She tossed him a pack of tissues from her handbag. 'Mr. Cassidy, once you've agreed to settle up with *me*, I'll bring you up to speed with our plans.' I gripped my own hands together as if in prayer; I didn't want them seeing me tremble. 'And if you feel inclined to importune me further by making yourself scarce on Tuesday, be aware the ports and airport are in hands *sympathetic* to my cause.'

'You're actually threatening me?' Janice and Pablo put on a pantomime of laughter for my benefit. 'And what the *hell* do you mean by "settle up" with you?'

Janice levelled another look of incredulity at me. 'I'm sure your uncle will advise you as to an appropriate agency commission, given the size of my client's offer.' She snorted once more. 'Pablo, get me out of here. This faded colonial backwater is giving me the creeps.' She patted his arm before starting down the stairs. 'I'll give you a minute to say "bye-bye" nicely to our host. Have a good evening, Mr. Cassidy.'

I thought for one moment of misplaced optimism that Pablo was going to pass me without comment, but as he drew level, he shot out a hand the size of a roasting dish, grabbed me by the shirt front and shoved his face into mine, blood still bubbling from his left nostril and down his upper lip. A fat pink tongue appeared and licked it away.

'Yes, Pablo?'

'Cassidy.'

'Mm?'

'Don't. Fuck. With. Me. *Comprende*?'

I nodded my head, any witty riposte eluding me. The monster thrust me against the balustrade and stalked off after his boss.

I turned at the moist, slapping sound of Kenny the crapaud lolloping across the floorboards to inspect a drop of fresh Venezuelan blood. The amphibian and I locked eyes for a second before his tongue too flicked out and the blood was gone.

12

I was roused at five a.m. from Pablo-infested nightmares not by squawking cocricos this time but by a phone-call from a screeching madman in East Sussex.

'Uncle, have you any idea what time it is?'

'I don't give a flying *fuck*, little black Sambo!' The man was beyond intolerable. 'They've reduced the bloody offer price an extra five percent! What's the big idea – if you even have one? Are you going to prevaricate until I'm forced to swap Shurland for a lovely bunch of fucking coconuts?'

'No, I just—'

'Don't "just" me. I was the one who *just* told you to get on with it and sign on the bloody line!' He was screaming so loudly I feared for his heart. 'And now you've managed to piss the buyer off with some cock-and-bull bollocks about Power of Attorney. As if anyone in the Caribbean cares about that! You could have signed my name – or William the bloody Conqueror's for all they well care. Janice Cordner is incandescent.'

'I know, but—'

'As am I.' Sighing, I put an arm through my mosquito net and switched on the bedside lamp. The usual something skittered away behind the curtain. 'Gabriel,' my uncle ranted on, 'do as you're buggering well told! This is my chance to get shot of that millstone but you seem determined to sabotage any deal!'

I lay back on the pillow. 'Right, listen, uncle. The reason I am dragging my feet is that—'

'So you admit it?'

'—is that in my opinion the whole thing stinks. They've got some monstrous scheme up their sleeve, I'm sure of it.'

'Oh, so you're the expert now in fantasy financial scams, are you?'

'No, but I've a hunch that—'

'In other words, you're imagining things.'

'Well, *you* explain to me their indecent rush to complete the purchase.'

'Don't know, don't care.'

'But you'd agree we have to run it past Max?'

I heard the sound of crockery smashing into a fire grate. 'Bugger Max!'

'Uncle—!'

'Don't be so bloody po-faced and dreary, Gabriel! If these people are willing to pay seven and a half million – considerably less now, thanks to you – then Max can take a running jump.'

'No, he can't. The contract will have to be dealt with properly or you'll have no come-back in law and could lose everything. I must at least have Power of Attorney or we're going to be sold down the river.'

During the subsequent squawking soliloquy I fought my way through the mosquito net and clambered out of bed. Yet another truncated night. The sore patch on my leg was looking better, I noticed, but the abrasion on my forehead and the supposed soucouyant bites were still painful to the touch. Lily had said yesterday that I was susceptible, but this was ridiculous: what was this place to have given me these unlikely wounds and welts in just a couple of days?

'Uncle,' I interjected when finally he drew breath, 'have you thought any more about my compromise Airbnb idea? Just selling off a corner of the estate? You'd still end up a millionaire.'

'Give me strength. It's like talking to a fucking armchair with you.'

'I'd really appreciate your support in this, uncle, at least until I've got to the bottom of what they're plotting. I don't trust them. And it's not just the house I'm worried about.'

A loud sigh. 'What are you blithering on about now?'

'Someone has to stand up for Lily and Churchill.'

There was a long pause during which I thought I could hear muffled voices. Was Neville covering the phone mouthpiece? Was he conferring with Mabel? I pressed on. 'Also, Janice is now demanding sweeteners. What am I supposed to do about that?'

When Neville spoke next, his tone was measured and cold, as intimidating as Pablo. 'Firstly, Gabriel, if *ever* I hear you mention those live-in, sponging savages again I shall personally see to it that your bollocks are severed and fed to the nearest stray dog.'

'Really—'

'Secondly, the client – as you should know by now – is none other than the legendary Buck McClung!'

'I am aware of this. Your point being?'

'He's an American billionaire, a man of influence and friend of Presidents past and present! Someone whose powerful acquaintance a normal, *ambitious* person would strive to cultivate.'

'Oh, I see. We're sucking up to random capitalists now, are we?' Far from feeling discouraged, my rising irritation with this impossible old man seemed only to increase my determination to defy him. I must be feeling better.

'Do not take that tone with me, sir!'

'I shall do what I judge to be right.'

'Is that so?' I heard Neville glug down what I assumed to be rum. 'Silly me, I forgot we can't expect St. Gabriel fucking Cassidy to involve himself in mere *worldly* matters, can we? No, he'd rather take the easy way out and skulk under some Old Testament rock waiting for his Saviour to return.'

'I'd ask you to respect—'

'Quiet! The owner of the largest tropical hotel-resort group on the planet actively wishes to hand me a colossal stack of readies for Shurland. You, Gabriel, are to see the deal through to a swift conclusion – as both he and I wish. Can you get that into your thick skull?'

'When I've found out what McClung is up to.'

'Sod you for a cowardly sack of shit!' I put the phone on "speaker", laid it on a chest of drawers and reached for a fresh T-shirt. Neville would blow himself out soon enough, maybe even die in the process. 'Sod your respectable petit-bourgeois caution and enable him! And of course Janice wants her cut! What sort of naïve arsehole are you? The wheels on the Caribbean bus need oiling or they won't *fucking* well go round and round.'

I pulled on some shorts, a gecko eyeing me from the underside of a rafter. 'Well, uncle,' I said, 'since you're so worldly-wise, perhaps you could tell me how much bloody Janice will want for her bribe?'

A squawk of derision. 'Bugger me if me nephew ain't swearin' now! Christ, what is the world coming to?'

'Answer the question!'

'How'm I supposed to know? Negotiate, man! Start at – I dunno – ten. She counters with thirty and you settle on twenty. *Thousand* dollars, before you ask. It's a drop in the ocean. Just pay her!'

'Me pay her?'

'Who else? I don't have the cash.'

'Nor do I!'

'Bullshit! You just sold your company!'

'But I can't just—'

'Oh, don't tell me: wifey won't let you touch her retirement nest-egg. Is that it?' I said nothing. 'If you don't dare face her down, take out a short-term loan! You'll get your money back soon enough.'

Not only was my own uncle using me as his stooge, he was also expecting me to pay his infernal bills. The telltale muscle above my left eye was quivering again, in former times a sign of tears to come but which I was now learning to recognise as a precursor of rage. I rubbed at it before trying a different tack: 'Well, uncle, if I'm stumping up the cash for Janice, that entitles me to—'

'Don't you bloody dare!'

I let it go, but was now more involved, whatever he said. 'Alright, but what about the Power of Attorney?'

'For Christ's sake, if you're insisting on all this bureaucratic shit, sort it out with Gibson. Just let me know when everything's signed. I don't want any more shitty emails from Janice Cordner.'

'I'm sure you don't.'

'Because, as of today, any further reduction in McClung's price is going to be covered from your own funds. That should focus your mind.'

'But—'

'Goodbye.'

A minute later I was on the balcony, my hands shaking and head spinning from frustration and anger. I could have done with a cup of Lily's tea. 'How can an old man be such a manipulative bastard?' I spat, leaning against the balustrade. 'I could wring his scrawny neck.'

Out to sea, dawn was daubing the rims of clouds in the palest of pinks and greys. Time to bite the bullet. I pulled out my phone and emailed Max, asking him to expedite a PoA. 'Please make sure I have it by tomorrow 4pm your time,' I typed. 'I'll pay whatever it takes.'

Next, I opened my online banking, grateful not to be in touch with Sarah; my involvement with what she would term 'such skullduggery' would have led to massive unpleasantness. With luck and a following wind I'd get it all paid back before she even noticed.

A footfall at the far end of the balcony. Hastily I wiped my eyes as Lily greeted me. 'Good mornin', Mr. Gabriel. What you doin' up so early? I hear you talkin' an hour ago.'

Just taking steps to betray you and Shurland, I thought. 'Just sorting out some banking,' I forced a smile.

'You bankin' on cellphone? Lors! I still go down Scarborough an' join de line.'

'All I need on this phone is my thumbprint and I can do whatever.'

A steups. 'Who call you so early?'

'Who do you think?'

'Mr. Neville?'

'Right first time. And he's not pleased. Janice and he are ganging up on me to get this thing signed and sealed.'

'You ax him about de birdin' lodge?'

'I did. He was not enthusiastic.'

Lily turned away to plump cushions. 'What you goin' to do?'

'No idea. But I must come up with something before tomorrow's meeting. I need time to think. Maybe I'll take the car and explore a bit; go for a swim further afield. Is there somewhere off the beaten track you can recommend?'

'Plenty places. I tell you after I make coffee.'

'I'd prefer your tea.'

'Oh, it run out. It have special ingredient from my friend Annesia. She livin' quite by Moriah. I seein' her nex' week.'

'That's a shame.' I opened my laptop. 'But now it's high time to google this 'Buck' character. Should have done it before.'

Five minutes' online research dashed any positivity Lily's excellent repast might have provided. It transpired that "Entrepreneur Buck McClung, major #MAGA Republican donor, and ally of 45th

President Donald J. Trump, is CEO of Tropitel, a global chain of high-end coastal resorts boasting properties from Tahiti to Mexico, Costa Rica to Papua New Guinea, Hawaii to Brunei." I'd seen such places advertised in the Sunday glossies: prim, "vernacular" wooden huts on jetties over clear blue waters – devoid of wildlife, I was coming to suspect – or vast and sterile hotel complexes in white concrete with colourful awnings, oddly-shaped swimming pools and a booming themed bar every twenty paces. I wouldn't be seen dead in such places. 'My God,' I heard myself take the Lord's name in vain as my worst suspicions were so graphically confirmed, 'is this what is planned for Shurland? It would be environmental devastation.'

I typed in 'Tobago Assistant Secretary Janice Cordner' and learnt that she was forty-six, had won a scholarship to study at the London School of Economics and was a "rising star" in Tobagonian politics. Before turning to "public service" she'd enjoyed a successful career in marketing and was now second-in-command to an Environment Secretary who had risen to power on his popular "Tobago, Clean, Green, Safe and Serene" campaign. 'Surely,' I muttered to myself, 'Janice must be on the side of Good here.'

'You talkin' to yourself, Mr. Gabriel?' Lily had arrived with the coffee.

'Was I? Bad habit.'

'What you discussin'?'

'That Janice Cordner surely can't afford to be seen getting into bed with a company like Tropitel.'

'Janice Cordner,' she flared her nostrils, 'she a *Baddis*.'

'Is that so?'

'Talkin' of gettin' into bed, she divorce three time already. Always lookin' for a new husband wid money.'

'Yes, so you said, but that doesn't necessarily mean she's out to destroy the planet, does it?'

A steups. 'You aware, Mr. Gabriel, existin' hotel in Tobago already empty?'

'No. Why?'

She was smiling sadly down at me. 'Because sweet T an' T have reputation for murderin' Europeans, you understan'? You nuh read de papers?'

'No. We Christadelphians don't involve ourselves in...' I stopped myself, hearing the smug pomposity of my words. That familiar tone of self-satisfaction was not something I felt comfortable using any longer. I cleared my throat: 'That does ring a bell.'

'You government blacklist us. English visitors is endangered species like our pawi.'

'Mm?'

'A bird. Only a few left in Trinidad Northern Range.'

'Ah. But presumably those murders were drug-related?'

'Truth. Retired folk wrong place wrong time. Dey witness shady dealin' on a beach an' nex' ting, dey get chop wid cutlash in bed.' She began to clear the table. 'My son, Trevor, police ax him what he know, but dey let him go.'

'Surely he wasn't involved?'

'Trevor make he own mistake.' Lily picked up the loaded tray. 'But I not botherin' you wid my family worries. You ain't have no children?'

'No, Sarah says it wasn't God's will.'

'God savin' you plenty heartache.'

I watched her shuffle away towards the kitchen and, the aftershocks of my call with Neville still reverberating in my head, turned and tried to focus on the loveliness about me. Five or six hummingbirds were squabbling for pole position at the sugar-water feeder and the motmot was sharing a blackened plantain with three mockingbirds. On the table-cloth three feet from me, a blue-grey tanager had joined the usual gang of bananaquits tweeting, bickering and pecking at the sugar-bowl. Beyond this merry mayhem, a bright green iguana scuttled along the balustrade in pursuit of a red and black butterfly; beyond him, cocricos hopped about in the bushes. All was at peace, the Caribbean glittering in the background, the sigh of the breakers just audible over the buzz of insects. Somewhere in the garden, Churchill was hacking away at undergrowth with his cutlass – just as he'd done for the past sixty years. How would I be able to live with myself, I thought, if I was complicit in allowing McClung to concrete over this earthly paradise?

Lily was at my shoulder. 'You lookin' thoughtful, Mr. Gabriel.'

I glanced over to where Pablo had pushed me about last night, imagining I could smell the brute's aftershave hanging in the warm air. 'Lily,' I said, 'I'm up against it as never before.'

'I know, Mr. Gabriel.' Those poor, belaboured cushions.

'On the one hand I have my uncle insisting I cave in to the economic and political might of Janice, McClung and that bastard Pablo.'

'Mr. Gabriel, you cussin' now?'

'Extenuating circumstances, Lily.' She steupsed. 'On the other hand, I have a duty to protect the future of Shurland. You see, in accepting Neville's mission, I became a pawn in the ambitions of a member of my own family wishing to cash in and throw you and Churchill on the scrap heap. After all the years of unstinting service you've given.' Lily put her head on one side and raised an eyebrow. 'I am so angry, Lily. So, should I stand aside and let "progress" do its thing? Join the mobs of short-sighted idiots who – as we've all seen on TV – deliberately burn down rainforests, destroy ecosystems and imperil the planet in the name of political and financial expediency? Would you ever forgive me? No, of course not. Why would you?'

'You will find a way, Mr. Gabriel, I know.'

'There must be a way of putting on the brakes without being beaten up by Pablo. I just need to buy myself some time to formulate a plan.' Lily was watching me intently over a cushion she was holding. 'At the very least I have to confirm what they're planning to do with the property. Maybe I can delay the Power of Attorney.'

Lily nodded. 'I never know lawyer to rush.'

There was a ping from my pocket. I pulled out my phone. 'Talk of the devil,' I muttered. 'A text from the solicitor.' I scanned the content rather than read it aloud – a wise move, given Max's tone. 'I see there's an email from you,' he wrote. 'Can't download it right now. Shite signal on clifftops. Having a few days away in N. Devon.' I smiled at Lily. 'You were right: the lawyers are indeed on our side.'

'Then go out an' explore, Mr. Gabriel. Great swimmin' at Arnos Vale jus' fifteen minute up de coast. And maybe on de way back you pass by Pennysavers and pick up some supplies for me.'

'Of course, ma'am. Glad to be of service.' Indeed, a sense of relief was seeping through me, despite the knowledge of how angry this delay to the Power of Attorney would make certain people. I had a breathing space, a little time to reflect on the best way forward, time for Caribbean saltwater to heal my injuries. If I could avoid the aggressive attentions of beasts real or imaginary, I knew my spirits would rally in anticipation of whatever Janice and Neville could cook up next for me.

Lily was speaking. 'Mind you is careful drivin' roun' dese island roads, Mr. Gabriel. No pickin' up any girls by de road, you understan'.'

'I wasn't planning to.' What had brought this on?

'I talkin' about de la diablesse, Mr. Gabriel, a devil woman lookin' to hitch a ride on lonely forest road.'

'Ah. Don't tell me: she sucks blood?'

A steups. 'No, Mr. Gabriel. La diablesse, she seduce driver – always a man ready to cheat on he woman!' Lily's eyes seemed to be out on stalks. 'An' she leave he to die deep in de woods, stuck in a picker bush.'

'Right, okay. But in the unlikely event I pick up a female hitchhiker, how do I tell if she is one of these, er, jabbless things?'

'Easy, Mr. Gabriel. One foot normal, but de other, hidin' in de long grass or under she long dress, is a cow hoof.'

I wasn't expecting that. 'Oh, I see. How fortunate I'm not planning on cheating on my wife.' I looked out to sea and struck upon an idea. 'But you know, Lily, it occurs to me that if a harmless roadside dalliance does present itself... and the only price to pay is a slow and grisly death in the forest, then it might be a price worth paying to get this crew of ne'er-do-wells off my bloody back.'

Lily wagged a finger. 'I never hear mo', boy. And how you cussin' so dese days. Lors, Mr. Gabriel, Tobago affectin' you!' She squeezed my wrist. 'All I is sayin', be careful when you drivin' – especially after dark.'

'I appreciate your concern.'

'You fetch your ting an' I make you a shoppin' list and mark where to go on de map.'

13

An hour or so later, following Lily's suggestion, I was snorkeling at a secluded and forest-clad bay down a hill from the village of Arnos Vale. Thankful to be feeling better at last – less nauseous, anyway – I was engrossed in watching from below the surface of the water how clouds of bright foam formed when waves smashed against dark rocks. My body buoyed up with the ebb and flow of the water, I floated without moving a muscle, observing shoals of tiny fish cowering in the lea of a cliff which plummeted to the depths beneath me. Despite everything, I felt almost at peace.

Until, as clearly as if something had tapped a fin against the glass of my mask, I knew I was not alone. Warily, I swiveled my head towards the open ocean. There, immobile against the azure nothingness, its long silver shard of a body flashing in the sunlight, hung an evil-looking fish. I knew the species at once because only a few weeks ago I had sat through an execrable B-movie called *Barracuda*. Its gory opening scene began to play in my mind right now. I had no way of judging how far away this one was was: if it was a king-sized specimen, it might have been a hundred yards off; if a tiddler, ten feet. But whether it was the creature's unblinking yellow eye or the unspeakable menace of its cruel and turned-down mouth – or whether indeed I was hallucinating the whole episode as a result of some post-viral after-shock – I was certain this vile missile of a fish was in league with Pablo, a man I would cheerfully have seen chewed up and swallowed by Jonah's biblical whale. Even underwater I could see the Venezuelan's eyes, smell his aftershave, feel those Cumberland sausage fingers of his gripping my shirt front. I heard his horrid voice hissing in my head: 'Meestah Cassidy, you comfortable white asshole in a black man's skin, how does it feel to be so weak, naïve and *dispensable*?' The barracuda flicked a fin. 'Sign the fucking paperwork, Cassidy, or face the consequences.'

I hung there in the void eyeballing what I took to be Pablo's fishy emissary, plucking up the courage to move my arms and edge backwards when something stung me on the hip and again on the shoulder. It felt like a flea or a bed-bug but was infinitely more threatening, being invisible. Was it a jellyfish? With a bubbling yowl, and pointlessly trying to slap at myself, I abandoned any remaining marine decorum, pushed my mask onto the back of my head and struck out in panic for the shore. Of course, the more I splashed and kicked, the more I imagined the barracuda sidling along behind me, biding its time behind a coral-encrusted submarine headland, whistling up reinforcements maybe, waiting for the moment to launch a coordinated attack. Exposed, I could *feel* those teeth sinking into the back of my calf – or worse, my neck – stripping flesh from me, bare bone gleaming white through clouds of red.

Soon I was puffing and blowing, spitting mouthfuls of water before me. Unused to such exertions, my arm and leg muscles rebelled but on and on I pounded, the beach seeming to remain as far away as ever. I twisted my head to left and right, taking heart from my snail-like progress against the trees clinging to rocks above the waterline. To use that Christadelphian euphemism, "if anything happened to me", there was little likelihood of whatever was left of my corpse being spotted by anyone. The coast hereabouts was devoid of any sign of human habitation – not a roof, pylon nor telegraph pole in sight: I might have been Robinson Crusoe swimming ashore from his wreck. But I was in no mood to revel in such unspoilt natural beauty because I was also enduring the continuing echo of Sarah's acrid voice in my head: 'You've only yourself to blame, Gabriel. These are your just desserts for not having read your Bible for days, not giving thanks before every meal, not saying your prayers at bedtime. Not to mention using bad language.' I flicked a piece of seaweed out of my hair, exasperated that even here, with so much else to contend with, my inner monologue was plagued by my wife's whining interventions.

I rested for a moment to allow a wave to lift me a yard or two further in. Sarah had a point: after less than a week away I had more or less abandoned forty years of Christadelphian ritual and compliance. In its place I was being challenged as never before to stand up to what amounted to a gang of mobsters headed up by my own uncle. Was it that, as Lily had just decreed, 'Tobago affectin' you'? There was some truth in this: I might as well have gone to sleep and woken up on Mars, so great was my sense of *dépaysement*. I was four and half thousand miles from home, beset with apparently insuperable problems and hosted by someone – Obeah woman and mother to two illegitimate grown-up children – who believed that an old crone could morph into a fireball, fly through the air and suck the blood out of innocent passers-by. Not to mention her nonsense about the la diablesse and children with feet on backwards. Regardless of what weird powers Lily reckoned she possessed, if anything was driving me to protect Shurland it was the example of her warm and kindly presence, her confidence in me, her delicious coconut bake, chicken pelau and herbal tea, and – most importantly – her determination to show me that Tobago was no longer to be pushed around by rich white folks from the other side of the planet. Pablo's barracuda was right to imply I had no clue what to do, but one thing was certain: I must face each battle to the best of my ability if I were to have any chance of winning this ill-defined war. For the first time in my life I had a fight on my hands, and I was ready. I had no choice. The consequences of failing to save this corner of Tobago were unthinkable. No amount of cosy Bible reading back home in leafy suburbia would relieve the guilt of allowing the ruination of the lives of people who cared for and guarded the natural habitat that sustained them. In enriching my uncle – and presumably myself when he eventually conked out – I would have become just like him, an abhorrent twenty-first century reincarnation of the cruel, greedy and careless colonialists of the past. And me, with no blood ties to the Cassidy family at all, a Ghanaian whose ancestors might well have been amongst the slaves who built the Shurland estate in the first place.

I swam another thirty strokes until I could hear the homely sound of waves sluicing up and down the steep sandy beach. Beyond stood a couple of bent palm trees guarding a ramshackle collection of down-at-heel hotel buildings. My inner debate concluded with an answer of sorts as my toes at last touched the bottom: my only option was to adopt a policy of – what should I call it? – positive prevarication. Try and persuade my antagonists that I was on board with their hateful plans but hoping all the time – like Mr. Micawber in *David Copperfield* – that something would eventually turn up to save the day. Sarah had often accused me of being constitutionally unable to make a plan and stick to it, so it wasn't too far from what would be expected of me.

My clothes and towel were safe where I'd left them on a low wall so I scrambled up the beach and dried off near where a blue boat had been drawn up above the waterline. On it were painted in large orange letters the words *Fish Is Fish*, a statement to which I felt no one could object.

I allowed myself a moment of self-congratulation for having both outwitted Pablo's barracuda and settled on a position. I deserved a beer. There must be something available in this wreck of a hotel. Trying not to scrape my new bites and stings, I pulled on my T-shirt and shorts, flung the towel over my shoulder and vaulted over the wall.

To my right stood a dilapidated building with steps leading up to a sagging balcony; to the left, a rickety covered bar area and swimming pool, now a repository for rotting vegetation and green water. According to Lily, this mouldering complex of buildings stretching away up the valley was all that remained of the once prestigious Arnos Vale Hotel. She'd told me in a whisper that the owner had for years been selling it off bit by bit, bed by bed, to keep his suppliers at bay.

Behind the bar, trampled amongst broken bottles and syringes, I found a sign optimistically declaring: *No Obscene. No Bare Back. No Illegal Drugs or Smoking.* I sighed and peered into filthy cupboards, a rusty fridge and a glass-fronted drinks cooler. Stepping over a desiccated crab with its shell peeled back, I resigned myself to the fact that there was nothing here for me but smashed light fittings, twisted wires and the grey salty dust of mould and decay. I fought off a sense of gloom with a moment of fantasy nostalgia about the long-gone Bright Young Things of the 'sixties and 'seventies dancing and wassailing the night away here without a care in the world. Had my uncle Neville been a regular reveller down here? Did he bring his new wife Beryl to the hotel to celebrate their wedding? One day I would ask him.

I stepped outside and walked towards the pool but even in the sunshine the whole complex exuded an atmosphere of dank desolation and sadness with only the muffled sound of the sea to disturb an eerie silence. Lizards and cockroaches roamed free and unmolested, bats hung in the rafters and endless birds fluttered between the encroaching trees and decaying buildings. Saplings were already pushing their way through cracks in the concrete. Even if I were to fail in my mission and McClung developed the

Shurland site, it would be only a matter of time, I thought, before Mother Nature reclaimed her own.

Mulling on this long-term silver lining – positive prevarication at its most protracted and rewarding – I inadvertently kicked a rusty beer can and sent it skittering across the paving. The din, amplified by these skeletons of empty buildings, roused the guardians of this ghost town. A pack of ravening dogs came spurting out of a shack some seventy yards away, howling and yapping with fury at my presence. Was everything in Paradise out to get me? The leader was closing in at speed, a long pink tongue flopping and drooling over a set of savage teeth. It was too late to run.

A piercing whistle brought these hellhounds up short and panting. 'Here!' A large man in overalls had appeared in a doorway and was looking over at me. One or two of the pack trotted whimpering back towards him. He was swinging the obligatory cutlass, tapping at the side of an oil drum with it. Sweat trickled between my shoulder-blades. 'What you doin' here, bro?' he shouted. 'Private property. You cyan' read?'

I raised my hand. 'I'm really sorry, but I've just been swimming and was wondering whether there might be any chance of a beer.'

The man emitted a sound like a car backfiring and lumbered knock-kneed towards me, skirting the remains of two engines on blocks, a stack of old tyres with creeper growing through them and innumerable chunks of rusty scrap metal. He sported a scrabby grey beard, a toothless grin and a grubby baseball cap worn backwards. 'Eh-ehh,' he stated, looking me up and down. 'You is no Trini.'

'No.'

'Where you from, bro?'

'The U.K.'

'Ehhh.' He ran an oil-stained finger along his cutlass blade. He must be at least as old as Churchill. 'You upsettin' my pothound.'

'Potong?'

The man bent to stroke a dog's head. 'Dey upset.'

'Oh, right. These are your, er, pothounds, are they?' Three of the malnourished mutts were licking the salt from my bare legs. I bent to fondle the head of one of them. 'Listen, I'm really sorry to disturb but if there's nothing to drink here I'll be off. Sorry, my name's Gabriel.'

The man put his head on one side. 'Gabriel? As in de Angel?'

I sighed, reminded of Max – and of tomorrow's need for a Power of Attorney. 'Indeed.'

The mechanic pulled a crumpled card from a pocket. "Winston Frank. Secondhand Car, Repairs and Bodywork". We bumped fists. 'My workshop,' he explained, jerking a thumb over his shoulder, 'in de ol' hotel reception. I got plenty car for sale, but no beer here since 'ninety-eight. If you was here earlier ago, I could o' offer you sea-moss, but I jus' finish him out an' it take time to prepare.'

'What's sea moss?'

'Non-alcoholic. Fishermen drink. It have special seaweed, condense milk, vanilla, anis an' so. But if you thirsty, I open a coconut, yes?'

'No, really, that's—'

But Winston was already shambling off to the other side of the swimming pool where brown coconuts the size of rugby balls lay strewn upon the flagstones under a tall palm. Ignoring these, he reached up with a fifteen-foot bamboo pole and knocked down a fresh bunch of greeny yellow ones. He selected one and I followed him into the shade of a dilapidated hexagonal pavilion. There he placed the coconut on the rail and, with six or seven deft blows with his cutlass, proceeded to chop chunks of flesh from one end. I was astonished at the dexterity he demonstrated with such a long and unwieldy tool. Then, with one lateral blow, he whipped off the top like a boiled egg and presented it to me.

There was a hole the size of a ping-pong ball in the top. 'You try, bro.'

'Thanks so much.' I took it in both hands and inspected it. 'You know, coconuts where I come from are hard, brown hairy things. Nothing like this.'

'It fresh, Angel Gabriel. You drink.'

I tipped it up and took a sip. 'Oh, gosh, that's amazing – like warm nectar. I've never tasted anything like it. Thank you so much.'

'You're welcome.' Winston was eyeing me up and down, one hand in a dog's mouth, the other swinging the cutlass. 'So you vacationin' in sweet T an' T?'

'Business, as it happens.'

'Stayin' at de Kariwak Village? Coco Reef?'

'No, at a place called Shurland.'

'Eh-ehh! Lily, she lookin' after you?' Despite his missing teeth, Winston steupsed.

'Well, yes, actually, and I—'

'Lily an' me, we ol' friends! You take her sometin' from me? Save me a trip?'

'Of course.' I walked with Winston and his troupe into the workshop where he cleared a space on a table and began decanting some pinkish powder from an old paint pot into a plastic bag. The room reeked of engine oil and rotting fish.

'I jus' makin' pacro for Lily,' Winston said. 'I is her sole supplier.'

'Ah.'

'You know pacro?'

'Afraid not.'

'So, I prise de material – Tobacco whelk – from de rock.' He indicated a bucket of grey, limpet-like shells the shape of woodlice. 'Scrape off de slime, dry it nice-nice in de sunshine an' grind to powder. Pacro.' He shook the bag and tied it off.

'Which is used for...?'

Winston winked. 'Pacro good for de back, bro.'

'Say again.'

'Aphrodisiac. I give you good price.'

'Oh! Right. Well, actually, I'm fine—'

'Eh-ehh. So, Angel de black Englishman doh need no pacro from Winston?' He pulled a face and made to high-five me. I wasn't ready of course and the flat of his hand bent my thumb back. 'Tell dat Obeah woman she go pay me four hundred fifty dollar later.'

'I could give you that now if you like – and she can pay me back.' I unzipped my shorts pocket and gave him five hundred-dollar bills, a sum that wouldn't break the bank at the present exchange rate. 'That's all I've got, I'm afraid. Sorry it's a bit wet.'

Winston reached behind what must once have been the reception desk and produced a rusty tin. 'I give you change.'

'Please don't worry. You've been very kind and I must be off.'

'Dat your hire car?' Winston pointed through a cracked windowpane to where my trusty Honda squatted in the shade.

'Yes. You saw it?'

'Been maccoin' you since you reach. Winston see everyting.'

14

I collected my car keys from where I'd squirrelled them away under a log, grabbed my camera and phone from the spare-wheel well and drove back up the hill. Negotiating a bend in the narrow lane, I came across a police car parked by an upturned boat. The thickset copper inside wore mirror shades so ostentatious I could see my Honda in duplicate nosing past. It was reassuring to see an officer of the law but he did not return my wave.

Eventually, I left the village behind me, avoiding gaggles of kamikaze chickens, a series of massive potholes and even a pair of elderly men playing chess at a table in the middle of the road. With no fixed route in mind, I was intrigued by signs to Moriah and followed them simply because it was there that, in the Book of Genesis, Abraham was directed by God to sacrifice his son, Isaac. Mulling over that story, I was soon lost in a labyrinth of tortuous sandy lanes through lumpish green hills clad in low brush.

I was oppressed by the searing afternoon heat. The Honda's wheezing air conditioning was no match for such ferocity so I opened all the windows to maximise the through draft. The breeze was welcome but left me parched. I tried to distract myself by imagining a nice, airy café perched on a hilltop somewhere, waiting for my custom, but low blood sugar soon began to take its toll. Gloom and anxiety took root once more as I thought about how my chosen path of least resistance meant that I would be heading into tomorrow's meeting empty-handed. Moriah ("Land of the Vision" as it's ironically known in the Bible) was proving more elusive than ever so I turned back under a sign for Castara, Parlatuvier and L'Anse Fourmi, all villages up the north-west coast of the island.

Forty minutes later, after dozens of random yet promising-looking turnings, I had established that Tobago – unlike, say, Devon and Cornwall – did not cater for the hot and care-worn traveller craving a cold drink and a chocolate brownie. I passed three boarded-up roti shops and a tiny supermarket skulking behind a façade of metal grilles. In the end I stumbled across a cheerfully-painted wooden stall opposite a car on its side with its wheels removed. This oasis – fortunately no mirage – was run by a vivacious lady in a smart black apron and white shirt, a board behind her declaring *We have cold drinks too – Thanks for stopping by – We appreciate it.* I scanned the exotic assortment of items on display and relieved her of a packet of Dixee Peanut Butter & Chocolate Biscuits, two small bananas (she called them 'figs'), a bag of "Bene Sticks" and two cans of ice-cold lemon, lime and bitters. She tried to fob me off with some iffy-looking star fruit and something hard and citrussy but I declined, citing poor digestion. When I asked her for directions to Scarborough, her gesticulations were good-humoured and flamboyant but left me none the wiser.

Another hour or so and I was becoming familiar with too many landmarks – viewed from both directions: a half-built house, part-painted purple and part-covered in bamboo scaffolding; a defunct green Landrover under a tarpaulin; the Jeremiah Praying School and a rusty yellow car so long abandoned at the roadside it had vines growing through it. At my third encounter with an ominous sign which read *Warning: Depression Ahead*, I let out a new expletive – 'Damn and blast!' – one favoured by my old payroll clerk at Hillcrest Insurance Brokers when his computer crashed.

I pulled over at a hairpin bend where the road widened for no apparent reason into a lay-by large enough to accommodate two articulated lorries. (Not that such vehicles could exist on this island; the heftiest truck to impede my progress so far had been a bright yellow three-tonner tantalisingly stenciled *Get behind a real beer: A real beer is Carib.*) I looked at my tourist map one last time, but the flimsy fold-out showed only a fraction of the streets and lanes which in reality festooned the hills between endless unmarked hamlets. I scrunched it up and tossed it into the back of the car.

I killed the engine and closed my eyes, a sense of impending doom augmented by a growl of thunder. A heavy mist seemed to have settled over me and I sensed I was wasting my time out here, that somehow I should be back at Shurland where I would feel less exposed. With a cup of Lily's tea in my hand, I thought, I'd be able to work out what I was going to do.

At the bottom of the valley below me, palm trees punctuated shimmering green clouds of bamboo. Above, colourfully painted houses propped on concrete stilts clung improbably to the steep slope. It was deathly still and behind the ridge the sky glowered dark and menacing. I climbed out, stretched and plonked myself down on a concrete crash barrier which some local council bigwig had caused to be painted in neat black and white warning stripes. A gang of anis – to my eye ugly black birds with craggy beaks – were fossicking about in the bushes below but I was too preoccupied even to think about photographing them.

I clambered back into the oven-like Honda and forced myself onwards. After a series of impossibly tight corners, I found myself opposite the Moriah Rumshop. I called over to a gaggle of villagers lolling on benches in the shade and asked them for navigational clues. They responded in a patois so thick I was at a loss to understand them, so a cheerful and muscular young man was deputised to give me the benefit of their deliberations. Pointing ahead, he explained: 'you go so, den straigh'-straigh' dong Mason Hall 'til you meetin' Claude Noel Highway. Better hurry, bro,' he added, slapping the roof of the car. 'Storm, it reach soon.'

My guide had omitted the detail that his recommended route forked every half mile or so. I always chose the widest looking option, but twenty minutes later I had once more lost all sense of direction. I switched on the headlights and followed a wide, recently surfaced road leading between a deserted sports pitch and Mason Hall Secondary School, a modern three-storey building which wouldn't have looked out of place in a London suburb. A half mile later, the tarmac had evaporated and I was bouncing uphill over a rutted track through clumps of waving bamboo thirty feet high.

Ahead suddenly was total blackness. I slammed on the brakes. In the dim glow of the headlights, the track seemed to curve away downhill to the right. In daytime, on a dry afternoon perhaps, I might have risked it, but in the pitch black and with the Honda being buffeted by gusts of wind, it would have been sheer folly to proceed into what might easily have turned out to be a valley of death. Especially if it began to rain.

I fumbled for the ceiling light and pulled out my phone. No signal. 'Oh, well done, Gabe,' said a voice – Sarah could always be relied upon to improvise unhelpful commentary at times of crisis. 'Good work. I wonder whether you can see fit to turn this car around without tipping us into the void.' I needed no wife to stir the cauldron of self-loathing. I tried to jam the gear lever into reverse without depressing the brake pedal. The car screeched in protest, red lights pinging on all over the dashboard. This was the last straw in my litany of poor decisions. 'You bloody *arsehole*, Gabriel!' I yelled. 'Why couldn't you have just—'

A sharp bang on the car roof. 'Jesus *Christ*!' Ahead of me, three – no, four, *six* pairs of yellow eyes flashed in the headlights.

Another thump on the roof. 'What the—?' A diabolical grey face leered at me through my side-window. Whipping white dreadlocks, bulging eyes – an acreage of wispy facial hair. The car was rocking. Why was I hallucinating again? With trembling fingers I felt for the switch and locked the doors.

'Eh! Open up!' The hammering over my head became more insistent.

'Go away!'

The monster was rattling at the door handle. I'd fallen into the pit of Hell again. 'Bro, what you doin' here?' came his cry. 'You lost?'

'What?'

'Open de door! I doh bite.'

Breathing hard, I released the lock and the door flew open. The man outside was guffawing at my terror. He leant into the car and, with an efficiency of purpose I had not expected, shot out a hand in a bid to grab my camera from the passenger seat.

'Ah! No, you bloody don't!' I seized the scrawny wrist and banged it hard against the steering wheel, the shock making my screeching attacker withdraw, leaving behind him a sickening stench of goats and alcohol. Something was telling me I'd met him before. I slammed the door shut, locked it again and fumbled for the ignition key. But trying to start the car in "Drive" only released the locking system again. The door flew open and I was grappling with a hairy great goat, its hooves scratching my bare thighs as it strove to join me in the car. 'Get it off me!' I shrieked at the old nutcase outside, but he took no notice, merely nursing his arm and gibbering inanely. And then I remembered where I'd seen him before: it was Lester, Ben Gunn's body-double from the beach.

The invading goat had by now pretty much established itself a base-camp on my lap. It was sniffing about, rooting under the handbrake and chomping on the remains of my sesame sticks, packaging and all. Pinioned in place by my seatbelt and the weight of this malodorous ruminant, I flung out my right hand, grabbed what turned out to be a dreadlock and yanked hard.

Caught unawares, Lester's ridiculous face was soon as close in to mine as I could tolerate; close enough, I hoped, not to be able to defend himself with his cutlass.

'I know who you are, *Lester*,' I snarled, 'and Trevor will be very unhappy to hear how you tried to rob me! As for the Obeah woman... I wouldn't fancy your chances with her! Now get this bastard animal out of my car, *bro*, and back off!' I shoved hard on his forehead with my fist and Lester fell backwards onto the grass.

My threats struck home. He was soon on his feet again, fawning and scraping like any Gollum cornered under the Mountains of Mordor. Obeying me, he seized the goat's haunches and tried to haul the beast out of my car. 'Come *out*, Randell!' he squawked. 'Leave de fella alone! He doh harm you.' But Randell was deaf to these entreaties and gave Lester a mighty double kick with his back legs. Seizing my half-packet of biscuits in peg-like teeth, he hopped backwards into the darkness where the other Billy-Goats Gruff were doubtless waiting to fight it out for the spoils.

Lester now dissolved into a grossly over-acted display of self-recrimination, tears plopping into his matted beard. 'Yeah, man,' he uttered at length, 'I sorry, I no recognise you. Where's you headin'?'

Stunned by this second unexpected descent of mine into physical aggression in recent days, I decided in victory to play it sulky and sarcastic. 'Nowhere fast, thanks to you.' I was about to enquire after his dead chicken but thought better of it. 'I'm trying to find my way home to Shurland. No idea where I am.'

'You completely lost?'

A flash of lightening and a colossal clap of thunder set the goats into paroxysms of bleating. Raindrops as heavy as marbles smacked onto the car. Ignoring the oncoming storm, the goatherd went into a tirade of gibberish which, interspersed with bursts of laughter and windmilling attempts at semaphore, left me clueless. All I gathered was that the track ahead led to what sounded like 'Hill-bro-dam'. I sacrificed a small denomination note in the hope Lester would make a more articulate suggestion, but in the end I'd had enough. Loath to spend the night with him and his flock in some dripping hovel, I thanked him for his time and expertise. I put the car into reverse, turned round and nosed back the way I'd come.

The skies opened as I edged into the dark bamboo tunnel again, but despite appalling driving conditions I managed to return to the school without further incident. From there I followed a sign I'd missed earlier towards Scarborough, heading up a hill away from the street lights and into darkness once more. Soon I was rattling over the loose planking of a narrow iron bridge. On the far side, in a flash of lightning, I jumped at the sight an enormous black cow chained to a tree at the roadside, the diabolical great bovine shaking its horns at me as I passed. The storm finally broke, unleashing its wrath upon my poor old hire car. On all sides, lush vegetation lashed and flailed under the onslaught of wind and water, torn leaves ripped and whipped away, branches hurled in my path. A ten foot palm frond smacked onto the pitted asphalt just ahead and, with a horrible grating noise, entangled itself in my wheel-arch. In that second, almost dead ahead, I saw a flash of white, the curve of a leg and the bat-wing edge of a red umbrella. I stamped on the brake pedal, my heart pounding. 'Jesus wept!' I yelled. The car slewed to the right, a front wheel clunking into what must have been an absolute Grand Canyon of a pothole concealed beneath the torrent. A second later and I'd have mown down whoever it was. *Come to sunny Tobago*, they'd said!

The passenger door was flung open. I was being car-jacked for the second time in forty minutes. My first thought was oddly ethereal, given my plight: how churlish a God would it be who exacted revenge for my spiritual absence by playing games at my expense, especially as I was on a mission to make a positive contribution to this island corner of His creation. My second thought proved Lily's point about how susceptible and *suggestible* I was: instinctively I had seized my camera, braced to use it as a weapon in mortal combat with one of her la diablesses. After all, I reasoned, I'd been rebuffed by the Phantom and dive-bombed by a soucouyant so was it not high time to be seduced and slain by the la diablesse too? A neat if improbable solution to my problems.

A girl in a white dress and hair running with water had thrust her head into the car. 'Goodnight!' she cried, out of breath. Yes, I noted, she had a certain damp la diablesse beauty, and no, I couldn't see whether she sported a cow hoof. Perhaps mystified at my indecision she shouted, 'Excuse, fella, can I get in?'

Before I could reply, she had folded herself into the seat and plonked a large red raffia bag on her knee. 'Good night to you too,' I managed.

'Lors! Rain fallin'!' she exclaimed, banging the door shut. She was battling with the umbrella, her matter-of-fact and friendly tone thoroughly disarming. Of course she was showing not a single sign of turning vengeful seductress. Brought to my senses, I determined to remain calm for once in the teeth of aggressors, especially imaginary ones. I flicked on the ceiling light and made much of keeping my camera safe and dry, lowering it and placing it carefully – as any photographer would – on the floor behind my seat.

The girl pushed a ringlet of dripping hair behind her ear, assessing me with enormous brown eyes. 'Whooo,' she exhaled, her grateful smile revealing a flash of perfect white teeth and cheeky dimples. 'Tank you for stoppin'. No bus passin' tonight, so I grateful for de ride. We right behind God back.'

'At least I didn't run you over,' I said. 'I thought for a moment you were a la diablesse!'

She shrieked with laughter at this. 'No, fella, you mistakin' me! Sorry to disappoint!' She tugged a silk scarf from her bag and mopped her face with it. 'You English? I hear accent like yours at work, but I not expectin' it from—ehhh.' She trailed off.

Plus ça change. 'A black man?'

'Eh.' She whooped again with unapologetic laughter. 'So, I visitin' my friend Ezrah. I ent see de cloud reach.' She wrung out a corner of her dress. 'Why it smell so bad of goat in here? You eatin' roti?'

'Long story.' I risked taking my eyes off the road to glance at her. 'Lost my way and asked a goatherd and, well, there were incursions, if you follow me.'

'Eh-ehh! You a crazy guy!'

'What I mean is, the old man wasn't much help since I'm still—well, not to put too fine a point on it...'

'Lost?'

'Completely.' I negotiated another fallen branch. 'Where are you heading?'

'Crown Point.'

'By the airport?' I swerved around a landslip of reddish mud and rocks. We banged into another crevasse.

'Mind de hole,' she shrieked. 'De road all mash-up.'

'You think?'

She laughed at this. 'So, yeah, I have apartment along Ol' Road.'

'I'll take you home in exchange for guidance out of this maze.'

'Deal,' she replied, laughing again. 'But you speak funny.'

The storm was abating as we drove through a village called Whim and emerged from the dripping hinterlands at a T-junction I recognised not too far from Shurland. Ten minutes later, following my cheerful passenger's instructions, I swung left past Drunken Joe's (*Get drunk here*, blared the floodlit signage) near the airport. The girl pointed to the right. 'I work down there. Kariwak Village and Hotel. My place here on de left.'

I bumped over the kerb indicated and pulled up on the forecourt of a two-floor concrete building painted bright green and clad with rickety-looking balconies and balustrades hung with creeper. I climbed out and opened the door for my passenger.

'Tank you, my friend,' she said, seizing her belongings and swinging her legs out. No cow hoof in evidence.

'What your name, Mr. Englishman?'

'Gabriel Cassidy.'

'So.' A hint of amusement lit up her face and I saw in the dazzling light of a security lamp that her eyes were bright blue. 'Yvette,' she said. 'Maybe if it de Lord will, we meet again.' She seemed about to say something else but thought better of it. 'Have a bless night, Gabriel.'

I watched her saunter across the yard. She unlocked a tall metal grill at the foot of a staircase, turned briefly to wave, then disappeared.

I reversed into the street and made my way slowly back to Shurland. As I turned up the steep driveway it occurred to me that I had never travelled alone in a car with any woman other than my wife. It didn't bear thinking about, I smiled to myself, what Sarah would say on the topic of my picking up a stranger, a *girl*, on a dark and stormy night.

The tempest had passed as I parked the now very muddy Honda under the samaan tree. My camera wrapped in a towel, I grabbed the rest of my stuff and ran up the staircase to the balcony. As before, my Shurland welcoming committee was in place: Kenny the crapaud squatting in the doorway and Lily in the kitchen. 'Merciful Lord,' she shrieked, waddling towards me but recoiling at the last moment, 'but you stink, Mr. Gabriel! What you bin doin'? Muckin' out de farmyard?'

'Lily, there've been adventures. But thank you for waiting up.'

She sniffed and let out a bellow of horror. 'Give meh dem clothes and – I beggin' you – take a shower! Afterwards you eat a vegetable curry an' you tell Lily where you been so long! It pass nine o'clock!'

'Yes, ma'am,' I said, heading for my room.

'You nuh make it to Pennysavers?'

'Ah no, sorry. Things got a bit out of hand. But here's a bag of pacro from Winston. I've paid him for it.'

'You saw ol' Winston? I pay you back.'

'No need.'

She put her nose in the bag. 'Oh, he smell nice an' ripe! Winston tell you what it good for?'

'He did imply something.'

Lily steupsed. 'Dat Winston!'

'You didn't manage to find the missing ingredient for your tea, did you? I could really do with a cup.'

'No, I try, but my frien', she in Trinidad wid her son. But I tinkin' you should have no more. You allergic to an ingredient: maybe cinnamon. It happen sometimes, you understan'.'

'Then I'll settle for a Stag.'

Lily turned to open the fridge. 'Oh, Mr. Gabriel, someone visit you earlier. I ain't see him, but Churchill tol' him you out.'

A surge of adrenalin brought me up short. 'A visitor? Not Pablo, I hope.'

'No. Police officer. He come back in de mornin'. You in trouble?'

15

Churchill's dogs woke me from nightmares of temptresses dancing at a parade of barracudas masquerading as dentists. It was hardly even light, but downstairs I heard the rumble of voices. Someone was climbing the steps to our balcony. A peremptory rap on a windowpane; the rattle of the French windows opening. Clumping, uncertain footsteps across the floorboards.

Bleary-eyed, I pulled on boxers and a T-shirt and quietly opened my bedroom door. Holding my breath, I crept round the internal balcony until I could see into the kitchen. The intruder was a beige-uniformed policeman, the one who had called last night, I assumed. I recognised him at once. On his head were perched the same mirrored shades I'd seen on him yesterday when leaving Arnos Vale. As an added surreal touch he was rooting about in a cupboard. I observed him from behind a pillar, trying to marshal my thoughts. The man seemed very sure of himself.

I cleared my throat and marched down the corridor. 'Er, can I help you?' I was certain this copper was not within his rights to be making free with a brand new packet of best Brazilian Arabica in a private kitchen at 6.15 in the morning.

The man lifted his head from the task of lighting the gas under a kettle. 'Good day,' he called. 'Beautiful mornin'.' His words were slurred and, as I drew nearer, I detected a miasma of alcohol.

'That's as maybe,' I snapped, 'but you're trespassing. Or do you have a search warrant?'

'Eh-ehh,' came the predictable retort. 'No problem! Lily an' me, we was at school together.' He struck another match and set fire to the spent pile in a chipped saucer beside the stove.

I stood my ground. 'What the *hell* do you think you're playing at?' I grabbed the miniature bonfire and emptied it into the sink.

Before the policeman could answer, a tornado in the form of Lily whirled screaming over the floorboards behind me. I had not heard her coming up the stairs. 'What in God name you doin' here, Cleve? Get out my kitchen! You dare come here disturbin' innocent folk before sunrise?' She swept past me and snatched the matchbox from his hand. 'You crazy? Dis a wooden house!' She sniffed loudly and raised her eyebrows. 'Oh-ho! Maybe you wearin' a nice ironed uniform, but you is drunk, Cleve. You breath stink!' She smacked his shoulder. 'An' you poor, long-sufferin' mother, she assure me you on de wagon! You wait 'til I tell her.'

The obnoxious officer made a great show of tucking his shirt into his trousers, a dark triangle of hairy belly appearing above his belt buckle. A pair of handcuffs jangled. 'Eh, Lily,' he smirked, 'you won' be tellin' she nothin'.'

'Dat right?' snorted Lily. 'Why not?'

Alcohol-infused sweat beaded Cleve's brow. He pulled a fold of squashed papers from the back pocket of his trousers. 'Because, Lily, you harbourin' a member of—' He paused, fixing me with rheumy eyes.

Lily enquired, 'Of what?'

His moist lips parted into a leer of triumph. 'Of de criminal classes, Lily Pitt.'

'Oh, don't be ridiculous,' I said, my stomach knotting.

He was gloating. 'You is Mr. Cassidy? Mr. Gabriel Cassidy?'

'Yes.'

'Well, I sees you trespassin' yesterday on private property.'

'What?'

Cleve fondled the butt of a pistol protruding from a leather holster. 'You was at de Arnos Vale Hotel. You doh remember? Tax your brain some, Mr. Cassidy. I have sign' witness statement. I collec' it myself.'

Lily piped up. 'You talkin' about Winston, Officer Cleve? Yes, Gabriel was pickin' up someting for me.'

Cleve exhaled, unimpressed. 'Right,' he drawled, spreading his paperwork on the counter and visibly puffing up with self-importance. 'I hereby authorise, Mistah Gabriel Cassidy, to issue you an Official Warning. You require to confirm you read it and accept its *implication* by signin' here, here and here.' His finger left three damp stains on the paper.

'This is bollocks and you know it. What "implication"?'

'Implication imply no *explanation*, sah.' Someone had been rehearsing this insufferable policeman.

'Excuse me,' I muttered, stepping round him to turn off the gas before the kettle started to whistle – or before alcohol fumes caused an explosion.

Cleve was enjoying his moment of power. 'You makin' coffee, Lily Pitt?'

'No chance.'

The officer steupsed and produced a pack of cigarettes from his shirt pocket. With theatrical deliberation, he lit one. 'Mr. Cassidy, I also authorised – as a goodwill gesture, you understan' – to waive this first infringement, provided you sign de documentation.' He blew smoke in my face, of course, but I ignored it. 'Next time, however, we bring de full weight of de law down upon you shoulder.'

I glanced at Lily, She shook her head, lips pursed. 'Sign, Mr. Gabriel,' she murmured. 'Police an' dem, dey thrive on paperwork.'

'Okay.' I snatched Cleve's biro and signed in triplicate. I had never been in trouble with the law before. The situation reminded me of my father being "disappointed" in me forty years ago when I forgot to bring my Bible to a Sunday meeting. I took a deep breath and pasted on a mock-apologetic smile for the policeman. 'This too shall pass,' I hissed.

'What you say, Mistah Cassidy?'

'Nothing.'

Cleve refolded and pocketed the papers. At the top of the stairs he picked up a peaked cap he had left on the balustrade and, with absurd theatricality, placed it on his head, the shades dropping onto his nose. How often had he practised this routine in the mirror, I wondered? I wanted to smack him. 'Eh, Mr. Cassidy,' he oozed, favouring me with a gleeful smirk. 'I hear you is limin' wid people in high places.'

'Liming? I'm not familiar with the word.'

Cleve raised both eyebrows and cocked his head in disbelief at Lily. 'Limin', Mr. Gabriel,' she said. 'It mean hangin' out.'

'Exackly, tank you, Obeah woman.'

There was a dull ping from the region of Cleve's not inconsiderable backside. He pulled out a phone and smiled at the screen. 'What I is sayin', Mr. Cassidy, is dat I am aware you have *influential* friends in our Tobago House of Assembly.' Searching for his car keys, the man contrived to drop a roll of banknotes. 'Assistant Secretary Cordner, for instance,' he said, bending stiffly to gather up the money, 'she a powerful woman, but *unaccustomed* to delay. Irregardless whether you is a rich black Englishman.'

Cleve wiped the sweat from his upper lip, turned and stamped down the staircase. Lily and I watched him drive away, blue light flashing. Our motmot alighted at the bowl of fruit and began pecking at a chunk of watermelon.

I said, 'So, Janice and Pablo have their tentacles everywhere on this island.'

'You better take care. Officer Cleve, he may be a drunk, but he know everyone. You saw dat money? He not averse to bobol.'

'Say again?'

'Bribery. Jus' like Assistant Secretary Cordner. She have a reputation.'

'Oh, great. Excellent. Super.'

A hand on my back. 'You okay?'

'I'm fine, Lily, just congratulating myself on getting mixed up in all this. What a confounded idiot I am.'

'I make some coffee, Mr. Gabriel. You go sit on de balcony.'

In the garden below, an iridescent green jacamar flashed back and forth collecting insects from its spot on a breakfast twig. Beside me, buzzing about my head, the hummingbirds were already getting stuck into their daily battle for supremacy around the sugar-water feeder. But I was in no mood today to appreciate these tiny jewel-like birds; clammy waves of anxiety were coursing through me. It was obvious that Janice Cordner had orchestrated this police visit to intimidate me.

I sighed and leant against the balustrade wondering how best to proceed. My eye was caught by a newcomer, a curved-beak Hermit hummingbird standing its ground against three smaller Copper-rumped ones. Inspired by the tenacious spirit of the bird – like Robert the Bruce and his spider – it occurred to me that although I might be out of my depth it would be a sorry business indeed if I took the easy way out and caved in to pressure from Janice.

I was aware of Lily pottering about in the kitchen, that she'd been chatting and laughing with someone on the phone. It was doing me good, I knew, to be around someone so cheerful and ebullient. I glanced at my phone half willing an email from Max to pop up, the one that would usher in a Power of Attorney in time to assuage Janice and Pablo. Nothing. 'So Gabriel,' I murmured to myself, 'what's the plan? Still just hoping for the best or are we officially going with positive prevarication?'

A warm hand on my shoulder made me flinch. 'Mr. Gabriel! You okay? I been calling you. Breakfast is ready.'

'Sorry. Miles away.' I struggled to my feet.

Lily took my elbow and led me to the table. She was smiling idiotically. 'So, Mr. Gabriel, you didn't listen to me?'

'Eh?'

'What I say about de la diablesse?'

'Mm.'

'Lucky you not dead in a picker bush.'

Was she endowed with clairvoyance? 'How on earth did…?'

'Tobago small island. I jus' talkin' on de phone.'

I decided to make a clean breast of it. 'Well, the thing is, when last night's storm broke I almost knocked a girl down. Clearly, it being pitch black and pouring with—'

'Lors, it rainin' bucket-ah-drop!'

'If you say so. But anyway, I couldn't refuse her a lift.'

'Hold up, there! You check no cow hoof?'

'Actually, I did – credulous bloody fool that I am.'

'Eh-ehh.'

'Lily, obviously I gave the poor thing a lift home. She was soaked.'

'She work at de Kariwak?'

'Again, how did you know?'

'She tell me herself jus' now on de phone. She know all de time you is my guest.'

'But how—?'

'I know her,' Lily said, her voice dripping like the honey from my knife onto the tablecloth, 'because Yvette, she my daughter.'

At eight-thirty, Max's reply arrived from his personal email address. I opened it with thumping heart.

Sorry, Angel, seen your mail now. Unfortunately, solicitors being what they are, Powers of Attorney cannot be produced overnight. Think fourteen to sixteen weeks. Paperwork has to be approved by the Office of the Public Guardian. There's about as much chance of rushing that lot as your blue Caribbean freezing over. Also, what about other conveyancing formalities such as searches? Do you wish me to put those in motion?

Sorry again for lack of positive news. M

'What your lawyer say, Mr. Gabriel?' Lily was going through her nervous cushion-plumping routine.

'Up to four months for the Power of Attorney,' I replied. 'Shurland earns a stay of execution.'

'Praise de Lord.'

'I suppose so.' I refrained from telling her how frosty today's meeting would be as a result. 'I'll just have to brace myself and explain the situation to Ms. Cordner, won't I?'

'Tell her tings out of your hands.'

'Exactly. What's the worst that can happen?' I dared not imagine. A palm tanager fluttered away as my phone buzzed. The "No Caller ID" sent a rush of adrenalin through me.

'Pablo, good morning.'

'Everything ready?'

'Well, I've been in touch with our solicitor and—'

'You bring all documentation, *sí?*'

'Are you not coming here?'

'Change of plan. We meet near the site of development. Like before.'

'Proposed development, Pablo.'

'As you wish,' said the Venezuelan. His rumbling tone put me in mind of a volcano on the cusp of eruption. 'Also, Mr. McClung, he no like your game-playing, Meestah Cassidy. *Comprende?*'

'Absolutely.' A whistling louder than the din of cicadas was swelling in my inner ear.

'Until midday, Meestah Cassidy, at Rocky Point above Back Bay.'

An olive-coloured woodpecker with a red head was savaging the bark of the samaan tree. 'Got it,' I said.

I showered until the water went cold and rusty and an hour later presented myself for inspection in the kitchen where Lily was doing something aromatic with pimento peppers, shadon beni and herbs. 'Right, I'm off,' I declared. 'Wish me luck. Do you think the blue-shirt-pale-chinos look is sober enough for the occasion?' I didn't believe my forced bravado, and I was sure Lily didn't.

'You sea-bathin' after?' She pointed to the rolled towel under my arm.

'Assuming Pablo hasn't tied me to a tree and beaten me to death for refusing to sign, then yes. I'll stop at that beach at the bottom of the drive.'

'No snorkelin' at Stonehaven Bay.'

'You know what?' I said grimly. 'I'm giving snorkeling a rest.'

16

Twenty minutes later, I parked the Honda in the shade near the Private Property sign. Opposite and above me, four tin-roofed shacks on stilts clung to the sunlit and wooded hillside. In stark contrast to these impoverished yet colourfully painted dwellings, the presence of Janice's shiny official SUV before me was incongruous and distasteful. The sleek, black ostentation of the vehicle reeked of self-satisfaction, injustice and inequality. The very sight of it inspired a surge of rage. 'And what a prime example of a worldly, conscience-free politician you are, Janice,' I muttered to myself, killing the engine.

Banging the door shut, I stood there for a moment with the midday heat beating down on my head. It struck me all of a sudden why Christadelphians decline to exercise their right to vote; why indeed they refuse to go to war at the behest of mere kings, queens, dictators or – worst of all – professional politicians. God's plan for mankind does not, it is suggested, require us to take any notice of puffed-up, self-promoting and vain people with mere earthly power like Janice Cordner. It is even argued by the more strait-laced members of the Ecclesia that by voting for one or other politician you might unwittingly put yourself in the invidious position of voting against God's own wishes. I locked eyes with a large, hump-backed cow tethered nearby. It had a dirty-white cattle egret balanced erect on its shoulder. 'Thing is, Gabriel,' I said, addressing this seemingly benign duo, 'the time for self-imposed political exile is over. Now you must stand up and fight, so face your demons, lose the sophistry and get a grip.' The cow gave a vigorous shake of its head and dislodged the egret which flapped to the ground to wait for insects.

It was eight minutes to twelve so I jammed on my hat and set off between tall grasses down the track I'd used two days ago. Hearing a voice, I paused behind a clump of bushes and parted some branches. Waddling about not fifteen feet from the burnt-out car, Janice was on her phone belittling some minion on the topic of dwindling Party membership. Attired today in a luminous parrotlet-green suit, matching shoes and black tights, she looked utterly out of place in this arid tropical brushland. She reminded me of one of those roly-poly Humpty-Dumpties my mother used to knit for fundraising Christmas "fayres". Pablo was standing guard at a respectful distance against the trunk of a palm tree, his suit gleaming in the dappled sunlight. He soon spotted me and, at a nod from him, Janice wound up her phone-call.

'Mr. Cassidy,' she called, 'you are commendably punctual today.'

I lifted my hat. 'Good day, Assistant Secretary.'

'I see that, like us, you have wisely left any paperwork in the car.'

'Well, I—'

'You remember Pablo, of course.'

Pablo lifted his sunglasses enough to reveal a strip of pink Elastoplast stretched across the bridge of his nose. 'Once seen, never forgotten,' I said, my heart sinking under his barracuda-like glare.

Janice was squeezing my arm. 'Let's walk and talk in the American style. The weather is perfect and the scenery exquisite, do you not think?'

'Absolutely.'

She flapped a hand at the shell of the car. 'So regrettable though that people think it appropriate to abandon this sort of excrescence in such a beauty-spot. In fact, Pablo,' she snapped her fingers and glanced over her shoulder, 'make the necessary arrangements to have it removed, would you?' Expressionless behind his Mafia shades, the man inclined his head. 'Mr. McClung insists,' went on Janice with a tight smile, 'that as a courtesy to you and your uncle, I show you the view – and reveal his plans – from the escarpment.'

'So thoughtful,' I said, breaking into a sweat. 'You lead the way.' I said nothing about the harrowing scenes I'd witnessed here two days before. No point in stirring the hornets' nest, especially as the queen and her chief drone seemed benign today. We were passing my former place of concealment. This time I read the sign: "Manchineel Tree. Poisonous. Do Not Touch".

Janice parted some bushes and beckoned me to join her on the cliff edge. We were only a few yards from the top of the path I'd climbed to escape the snake-man. 'God have mercy,' she hissed, staring down.

'What's the problem?'

'Take a look for yourself.'

Was she planning on hurling me to my doom? 'Mm,' I murmured, my hand clamped to the stem of a sapling. 'Lovely view.'

'Do you not see what I'm seeing, Mr. Cassidy?' She flung an arm out. 'Or not seeing.'

I looked across at what I knew from the map was called the Lagoon, a wide bay of bright blue water and tree-lined coastline extending to the iconic beach of Pigeon Point. I'd seen pictures of it in holiday brochures. High above, frigate birds soared, angular black shapes reminiscent of their pterodactyl forebears.

Janice was frantically texting. I asked her, 'So, what am I missing here?'

'Sand,' she snapped, jutting her jaw. 'Down here, just below us. Two days ago that was a wide sandy beach ideal for surfing and water sports. Today, it's nothing but rocks. Last night's storm has washed away one of your most valuable assets.'

'Gosh, you're right, it's gone.' On the far side of Mount Irvine Bay where it was less sheltered, waves were still smashing against the coastline, sending up huge plumes of spray. 'It was a lovely spit of sand.'

'Quite so, Mr. Cassidy,' she continued, pulling down her shades and peering up at me over them. 'Which is going to be expensive for you and your uncle.'

The lunatics really had taken over the asylum. 'How so?'

A hand the size of a pizza gripped my left shoulder. Pablo had finished his call and snuck up behind me. I wriggled out from under his grasp. Janice went on, 'Because in order to recreate the surfing beach so dear to Mr. McClung's heart, we'd have to construct a concrete breakwater and import replacement sand.'

'Are you bonkers?'

'You know what, Pablo,' Janice sniffed, ignoring me, 'I might suggest to Buck that we dynamite some of what we're standing on. No one would miss it. That way we could generate enough ballast for the breakwater without going to the expense of having to bring in too much concrete. Using local materials would keep things more organic. What do you think?'

'Good idea, boss.'

'And save our friend here a great deal of money.'

'What's it to do with me?' Pablo's hand was again on my shoulder. He could so easily push me over the edge onto the sharp, newly exposed rocks below. 'I'm afraid I don't follow.'

Janice was stroking my wrist, making my flesh crawl. 'Obviously, Gabriel, Mother Earth's interference in our plans was unforeseeable—'

'Ah, well, not entirely, given what we know about global warming and extreme weather conditions.'

She ignored me again. 'So obviously we'll now be obliged to re-cost the works taking into account this marine infrastructure. At a reduction in the offer price, of course.' Her phone pinged and she read the text, her other hand now actually holding my wrist. Perhaps she was the one deputised to dispatch me after all. Despite my recent resolution to fight, a wave of adrenalin assailed me; these two were a demonic double act. 'That was from Mr. McClung,' she went on with a brief smirk, 'and he agrees with me that a price reduction would be only fair, given this new set of environmental circumstances. As I said, Mother Earth's unilateral decision to downgrade our proposed facility obliges us to find some way of curbing the sand's inclination to escape. It's happened once as you can see: it could happen again.' She produced an iPad from her handbag and flicked open an aerial view. 'Perhaps now would be a good time to clarify the situation with this ground plan. Here's Pigeon Point and...' she widened the image with two fingers, 'the lagoon and surfing beach. Our breakwater would run, I imagine, across here.'

'Your proposed devastation of the lagoon aside, what are all these red blocks inland?'

'Hotels. In yellow are the avenues connecting them with each other – and with the beach.' She sniffed. 'How does the plan strike you?'

I could have done with a beer – or something stronger. I almost shouted, 'But there are four hotels! I thought it was only supposed to be one. And what are these little orange squares dotted about further inland?' I seized the tablet. The map was like a Monopoly board.

Janice replied, 'Executive villas, Mr. Cassidy.'

'But where is Shurland?'

'Shurland? This is all Shurland.'

'You know what I mean: where is the house?'

'House?' Pablo pushed in and raised a quizzical eyebrow. 'What house?'

151

A stab of panic as the penny dropped. 'Oh, for Christ's sake—'

Janice took back her tablet and smiled expansively. 'Pablo, I thought Mr. Cassidy was his uncle's man in Tobago, but obviously not.' Pablo grunted his equivalent of merriment. It would have been an unwise decision given how I valued my own physical safety, but I'd have loved to smack his face into a tree trunk. Janice turned her gaze to an area of virgin mangroves and forest that extended between where we stood and the more urbanized end of the island near the airport. 'Allow me to explain, Gabriel. Down here is nothing but useless forest and mosquito-infested swamp.' She prodded at my neck with a purple-varnished claw, her nostrils flaring. 'I see you've already been bitten, so you understand the inconvenience.' Her voice was bubbling like soapsuds leaking from an old washing machine. 'But if you're still suffering colonial qualms and scruples, just answer me this: is Shurland in its present form earning its keep?'

'I've told you, I have plans to create an eco—'

'So, no, then.' I was about to remonstrate further but Pablo's hand was on my back once more. 'So, what's to be done, Mr. Cassidy? At only fifteen minutes from the airport, it's a golden opportunity for growth. Your uncle and Mr. McClung are in agreement on this: Mother Earth must be *tidied up*. As you've seen, Buck is not planning a stand-alone facility but a four-hotel complex plus eighty villas all the way...' she swept her arm inland '...across there, up into the forest to the top of the hill. Imagine the views towards Trinidad.'

'So, the historic plantation house itself is to be obliterated, together with mangroves, forest, wildlife and everything else?'

'Oh, Gabriel, you are so old-fashioned. Positively stone-age. Don't worry about our despoiling the environment a bit: the north-east of the island is covered with enough of that natural UNESCO bio-sphere shit to last a lifetime.'

'I know that, but—'

'Besides, Tropitel's architects always make a point of reforesting their facilities with palms and bougainvillea to offer guests some well-earned shade for their dollar.'

Pablo refolded his arms and assumed his favourite bouncer stance. I looked from him to Janice. 'This *is* your idea of a joke, right? You'd never get away with it. Ecologically speaking, it would be a disaster.'

Janice glanced at her phone which had pinged again. She sniffed and snorted. I wished she would blow her nose: this constant clearance of her eustachian tubes was repugnant. 'Be that as it may, we two must bring matters to a conclusion, Mr. Cassidy. Buck informs me that Tropitel is reducing its initial offer by fifteen – one five – percent to take into account the costs of sandscaping, if I may coin a phrase. Assuming this is acceptable, and bearing in mind the extra administrative time I personally will be required to put in, I will also be looking to improve the arrangements as regards myself.'

'Oh, don't be—'

She held up her hand. 'Remember, I am the one charged with easing the project through Government – before, as I said, Mr. McClung's arrival next Wednesday. I'm confident I can still achieve this, but everything has its price.'

Pablo seized my shoulder again, exerting just enough force to assure me that tossing me over the escarpment would be a mere bagatelle for him. 'Oh, absolutely' I whispered.

A Hispanic voice in my ear. 'What you say?'

I spoke carefully so as not to choke on my words. I was mindful of my strategy of positive prevarication. 'I said: absolutely.'

'I'm so glad we're in agreement,' declared Janice, pushing her way back through the bushes. 'Pablo's assistant Newton will bring round the amended contract later today. Then we'll sign off in the morning.'

We had passed the burnt-out car when Pablo cleared his throat. 'Meestah Cassidy, you met Officer Cleve this morning?'

'He has you in his sights for trespass, as I understand it,' stated Janice over her shoulder. Seeing her totter along this uneven track was beyond absurd.

But Pablo hadn't finished: 'You saw Cleve is a smoker, *sí*?'

'Your point being?'

'Smokers can be careless.'

'That's a bit of a generalisation, isn't it?'

Janice interrupted. 'Pablo is hinting that with things being so combustible in the Caribbean, especially in the dry season, accidents can – and *do* – happen. That car we passed is but one small example but, you know, antique wooden plantation houses are particularly susceptible to conflagration.' I stared at her in disbelief. 'Especially at night. It would be unfortunate if Cleve inadvertently cremated that woman and her stupid old father during routine nighttime patrols.'

Beads of sweat were dribbling down my back, white spots dancing in my eyes once more. I had to draw this encounter to an end before one of them smelt my fear as clearly as I could. I swallowed, looking from one to the other. 'I suppose people like you are used to issuing threats on behalf of your superiors.'

Janice was out of breath. 'I advise you to choose your words with care, Mr. Cassidy. You don't want your words to be misconstrued.'

My turn to ignore her: I had "ocular wool to pull", as my father used to say. 'I'll bear it in mind,' I said as airily as I could. 'And in the meantime I look forward to receiving the amended contract this evening. It'll need scanning and sending over to the U.K., of course.' Now I'd supposedly agreed the price, they'd be thinking they were pretty much home and dry. But events would take a turn for the worse when I told them the Power of Attorney was going to take weeks, that I still couldn't sign on the line. I was certain positive prevarication would have its price.

'Glad to see you've decided to take a professional line at last. I appreciate it.' The woman was smiling, but in the manner of a hyena. 'So, how do you plan to spend the rest of your day in Paradise? Chasing birds perhaps?'

'Maybe. After a swim.'

Janice snorted so deeply it made my eyes water. 'I wouldn't advise it. The sea is still rough after the storm and there'll be dangerous undercurrents. It would be such a tragedy – and a great inconvenience – to lose you just now.'

We were still a couple of hundred yards from the cars. Over to the right, a gaggle of squawking and ugly grey-black turkey vultures with bald pink heads were hopping and flapping around something concealed from us on the edge of a patch of scrabby woodland.

Janice's hand was on my arm again. 'I wonder what those corbeaux have found.' She held a hand to her nose. 'Do you smell something, Pablo?'

'*Sí*, Assistant Secretary.'

'Can you smell it, Mr. Cassidy?'

I sniffed but could only smell the Assistant Secretarial perfume with which the air was laden. 'Not really.'

'Something the matter with your nose? Here.' She dragged me to the right. 'What about now?'

I sniffed again, wondering how long I had to continue this tight-rope of play-acting with them. There was indeed a faint hint of putrefaction in the air similar to that dead-mouse smell in our attic when I haven't checked the traps for a while. 'A dead animal?' I suggested.

Janice pointed imperiously. 'Pablo, check out those bushes. See if there's something we need to get one of the fellas to deal with.'

Pablo nodded and sauntered away, the slightest trace of a smile playing about his lips. Seeing this besuited bouncer picking his way through tall grasses and fallen branches might have been

155

under any other circumstances comedy gold, but today I was in no mood for a scene from *Carry On Up the Jungle*. Janice had taken my arm and was whispering with forced theatricality into my ear. 'Someone can earn himself a day off in exchange for burying a dead dog, you know.'

'Is that a thing in Tobago?'

'Certainly.' She was looking at me as a cat eyes a goldfish she's clawed out of an ornamental garden pond, unsure as to whether to lick first or go straight in for a bite. Lily was right to call her a Baddis. She spoke: 'Pablo seems to have taken a dislike to you, Gabriel.'

'You think?'

'It was perhaps rash of you not to let him play with your camera the other night.'

'Nobody touches my rig.'

'Where Pablo comes from, they find it hard to forgive personal slights.'

'So I gather.'

Janice cleared her congested tubes again. 'And then you humiliated him further by making his poor nose bleed. I was quite impressed, to be honest.' She tried to touch my cheek but I flicked my head aside. 'I see you can be quite the man under that coy façade of British dotishness.'

'It all depends upon the level of provocation.'

'Pablo is a man who bears lifelong grudges.' The woman was insufferable.

'I do appreciate your insights.'

Seven or eight squawking corbeaux rose into the air with a clatter of wings as Pablo pushed aside the leaves of a banana plant. I saw him stand stock still for a moment looking at the ground. 'This no dead animal, boss,' he called, his voice matter-of-fact. 'You better look.'

Janice sighed. 'I am not dressed for hiking, Mr. Cassidy, but we'd better do as the man says. Here, let me hold your hand – I don't want to fall and cause a scene. Help me over this branch.' This was absurd. What did I think I was doing, holding her horrid, plump, clammy hand? I swung her past me and for a moment her green bulk blocked my view. 'So, Pablo,' she was saying irritably, 'you've dragged me over here. Let's see what all the fuss is about. It had better be worth it or...' She stopped, crossing herself. 'O Lord preserve us.'

I edged round her and stared. Under a bush ten paces away was the corpse of a skinny young man. He lay on his back amongst leaves and twigs, clouds of flies buzzing around his head. He couldn't have been more than seventeen or eighteen and was clothed in only denim shorts. His dusty torso was grazed and gashed, the greyish flesh of his face ripped and contorted into a hideous leer. One of his eyes was gone but worse still, giant brown ants had already invaded the socket. I'd seen any number of ghoulish faces conjured up by prosthetic make-up artists and special effects experts in films, but the sight of this mutilated lad was my first real-world horror. Bile rising, I removed my hat. And then a gust of warm wind huffed the stench of the poor lad's putrefying flesh towards me and – I am not proud to say – I grabbed a dead branch, bent over and retched.

How long I hung there I have no idea, but as I straightened up, silvery mists were swirling in my peripheral vision. Through the fog, I saw the beast Pablo grinning at my discomfiture. Expressionless, Janice passed me a pack of tissues.

'Without touching the body, Pablo,' her voice was echoing in my head, 'can you see how he died?'

'Shot in the eye, boss.'

'Drugs, I suppose?'

'*Sí.*'

'Something to do with the burnt-out car, perhaps.'

'Maybe.'

'There's no blood on the ground, but isn't that a shoe over there?' She pointed. 'The grasses have been flattened so it's obvious to me, Pablo, that the body was dragged here and left to the mercy of the vultures.'

'I agree, boss.'

The mists cleared and I understood. I had seen that grieving family searching this very area only two days ago. Had the body of their lost relative been here, they would surely have found it, or at least seen the circling vultures. A terrible thought flashed into my head: Janice's henchmen had placed this cadaver here as a warning to me for what was in store if I didn't play ball. This would explain why this appalling woman had insisted on meeting me here rather than at Shurland.

I wiped my mouth and handed her back the unused tissues. 'Thanks, Janice,' I muttered, not trusting my voice. 'This is all a bit much for me.'

The Assistant Secretary nodded and pulled out her phone. On no account must I let on I knew what they were up to. 'I quite understand, Gabriel. It's not what a Brit expects to come across in Paradise. I'll call the Commissioner of Police. He's a close personal friend and can be relied upon to be discreet.' She walked back a few paces towards the manchineel tree.

I was alone with her henchman. He was rolling the dead lad's head from side to side with the tip of a shoe. 'A clean death,' he announced.

'Ah.'

'Your first, Meestah Cassidy?'

'My first murder victim, if that's what you mean.' I'd seen both my parents on the undertakers' slab but I wasn't going to share this information with this monster.

'You know,' he grunted before spitting on the corpse, 'his sort die when they stand in the way of progress.'

'I thought you said it was a drug-related crime.'

'I did, *sí.*' He pulled off his shades and polished them on a handkerchief embroidered on one corner with his initials.

'Maybe he no pay for his ganja on time,' he went on. 'But he pay the price now. *Comprende?*'

Glancing over to check Janice wasn't looking, the beast grabbed my neck. He could, I was sure, have shaken the life out of me as easily as a fox a baby rabbit. He pulled my face up to his. 'I no forget,' he hissed, his breath reeking of yesterday's garlic and tobacco. 'No one hurt Pablo and live to old age.' The ferrous grip tightened on my jugular; I was being lifted bodily upwards. 'I tell you once, I tell you again: Don't. Fuck. With. Me. *Comprende, amigo?*' I managed a noise akin to a death rattle. '*Bueno.*'

Dropping me, Pablo barged past to rejoin his boss. I stood for a moment swaying and gasping for breath and then, with a final glance at the murdered youth, pulled on my hat and retraced my steps to the path. When I emerged from the undergrowth, however, there was no sign of my tormentors. I slumped down in the shade of a bush. In the distance, I heard car doors banging.

They had gone.

Sitting there in the grass I wondered how was I to avoid a similar fate to the assassinated boy's if Pablo – yes, and Janice too – were this determined to bring me low? This good-cop-bad-cop routine of theirs would pose well-nigh insuperable challenges even for the most bullish and battle-hardened of vigilante heroes; but since I had never thought of myself as an Arnold Schwarzenegger or a Liam Neeson, I would need to dig deeper than ever before if I were to prevail.

A cacophony of squawks: a gaggle of the corbeaux who had been patiently circling overhead had flapped down and landed in the bushes to continue their interrupted feast. I rolled onto my side and threw up once more.

17

Ten, twenty minutes or an hour later – I have no idea – I was back at the Honda. Inside it was like a pizza oven, my nausea exacerbated by the chemical stink of the deformed pink sea-horse air-freshener dangling from the rear-view mirror like a half-chewed piece of bubblegum.

Lord alone knows how I drove but later still I was stumbling in a daze across the hot, white sand of Stonehaven Bay. The beach was no picture-postcard paradise that day. The thunderous procession of rollers crashing over rocks and up the sand was overwhelming; spray hung in the warm air and hissing grit stung my calves and ankles. A hundred yards out to sea, a speeding pelican rose, paused, then plummeted into the grey water to reappear seconds later to swallow its catch. High above, those frigate birds continued to circle watchfully on tropical thermals.

Janice had been right: the sea was still out for retribution, on a mission to redistribute that sand so important to McClung's plans. Torrents of storm water had cascaded down from the road and hewn miniature cliffs on the beach where only a couple of days ago there had been a smooth slope down to the water's edge. I was momentarily heartened by the thought that Nature would one day prevail in some form, just as she was doing at the ruined Arnos Vale Hotel. Whatever McClung did, however much mankind determined to destroy his only home, the planet would show him who was boss in the fullness of time.

Swimming was out of the question but I thought I might still be able to wade near the edge to cool off – wash some of the stench of corporate corruption from me, not to mention the horrible vision of that decomposing corpse.

I would have expected the beach to be deserted in such inclement weather conditions but my eye was caught by a flash of red through the branches of a fallen sea-grape tree, its trunk whitened and smooth under the constant depredations of the climate. Warily, I edged forward for a better look. The red thing was a raffia bag I recognised. And then, with a shriek of merriment, a slim figure in a blue swimsuit – the owner of the bag – burst from the bushes and sprinted down the sand towards the breakers.

Yvette.

Only a suicidal fool would brave such breakers. 'Yvette, don't!' I yelled. 'Come back!' The nuisance girl however had other ideas, either deliberately ignoring me or unable to hear above the din of the ocean. She pelted into the water until waist-deep in foaming backwash. Dwarfed by the oncoming seas, she stood braced for a second, a fragile and vulnerable figure silhouetted black against a wall of green-grey water. Rooted to the spot in utter dismay, I saw her dive under that colossal wave. I waited and waited for her to emerge – as so many such foolhardy swimmers might do – further out to sea, beyond the breakers. For what seemed like an eternity, I fearfully scanned that turbulence for a glimpse of a curly black head, a flash of blue, a waving hand. Nothing.

And then I saw her, swept way over to the right, on her feet once more but struggling to stand. I shouted again but the next wave was upon her and she disappeared into the maelstrom.

There was no time to make a plan. This was no British beach with its neat posts at regular intervals bearing orange-painted life-rings. I rolled my phone into my shirt, hurled the bundle to the ground and pelted down the sand into the water. I was determined to reach her before she was dragged any further to the right and smashed to a pulp on the jagged teeth of a rocky outcrop. A glimpse of blue swimsuit in the foam and my flailing hands found hers. I dragged the girl towards me, seized her under the armpits and lifted with all my might. I knew I had to brace myself before heaving us both up the steep sandy incline to safety. The sea though was having none of it and I turned to see another monster wave, the height of a London bus, rising behind us. It smashed down, sweeping our feet from under us. Still locked onto Yvette's wrist, I rose to my knees only to be submerged and tossed by yet another mighty wave breaking over us. Acrid salt stung in my nose and the back of my throat as I was turned over once, then at least twice more. Inevitably, my grip on the girl was lost but in the teeth of a premature and watery death, I threw myself towards her floundering body and managed to grab her by the arm again.

'I've got you!' I shouted. 'Come on! Stand up!' And then I too was on my knees being dragged towards those rocks. 'Yvette! One last effort or we're screwed!' I threw another glance over my shoulder. The horizon was rising again. We had mere seconds before the terminal blow would fall. I hooked my arm under hers and hurled myself at that slope, my legs pounding to gain some traction against the tug of water and the downward movement of sand underfoot. 'Let's go!' I screeched. 'One, two and... Now!'

Six inches of black stone protruding from the wet sand saved us. I grabbed it with my left hand and with this solid purchase, resisted the backwash of that next wave. With the water sluicing under us in preparation for the next onslaught, I made a supreme effort to rise to my feet and, struggling backwards, dragged the girl up the beach to safety.

'Yvette, for heaven's sake!' I gasped, lowering her to the sand and throwing an arm round her shoulders as she coughed and spluttered, 'what the hell were you doing? Trying to get us both killed?'

'N-no, Gabriel,' she sobbed. 'I so stupid.' She was shuddering now, cold despite the warmth of the milky sun. 'Tank you. You save my life.'

'Just as well I did because your mamma would have taken a dim view had I turned up for supper with the corpse of her daughter slung over my shoulder.'

Yvette sat up and stared at me, blue eyes bright with tears. I immediately regretted my flippant tone, a reaction perhaps to my having for the first time in my life had occasion to haul someone from imminent death. 'Please don' tell my mum what happen,' she said, her voice almost inaudible above the roar of the waves. 'She tol' me you might be dong here so I taught I surprise you. But if she find out, she go vex.'

I brushed at wet sand on my ankle. My ears were singing and any number of recent abrasions were stinging from contact with saltwater. 'Your secret is safe with me, Yvette,' I declared, forcing a grin despite my absolute exhaustion. 'But it was lucky for you there was a lifeguard on duty. I'm surprised there's not a red flag up when the sea's like this.'

She turned away from me, seemingly focussed on twisting a small shell between her fingers. In the moments that followed, my thoughts flashed back to Janice and her terrible plans and what would happen to Shurland, Lily and now, by default, Yvette too. It was almost impossible to concentrate given this latest unnecessary development, but I was trying even then to compose in my head an email to update Max. He might have an idea of the best way forward.

Yvette interrupted my train of thought. 'Listen, Gabriel, can I buy you a drink? Dat de least I can do, an' I wan' get away from dese waves. It have a café jus' along de beach. My brother, he comin' in an hour so we have time.'

'Who? Trevor?'

'Of course.'

After the ordeal in the water, I had no energy to deal with the likes of him. 'Well, I don't know, maybe I ought to be getting back. But why don't you just let me drive you home? Or come up and see your mum. My car's right there.' I pointed up the beach to where the Honda was parked under some trees.

'Oh no, I cyan' be upsettin' my brother. Once you make plan wid Trevor, he nuh changin' it.' She flashed a dimpled smile at me, more like the Yvette I'd met during the storm. 'Come on, jus' one drink. I owe you.'

No point in arguing further, I thought. If today I was destined to play the Good Samaritan, then who was I to decide at this late stage to pass by on the other side of the road from a beer? It wasn't every day one saved a life or faced such a succession of crises. 'Alright,' I said, 'just one.'

Five minutes later I wearily followed her up a flight of broken concrete steps to an open-air café I hadn't noticed before called *Breezes*. The place nestled behind wind-battered trees on the seawall. Although devoid of customers, it looked promising, boasting a white awning, discreet Caribbean music, starched tablecloths and a petite waitress labelled Annesia decked out improbably in a dark uniform reminiscent of an air stewardess. Although she had not been trained in the art of natural proactivity in the presence of a paying customer, Annesia led us to a table in the corner overlooking the beach. She adopted such an unhurried way of walking that we were obliged to stop and wait twice before reaching our destination. 'Is a Trini ting,' Yvette explained when I queried it. 'You walk too fast – like European an' dem do – you raise a sweat. Nobody want dat.'

We ordered two beers, a chicken sandwich to share and two bowls of ice-cream – coconut and rum-and-raisin. So much for just one drink, I mused: saving people was hungry work.

For the next half hour I maintained some semblance of small-talk in spite of my desire to be silent and think. I lectured poor

Yvette on the topic of the various birds scurrying about at the water's edge below: sandpipers, a comedy green heron wandering aimlessly and a little gaggle of ruddy turnstones. I assume to change the subject, she in turn waxed enthusiastic about an unemployed young man she had her eye on. He lived further up the island near somewhere called Argyle Falls and had assured her that his prospects were good despite a great deal of evidence to the contrary. It was not my place to suggest to Yvette that she might like to avoid following in her mother's footsteps and risk having a baby out of wedlock, so I kept my south-London morality to myself. Perhaps they had different and more relaxed views of long-term relationships here.

Despite watching Yvette smiling and chatting away, my mind drifted intermittently to images of vultures flapping about a mutilated corpse. I almost plucked up enough courage to share my woes with her but decided not to, given her brother Trevor's involvement in local drug supply. Might he have had something to do with the murder? It wasn't a question I could very well ask his innocent sister.

Yvette's face clouded at the insistent sound of a car horn. 'Trevor early,' she sighed, already on her feet. 'I should go.'

'Right. He didn't strike me as the patient type.'

'You know him?'

'Didn't your mum tell you? I bumped into him on the beach a few days ago. Not a particularly uplifting encounter, but the mention of Lily's name soon sorted things out.'

Yvette picked up her bag. She spoke very quietly. 'You know he an addict?'

'I guessed.'

'Also, he usin' cash from one addiction to feed another.'

'Which is?'

She paused. 'Trevor have a special seat reserved at de casino.'

'Ah.'

'He does loss a fortune every month.'

'Don't tell me he gambles his drug takings.'

'Sure ting. He loses an' nuh pay he supplier. Dat is why he always vex so.'

'A complete bloody disaster area.' Bad language was becoming second nature to me but still I hadn't been struck either dumb or dead.

Yvette raised an eyebrow. 'You talk crazy, Gabriel. Come on.'

We threaded our way across the restaurant, Yvette fumbling for her purse. I reckoned our meal would be the equivalent of a week's wages for her. 'Allow me.'

'You sure?'

'I insist. My treat.'

'You a gentleman.'

I passed a handful of damp notes to Annesia who nodded her thanks and murmured 'Have a nice day, allyuh.'

Outside in the lane, a low-slung, metallic-purple car with shiny wide tyres and blacked-out windows reverberated and boomed with unspeakably loud thumping music. I opened the door for Yvette.

Trevor yelled at his sister. 'Where you bin, gyal? Ent I tell you to never make me wait?'

'I is exackly on time, Trevor!'

'Who de fuck is dat?'

I bent down. 'Good afternoon, Trevor.'

'Yam-yam! Sorry, man, didn' recognise you.'

'No worries.'

A sinewy hand emerged to seize Yvette's bag. 'Get in, gyal. I late for an important meetin'.'

Yvette's face was crumpling under what I took to be the weight of family history. I might one day find the courage to have words with this Trevor bully. 'Bye, Gabriel,' she whispered. 'Tank you for lunch – an' everytin'.'

Trevor's face leaned into view again. 'Eh, Mr. Gabriel, man, you have spare dollar? I short two hundred for my meetin'.'

Yvette looked mortified but I straightened up and winked at her. I unzipped my shorts pocket and made a show of not finding much in there. It would be worth seven or eight quid to pacify the man and make Yvette's journey home less unbearable. 'Sorry, Trevor,' I lied. 'Only got a hundred.' I handed it over.

'Yah man, no problem!'

Trevor stamped on the accelerator and the car sped away in a cloud of fumes.

18

'Oh Lord, Lily.' I said as I flopped into an armchair fifteen minutes later. 'What a day.'

'How was de meetin'?'

'Awful.' I fanned myself with a stained Carib beermat. 'But I think I've managed to stall them.'

'I know you would o' find a way.'

Deciding to spare her the grizzlier details of my conversation with Janice and Pablo, I forced a jovial smile and said: 'On the bright side, I had an impromptu lunch-date.'

'Dat so?'

'Uh-huh. With a certain young person.' I was trying to catch her eye, but she was busy sweeping.

'Yvette,' she murmured finally, with a guilty look. 'She a good girl.'

'Without doubt. A credit to you.' Lily's smile of maternal pride melted my heart. 'Pity the same can't be said of her chauffeur.'

'You see Trevor?'

'I've heard all about his troubles.'

Lily steupsed. 'My poor baby. I ax de Lord every day where I went wrong with him.' The cushions were taking an absolute pummeling now. 'But no mo' talkin' 'bout him: I got an invitation for you, Mr. Gabriel.'

'Really?'

'Tonight I perform a ceremony.'

'Oh, I don't think I—'

'Dey bringin' me a boy call Darryl so I can remove it.'

'Remove what?'

'He demon.'

'Ah.'

'So, you come see me work?'

'Ah well, I—'

'Take your mind off Janice Cordner? It start nine o'clock in de old slave quarters.'

'I don't think so, Lily, thanks all the same. It's just that, how shall I put it? – exorcisms aren't really my cup of tea. Not much call for that sort of thing in my part of south London.' I didn't mention I was expecting delivery of the sales contract.

'You be surprised what happenin' on your own doorstep, Mr. Gabriel.'

An hour or so after sunset, with Lily preparing downstairs and 'communin' wid de spirits', my solitary supper was disrupted. The peace was desecrated by the rhythmic thump of a bass line, the rattle of a diesel engine and Churchill's dogs going mad. I pushed away my callaloo soup, stepped across the balcony and leaned with some trepidation over the balustrade. The visitor had better not be Cleve again. I couldn't cope with his supercilious grin and arsonist tendencies. Not now.

However, this was no police car but an even more ostentatious Hyundai truck in metallic red reversing at speed to the bottom of the staircase. The music was snuffed out but the engine continued to belch blue-grey fumes into the floral-scented evening air. The driver's window slid open to reveal an unsmiling moon-like face under an orange baseball cap worn backwards. Pablo's errand boy glared up at me.

'Good night,' I said. 'You'll be Newton?'

'Ri-ight,' he drawled, his tones oddly thin and reedy for such a mountain of a man. In children's animation movies, Newton might have voiced that weaselly purple baddie called Randall in *Monsters Inc.*; physically, though, he was more *Jungle Book* pachyderm. 'Gat package for Mistah Cassidy,' he squeaked. The window closed again.

I could see that carrying packages up flights of stairs was not in Newton's job description so with a weary sigh I descended to lawn level. The music had been turned on again and I could feel the car vibrating with it as I laid a hand on the gleaming roll-bar. The dark glass dropped once more and a hefty A4 envelope was handed wordlessly to me. I took a breath to thank him, but Newton had already gunned the accelerator.

'Well, Kenny,' I said glumly, stepping over the crapaud who had taken up pole position on the bottom step, 'looks like I've made another friend.'

I finished my dinner, trying not to get grease spots on the contract I was reading. It seemed simple enough – too simple in all likelihood – but I did notice with a sinking heart that McClung had stood by his threat to reduce the offer price. Neville would be apoplectic.

By eight-fifteen, I had photographed each page and emailed it over to Max. I added a cover note in the name of positive prevarication: 'Please work as much of your bureaucratic magic as is legally convenient. This whole business stinks and I could use as long a delay as you and a Power of Attorney can generate.'

Half an hour later, I heard cars drawing up in the woods behind the house. Lily's ritual would be beginning in a minute. Absurdly, I felt a twinge of regret about turning down her invitation. Still, I thought, having said No, I couldn't very well just turn up – even if I could find my way in the dark through the woods to the slave quarters. I settled for fetching my camera and laptop and installing myself at the dining table. Some earnest uploading and editing of bird photos would keep me from temptation and deliver me from Evil.

A floorboard creaked behind me and I spun round, heart pounding. 'Yvette! Don't creep up on me like that!'

'Excuse, Gabriel.'

'Are you trying to frighten the life out of me – for the second time in a day?'

The girl had changed into a seemingly Westernised outfit of black vest, floral leggings and black suede pumps. Sarah and I had occasionally seen girls dressed like her queueing outside south London nightclubs as we drove home late after church meetings. She was smiling, one eyebrow raised, looking very much like her mother: 'I jus' come to say is time to go.'

'Go where?'

'Exorcism, of course.'

'But—'

'Come on, fella. Doh be so... what de word? It begin with B.'

'Boring?'

'*British.*'

'Woah!' She had a point, but conscience told me to try one last stand. 'Thing is, much as I'd like to attend, I'm not in the market for headless chickens, goat's blood and what-not. Not really my cup of tea. We Christadelphians, you know, we don't approve of such—'

'Gabriel, stop! Don' play dotish!' She put her head on one side. 'Mother, she believe de same God as you! She attend church on Sunday jus' like you. She tol' me you already had this argument.'

'Ah, well—'

'It okay by me whether you believe or not.'

'That's rich coming from a good Christian girl like you.'

Her laugh was as carefree as it was infectious. 'I no more a Christian dan you.'

'Oh now really, Yvette, that's going too far—'

'Gabriel! Get your shoes!'

Five minutes later we were picking our way in dappled moonlight down the drive and along a path into the woods. People were talking in hushed tones near silhouettes of parked cars.

Leaves and branches flicking our faces, Yvette led me towards firelight until we emerged into the paved courtyard of the ruined slave quarters.

I said, 'You heard I had an adventure here the other day?'

'Mother tol' me you had a close encounter wid de residents. She often see dem too.'

'Obviously I know now I was hallucinating. I wasn't well.'

A steups in the darkness. 'Dat so?'

'Are you saying I really did see them?'

'For you to decide, Gabriel.'

We stepped round the edge of the yard. A brush had been left lying over a pile of leaves, petals and twigs. 'My grandfather, Churchill, he sweep up before de ceremony an' light de fire.'

'Actually, I saw him here that night. He reckoned he was hunting.' We took our places on a log just outside the circle of light thrown by the fire. 'I say, these cicadas are deafening.'

'Eh-ehh, Gabriel.'

'What?'

'We say "cigalles".'

'Oh, right.' I leant back against the trunk of a tree towering above us, its canopy silhouetted against the moon, and looked around. This crumbling skeleton of a building was all that remained of a miniature fortress built presumably by slaves for their own incarceration. The roofing timber was long gone, reduced to sawdust by about two hundred years of industrious insect life. Saplings and scrubby bushes had thrust up here and there through the flagstones, forcing them in places almost to the vertical. The walls had long since fallen prey to cascading foliage, creepers insinuating their roots between the bricks in their determination to dislodge the rendering and prise them apart. In a century or so there would be nothing left of this supposed hub of a slave rebellion. What was I even doing here, I wondered? Why was I so determined to ignore my own better judgment? To please Lily and Yvette? What was the matter with me? It wasn't only Tobago 'affectin'' me, as Lily put it; her people too were starting to insinuate themselves under my skin.

A loud whisper interrupted my thoughts. 'Dis really where you come de other night?'

'Absolutely.' I pointed over to the left. 'I knocked myself out on that wall over there. There'll be my DNA on a brick if you look closely. When I came to, I remember feeling around and finding a pile of ash.'

'I understand. But you see de loops?' She indicated a series of rusty iron rings set in the brickwork.

'Yes.'

'Dat where de slave chain up when he not workin' de plantation.'

I saw again those ghostly apparitions, the woman and the dog, all products of my illness. 'I don't think I should've come,' I said.

'Gabriel, you safe with me.'

'I know, but—'

'Sshh. It startin'.'

A door concealed behind a bush creaked open and I counted eleven family members file in and settle themselves on the flagstones, their faces solemn and timorous in the firelight. Last to arrive was a tall, gaunt man with greying temples. In his arms was a boy of about five who seemed half asleep.

'Dat Solomon, Darryl father,' whispered Yvette as the man set the boy on the ground facing the fire. 'Lors, he so tiny! But he nine year old – floppy like a rag doll. He bin lethargic and sleepy for months. Doctor cyan' do no more. Dat why de family now tryin' Obeah.'

A twig cracked close behind me, a firm hand gripping my right shoulder. I spun round, heart pounding again. I was a nervous wreck. 'Welcome, Mr. Gabriel,' whispered Lily who had been concealed behind our tree. 'So glad you here. Yvette, you done good, gyal.' The Obeah woman stepped forward into the firelight.

I hissed at Yvette, 'Always hated immersive theatre.'

'Sshh!'

In terms of production values, Lily made an imposing figure. Adorned in a plain, purple dress and tall blue turban, her feet were bare, and round her neck hung a string of shiny black beads. She stood behind the fire and held up both hands as if in benediction. The gathering fell silent, heads bowed. At length she spoke: 'Mr. Solomon, you has de dollar I ax?' The father handed Lily an envelope which she secreted in her bosom. 'So let us begin.' She flung an imperious gaze upon the assembly. 'Whatever you God, min' you pray to him while I remove demon from dis boy. I cyan' do it alone!'

She reached between the rusting bars of a low window and produced a half calabash, stirring its contents with her fingertips before muttering some incantation and flicking a handful of powder into the fire. A shower of sparks shot up.

'Incense,' came a low voice in my left ear. 'Dry herb an' seed.'

'The influence of Catholicism permeates e'en into this benighted spot.'

'What you say?'

'Nothing.'

Solomon had assumed a crouching position behind his terrified son, holding him upright by his skinny shoulders. Lily threw another handful of stuff into the flames then replaced the calabash. At her feet, the family cowered as her gaze swept over them. With portentous deliberation, she faced the child, took three steps towards him and raised her arms again. Slowly, she spread her fingers, holding the pose with her eyes shut. Almost inaudible, she began to utter unearthly sounds, half speaking, half chanting words in a language alien to us all. Adrenalin surged in me, a frisson of fear lifting the hairs on the back of my neck. Yvette whispered, 'She contactin' de spirits.'

From her robes, Lily produced a shiny wooden pipe – not unlike the one my old dad used to smoke. She pointed its stem at one of the men seated by the fire. He scrambled to his feet, produced a lighter and lit the tobacco. Lily sucked and puffed, leant forward and blew a cloud of smoke into the child's face. Poor Darryl closed his eyes and struggled, rolling his head from side to side trying to escape, but his father had him tight. Tears rolled down the little mite's face as he fought and coughed.

Emitting deep moans which rose to diabolical whoops, Lily began windmilling her arms over the boy's head. 'Open yuh eyes, Darryl!' she taunted. 'Open!'

Not that I could imagine such circumstances in London's leafy suburbia, but had I come across a child being treated in this way at home, my conscience would surely have dictated that I intervene. Or at least call social services. Here, though, I was sure I should have perished by cutlass had I dared rise up to stop this abuse. I was trembling with the horror of it. Never had I known such conflict within myself. 'Yvette, what in God's name does she think she's doing?'

'Removin' evil spirits. Darryl eyes closed, meanin' de demon sealin' dey self in.'

'You cannot be serious?'

'Sshh!'

Lily was chanting more loudly now, swaying from foot to foot like a sumo wrestler. Pipe abandoned but arms still outstretched, she gave a single balletic twirl, her dress fanning the flames. She pointed again at the lighter man who tossed her over a handful of long twigs bound together at one end. This rudimentary broom was then brandished over the boy. The family set up an insistent and rhythmic wail, urging the Obeah woman on.

'Yvette! This is dreadful! Don't tell me she's going to—?'

'Is a cocoyea broom.' My companion grabbed my face with both hands. 'Listen: in Obeah it use to beat out demon.'

'Christ have mercy on us all.'

175

Lily started by flicking the twigs over the boy's shoulders, arms and torso, softly at first – almost a tickle – but then increasing to a full-on assault, slashing and flailing at him. I wanted to turn away – run away – but move I could not for Yvette's arm had slid over my shoulder and was holding me in position against the tree trunk. The little boy's anguished shrieks echoed round the forest as blow upon blow rained down upon his emaciated frame. Solomon was still behind him, pinioning his son to his chest, but the lad's desire to escape showed no signs of abating. He was writhing and kicking so hard I was certain he'd soon break free. But Lily was powering through, the stubby fingers of her left hand waggling as she applied that birch with her right. There was something inexplicably – shockingly – powerful about her.

'Time for dis demon to fly,' she boomed. 'Time for de obi seed!'

I wrenched my gaze away to look at Yvette. 'What now?'

'She extractin' demon.'

Lily flung down the whip, dived at the boy and grabbed his legs. For a minute or so, she and Solomon fought the lad as he kicked and curled and twisted. How could such a tiny weakling of a child be holding his own against two adults? Whence did he derive such strength? It was just not possible. And then Lily dropped onto him, those matchstick legs trapped under her bottom. She brandished something tiny between forefinger and thumb and the family's chanting escalated to a series of rhythmic yells. Taking advantage of the boy's next scream, Lily pushed whatever it was down his throat and clamped his jaw shut until he had swallowed it. I'd rather give an aspirin to a grizzly bear than force-feed an obi seed to any child possessing such unearthly and diabolical strength.

Still straddling the child, Lily grabbed the broom again and raised it. At the sight of it, the boy stiffened, sucked in a monstrous breath and let fly a sound which turned my blood cold. In a woman it might have been a high-pitched scream; in a man, the deepest of leonine roars. My ears rang with Darryl's cry of rage and defiance. And above it all came Lily's voice, bellowing into the child's face as she continued to belabour his chest with the broom: 'Out now!' she commanded. 'Back into de pit of Hell!'

The boy's tongue shot out, horrible and long like a green mamba, flicking and twisting in the light of the flames, trying to lacerate Lily's face. Since she was leaning back it was as powerless against her as if she'd pinned it to the earth with a barbecue fork. The terrified family wailed and hid their faces. What black magic barbarity was this? The boy was going to die. I leant forward and drew breath to yell, but Yvette, both arms around my neck – and a determined hand against the side of my head – hauled me sideways into her bosom, her skin wet with tears, mine or hers I could not say. I peered out from under her protective arm like a toddler at a fireworks party, desperate to hide but determined to miss nothing.

The serpentine tongue had gone, but the boy's face remained grotesquely distorted. With a final otherworldly roar, he vomited over the flagstones before collapsing backwards between his father's knees. Lily threw aside the whip and stood up, breast heaving. A woman I took to be the mother sat with popping eyes, hands clamped over her mouth.

No one moved. Apart from the beating of Yvette's heart in my ear, all was still. The cigalles had fallen silent out of respect for the dead.

An amazed murmur of 'Darryl?' from someone near the fire. The poor little fellow was stirring. He sat up and looked round, eyes bright, the former lethargy replaced with an energy I would not have believed possible had I not witnessed it for myself. He turned to his mother. 'Mammy,' he said, reaching out a hand. 'I hungry.'

Lily threw back her head and cried thanks to God. Then she bent forward and gathered the boy into her, rocking him from side to side and weeping. 'Demon, he gone!' she cried, standing

Darryl on his own two feet. The family were also up and embracing each other in joy and relief. Lily turned to them: 'My work, he done! Spirit has heal de child. Blessins on you, Darryl!' She beamed down into the boy's face and pressed a farewell kiss on his forehead before handing him to his parents. 'Solomon an' Miriam,' she said, 'take good care of him, for he life is renew!'

Ecstatic, the family pressed in, some in their gratitude grasping the hem of Lily's dress to kiss it, others launching themselves on the smiling boy, smothering him in their loving embrace. Lily detached herself and disappeared with a final theatrical flourish through the broken doorway to a volley of cheers and waves. The exultant father kissed his son, lifted him to his shoulders then led the jubilant procession out of the clearing towards the cars.

As the sounds of jubilation faded, Yvette murmured, 'Well, my cynical Englishman, what you say now?'

I found my voice: 'On the one hand I'm in a state of utter shock having just witnessed what I'd describe as child abuse on a breathtaking scale. On the other hand, something did just happen and, well, the family do seem happy.'

She steupsed. 'So, what would Christadelphian call it? Magic or miracle?'

'Ah, now, I'd need some time to—'

'Yvette!' Lily was calling from backstage. 'You there, gyal?'

'Comin', Mother.' Yvette stood and smoothed down her vest. 'Gabriel, I must go an' help her back to de house. Could you stamp out de fire?'

'Sure.' I didn't move.

'You stayin' to soak up de atmosphere?'

'Just a few minutes.'

Cars started up and were driven away; Yvette and Lily's voices faded. Undeterred by the bizarre and noisy antics of homo sapiens, the forest resumed its normal nocturnal din: the buzz of cigalles, the tiny peep-peeping of miniature tree frogs and the eerie, guttural croak of Kenny's crapaud friends and relations in a nearby stream-bed. Moths and bats fluttered above me and I spotted a tarantula sidle out of a broken bamboo stalk to lie in wait for its supper. Less alarming – but stunning in their regimental discipline – were the thousands upon thousands of leafcutter ants parading in and out of a hole in the earth. Theirs was two-way traffic (driving on the right, I noticed) which followed an agreed highway over roots and stones before heading up a tree trunk to my left. Those in the descending lane held aloft snippets of yellow petal harvested from high in the forest canopy. I could have watched their unquestioning labours all night.

I remained on my log for maybe forty minutes gazing at the local wildlife in the glowing embers of the fire and the moonlight. Was there any real difference, I debated with myself, between the belief system in which I had been educated and that of these Tobagonians? – setting aside the assault and battery of a small boy, of course. Before this trip to the Caribbean, I had accepted without question that my spiritual nourishment should derive from the Bible, itself a set of translations of stories scribbled down by possibly unreliable sources a couple of thousand years ago. These I had believed involved the teachings of a man – poorer in material terms than many of the people I had met in Tobago – himself supposedly the Son of God, who gave up his life to save us miserable sinners from everlasting death; a man who could turn water into wine, multiply loaves and fishes to feed the five thousand and, miracle of miracles, raise the dead. Was there anything more or less rational in this series of scientifically unlikely circumstances than in what I had just witnessed here? Were spirits of the forest such as soucouyants, the phantom and the la diablesse any less relatable as fictions or fantasies than tales of Jesus Christ's miracles?

I stood up, patted down my trousers for inquisitive insects with sharp incisors and stepped over the ant trail towards the fire.

I have never been much of a thinker or philosopher – a prerequisite, some have argued, for long-term membership of any religion – but, crouching down there in the ashes, I knew it was time to prioritise reeling in and sorting into some semblance of order the clues I was being presented with in Tobago; clues which might lead, I knew, both to upheavals at home and a new way of thinking.

A distant flash of light in the treetops. I hadn't heard a car, so were we in for another storm? Time to head back. I flicked on my phone torch and stamped out the embers. Another thought struck me: if I was subliminally looking for a way out of my staid and compliant life in London, why not *commit* to the protection of this tiny corner of a beleaguered planet? Surely, all I had to do was to take a firm stance, say No and that would be that. So far, my performance in battling the grim quartet of Neville, Janice, Pablo and McClung had been lacklustre at most, even allowing for my illness, Pablo's threats and my stated adherence to positive prevarication. It was now high time to take action, get a grip and stand up for the people for whom I was starting to feel real affinity and compassion. But what of my Faith, I wondered, given how I had hardly spared God a thought since I arrived here last week? A few days away from my Bible, wife and fellow Christadelphians seemed to have sounded the death knell for forty years of inauthentic existence on my part.

I picked my way along a rough track downhill and followed it with some trepidation until to my relief I came out by the cocoa house Churchill had shown me the other night. This time, though, the door that had been locked before was slightly ajar and I thought I heard a rustling sound from within. If it was one of Churchill's rodents – agoutis, hadn't he called them? – I'd better chase whatever it was out and lock the door again. Creeping up, I pushed open the door and shone my light inside. Straight ahead was Churchill's bushwhacker, a collection of garden rakes and forks and a chaos of twisted hosepipe. The rustling continued, louder now. I took a step into the shed and threw the beam of light to my right. Stacked on two pallets against the wall were dozens of white brick-shaped plastic packages sealed with brown tape. What on earth could they be? Bags of cement or fertiliser? Odd that there was a distinct smell of alcohol in there too.

A metallic click and I was dazzled by a beam of light pointed straight into my eyes. I could see nothing but flashing images of the capillaries on my own retinas.

'Eh-ehh, boy, look who jus' drop by.' I recognised the voice behind the torch.

'Officer Cleve? What are you doing here?'

'I goin' to ax you de same question, Mr. Cassidy. You dong here checkin' you stash?' He belched a bubble of alcohol fumes.

'I have no idea what you're blithering on about. And stop shining that bloody thing in my eyes!'

Scuffling footfalls behind me. In a panic, I turned, but too late: I had been outmanoeuvred by more men lurking in the shadows outside. I was seized by the arms, dragged backwards out of the shack, spun round and shoved hard against the wall. Struggle as I might, I could not summon even half the strength a small boy had demonstrated during his earlier ordeal. In the end, unseen assailants succeeded in cuffing me.

'Look, Cleve, you corrupt arsehole,' I yelled, 'what the hell do you want from me?'

'Mr. Cassidy, you comin' quietly?'

'No, why the *fuck* should I? This is a bloody outrage!'

At a signal from Cleve I was felled with a blow to the back of the head.

19

'Eh, fella, you wakin'?' The far-away echo of an unfamiliar voice, rasping and slurred, broke into the roar of traffic and wailing sirens outside. 'Yeah, you! I addressin' you.'

I tried to answer, but no sound issued from my parched throat. Whoever it was would have to wait. My head throbbed as never before. I forced open my eyes, tried to focus. Frayed, stripy material bulged through a diamond pattern of wire bed-springs above me. I was lying fully clothed on a metal-framed bunk bed. To my right, a low table adorned with a chipped enamel jug and two mugs, a green plastic chair with one bent leg, a galvanised slop-bucket with a pile of old newspapers beside it. Smelling far worse than a dormitory at a summer camp for Christadelphian children, this hell-hole reeked of urine, excrement, generations of dried sweat and, as if pouring from the upper bunk, wafts of alcohol fumes.

I placed a tentative finger on a lump on the back of my head. The skin wasn't broken but it felt as if I'd been whacked with a telegraph pole. I licked my cracked lips. 'Fucking bastards.' How soon had I become inured to using such a profanities. I wasn't even sorry.

The upper bed-springs creaked. 'What you say?'

'Nothing,' I croaked. What the hell had happened to me? One minute I'd been walking back to Shurland and now I was in some vile dungeon.

The grizzled face of a man appeared, the whites of his eyes the colour of egg-yolk, his dusty complexion reminiscent of a mildewed milk-chocolate Easter egg. What must I have looked like to him? 'Lors, you lookin' like shit,' came the answer.

'Hardly surprising.'

'Eh-ehh, you ent talkin' like a Trini, fella! Why you in here?'

'Not a bloody clue. I wouldn't know where to begin.' I reached for my phone but it had gone, together with my belt. Suicide was the last thing on my mind, but the implications of being unable to contact either Max or Lily were far more serious: I was alone and vulnerable.

'Begin at de beginnin'. We gat plenty time.'

A scraping outside the studded metal door and a tray of bread and coffee appeared through a flap. My cellmate climbed down the ladder and urinated long and loudly into the bucket. He picked up the tray and placed it on the table, took a slurp from one of the coffees and offered me the other. With extreme caution, I swung my legs off the bed and took the mug.

'Thanks.' The coffee wasn't bad, considering, although I'd have preferred a cup of Lily's tea.

The man had assumed the role of host. He dragged over the chair and grinned at me, sporting a single gold tooth.

'Meh name Devon, bro.' He pronounced it like Yvonne.

'Gabriel.'

'As in de Angel?'

I sighed. 'I suppose so.'

'You from England?'

'What is this, the Spanish Inquisition?'

'Only makin' conversation. I meet plenty interestin' people in jail.'

'You telling me I'm actually in jail?' This made no sense. 'Christ.'

'Where you tink? We at Central Police Headquarters, Scarborough, bro. Lower ground floor.'

My heart sank. 'You're bloody kidding.'

My companion exploded in laughter so violent that the bent chair leg buckled, hurling him to the floor and almost upsetting the slop bucket. 'No, I jokin' you,' he cried, picking himself up, flinging the now useless chair into the corner and joining me on the bottom bunk. 'Dis in reality is de bridal suite at de Magdalena Beach Hotel.'

A fluttering and tweeting above us. I craned my neck to look up, making my head hurt. A small brown bird with a pale chest was building a nest on a ledge where the sloping ceiling met a tiny, barred window.

My companion followed my gaze. 'A dove, bro.'

'A house wren, I think, actually. Ironic that so tiny a creature chooses to roost in a place of incarceration.'

'Is de Lord will.'

'Right.' Proof if ever it were needed that religion insinuates itself even into the world's darkest corners. 'And what are you doing here, Devon?'

'De police and dem, dey foun' me dong by de docks las' night. Too much rum wid de fellas. My gyurl, Anika, she go report me missin' soon.'

'Poor woman.' I immediately regretted the hypocrisy and judgmental tone of my response: who was I to talk, given how I had elected to be out of contact with my own wife for so long? 'So you're giving your lady a night off, are you?'

'Eh-ehh, you a mind-reader? I doh know my Anika long, but she wa meh make baby wid she. She tenth child! Dat never happenin', bro.'

'Your Anika clearly has no views about overpopulating the planet, then?' I managed a smile.

'No, man.' He reached across and shook my hand. 'I like you, Angel Gabriel. But why you here? You rob a bank?'

'If only.' A dirty grey rodent the size of Kenny the crapaud scuttled out of a hole at floor-level and disappeared under the bed. 'I reckon I've been well and truly framed. That much I've worked out.'

Devon roared with laughter again, putting his arm round my shoulder. 'Right. And I was sober.'

'No, really.'

'Okay, Angel Gabriel, who frame you?' He had taken to shaking me to emphasise each syllable; this invasion of my personal space was both condescending, irritating and painful, given the fragile state of my head.

'People with power and influence, I'm guessing,' I replied. Devon was peering with a mixture of incredulity and amusement into my eyes. His presence – coupled with what was dawning upon me to be the monstrous injustice of my situation – filled me with impotent rage. I clenched my jaw against any eruption and shrugged off his arm. 'Devon, could you just do me a favour and leave me alone a bit? I don't want to talk about it – I just need time to think – and my head really hurts.'

Devon steupsed. 'I see you could be dangerous when you angry, Angel.' He stood up. 'But whatever you lyin' an' delusion, de Lord Jesus, he love you. He forgive all sinners. You mus' repent. You wan' join me in prayer?'

'Kind offer, but I'm fine. In fact, I'm pretty much done with religion for the moment. I'm too pissed off now to listen to cosy fairytales.'

His eyes bulged. 'You doh mean what you say.'

'I shouldn't be so sure, given what I'm going through.'

'You is in a dark place, Angel. But de Lord comin' to your aid.'

'I shan't hold my breath. It'll be up to me – and my friends – to get me out of this mess.'

'Human weakness an' vanity. Only de Lord can provide.'

'Mm.'

'De Lord Jesus Christ, he take his own cool time.'

My right hand had clenched into a fist of its own accord. I fought with the urge to knock that gold tooth out. 'Devon, if you really want to know, I've been framed by a corrupt police officer, knocked unconscious and lost my phone. And that was just last night. In recent days my life has been threatened more than once and—'

'How long you been in T&T?'

'A lifetime, it seems. Five days.'

'You mixin' wid de wrong people, Angel.'

'Not only that, but I'm being manipulated by powerful, self-seeking people who wish to destroy the planet to line their own pockets.'

'Welcome to Tobago.'

'And now you're suggesting I trust in Jesus Christ – someone about whose efficacy in practical terms I've always had my doubts, I'm coming to realise – to extract me from this putrid swamp?'

'Yah man! Remember Psalm 37: *Commit your way to de Lord; trust in him an'*... eh-heh... call dat George.'

A turn of phrase I hadn't heard before, but I knew what he meant. I dragged another "proof" from the recesses of my mind: '*Blessed is the man who trusts in the Lord,*' and all that, '*whose trust is the Lord.* Jeremiah 17:17. Yes?'

'Truth, bro!'

'Listen, the reason I'm slightly sceptical about religion now is that only last night I watched a ceremony where, by sheer force of conviction, belief or magic – whatever you want to call it – an Obeah woman cured a child.'

'You acquainted wi' de Obeah woman?'

No point in going into it all now. 'And the way I'm coming to see it is that there must be as many different gods out there as there are ways of worshipping them; an infinite number of explanations for existence and death conjured up over millennia by a sometimes desperate yet always super-imaginative human populace. Endless fictions to answer unanswerable questions.' I picked up and sniffed at a dry-looking bun from the tray. 'What then is a rational man to believe? Is an Obeah woman more or less right in her beliefs than a Muslim or a Buddhist, a Catholic, a Jew, a Sikh, a Seventh-Day Adventist or a Christadelphian? – I'm drawing the line at Scientologists and Jediists.'

'Eh-ehh.' I bet Devon wished he'd left me to sleep it off.

'It's *all* about stories, isn't it?' I ranted on, my head clearing by the second. 'Stories made up to counter our natural fear of the unknown: of death; stories designed by those in positions of power to subjugate the rest – to sway the opinion of the credulous masses. Well, I have lived under the jackboot of manmade religious compliance for too long and I'm here to tell you right now, Mr. Devon, that I'm finished with it. It's up to me to sort out my own shit.'

Devon wagged his finger at me and steupsed again. 'In my opinion, dat knock on de head leave you deluded. Or maybe you is here because Obeah woman leave you here. You givin' me a headache now. I goin' an' sleep.' And with that, he climbed back into the top bunk, lay down and faced the wall. So what if I had offended him?

I stretched out my neck on the filthy lump of foam-packed cloth that passed for a pillow. There was no chance of sleep what with the sledgehammer banging in my head and someone on suicide watch rattling every ten minutes at the peep-hole in the door. I was soon railing against Janice, Pablo, Neville and McClung – not to mention the corrupt Cleve – although in here at least I knew I was safe from their machinations.

At some point, the door was flung open and we were joined by a burly and blue-uniformed warder laden with weaponry.

'Devon Wright? Someone claimin' she you wife downstairs.'

'Anika here already? Oh lors.'

The warder laughed and banged on the iron bed with his truncheon. 'Come on, down!'

'She mighty angry?'

'Yessir. Spittin' feathers!'

No sooner was Devon out of sight than another guard presented himself in the doorway. 'On your feet, Englishman. Visitor.' The warder stood to attention.

'Really?'

A surge of hope turned to abject misery as a colossal and familiar form filled the door-frame.

'Meestah Cassidy.'

'Pablo.'

My foe peeled off his shades and tucked them into his breast pocket. The damage wrought on his nose by seven kilos of camera was less pronounced now but given the fresh bead of blood perched on the bridge of his nose, I suspected Pablo had been picking his scabs. He was in a black suit today and had affected a nasty green tie over a pink shirt. He kicked the cell door closed and thrust his jaw towards me. 'Have I given you enough time to understand the delicacy of your position, Meestah Cassidy?'

Here was final confirmation that Pablo, Janice and Cleve were all in this together. I formulated my reply as carefully as I could. 'Yup, I'm pretty much up-to-speed with your politically and financially motivated corruption and coercion tactics. You have caused me to be assaulted by a posse of tinpot three-for-one bribable policemen and banged up in jail. I'm sure you're breaking every rule in the Geneva Convention and—'

'Quiet!' Pablo snorted, a muscle in his jaw twitching. 'You do not learn your lessons.'

'I see what I see.'

'Mr. McClung and Señora Assistant Secretary Cordner not appreciating your continuing amateur tricks to delay the Shurland deal.' Pablo reached behind him and pulled the warder's black steel truncheon from his waistband. He began tapping it into the palm of his hand.

I eyed the weapon. 'It's surely not in your job description to use that on me, is it?' My forced smile was not reciprocated. It was going to be well-nigh impossible to pull the wool over this beast's eyes, but I decided to give it a go and try to remain outwardly calm. 'As far as I was concerned, Pablo, my job was to come to Tobago with the task of agreeing a price for—'

'Shut it, Cassidy! I explain: Mr. McClung a businessman. His shareholders, they expecting a healthy dividend and—'

I held up a finger. 'Ah, now I see.' Tropitel must be in financial trouble; hence the rush to seal the deal. I wracked my brains to remember what I could of the worldly machinations of the stock market. 'So,' I went on, keeping a weather eye on the truncheon, 'McClung the Great must be seen to demonstrate confidence to the markets, is that it? And hopefully the announcement of a Shurland deal in the end-of-year report will boost the share price. I imagine McClung's probably planning a rights issue to raise cash.' I had almost convinced myself, but Pablo's mask-like face might have been rendered in burnished bronze. 'Like I said, my friend, I get it. I wasn't born yesterday.'

'You have one week to sign, then we start work. *Comprende*?' The Venezuelan was stroking the truncheon with the tips of his sausage-like fingers. 'You already in *la mierda profunda* – deep shit.'

I tried one more tactic, appealing however hopelessly to his better human: 'Pablo, think of the children's future, the ecological impact and—'

'Enough, asshole!' He took a step towards me shaking his enormous wrecking ball of a head. He was so close I was gazing straight at the fake, elasticated Windsor knot of his tie. 'For your information, Meestah Cassidy, Mr. McClung arrive next Wednesday. By Tuesday evening you giving me the signed contract, deeds and keys to Shurland.'

'And by what magic do you intend me to achieve this feat?'

'Simple.' He produced a folded sheet of A4 from an inside pocket. 'Here's your flight reservation.'

'Fly direct from jail and collect two hundred pounds? Is that it?'

'Señora Assistant Secretary Cordner has—'

'Oh, cut the obsequious crap! We both know her name's Janice.'

I saw him flinch at this. 'Señora Assistant Secretary Cordner has intervened.'

'How thoughtful, considering she landed me in here in the first place.'

'Despite your recent crimes of trespass, drug-dealing—'

'Piss off.'

'You are to be released on, eh, compassionate grounds.'

'Which are?'

'That your uncle is dangerously ill.'

'How very convenient of him.'

'Your ticket and boarding pass will be with Angela at Kariwak Hotel. Your flight is 1600 hours on Friday.'

'What, the day after tomorrow?'

'*Sí*. You return Tuesday.'

'Go boil your head.'

'Also, I have a personal message for you from Mr. McClung.'

'Not interested.'

Pablo grabbed me by the neck and shoved me against the wall. 'I don't know why, but he flying you Business Class.'

'Do thank the patronising old cowboy but tell him I'm not going anyway. You can't make me, so sod off!'

'Your choice.'

In two lightning moves, astonishing in a man so hefty, Pablo jumped back and struck me with the truncheon across both shoulders. I put up my arms to protect my face but was powerless against the succeeding blows that rained down upon my ribs, hips and thighs. And then he had me by the neck again, bending my head backwards over the sharp edge of the top bunk. 'Also,' he snarled, his garlicky breath hissing with the sudden exertion, 'do not let your uncle die before he sign, *comprende*?'

'You suggesting I'd murder my own relative to thwart your plans? You really are a band of fucking sickoes.'

I lost count of the blows after that. I know that during my beating I yelled and screamed but no one came to my rescue. I remember at one point his slab of a hand holding my face down in the contents of the slop-bucket I'd kicked over in the struggle.

Finally the monster stopped to catch his breath. He towered over me as I lay curled foetus-like and quivering in spilt excrement. Through my pain and anguish, I was gratified to see glistening splashes of bodily fluids on his shoes and trousers.

'Now we understand each other, Meestah Cassidy.'

'Alright, I'll do it, you bastard! Just fuck off and leave me alone.'

'*Bueno*.' The gritty sole of his boot twisted onto my cheekbone. 'Enjoy your flight. We'll be with you all the way.'

He landed a final kick to the side of my head.

20

'Welcome to Gatwick,' came the cheerful announcement, 'where the local time is nine-forty-six and the temperature a bracing three degrees.' A mere twenty-six degrees cooler than when I had boarded the aircraft. Through a rain-flecked window, planes stood sullen, dripping and resentful on the gleaming grey concrete.

I scrumpled up my blanket and removed my headphones, taking care not to exacerbate the bruising on my temple. It was one of today's many bitter ironies that I should be grateful to McClung for flying me Business Class. His condescension had allowed me at least some sleep, some vestige of comfort after my battering at the hands of his hired thug, but I still felt dreadful. There was not a single part of my body that didn't hurt: my head was swollen, both shoulders were badly bruised and I hardly dared touch a particular spot on my ribcage. From pacifist Christadelphian retired insurance broker to being imprisoned, beaten and broken within a week.

While the crew and ground-staff faffed with doors and exit ramps I unfolded the article I had torn out of a newspaper in the departure lounge. Guilt and anxiety ebbed and flowed as I re-read the piece.

Tobago Tropitel Threat

Hotel multinational Tropitel owned by Texas billionaire and impeached former Republican Party lawmaker Bill McClung has set its sights on Tobago, threatening wetlands, mangrove and prime forest near Mount Irvine and Black Rock. In imminent danger is an area half the size of the island's capital. According to sources at the Planning Department, McClung's corporate ambition has by no means been sated with recent hostile acquisitions of coastal land in Barbados, Grenada and Antigua.

The Tobago House of Assembly is now being asked to fast-track an application to construct four 150-room hotels and a complex of 80+ villas complete with pools, bars, executive helipad and golf course. Planned for the waterfront are three 24/7 bars and a boat-station to accommodate watersports such as jet- and water-skiing, and more leisurely tourist pursuits such as glass-bottomed boat-trips to Buccoo reef and night-time bioluminescence paddle-boarding.

However, the threatened coastal mangroves provide breeding grounds for the fish that sustain that very coral reef. If they are removed the reef will also die. In addition, such a development will destroy the tranquil allure of nearby world tourist hotspot, Pigeon Point.

Officials are expected to rubber-stamp the plan despite the Government itself being required to fund and build the project. Sadly, we have seen this so often before: money will even now be changing hands to oil the wheels of this ecological catastrophe. Bobol is part of everyday life in Trinidad and Tobago. [Malika George is a conservationist and wildlife photographer]

I stuffed the article into the back of my passport. Might not Neville be persuaded to change his mind if he read it? I doubted it.

I rubbed my thumb over the new crack on my phone's screen. Pablo had thought fit to return it by chucking it at me as I'd lain on the floor of the cell. Checking no one was looking, I took a selfie to inspect the damage. My face seemed far larger on one side than usual and my right eye was bloodshot and half-closed. One of my front teeth was chipped. 'Jesus Christ', I muttered, 'I look like the bloody Elephant Man'.

So keen was I to avoid awkward looks or questions, I remained slumped in my seat whilst the cabin burst into life with people stretching and heaving luggage down from overhead lockers. Out of habit, I flicked open Sarah's WhatsApp page to report in – not something I'd done in what seemed like a lifetime – but closed the app at the sight of her last message about leaving my Bible behind. I couldn't face my wife. Not today, not ever perhaps, and certainly not looking as I did. I was in no mood either for her conditional sympathy or that well-worn whine of a lecture: 'We in The Truth can afford to turn the other cheek, Gabe, because all this silliness is part of God's plan.' This illogical denial of responsibility had been easy enough for me to swallow in the old days of blinkered, middle-class comfort, but having recently experienced the sharp end of life – and with the indentation from Pablo's jackboot still palpable above my ear – things looked very different now.

My bag slung over the less damaged shoulder, I left the aircraft and limped painfully the three or four miles to Gatwick's Passport Control. During this interminable hike, I dwelt upon how I'd changed in other ways too: at a pinch, I thought, I might be able to forgive Janice and Neville, but Pablo I actually wanted dead. Dead. 'How fucking *dare* he?' I spat, equally uncharacteristically kicking an empty drinks bottle ahead of me along the travellator instead of picking it up and putting it in a recycling bin. 'Because of that *bastard's* bully-boy tactics, I'm now on a mission to betray both my morals, a group of people who have done no wrong and any concern I might have for the planet. What else can I do?' I hissed through clenched teeth, gazing out at parked aircraft through the rain-flecked plate glass of the corridor. 'Accidentally mislay the sales documents or abscond with them to New Zealand or Canada? Pointless rantings', I concluded aloud, pausing for breath at a trolley stand, 'because if I don't do their bidding, Ms. Cordner and Pablo will more than likely have Lily, Churchill and Yvette bumped off and send in Cleve to burn Shurland to the ground.'

In the queue at Immigration, I emailed Max and begged him to drop everything, track down the Shurland deeds and meet me at my uncle's house at teatime.

An hour and a half later, I was sitting disconsolate and aching all over on the train to Wadhurst, the nearest station to *Badger's End*. I glowered out at the misty grey vistas of English suburbia: in a street below, cars and lorries were gridlocked around untended roadworks. I gazed down at the ubiquitous warning signage, the temporary traffic lights, the neat white lines painted on smooth tarmac. Everything looked so different, so alien now. Such a contrast to driving conditions in Tobago where, in the absence of Health and Safety, all you were expected to do was follow an unspoken agreement to keep your vehicle out of potholes and, as Lily had put it once, 'doh bounce nobody'. I closed my eyes and remembered the warmth of the Caribbean sunshine, the brightly painted and dilapidated chaos, the people – Yvette and Lily in particular – and, of course, Shurland. If anywhere on Earth could be a future home for me, I realised with a jolt, then Tobago was the place.

Past Tunbridge Wells, Max rang to say he was available this afternoon to witness signatures. 'Curiously, Angel,' he said, 'I phoned your uncle only a couple of days ago. The old boy seemed pretty chipper about the sale – especially at the price they're offering. But it's as well you came back: Powers of Attorney can take months.'

I paid a taxi-driver over the odds to drive me the short distance to Neville's house where, to my consternation, an ambulance was blocking the driveway. A man's face appeared at the kitchen window and made me jump: had Pablo's stooge Newton beaten me to it? Was that what he'd meant by saying 'we'll be with you all the way?' But when Mabel opened the door to me, she introduced the stranger as her husband waiting to take her home. She didn't seem in the least surprised to see me, nor did she make comment about my facial disfigurement.

'What's going on?' I asked, sloughing off my coat and throwing it over the bannister. 'Why the ambulance?'

'Your uncle had a bit of a fall dis afternoon,' Mabel explained in what I now knew to be a Trini accent. 'Cut open his poor head on de fireplace. I waitin' to see if dey goin' take him to hospital.' There was something about this woman I couldn't put my finger on.

A ring at the front door and Max walked in. 'Christ, Ange, what the hell happened to you? Fall out of the plane?' He peered at the bruise above my right eye. 'Or have you taken up boxing? You look like absolute shit!'

In the fuggy sitting room, two medics had just finished bandaging Neville's head. Ignoring me, my uncle jabbed an imperious finger at Max. 'Gibson, take the minions to the kitchen and see that cook gives them a hot chocolate and a biscuit for their trouble' His voice sounded querulous and coarse.

My head pounding afresh, I stepped back into the hall. 'Max,' I whispered, 'I have been risking life and limb in Tobago and have witnessed firsthand the sort of mayhem the old bastard clearly relishes stirring up. Look, I have the bruises to prove it: imprisonment, police brutality and physical coercion. You know the sort of thing.'

'Ange, what the—?'

'So I'm giving you fair warning that right now I'm in no mood for Neville's outrageously racist and colonial treatment of professional care-workers... not to mention his utter, *utter* obnoxiousness. I would be loath to kill him in his own home – indeed I have been requested to refrain from doing precisely that – but in the mood I'm in, anything could happen. Why couldn't he have just saved us the trouble and bloody conked out years ago? We'd all have been let off the hook and been able – for a while at least – to avoid the acts of greed and vandalism I'm being asked to enable.'

'Angel, what's been happening? You're sounding delirious.'

'And what's even more ironic is that if he's still unwell tomorrow we'll never get him to sign anything anyway.'

'I'm sure he'll be better after a night's sleep.'

'But, Max, if he isn't, then Shurland and two people we owe are...' I leant my head back against the wall, springing forward again as I put pressure on a bruise '...well, not to put too fine a point on it: *fucked.*'

'Whoa, Ange! Such language from you! What is going on?'

'Feeling differently about things, mate. But I'll be fine.'

My old friend scratched the back of his hand but chose to ignore my last comment. 'You mentioned "two people we owe". What am I sensing here?'

'Can we discuss it tomorrow?'

The paramedics came into the hallway and began packing away their equipment. Mabel closed the sitting-room door and disappeared towards the kitchen. The news was that my uncle was sedated, comfortable and asleep. I wondered whether it was up to me to apologise for his behaviour, but they looked unfazed – as if this was all in a day's work – so I let it go.

'We've run some checks,' said one. 'Blood sugar, heart, blood pressure and oxygen – and he's alright for now. Could you sign here, please?' While I did as I was told, I felt her casting an eye over my own injuries. 'Would you like me to dress the worst of these?'

'Do you think they need it?'

'Better safe than sorry, eh?'

When I had been patched up to the paramedics' satisfaction, Max and I watched the ambulance leave. 'Can I drop you at a station, Angel,' he asked, 'or are you planning on walking home from here? I imagine Sarah's killed the fatted calf for the Wanderer's return.'

'Actually, she doesn't know I'm in the country.'

'Say again.'

'You heard.'

He blinked. 'Gotchah, mate.'

'I would be grateful if you could take me to somewhere I could roost for the night. I'm bloody knackered.'

'I'll drop you at the Queen's Inn at Hawkhurst and pick you up in the morning at ten-thirty. How's that for a plan?'

'Thanks.' Climbing gingerly into his car, I glanced back at the house. Once again, Mabel was on the phone at the window. The penny dropped. 'Max,' I said, needing to tell someone, 'I'm of the opinion that Mabel is a spy in the pay of my adversaries in Tobago.'

'And I'm of the opinion you're in serious need of sleep. You've become paranoid since we last met. Now sit back and close what's left of your eyes. We've not far to go. And by the way, what is that horrible smell?'

A quarter of an hour later, and not smelling anything I could identify, I checked in at the pub and, once in my room with the door locked, stripped off and stood in front of the mirror. In addition to my head and shoulders, the areas around my ribs, lower abdomen and right kidney shrieked injustice. I collapsed into bed needing to try – if only for a moment – to rinse my mind clean of Neville, my guilt about the impending sale of Shurland and of everything to do with Pablo and Janice.

I had only meant to put my feet up for a few minutes before going down for something to eat, but in the end slept two hours. I was awoken at eight-fifteen by a roar of carefree laughter from the public bar below. I rose stiffly and creaked across the sloping sixteenth century floorboards to take a shower in a bijou-beamed bathroom overlooking the car park and main road. It was raining again outside. A pair of grey-brown wood pigeons were bickering in the tree opposite: lamentably dreary creatures compared with Shurland's brightly coloured motmots, bananaquits and iridescent hummingbirds.

Feeling slightly more human but still aching all over, I wandered back into the bedroom. I could definitely smell something now. Was this what Max had been complaining about in the car? Sniffing like a terrier, I checked the soles of my shoes and finally traced the source of the stench to my rucksack.

'What the hell?' I murmured, pulling out my laptop and emptying the rest onto the bed. I rummaged through the pile and found nothing untoward; after all, I'd only packed the bare minimum. The smell persisted so I plunged my hand deep into the bag and felt around until my fingertips encountered something alien under the suspended laptop compartment. With an increasing sense of foreboding, I extracted a parcel about ten inches long. It had the feel of a broken stick of seaside rock and had been bound loosely in bubble-wrap and sealed in a black plastic shopping bag. The appalling stink was not unlike that of the rotting cadaver on the clifftop. Almost gagging, I opened the sash window and unwrapped the package on the wet sill.

Inside was a hairy sheep or goat leg, hoof intact, sawn off below the knee joint. It was crawling with maggots.

'Dear God! The bastards!' I slammed shut the window and ran to wash my hands. I disconnected my phone from the charger and took a series of photos of the excrescence through the window pane. 'Janice,' I texted, 'is this is your idea of a joke? I'm here in the U.K. as instructed. My uncle's at death's door. So back off.' I pressed "Send" before I could change my mind about the tone. Cleve's stooges at Airport Security must have tampered with my hand-luggage whilst pretending to check it for bombs, toothpaste and illicit bottles of water.

Ten minutes later I was downstairs, tucked away but not particularly snug in a corner by a log fire. It had been my intention to appear relaxed and calm but the first sips of Harveys Bitter were spoilt by the unmistakeable whiff of decomposing animal on my fingers, the rank odour reminding me of that mad goatherd Lester. I looked around to see if my fellow diners and drinkers were holding handkerchiefs and scarves over their faces to ward off the stench. They weren't, obviously, because they were too busy pretending not to be curious about my presence – let alone my 'mash-up' appearance. 'Why would a black person venture so deep into provincial Brexitland?' and 'Did he really deserve to be beaten up quite so badly by his horrid, druggie accomplices?' were written all over their smug Caucasian faces.

My phone pinged. A message from Janice accompanying a photo of Big Ben.

'Thx4 message. The clock is ticking. Enjoy ur stay.'

21

Still awake at three in the morning, I blamed in turn my ill-advised afternoon nap, the steak and kidney pie, the beer, the thought of that decomposing hoof on the windowsill, and jetlag. Above all, I dreaded having to face Neville in the morning. After maybe three hours of bilious sleep I gave it up as a bad job and, smelling bacon, pulled back the curtains. Rain still beat against the panes. 'Stupid country,' I groaned. The goat hoof had fallen off the windowsill and must have wedged itself out of sight in fronds of wisteria.

At ten thirty, after my substantial yet lonely English breakfast, Max arrived to drive me to Neville's. He took one look at the state of me and started in. 'Bloody hell, Ange! Have you caught some tropical disease? You seem more dead than—'

'I'm fine, Max. Didn't get much sleep, that's all.'

'I see. Well, that envelope on the back seat contains the Shurland deeds as requested.' We pulled out into a traffic jam of cars queuing to get into the Waitrose car park. 'I've given that so-called contract the once-over.'

'And?'

'I'll be raising a few points before I allow your uncle to sign off.'

'Whatever, Max, but let's just get this over with. I'm under real pressure to expedite the sale.'

'But I thought you wanted to delay it as long as possible. Why the sudden rush?' He accelerated through a set of red lights.

I fingered the bruise on my head. 'Change of circumstances, change of heart.' I said, without looking at him. 'I really don't want to talk about it. Not right now.'

Max was silent for a moment. 'Need to know basis, is that it? Well, you're the boss.'

We pulled up outside *Badger's End* with ten minutes to spare. Buffeted by the wind and rain, the old place looked even more down-at-heel than before. Max turned to me. 'Ange, I need to call my sister before we enter the lion's den.'

'Who, little Donna? The twelve-year-old who came to visit you at university?'

'Well remembered. It's her birthday today.' His fingers skittered over the phone screen. 'She works at *The New York Times—*' Max held up a hand. 'Rise and shine, birthday girl!'

I had always envied friends and acquaintances surrounded and bolstered by siblings. Sarah and I shared only-child status – about the only thing we had in common.

At one minute to eleven I grabbed the paperwork and followed Max up the stone steps to the front door: the march to the scaffold. 'No doubt,' I remarked, 'the spy will be on duty today.'

'Don't be so fricking paranoid.'

'Bet you a tenner,' I whispered just as the door opened. 'Ha! Mabel! Thought you might be here! Good morning, and how is the patient today?'

The shameless woman was already eyeing my envelope. 'Oh, much better, tank you, Mr. Gabriel. Come in. It so wet, eh? You wan' coffee?'

'That would be kind.' I turned to my companion and hissed, 'You owe me ten quid, Max.'

'The sooner you get a decent night's sleep, Ange, the better.'

*

Neville looked frail, the bandage round his head lending him the appearance of some Dickensian phantom. He had been propped like a retired scarecrow in his chair, the pristine white of the pillowcases only adding to his pallor. 'So,' he began without a word of salutation, 'you've finally condescended to pull your fucking finger out, have you, Gabriel? Having managed to piss off pretty well everyone concerned.' He favoured me with a brief glance. 'And what's the matter with your bloody face? Wifey been kicking off again?'

'Uncle, I—'

'As for you, Gibson, you're a bloody disgrace to the profession. Dithering and delaying because of a bloody Power of Attorney? You should have thought of something as obvious as that before my nephew left the country!'

'Mr. Cass—'

'The Cordner woman is furious with me for entrusting the conveyancing to a such a bunch of sodding amateurs.'

Max stood his ground. 'Really, Mr. Cassidy, there's no need to take this tone with me. My father I'm sure will attest that—'

'Oh, don't start with your mealy-mouthed solicitor shit! It's bad enough having to deal with this tosser.' He glared at me. 'Christ, Gabriel, find me a pen and let's have that contract.' I glanced apologetically at Max. My uncle was vile. His dementia might be erasing any residual redeeming features, but really, what was I doing enabling him to destroy a planet he himself was about to vacate? I slid the contract out of the envelope and passed it into his papery, almost translucent hand. With surprising dexterity, he flicked the pages until he reached the one detailing the reduced price. 'Aha!' he squawked, jabbing a finger at it. 'Are you determined to kill me off in advance, Gabriel? That's the second reduction they've made.'

'Uncle, this was beyond my control.'

'Don't give me that—'

'It's the bloody truth, Neville!' I was shouting at a family member for the first time in my life. My ordeal with Pablo seemed to have opened the floodgates. 'Just be quiet and bloody listen for once! A tropical storm has washed away part of their proposed surfing beach and—'

'Lies! Storms don't wash away beaches!'

'This one fucking well has!' I smacked the back of the arm chair sending up a cloud of dust. '*Christ!*'

Neville's voice rasped, 'Blaspheming nephews on the other hand can fuck up the simplest of tasks!'

Max held up his hand. 'Gentlemen!' We turned and stared like naughty schoolboys caught pillow-fighting after lights-out. 'If I may, there's another problem. I've been looking into the financial and legal implications of selling Shurland.'

Max had started to outline these to me in the car but, preoccupied with my own plans for the short-term appeasement of Pablo, I'd told him to save it for the meeting. Neville turned on him an icy glare. 'And?'

'The property is in the south-west zone of Tobago—'

'I am aware of that, Gibson.'

'Where it's illegal to sell land except to a Trinidad and Tobago national. And in the local currency.'

Neville's grizzled chin jutted. 'Your point being?'

'Well, this policy was adopted precisely to discourage foreign investors such as Tropitel buying up prime real-estate to the detriment of potential local purchasers.'

'Who couldn't afford the going rate anyway.'

'That notwithstanding, Mr. Cassidy, the sale is a non-starter because Tropitel is not permitted by law to buy Shurland from you.'

'What self-serving wank you solicitors talk.'

'As for their contract, it's nothing more than a hotch-potch of legalese-sounding jargon which, when examined closely, is as watertight as my sock.' Max cleared his throat. 'In my *professional* opinion the sale cannot go ahead.'

Neville snorted. 'Here endeth today's lesson.'

'There are, however, other money-making possibilities we might discuss, Mr. Cassidy. Only last week, for instance, Gabriel was suggesting turning Shurland into an upmarket Airbnb or ecolodge. In his opinion, it would be an absolute goldmine. And in the meantime, to raise you some cash, one or two plots near the village might be sold off legally – to local buyers.'

Neville levelled a look of absolute loathing at my friend. 'I am going to pretend I didn't hear that, Gibson. I'm not going to give you the satisfaction of seeing me rise to the bait.' His voice was almost inaudible. 'But let me address your other point, you arrant dickhead.' With a sudden roar of fury he slammed his fist down on the side table, the veins at his temples pulsing.

'Uncle, stop it,' I cried. 'For God's sake! You'll do yourself a mischief! Ms. Cordner has made it quite clear what will happen to Lily, Churchill and Shurland itself in the event of your demise before the sale goes through.'

But Neville roared on: 'You're not making any sense, you wanker, so shut up! I've told you both 'til I'm blue in the bloody face: I'm not selling to some Johnnie savage at a peppercorn price! Nor do I give a turd in a blender about your parochial Trini legality bullshit, Gibson! I am selling on the fucking *global* market!'

'But, Mr. Cass—' Max reached out a hand which was batted away.

'Shut it! Can't either of you be relied upon to do as you're fucking told?'

I managed to place a hand on my uncle's trembling arm. 'What Max says is true, uncle. As you are aware, I did initially flirt with the idea of persuading you to have nothing to do with Tropitel's plans – which I considered morally repugnant. I opposed them on environmental, social, ecological and historical grounds. In fact, I found a most persuasive piece in the paper to back up the argument against.' I opened my wallet and laid Malika George article on his side table. 'You can read all about what a catastrophe such a project would be.' Bang on cue, the door opened behind me and the carer-cum-spy brought in a tray of coffee and chocolate digestives. 'Thank you, Mabel,' I said.

'You're welcome,' she replied, leaving the room again but not quite closing the door behind her.

My uncle seized a biscuit and bit into it, crumbs tumbling inside his pyjama top. 'Gabriel, don't say you've gone all green on me now, you hypocritical little shit. Your carbon footprint is already colossal! You've just flown to Tobago and back and presumably you're planning on flying back *again* – unless you've hired a pedalo from Portsmouth to save the planet.' His breath was rattling in his throat. He turned on Max. 'And my nephew is a man with a gas-guzzling bloody Aga in his house. Jesus wept.'

Time to wheel out my positive prevarication card. What else could I do but kick this problematic can a little further down the road? 'You're right, uncle, to accuse me of rank hypocrisy. But in my defence I've been thinking the Tropitel project is small-fry compared with deliberately burning the Brazilian rainforest or the summer fires in California, Spain and Australia.' I glanced apologetically at Max. 'In fact, I've come round to the view that the economic value-added to Tobago is greater than the deleterious effect of removing a few old trees, swamps, agouti and birds' nests. I see that now. The advance of capitalism: it's all good.'

Astonished at my volte-face, Neville was beaming at me. 'Now you're talking, lad.'

'So I will finish the job, uncle.' I glanced meaningfully at Max in the hope he would somehow catch my drift, but he was reddening at the collar. 'One other thing, I should add that Lily and Churchill – not to mention their daughter Yvette – are absolutely distraught at being ejected from Shurland after all their years of service. I have assured them they'll be rehoused.'

Neville emitted a guttural noise of disgust. 'Fine! Sort out some shack for the buggers in Black Rock and honour will be satisfied.'

'Thank you, uncle.'

'If not, there's still plenty of jungle left in Tobago for the likes of them to swing about in.'

'Uncle, will you pack it in with this vitriolic racism?'

Ignoring me, Neville went on. 'I'm glad you've seen sense at last, boy: imagine it, a beautiful tourist heaven named after me! After *you*! The Tropitel-Cassidy resort! That's what they're offering, and even at this bastard lower rate, it's a generous deal.' He raised both arms. 'The march of progress across a primeval bog peopled by fucking piccaninnies! What's not to love?'

'Quite,' I whispered. What had I unleashed? And what about Max's objections? The repugnant old monster was in his element. He reached out to squeeze my hand but I withdrew it for fear I might haul him bodily out of his chair and smash his head open – properly this time – on the brass fender. 'I'm so proud of you, Gabriel! You are clearly not the weak, unimaginative and compliant Christadelphian male I took you for – like your arsehole of a father was. You've seen the light at last and become a man of the world! The real world.'

The landline rang in the hallway. I heard Mabel answer: 'Yes, sir, he is. I jus' put you on loudspeaker.' She popped her head round the door. 'Mr. McClung for you, Mr. Neville.' It was surely no coincidence that the old tycoon should ring at precisely this moment. Mabel was definitely a spy: she'll have been texting Janice.

Neville grabbed the phone. 'Buck! Good to hear your dulcets at last.'

'Whassat you say, Cassidy?'

Neville shifted in his seat. 'How are you?'

'Listen, y'know darn well the Shurland project cannot proceed 'til those governmental bastards in Tobago sign off on it.' My nemesis had a disconcertingly caricature Texan drawl which made my flesh creep. 'From what ah understan', your people've bin employin' all kinda delayin' tactics.'

'As it happens, Buck—'

'Enough of your BS, Cassidy. Jus' sign on the line, git your agent back to Tobago, have him pay Cordner her commission

ASAP and let's git the deal done! It's a great deal, the best deal. Let's do it, friend... or else!'

Neville was almost simpering. 'I was trying to tell you, Buck, old boy, that my nephew and the lawyer are right here listening. You catch us on the very cusp of signing.'

A pause. 'Dat right?'

'Indeed, everything is under control. Absolutely.'

Max leant towards me and whispered, 'I certainly hope you know what you're doing, Ange.'

'Trust me, mate.'

Neville was looking better than I'd seen him in years. 'And yes,' he was saying, 'I'll get Gabriel to sort out the Cordner woman pronto.'

'Great. Ahm relieved, Cassidy. Got a call on the other line. Bye for now.'

Neville turned a triumphalist gaze upon me. 'So, Gabriel, you heard what the man said. Get your arse back out there and pay the woman off.'

I moistened my chapped lips. 'I understand the need, uncle, but you are aware this is nothing but bobol pure and simple.' I felt the solicitor looking at me as if sizing me up for a straitjacket. 'It's official, Max, I'm to bribe Janice to influence the ladies and gentlemen of the Tobago House of Assembly. "Bobol" is Trini for "bribe".'

Neville was rooting in his pockets for his flask. 'Christ sakes, Gabriel, you'll get it all back when the cash hits my bank account. Plus – what shall we say? – two percent for your trouble. And think of it, if you play my cards right for me you'll be in line to inherit a fucking mint. I shan't last forever, you know. My property will be coming either to you or – if you manage to screw up even at this late stage – the local cat rescue centre. Think of Janice's sweetener as an investment in your own future security.'

My phone pinged again. Another message from the woman in question which turned my stomach. '*Buck not convinced*,' I read. '*Make Neville sign and confirm.*'

'Anything important?' asked Neville.

'No. Just the car-hire people.' I put the phone on silent and slipped it into my pocket. 'Here's a pen.'

A minute later the documents were signed and witnessed by Max and me. Neville called for Mabel to bring in a bottle of Champagne and four glasses. 'By the way, boy,' he asked, 'who's this Yvonne you spoke of?'

'Yvette is her name, uncle, Lily's daughter. But what's it to you? I thought you didn't care about the slaves as you call them.'

'The creature Lily had a daughter? How old?'

'Early thirties.'

Neville began rubbing the back of his hand. 'Christ alive, I'd no idea she'd been knocked up. Still, a toast!' We raised our glasses. 'To the future of Tropitel in Tobago.'

The fizz consumed, Max and I made a move, he saying he'd come back to Hawkhurst to sample the wares of the Queen's Inn. I gathered up the documentation and before leaving, shut myself in the cloakroom to photograph the signature page and send it to Janice.

'Goodbye, uncle,' I said, passing his door a minute later. The old man didn't to look up. He was staring into the fire and tugging vacantly at an eyebrow, a cruise ship holiday website open on his iPad.

For the next three hours, in a move reminiscent of our ten short weeks at university, Max led me astray with alcohol in an attempt to loosen my tongue. 'But tell me this,' he said after I'd skirted round a justification for my marriage and career, 'why is it you come back here looking as if you've had a close encounter with the propellers of a cross-channel ferry, airily mention police brutality and yet still refuse to tell me what's been going on? And then you demand that the contract be signed in the teeth of your own advice.'

'Sorry, mate, but I have no choice.'

'Uh-huh.' He narrowed his eyes at me over his glass. 'Here's another question that's been bugging me: how come you're so keen to avoid your wife?'

I sighed and looked him in the eye for perhaps the first time that day. 'Because to be honest, mate, I intend never to see Sarah again.'

Max raised both eyebrows. 'We're getting somewhere at last. I take it there's a woman involved?'

'Don't be crass, mate, of course not, but there are people in Tobago – and a way of life – I think might suit me better long term. Put it like that.'

'That makes even less sense to me given your determination to sell Shurland and allow this beloved paradise of yours to be vandalised. I'll ask you one last time, Angel.' He sat back and folded his arms. 'What. Is. Going. On?'

'Look, Max, I understand your confusion but I'm up against the greed and malice of a powerful corporate world of professional planet despoilers. They'll stop at nothing to get their way. But I'm the only person Shurland has to rely on.'

'But there'll be nothing left of it! I'm still none the wiser.'

'Nor am I, mate, to be honest. I've no idea what I'm going to do but I couldn't *not* have Neville sign the contract because the bastards need to see I'm onside – for today at least. All I can do is go back and await an opportunity to spike their bloody guns before I meet McClung next Wednesday. I'm calling it positive prevarication.'

Max snorted and pushed away his glass. 'Well, good luck with that, Ange. But I have to say I never had you down as someone who liked playing with fire, especially not alone and with his eyes shut.' His phone beeped; he glanced at the screen. 'But I must love you and leave you: the little lady says she'll be back in an hour. Better just see a man about a dog.'

I watched him head across the bar then gazed for a minute or two out of the window at the relentless grey of the British winter. I pulled my wallet out of my jacket pocket. A grubby slip of folded paper fell to the floor and I picked it up. *Fog Angels Welcome You to Sunny Tobago*, I read. *For Best Jouvert, Book Online Today!*

A pang of regret – of nostalgia almost – as I looked at the beautiful butterfly-costumed girl on the flyer. 'I'd forgotten about Carnival,' I muttered.

Max was beside me. 'Still talking to yourself, Ange?'

'Old habits. Just wondering if I should change my flight so I can experience Carnival. I'll miss it if I wait for Janice's Tuesday reservation.'

Max took the flyer. 'Wow, mate, if this is what Tobago has to offer at Carnival time I'd get back there as soon as.' He thumped me on the shoulder. 'Think of what you might be missing!'

'I'm changing my flight right now.' I clicked on my booking app.

'You don't think your uncle will mind?'

'The sooner the deal is done the better as far as he's concerned.'

Max picked up his coat. 'Hang on, Ange, there's something else.'

'What's that?'

'You're nearly missing a trick here.'

'How so?' I was peering at the little screen. 'Excellent, there are still seats on tomorrow morning's flight.'

A hand gripped the back of my neck. 'Ange, leave that a second and listen. If all this cloak and dagger shit of yours is true, then if you return early you'll at least be able to sneak in under the radar of these people. That way you'll gain the upper hand – for a while at least.'

I pressed "Change Booking" and stood up to hug the man, a scintilla of hope slicing the leaden skies of uncertainty. 'Thanks, Max! That's the best idea I've had all day!' I handed him my debit card. 'Could you settle up for me while I pack?'

'Sure, but—'

'Then maybe drop me at the station on your way home? I won't be five minutes.'

22

We made a hair-raisingly bumpy landing at St. Lucia, and given how the runway seemed to end only a couple of feet from the sea I didn't begrudge the captain his decision to wait four hours for a thunderstorm to pass in order to fly on to T & T. As a result, I wasn't through Tobago Security until gone midnight.

To my relief, there was no sign of Cleve nor any of his Boys in Beige who'd been on duty last time. Indeed I was practically waved through Passport Control by a lady so preoccupied with applying colourful Carnival eyeshadow in glittering purple that she barely looked at her screen. Presumably the staff would not be under instructions to look out for me for another two days.

I emerged into that wonderful humid heat of the tropical night – so unlike Gatwick – and immediately ran into the cheerful lady from Ground Staff I'd met when I first arrived.

'Hi!' She was regarding me with arms spread wide in welcome, holding in one hand her hi-vis singlet.

I spluttered, 'Oh, hi, erm...'

'Maisha.'

'Of course. Sorry. I don't seem to have slept for a fortnight.'

'So I see.' She leant in to inspect the dark abrasions above my right eye. To avoid questions, I had removed my dressings before

Security at Gatwick. 'What happen?' she asked. 'You bin fightin'?'

'Yup. The missus pushed me down the stairs. You know how it is.'

Maisha shrieked with mirth, satisfied with my idiotic response. 'Gabriel, isn't it?'

'Well remembered.' We shook hands. It was good to be back.

'You here for Carnival? I taught you gone.'

'I did have to go back but, well, business being business, here I am in Tobago once again. I have a day or two free before my next meeting—'

'You come back special? You is a real Trini now!'

'Actually, I found your flyer in my pocket and decided to see what all the fuss was about.'

'Eh! Fuss, you callin' it?' She had a way of lowering one eyebrow and arching the other which I found both endearing and intimidating.

'My apologies, ma'am. I misspoke.'

'Well, you in time for Jouvert tonight. I jus' headin' by my brother bar. If you come wid me, Roots he sign you up for *Fog Angels*. Come nah.' I slowed to keep pace with my new friend who had already set off at that ambling Caribbean pace I had not yet learnt to emulate. 'Also, you need a costume.'

How unlike me, I thought, meekly to follow a relative stranger into the humming tropical night. Perhaps I did so because the promised costume would disguise me from the prying eyes of anyone in league with Janice, Pablo or Cleve.

We took a detour to leave my luggage in the Honda. To my surprise, the trusty old banger was still where I'd left it in a back street. I opened the boot and slid the Shurland sales contract with my phone, passport and wallet under the spare wheel. I locked the car and zipped the keys with a few notes and a debit card into my shorts pocket.

We were now walking up the main drag in the company of a whooping crowd of revellers ready to party. There was a vibrant, primal energy abroad, a frenetic and carefree atmosphere. I might have started to enjoy myself had I not imagined seeing one of Janice's spies in every passing face. 'Ehh, Gabriel! Wha' is de problem?' cried Maisha, perhaps seeing the rabbit-in-headlights look on my face. 'Go wid de flow. You in Paradise an' you unhappy? I never hear mo', boy!'

We moved through the throbbing, velvety darkness for half a mile or so until Maisha led me into the ChillOut Bar owned by her brother. As soon as I was introduced to Roots, this most hospitable of men plied me with a veritable vat of rum punch and a bottle of Carib to stuff down the back of my trousers. 'For emergency use, bro.'

'Roots,' shouted Maisha over the music, 'I find Gabriel at de airport. De white black Englishman I talkin' about.'

'Good night,' I shouted in the vernacular, remembering to do that Caribbean fist-roll hand-pump thing. 'Great to meet you.'

'Maisha tell me about you las' week. She say you make she laugh.'

'Really?' No one had accused me of that before.

'Where you stayin', Gabriel?'

'Up the road at a place called Shurland. With Lily Pitt.'

I saw rather than heard Roots steups in admiration at the quality of my social contacts. He looked momentarily sheepish. 'I know she gyal, Yvette who work at Kariwak.'

I shouted, 'Oh, she's quite a card, that one.' Roots looked blank. 'I mean, she seems to enjoy living life on the edge.'

'Oh, sure ting, bro. She be dong soon. She already pay her *Fog Angels* ticket.' He turned to bellow in his sister's ear. 'Maisha, fetch Mr. Gabriel a welcome pack!' I pulled out my Trini dollars. 'No charge, Mr. White Black Englishman. You is we honoured guest.'

'Thank you very much.'

'No problem.'

Maisha pushed me into a corner of the heaving bar and returned a minute later with an orange *Fog Angels* T-shirt. This she folded and snipped at with some scissors until all that remained were tassels and holes. In a trice, my own Mr. Obviously-Foreign Tourist shirt was off and stuffed behind the bar and I was transformed into a species of walking doily, the sort of perforated paper thing you might find under a Victoria sponge in a twee café in Tunbridge Wells. This was topped off with an operatic black eye-mask and yellow plastic beaker. 'For your beverages, Gabriel. When de parade move off we help ourself from de drink truck.'

'Really? Right.' I was utterly bemused, the rum punch in conjunction with a lack of sleep wreaking havoc with my judgement.

'Sit dong an' wait for me,' said Maisha, shoving me backwards onto a low stool. 'I goin' upstairs to change.'

Never before had I visited such an establishment, even in my student days. My partying experience to date had been limited to chaperoned Christadelphian discos featuring 'eighties hits from the BeeGees, Gloria Gaynor and (at a pinch) Michael Jackson, but here in the ChillOut Bar, all was new and exciting. *Enticing.* The place might have been heaving, the music deafening, but it didn't matter to me. The clientele was alive and jubilant, already dancing and swaying and – what would be the word? – *jiving* on the pavement to what I would normally have dismissed as a monstrous, thumping beat. The costumes were otherworldly too: one man and his partner passed me splendidly decked out as tribal warriors wearing nothing more than *Fog Angels*-orange loincloths, sharks' teeth necklaces and grass leggings.

I leant back against the windowsill and closed my eyes to savour the sweet and intoxicating scent of something I sensed would be illegal at home. The last time I'd smelt it was in the woods the day I met Trevor. I must have drifted off because a second later – or so it seemed – a hand on my bare shoulder made me jump.

I turned. Maisha was transformed. Gone were the utilitarian trappings of airport uniform, the tight bun in which her hair had been imprisoned. Instead, she stood before me in fishnet tights, her hair an explosive celebration of liberty, and her face made up fit for a night at the Oscars – barring perhaps the single white dot under each eye. The confection Maisha was wearing was nothing more really than two arrows of orange material plunging from her shoulders and harnessed with the skimpiest triangle of black gauze over her breasts. Never had I been in the presence of such exotic, erotic beauty. Imagine the fussing if Sarah had been able to see me now.

'Cat got your tongue, handsome?' enquired Maisha with a grin.

'So sorry, I—'

'No need to get up, Gabriel,' she purred, looking down at me from under long, dark green eyelashes. For a second I thought she was going to sit on my knee.

I pulled myself together. 'Let me get you a drink.'

'Why, tank you, Gabriel.'

Since Roots was passing with a plastic jug I was saved the trouble of barging my way to the bar. 'Hey, Maisha,' our host shouted, swaying to the beat, 'I see you dress to kill!' Icy punch slopped onto my bare leg. 'Also, I see you frien' can put away my rum punch. Here, Gabriel, hol' still!' He filled my beaker to the brim.

'Thanks, Roots!' He slapped my shoulder.

'But y'all better get outside now. It nearly three o'clock. We startin' jus' now.' And then he was gone, swallowed up by the gyrating throng.

I rose unsteadily. Maisha set her empty glass down on a shelf and we moved outside. I scanned the crowd for any faces I knew but decided – no doubt under the influence of Roots's excellent brew – that for these few hours, my personal troubles and hang-ups could be pushed onto the back burner. Pablo, Janice and their devilry could go boil in Hell as far as I was concerned – not that we believe in Hell, but you take my meaning – and besides, they were not even aware of my presence in Tobago. I was an anonymous and masked black man hiding in plain sight in a seething crowd of revellers. More to the point, I was in the company of a vibrant local lady I knew would protect me from any foe. I wondered fleetingly if I would spot Yvette in this crowd, or indeed anyone from Shurland. Right now I needed as many friendly faces in my life as I could muster.

'Now, big fella,' declared Maisha as we mingled with the throng, 'it time to get on bad.' She pointed to a truck piled high with massive speakers fixed to scaffolding. 'We follow, we drink and we chip.'

'Eh?'

'Like this.' She showed me a sort of left-right shuffle move, one arm in the air. 'Understan'?'

'Got it.' My body was being swept along by the intoxicating rhythm of the music and I was no longer in charge. 'Maisha,' I shouted, throwing up an arm, 'thank you for inviting me!'

'You're welcome!'

With a burst of amplified drumbeats, the *Fog Angels* procession began to move off, the crowd "chipping" and jumping as one, a sea of dark heads and hands bobbing in time to the invigorating soca music booming from the truck. We were passing an NP petrol station I recognised and, looking around, I saw our band of orange-clad dancers stretching away into the darkness.

Someone grabbed my arm. It was one of Trevor's lads from the beach, the one with the starter-pack goatee beard. 'Yah man, you wan' ganja?'

'Oh, no, not really, thanks, I—' A cigarette was stuck between my lips.

Maisha yelled, 'Go on, Gabriel! Take a drag!' I sucked, choked and felt instantly nauseous. 'You like it?'

'Nah.'

I saw Maisha steups. 'You is Mr. Susceptible!'

The music from the truck had become even more deafening. Roots had clambered up and was dancing on top of the speakers, bellowing the lyrics into a microphone: 'Are you ready-ready? Are you ready for it? Yuh wan give me dat? Doh hold back! Wine it up! Ride it front to de back! No long chat! Just come to me!'

Maisha and I danced and cheered with everyone else.

'We need more rum!' she shrieked, her face alive. 'Come!' She grabbed my hand and tugged me through the crowd towards a long, flat-bedded truck serving as a mobile bar. It was a simple idea: the vehicle rolled forward at walking pace while we held up our two interlocking beakers, shouted 'Rum and Coke, please!' and came away seconds later replenished – and with no money having changed hands.

All at once, something was rolling and squeezing against me. I looked down, appalled. A girl, bent almost double, was actually grinding her buttocks into my groin. Push her away I could not, not without handling her wobbling backside or hips. She was too engrossed in her own world of noise, rhythm and movement to take any notice of my attempts to back away. Besides, the revellers behind me were pushing me inexorably onwards and even by tonight's standards I felt myself being edged out of my comfort zone. This was too much.

'Er, excuse me!' I tried, flapping my hands in the air to avoid accidentally touching her partially naked form. 'Hello, miss!' I was making no headway so in desperation looked round for Maisha, spotting her at last having an energised exchange with someone to my right. 'Maisha! Help!' My voice sounded absurdly squeaky and panic-stricken, even to me. 'I'm being molested!' Maisha swung round and took in my discomfiture with another shriek of laughter just as my plump assailant decided she'd had enough of me and bounced away to ply her trade on a skinny woman to my left. 'Maisha!' I shouted in her ear as she drew near. 'This whole gyrating bum thing... is it normal practice?'

'Of course, Gabriel! Doh dig no horrors! We all winin' here tonight! Now, listen, fella, time for you to loosen up an' unwin' yourself!' She stepped in front of me, turned away and, gleefully

219

watching my reaction over her shoulder, proceeded to waggle her own ample bottom into me just as the other girl had done. 'Nobody never wine on you before, Gabriel? Jus' hold my hips an'—'

'Oh, but really, I don't think I—'

'Pull me into you, fella! It Jouvert! Time to let go, Englishman!'

I hesitated half a second before knocking back my beakerful of rum and Coke. 'Alright, let's do it!' Casting out the last of my British scruples, I grasped Maisha's hips and for a long moment of Caribbean madness we wined and whooped together. For the first time in my life I felt as if my Lane Control Assist had been disabled allowing me to steer unimpeded out of the middle lane and into the fast.

'Now you really livin'!' Maisha yelled, out of breath. 'Also, you movin' so well! You is a natural!'

I filled my lungs and threw back my head. *'For all that is in the world,'* I bellowed to the whole island, *'the lust of the flesh, and the lust of the eyes, and the pride of life, is not from the Father but from the world.'*

'Gabriel, you quotin' St John Gospel right now?'

'Absolutely! For as of tonight, Maisha, I declare myself a citizen of the very world old John-boy so despised. Thanks to Tobago and thanks in particular to you! And for the first time in my life, I am drunk! Drunk on joy!'

Maisha straightened up and, still gyrating to the ear-splitting music, raised her beaker. 'I drink to dat, Gabriel!'

I was about to suggest another visit to the mobile bar when a great cry of exaggerated terror went up and, out of the darkness, I received a faceful of what seemed to be powder of some sort. Despite my mask, some went in my eyes and I swallowed a lot more, making me choke. It had apparently been thrown by a scrawny little bloke wearing a costume of raffia and coloured paper. However, thrusting his way through the crowd and towering above us all was a horrific man presumably on stilts, his

220

face painted in gold and black with one eye dripping with blood. 'Maisha,' I cried, spitting blue gunk. 'What on earth is he?'

'A moko jumbie! He in league wid de Devil, so take care!'

The fiend, rocking and cackling above me, made my flesh creep – even in my current state of euphoria. He wore an elaborate black wig and a bat-like costume made of sticks and feathers. I could just make out a pair of horns against the grey light of dawn. With a diabolical laugh, he tipped back his head and took a slurp from a plastic bottle. He then raised a flaming torch and blew a sheet of flame over our heads. I was not the only one to scream. But alarm gave way to merriment as his diminutive assistant hurled more powder about, coating our sweating bodies in purple, blue and pink.

My eyes stinging, I pulled off my mask. Maisha grabbed my chin. 'You is cryin'?'

'Powder in my eyes.'

'It only paint, Gabriel. It wash out.'

Through my tears, I saw the moko jumbie turn at the sound of my voice. He leered and pointed at me, laughing and lurching from side to side on his stilts whilst gesticulating with his torch. There was something familiar about this gangly brute, but I was in no fit state to work out what. I was glad to see him stalk away and terrorise someone else.

Maisha helped me over the storm drain and sat me down on the grass verge bordering someone's garden. Men were urinating into bushes further up the driveway. 'You okay, darlin'?' She sat very close and dabbed at my eyes with a tissue from a tiny silver bag slung over her shoulder.

'I'll survive. Why d'you suppose that bloody creature picked on me?'

'Probably he hear you accent. Couldn't believe a black man wid a voice like de BBC World Service. Listen, you wan' go on? Dey paradin' dong towards Pigeon Point for breakfas' and more limin', but you lookin' like you need some sleep. An' you head bleedin' again. My place only down so.' She gestured behind us. 'We go back and catch a couple hours?'

Ten minutes later, with the sun rising over the rooftops, Maisha led me up to a bright yellow building and unlocked her front door. 'Welcome, Gabriel. Shower on de right.'

23

It was gone midday when Maisha pulled up the blinds and opened the doors to a shady first-floor balcony. I rolled into a seated position on my sofa. She had pushed her hair up into a red and white brimless cap and was wearing a sort of romper suit to match. 'Come out an' sit here,' she said, indicating a white plastic chair. 'I make us some breakfast.'

Rubbing my eyes sent an excruciating pain through my head. 'Can I help at all?' My voice was little more than a grunt.

'No.' She touched my shoulder and smiled. 'You ent even lookin' like you could boil an egg right now.'

I pasted on a grateful grin and sat for ten minutes with my eyes shut until the sound of a car pulling up in the street below brought me to my senses with a jolt. Had they found me after all? I parted an explosion of pink and white bougainvillea and squinted down bleary-eyed. False alarm: it was only a taxi delivering neighbours home after a night on the tiles.

Maisha and I made short work of a plate of delicious fried breadfruit chips she had rustled up. To follow, a bowl of yoghurt, honey and slices of fresh pineapple.

After a long silence, I glanced up to see her studying me over her coffee cup. In contrast to how I was feeling, she looked so contented and at peace in the dappled light. If only she knew what was churning around in my mind. 'Nuh so talkative today? You okay?'

I grimaced. 'Never better – apart from a jackhammer at work between my ears. Sorry, I'm not very good company. Perhaps I'd better make a move.'

'No rush, Gabriel.'

My eyes were constantly drawn to the rooftops of the pink and orange houses opposite, and of course to the street below. I suppose I was subconsciously checking for concealed marksmen and sleek black limos loaded with Janice's thugs and spies. Maisha turned her head suddenly and followed my gaze. 'Eh, what you keep lookin' for?' There was a touch of irritation in her tone. 'We expectin' company? What's up?'

I put down my coffee cup and said, after a moment's hesitation, 'Listen, Maisha, I'm really sorry, but I've got myself mixed up in some pretty serious shit.' Her brow creased. 'It was probably a bad idea – irresponsible of me, I mean – even to come back to your apartment. I don't want them to find me here and have you implicated – or hurt. I'd never forgive myself.'

'Who de fuck "dem"?'

I paused. 'A powerful multinational corporation steeped in financial expediency and – what's your word? – bobol.'

'Jesus. You serious?'

'Put it this way, I spent last Wednesday night in a Scarborough police cell. Hence these bruises.' I lifted the T-shirt she had lent me. The area below my right armpit looked like a cheap piece of installation art left out in the rain.

'You shittin' me.' Her eyes were wide. 'What you goin' to do?'

'Once I've touched base with Lily I'll—'

'You wan' me to call de police?'

'No. Anything but that.' With an effort I stood up.

'I ent likin' what I hearin', Gabriel. I come wid you as personal bodyguard but I start my shift in an hour – an' I in no position to lose my job. I could call in sick, but nobody believe me at Carnival time.'

'That's very kind, but I wouldn't dream of letting you become any more involved. It'll sort itself out one way or another – at least, I hope so. Things are coming to a head the day after tomorrow. Right now, though, I'd better be off.''

I changed back into my Jouvert shirt and at the front door, Maisha put her head on one side. 'Take care of yourself, Gabriel,' she smiled, pushing a piece of paper into my hand. 'My phone number.'

'I'll be in touch. Thanks so much.' I turned and headed slowly back towards where I'd left the Honda.

It was only as I passed the entrance to the Kariwak Village Hotel that I realised I'd not seen Yvette last night. Maybe she'd decided after all to spend Jouvert with her new love interest up the island.

Heavy thunderheads had blown in from the north-west and splats of rain were already clanging on the car's dusty roof as I grabbed my valuables from under the spare wheel, climbed in and switched on my phone. There was a cheerful message from Max hoping I'd arrived safely and another from Janice that made me feel a little better: the Baddis – I had remembered Lily's term for her on the flight over – was under the impression I was still languishing in London. It pleased me to think how, sitting here anonymously in my claggy *Fog Angels* garb, I had one over on her and her henchmen.

I started up, switched the windscreen wipers to full and, dodging drenched and staggering revellers, headed out of Crown Point. Now I was away from Maisha's pleasant and distracting influence, sickening anxieties about Shurland rose within me like a great grey wave laden with dead seabirds and plastic waste.

The main road north-east up the island along which we had paraded last night was now blocked by gangs of dejected-looking workmen standing around in the downpour with brooms and wheelie-bins. I took a random right in the hope of finding a way through but the backstreets too were thronged with people scuttling for shelter. A black truck appeared out of nowhere behind me and blared its triple horns. I pulled over and it roared past me in a cloud of spray. 'Bloody idiot!' I yelled, making my head hurt. I followed in its wake round a corner and was in time to see it career into a flash flood, a torrent of water cutting across a dip in the road. The truck ploughed on, setting up a two-foot bow-wave. I judged that my low-slung little Honda would be no match for such adverse conditions so I swerved into the side with the intention of turning back. Beleaguered and drunken revellers jostled past and in my mirror I saw another car screech to a halt behind me, its metallic purple livery and blacked-out windows oddly familiar. I was too tired to think where I'd seen it before.

A loud thump on the roof, a fearsome face leering in at me through the misted passenger window: a woman in a bright red dress, bare arms jangling with bracelets and bangles, a mop of crimson-gold Rasta hair and an absurd straw hat. Before I could slam the car into E for Escape, the door flew open and the creature had flung herself inside. Hat off, she gripped the back of my neck and pressed her forehead to mine. 'You comin' wid me, fella! We go make love like de Devil his-self!' Her eyes were wide, hideous lips seeking my own.

'Oh no you—!'

'Shut de fuck up!'

Was this the la diablesse Lily had warned me about? I managed to pin the creature back against the passenger window. Blood-red lipstick was smeared across her cheek, and twists of black and white make-up ran in rivulets down her ghoulish face. Foulest of all, the car was filled as once before with a rank stench that turned my stomach. Remembering the severed foot in my luggage, I threw a panicked glance at the intruder's legs. 'Jesus

Christ!' I screeched, my worst fears confirmed. 'You've got a fucking cow's hoof!' This was no hallucination.

She squawked with cackling laughter and tried to belabour my face with her nails. 'De la diablesse come to he who sin, Gabriel Cassidy! Now drive!' My seatbelt clicked undone.

'But the flood—we can't!'

The beast-woman tugged at a silver chain round her neck. A shark's tooth the size of my middle finger was pressed into the flesh just below my left eye. 'I said, drive!'

We shot forward down the slope and into the water. Such was our velocity that we were through in a second, water sluicing over the bonnet and spurting through gaps in the door-seals. Although I fought for control, the monster elbowed me in the face and tugged the wheel to the left. We crashed through a low fence and into a field. My door flew open and I was dragged out into the mud and chicken-shit.

'Okay, Trevor, sweetie,' came a triumphant cackle, 'he all yours!'

With rain smashing into my eyes I caught a glimpse of the jeering face of the moko jumbie from the night before. A powerful smell of gas then blackness.

24

When I regained consciousness, I found myself like a single-use plastic bag, abandoned in the branches of some horribly spiny bush six feet above a wooded slope. I was scratched and bruised, my exposed skin tingling with insect bites. Somebody – that bastard Trevor presumably – must have hurled my unconscious body over the edge. The only good news was that the wind had dropped and it was no longer raining.

I managed to retrieve my phone without dislodging myself and falling further down the tree. I squeezed my thumb against the haptic and in the split second before it died, I saw the time was 05.43. Lord, Shrove Tuesday already. Above the early-morning birdsong I could hear the distant throb of music. Carnival.

Trying not to move my aching head too much, I peered about me. Above, through the dripping undergrowth, I could make out the consoling and homely shape of my Honda on a sloping track and realised I'd been jettisoned halfway up the drive to Shurland. In the movies, I mused bitterly, this would be the moment when, just after we have been led to assume our protagonist is dead, a dusty and bleeding hand pushes through the rubble and the music explodes into triumphant C Major. Now would be the time for our hero to focus up, make good his escape and save the day.

In reality, though, I was no hero, this was no movie and I was unable to move.

Nonetheless, I forced myself to think in pragmatic terms. If I tried to sit up or reach for a branch to haul myself out, another five or six deadly twigs would ping into position to impale me even more painfully. How had Lily described the fate of her would-be adulterer? 'De la diablesse, she leave him stuck in a picker bush deep in de forest. To die.'

Lily.

She'd be preparing breakfast for Churchill only a couple of hundred yards away up the hill. 'Well, Mrs. Pitt,' I muttered aloud to a bespectacled thrush watching me with curiosity, 'since I'm stuck for the foreseeable future in this bastard "picker bush" of yours, I may as well tell you that recent events will place a not inconsiderable strain on our friendship. For reasons beyond my comprehension I have been bamboozled and abused by your son – and some floozy of his wearing a fucking cow foot – both of them choosing to conceal themselves behind costumes of local superstition.' In my frustration, I smacked a branch with my fist; a mistake, given the prickly nature of my cage. 'Trevor was right to take me for a susceptible bloody foreigner.' With a surge of impotent rage, I then reflected that between them my attackers had expunged any advantage I might have gained by flying back two days early. I was headed, in the words of Ozzyman the online Australian influencer (my guilty pleasure in the old days) for 'Destination Fucked'. I ground my teeth at the thought that I had done nothing to stop the sale of the estate; quite the opposite, in fact, because Bill *bloody* McClung was arriving in about thirty-six hours to sign off the deal; and here was I, stuck in a sodding tree like the proverbial old lady's cat. With no hope of being rescued by the fire brigade. Which started me fretting about whether the contracts were still safe in the car or whether Trevor had stolen them. God help me if he had. God help Tobago.

A pair of parrots squawked rhythmically overhead and, not six feet away, a rufous-breasted jacamar alighted on a twig, its green back luminous in a ray of sunshine. It cocked its head, a dragonfly clamped in its long black beak. 'I know, I know,' I stated aloud, 'you're right to be judgmental. I bloody deserve it.'

To my surprise, a familiar voice from somewhere above responded: 'Who dat?'

My heart leapt. 'Churchill! Thank God!'

'Mr. Gabriel?'

'Down here!' I could have wept for joy.

The old man belched a resonant 'Eh-ehh' and leapt down goat-like towards me through the undergrowth. 'Lors, Mr. Gabriel! We not expectin' you back 'til tomorrow!' He produced a half bottle of rum and waved it at me. 'Thirsty?'

'You're a saviour.' I reached out and took a swig. The liquor made my eyes water but I felt better.

Churchill took a slurp himself and belched again. He was eyeing me as if I was a species of monkey long considered extinct on Tobago. He flapped a hand at my orange costume. 'I see you join *Fog Angels*. Roots look after you okay?' I had never heard the man so garrulous. He was clearly as drunk as a proverbial – I had no idea whether they even had skunks in the Caribbean – but who was I anyway to sit in judgement?

'Roots was most hospitable, thanks.' I wouldn't bother Churchill with how I'd strayed the night at Maisha's. He was bound to know her too and jump to conclusions.

Churchill seemed to focus on me again. 'Say, Mr. Gabriel, why you in de picker bush? You so drunk you fallin' out your car?'

I clamped my jaw shut. I was learning that in Tobago events moved at their own pace even at times of crisis. 'Well, the thing is, Churchill, I stopped to take a leak and must have fallen over the edge in the dark. Silly old me, eh?' The man cackled with laughter at this fabulation, ninety percent pure-alcohol tears running down his grizzled cheeks. It was enough. 'Oy! Hullo, Churchill! Help me out of here!'

The man wiped his nose on the back of his hand. 'Cool yuh herbs, fella. I fetch meh cutlash.'

Fifteen minutes later he had cleared me a reasonably pain-free escape route out of the bush and hauled me up the slope to the driveway. I immediately checked my belongings. The rucksack itself was gone, but the contents (including the sales contract and my valuables) had been left strewn across the back seat. I wondered what had been Trevor's purpose in putting me through this torture? To steal the bag but not the contents made no sense at all.

The keys were in the ignition so I lowered myself gingerly aboard and drove us both up to the house, parking at the foot of the staircase. It was good to be home, despite everything. Lily did not make an appearance so I begged Churchill to put on some coffee. I dragged myself up the stairs, collapsed into a chair with the First Aid box and applied some disinfectant and Elastoplast to the worst of the gouges in my flesh. Kenny eyed me with studied indifference from under the sofa. My motmot and the mocking birds were looking in vain at the empty fruit dish and three hummingbirds were at war as usual over the sugar water.

I was thinking maybe I should offer to help Churchill when he surprised me by tottering in with a tray of breakfast for two. Give the man his due: he could certainly take his drink. 'Thank you so much,' I said, as he poured me a large mug of coffee. 'I couldn't possibly have managed by myself, not after the night I've had.'

'Churchill in charge when Lily not here.'

'Where is she? Sleeping off Carnival somewhere?'

For a second he looked shifty. 'Eehh, what happen was, she gone to Scarborough wid Trevor. Urgent business.'

'What, on Carnival Tuesday?'

'I doh know, Mr. Gabriel. Since Friday I bin fishin' by my ol' friend Cap'n Stanley.' Churchill was having difficulty buttering himself a slice of toasted coconut bake. I could smell the rum on him.

I persevered. 'You haven't seen Yvette either, then? Roots said she was due to join the band last night but I didn't spot her.'

'Maybe you miss she in de dark. Pretty gyal like Yvette wid some man. She battin' in her crease.'

A blue-grey tanager hopped onto my plate and pecked at a crumb. Churchill flapped a trembling hand at it. 'Listen,' I said, 'thanks for breakfast. You'd better get some shut-eye. I'm for the shower. Thanks again for rescuing me. I owe you.'

'You're welcome, Mr. Gabriel.'

As Churchill negotiated the staircase I saw him take another surreptitious swig from his bottle.

The sun was low when I awoke. Too stiff and bruised to move, I remained on the sofa wondering where on earth Lily had got to. The roar of a vehicle heading up the track made my heart thump. I made an effort and limped over to peer down from a corner of the balcony as an all too familiar purple car skidded to a halt. Trevor. Now what? He leapt out and I heard him kick open the door of Lily and Churchill's apartment downstairs. 'Wake up, lazy bastard! In de fucking car!'

'Okay, okay, boy!'

'An' de rich Englishman? He here?'

'Upstairs, Trevor.'

There was no time to escape: the man was pounding up the stairs two at a time.

'Hey, asshole! You comin' wid me!' The look in his red eyes was wild and dangerous. He reached behind him to jam a pistol into my neck while with his other hand he frisked me. 'Where your fuckin' cell?'

'Somewhere in the forest, I imagine,' I gargled, grateful I'd had the presence of mind to stuff it between the sofa cushions. 'It didn't survive the night. No thanks to you.'

He was leering at me, traces of moko jumbie make-up still evident on his skin. 'Don' play de dumbfuck, Cassidy. We goin' for a ride.' He lowered the gun.

'Can I put on shoes and a shirt?'

He spat on the floorboards. 'Alright, Englishman, but I is watchin' you.'

Minutes later I was in the back of the car with Churchill, a fresh rum bottle secreted between us. 'Trevor,' squawked the old man, 'as you grandfather, I ax you not to hurt Mr. Gabriel. He done you no harm.'

'Shut de fuck up!'

Trevor drove us at breakneck speed down the drive and slung a right towards Black Rock village. A mile later, with one poor iguana flattened and endless chickens scattered, we swung sharp left over the bridge towards Plymouth. Churchill and I were flung about as he cornered this way and that up the hill between half-built and dilapidated shacks heading for the beach at Arnos Vale. That ruined hotel would be as perfect a spot as any for the discreet disposal of any inconvenient witnesses. Bizarrely, it struck me that, given what day it was, I was being flipped like a Shrove Tuesday pancake; but from one frying pan into another doubtless larger and far hotter one. It was only a matter of time before I was into the fire.

It was almost dark as Trevor ushered me at gunpoint up a rickety outside staircase to what would once have been a lovely bedroom suite. It overlooked the beach where I had snorkelled with Pablo's barracuda. I was hurled to the floorboards where I rolled against some upturned piece of rotting furniture in the foetid blackness.

Behind me, Churchill stumbled up the stairs and was thrown against a wall. Trevor yelled, 'Sit dong an' don' move!' I judged from the screeching tenor of his voice that Lily's little boy could be on the cusp of insanity. What could be terrifying him? 'Oh, so you drunk again, *grampa*! I smell ya from here. What you hidin'? Hand it over!'

'Please, boy,' squeaked Churchill, 'let me keep it.'

'No fuckin' way!'

At the end of the struggle was a dull thud, a second's silence and the sound of a bottle smashing outside. I lay very still, my cheek pressed to the floorboards in the filth and grit.

A step behind my head; Trevor was breathing heavily. 'Cassidy, sit up! You give me no hassle an' I nuh hurtin' you.' He had a hand on my collar like a disobedient hound. 'Slide your fat arse dis way.'

Trevor ripped a length of electrical cable from the wall and bound my hands and feet with it. He then dragged me against a pillar in the centre of the room and tied me by the neck to it with a strip of old bedsheet stinking of mould.

'So, Trevor,' I managed to say. 'Is this the best accommodation Arnos Vale can offer?'

For my impertinence I earned a kick on the thigh. 'Doh try an' be clever, Cassidy. How de fuck you know dis place?'

'Your doting mother recommended it to me for snorkelling.'

'Well, no one know you here now, not even dat woman. You stay as a guest 'til de bats eat you eyes out.'

'Is that what the smell is?' I was aware of an acrid stench and a constant fluttering in the darkness overhead.

'Yah man. Batshit drive you crazy in de end.' He laughed at his own wit. He must have been high on something. This near madness of Trevor's was more frightening even than the sober and calculated violence meted out by Pablo.

I asked, 'What are you doing about Churchill?'

'When my associates arrive, we all takin' a nice family trip like in de ol' days when we was small.' His phone rang. 'Yah, my friend,' he cried with false bonhomie, nervous all of a sudden; obsequious even. 'Trevor gat everytin under control. Yah man, see you in two.'

Behind me, I heard Trevor kick Churchill back into consciousness and drag the whimpering old boy to the head of the staircase. Then, with a great deal of more abuse, he coerced him to his feet and down to beach level again.

I was alone. I tugged and twisted at my bonds but the man had tied me too tightly. A whisper from directly behind me. 'Gabriel!'

The hairs on the back of my neck bristled. 'Who's that?'

'Me, Yvette.'

'Yvette?' My heart leapt and I offered up silent thanks to any gods still awake and listening at this time of night. 'How in the name of—'

'I so sorry for landin' you in dis shit but Trevor, he crazy. I never thought he sink to kidnappin' his own sister.'

'What? But why?'

'Sshh!' A car screeched to a halt below. I heard Trevor ordering Churchill into the vehicle and Lily's unmistakeable voice hollering invective from inside. She was keeping up a constant wailing not unlike the din she had made in the forest last week.

A newcomer was whining: 'Trevor, bro, de Obeah woman, she boofin' meh!'

Trevor commanded, 'So gag de fuckin' ol' witch while I fetch de las' one dong.'

'Gabriel,' hissed Yvette, 'he comin' for me, so listen.' I tried to twist my head round but still couldn't see her. 'Trevor meetin' he boss at Hillsborough Dam in an hour or so – a monthly arrangement to hand over drug money. But dis time, he have a problem.'

'Which is?'

'Two hundred thousand TT. All gone by de casino.'

'He's lost twenty thousand sterling in a single month?'

'Yes, but Gabriel, when he sees you at Jouvert he somehow know how to save he ass. He found a way of replacin' what he owe, an' he handin' over all de cash tonight. An' he take me along for de ride, he say.'

'But why?'

'He ent tellin' me what he schemin' for me and mum. I guess he takin' granddad in case he took it in he head to warn you.'

'Yvette, I just don't get why your brother ambushed me of all people.'

Trevor was still shouting outside but a slight vibration in the floorboards told me he was on the staircase. 'He say he needed to access your phone.'

Hurried footsteps coming up the stairs. 'Try to forgive my family,' Yvette moaned. 'Please, Gabriel.'

Trevor burst into the room, his breath rasping. 'Allyuh happy in de bridal suite?' Crouching behind me, he switched on a torch and began cutting Yvette's bonds. 'Alright, pretty lil' sis',' he snarled. 'Up! You comin' to meet an ol' friend of mine. It my contention he goin' to love you.'

'Please, Trev,' began Yvette, her voice cracking with panic. 'Gabriel bin so good to us, cyan' you let him go?'

He slapped her. 'How many time I ax you be quiet, bitch-slut?'

I was having to control my breathing. 'Trevor, please don't hurt anyone tonight. As a favour to me.'

'Else what?'

'Else you'll answer to me.'

Trevor's scornful laughter at that moment sealed his fate as far as I was concerned. Hauling Yvette away, he paused at the door. 'Maybe I does owe you a favour, Cassidy. I see what I can do.'

'What are you bloody talking about?' I wrenched my head round, the material cutting into the flesh under my left ear. Trevor did not reply, and in flashes of torchlight I saw Yvette's face crumple as he dragged her out of the room.

I waited until the two cars had accelerated away up the hill before beginning to heave at my bonds. Soon I had stretched the bedsheet enough to be able to swivel my head half round and survey my prison. With eyes long since accustomed to the dark I could make out under the pale rectangle of a window chunks of upturned furniture and a broken metal bed-end to which Yvette had presumably been tied. The mattress had been thrown to one side. What might have been a car battery lay on its side six feet from my right shoulder. At least I'd been spared electric shock treatment.

In those late-night B-movies I might never again watch there'd be a shard of glass conveniently to hand. I stretched my fingers as far as I could but, in this unscripted dark reality, encountered nothing. Trevor had done too good a job for me to effect a quick escape and raise the alarm.

For a while I listened to the waves crashing on the beach below. I leant my bruised head against my post and replayed over and again what Yvette had said about Trevor needing my phone. I drew a blank. All I knew for certain was that Bill McClung was due in Tobago within the next few hours and that if I remained stuck here, my geese were as good as cooked. I doubted that Janice, Pablo and Cleve would delay the incineration of Shurland after reports reached them of my disappearance or death. All they had to do was retrieve the signed contract from the house before asking Cleve to apply a match.

Something lightweight, multi-limbed and *arachnoid* was crawling over my bare shin. I froze, hoping it wouldn't feel the need to explore up a leg of my shorts. A particularly large wave thumped onto the beach. And then another sound: the distinct tinkle of broken glass being kicked across concrete. A dog barked. Footfalls on the staircase and, seconds later, the blinding beam of a powerful flashlight in my face.

25

My pulse pounding against the binding at my neck, I turned away from the glare and listened for the terminal sound of a cutlass being withdrawn from its sheath. Or the click of a safety catch. Instead I heard a long steups and a rumble of amusement. 'Well, de Angel Gabriel.'

Relief surged through me. 'Winston, am I pleased to see you! But if anyone's an angel tonight, it's you.'

The old mechanic lowered the beam and waddled towards me. He dropped to the floor an enormous spanner he'd been brandishing, pulled out his cutlass and began to saw – with what I hoped would prove the usual Tobagonian dexterity – at the material round my neck. 'I should be axing you what you doin' here past midnight truss up like a roastin' chicken?'

'Long story,' I said through gritted teeth, the blade being millimetres from my jugular.

'I understan' someone in deep shit when I hear de Obeah woman hollerin' at stone-brain Trevor an' his friend. An' den I see poor Churchill drag out. He drunk again.'

'You saw them?'

'I tell you before: Winston, he always maccoin'. He see everytin'.' My neck released, he was about to set to work on my ankles when something stopped him. 'Hold still, Angel.' With infinite care, Winston edged the cutlass blade under a vast and hairy tarantula which had taken up position straddling my shoes. He lifted it for me to see. 'A real beauty, eh?'

I opened my mouth to say something to the effect of 'absolutely, it's a point of view' when the infernal thing sprang onto my shirt front. 'God almighty!' I squeaked, blaspheming without turning a hair. 'Get it off me!'

The spider gazed balefully up at me through myriad eyes as Winston once more lifted it away, reaching over to place it on the mattress. 'He won' harm you,' he gurgled. 'He prefer bugs.'

'Just untie me, please, Winston. I haven't time for a natural history lesson.'

'You in a hurry?'

'I'm going after Trevor.'

I waited for a steups that didn't come. 'You crazy?'

My feet were free at last. 'Probably. They're headed for the Hillsborough Dam.'

'De reservoir? In de hill by Easterfield? Take you forty minutes to reach. You gat a vehicle?'

'Can I borrow one?'

'Sure.' He was working at the binding on my wrists. 'Lily an' Churchill in danger?'

'Yvette too.' I flung away the wire. 'Thanks, mate.' I was already on my feet and stumbling to the top of the staircase. I grabbed the branch of an overhanging tree to steady myself. 'Trevor's on the war path.'

Winston spat. 'Dat boy never care a shit for anybody.'

Down the stairs we went, skirted the broken pavilion by the pool, Winston's "potongs" at our heels yipping with excitement. My saviour ran into his workshop, grabbed some keys and opened up some ancient Japanese banger parked round the back. 'Dis de best vehicle, Angel. Not too mash-up. You know de way?'

'Can you give me directions?'

He said nothing. He opened a back door and threw in his cutlass, spanner and torch.

Winston drove with immense skill for about half an hour. He seemed to know every hairpin bend, each pothole, and the smoothest route to take over swathes of unmade-up road. We swung round abandoned cars resting on bricks, avoided rolling into chasms where the road had slipped away and scattered any number of goats and cows grazing in the dark at the end of their tethers. I regained my bearings when we screeched round a corner between a school and a football pitch. I'd been lost down here that night in the storm when I encountered the mad goatherd and picked up Yvette. We revved through the bamboo tunnel I remembered, bumping and slithering up the incline to the spot where I'd been accosted by Lester a mere nine days ago. Winston braked, swung to the right and headed down the slope into the darkness, the track degenerating into nothing more than a ledge on the hillside. 'About half a mile to de reservoir,' he announced.

'I'd better walk the rest of the way.'

'You wan' me park up?'

'Please. Switch off the engine and kill the lights.' He did so and the sounds of the night closed in upon us like shimmering velvet. 'Also, can I borrow that spanner? In case I meet the la diablesse again?'

'What you mean *again*?'

'Another long story.' I threw open the car door.

'Take ma cutlass, Mr. Angel. He more use.' I reached over and grabbed it. It was the first cutlass I'd ever handled but I felt more secure than I'd done in days. No wonder they all carried one. Winston coughed. 'I not coming wid you?'

'Thanks, Winston, but I'd rather you waited in the car. If things go well, we'll be needing reliable transport out of here. I don't suppose Lily will be able to walk far.'

'You has a plan?'

'Nope. Wish me luck.'

'Take my business card. My phone charged.'

We shook hands and I left him. A moment later, the glow of Winston's cigarette vanished as I rounded a bend. As luck would have it I was soon walking on pitted tarmac and, apart from the usual Tobagonian hazards such as fallen bamboo, a leaning telegraph pole and an electrical cable slung waist-high across the road, I was able to make good progress in the starlight. I rounded another corner and saw the glint of something before me: Trevor's car. Beyond it, another vehicle, also unoccupied I found, presumably belonging to the stooge who had brought Lily. I knew from police dramas that you can let down a car tyre simply by pressing a stick into the valve. It took me only a few moments to disable both vehicles. I was encouraged by this minor triumph, particularly since the hissing of the valves was so effectively masked by the buzz of cigalles.

With infinite care, I crept another fifty yards down the road. A nightjar sputtered out of my path and an enormous cow chewing on the verge made me jump. But it was the sleek, dark shape of a third and horribly familiar car that gave me real pause for thought. It was the government SUV used by Janice.

Harbouring dark suspicions, I took the track into which the vehicle had been reversed. At its end stood what might have been a pumphouse. Pressed close against the wall, I peered round the corner. I could smell fresh water. Against the faintest of glows in the eastern sky I could just make out I was at the foot of a slope leading up to the horizontal top of the dam itself. A little to my left, silhouetted against the few remaining stars, were six figures, three further along the dam and three directly above me. Low voices wafted on the gentle pre-dawn breeze. Furthest from me I recognised Trevor's distinctive tones at once; another wasn't speaking, but the third I knew simply by the menacing breadth of his shoulders: Pablo. So, that was it. The Venezuelan used his employer's SUV to drive himself to meetings with his minions in the narcotics trade. Pablo was Trevor's boss.

My ears ringing and gulping for air, I pulled back and leant my head against the cool brickwork of the pumphouse. I needed to weigh up my options. Storm the dam alone I could not: one cutlass against at least three guns wouldn't really cut it. What would Harrison Ford do in this situation? Bide his time and see what transpired. I gazed before me down the valley where the blackness was broken only by the lights of what I imagined to be Water Company buildings. With Pablo to contend with, I now understood why Trevor had been so terrified. And who could blame him? I was trembling myself; a few minutes earlier and I could have walked clean into Pablo's arms. I already hated the sadistic Venezuelan for what he had done to me in that police cell, but when I considered how he earned his millions it made my blood boil. Yet my beating had had nothing to do with his dark trade: I'd just been rash enough – blind and trusting enough – to defy and inconvenience him in his lust for power and influence over Janice, his pet government official. Could she be aware of her chauffeur-henchman's moonlighting activities? If so, and she was indeed complicit, sufficiently self-seeking and corrupt to condone his nefarious deeds, it would quite be in character for her to demand her cut. And, standing there in the pitch black, this grotesque realisation made me all the more determined that, assuming I survived this present dilemma, she and McClung would never pull one over on me with regard to Shurland. Quite how I'd prevail, I'd no clue – any more than I had as to why Trevor and his la diablesse had attacked me in the first place. All I knew was that this time, I mustn't lose whatever advantage I possessed, however slim.

I gave myself a minute to let my heartbeat settle then poked my head round the corner again. The conference was still in full flow above me so I flattened myself into the grass and, cutlass in hand, slithered like a true pirate of the Caribbean up the slope until I was five feet below Churchill. I could see the old man's silhouette: he was standing swaying slightly behind his daughter and granddaughter. I made a low hissing noise and he turned his head. I pushed the weapon towards him through the grass and lay still again. Churchill had heard me and, waiting his moment, stooped to grab the blade and secrete it in the back of his Wellington boot.

I edged back down the bank, passed behind the pumphouse and elongated myself in the damp grass again. In the early light of dawn I could make out a bush about halfway between me and Pablo. I simply had to hear what he and Trevor were discussing, so with infinite care I crawled to within earshot. Predictably, Pablo was dressed for the occasion in his shiny suit, the vile outfit gleaming pinkish even in this flat pre-dawn light. As was the pistol he held trained on Trevor's chest. A torch flicked on and I saw a bag on the ground between them: my own hold-all stolen from the back of the Honda. I recognised the little yellow padlock with the key still on its ring. Given how unlikely it was that Trevor had set a la diablesse upon me simply to borrow a phone and steal an empty bag, what was he up to?

Pablo dog-whistled the third man: 'You,' he snapped, 'frisk this asshole and count the cash. I don' trust him. He is unreliable.'

'Yeah, boss.' I knew that high-pitched voice. It was Newton the driver who had so gracelessly delivered the contract last week. I watched his silhouette reach behind Trevor and find his pistol. With a grunt of triumph, Newton shoved it into his own jacket pocket. He then knelt, emptied the bag and began to count the cash.

Pablo was speaking with infinite menace. 'So, Trevor, you bring a gun to a meeting with *me*?'

'Hey, boss, I need it earlier an—'

'Quiet!' The barrel of Pablo's pistol tilted upwards. I could see it against a patch of sky between the trees. 'Listen good, Trevor. My contact at casino tell me you have a *problem.*'

'No, boss, I ent got no problem.'

'An addiction to gambling, I mean, Trevor. It make you unreliable, *sí*?'

'Boss, I bring what I owe you, yes? I always reliable.' He flung out a hand towards the money. 'No problem.'

'This time maybe. But what about next month? Or the next?'

'But—'

'Also, Officer Cleve tell me he found your shit stored in a fucking shack in the forest. Dis your idea of a secure location?' Newton laughed at this but Trevor did not respond. Pablo pushed the gun into his cheek. 'You still call yourself reliable?'

'Sure, boss, I—'

'So explain me this: why bring your entire fucking family here?'

Trevor forced a swaggering laugh. 'Listen, boss, I taught you like to meet my mother. She accompany me to de bank when I draw out de money today. She respectable, boss, indispensable.'

'Really?'

'Yeah, boss. De bank, dey believe a Obeah woman sayin' she buyin' Sugar-Shack… it a prestigious beach property, boss, in Charlotteville.' At least one of the ladies present was weeping.

'You telling me a bank is open at Carnival?'

Trevor sniggered and nodded. 'Oh, I knows people, boss. Dey oblige me, given de right incentive.'

'Uh-huh.' Pablo swiveled his head inexorably towards Yvette. 'And her?'

'Oh she my sister, boss. I keepin' an eye on she. Bring she along for de ride. I tinkin' she useful to you.'

'Is that so?'

'Sure, boss. I keep her away from rich-bastard Cassidy now he come back to sweet T an' T.'

Pablo's free hand shot out and gripped Trevor's neck. 'No. More. Fucking. Riddles.' Trevor was about to be lifted off the ground. 'What do you know of my dealings with that fool Cassidy?'

'He stayin' wid my mum – you know already – he gone but now he back in sweet T an' T. He wan' fuck my sister so bad. He *hard* for she.'

Pablo spoke slowly. 'You lying fucking bastard, Trevor. Cassidy flies in this afternoon.'

'Boss, I tellin' truth,' rasped Trevor. He was finding it hard to speak with those fingers I knew so well squeezing his scrawny larynx. 'Right now I got Cassidy safe-safe at secret location. You understan', boss, I need his thumb-print for accessin' his online bankin'.' Again he indicated the cash Newton was still counting. I bit down hard on my thumb to stop myself yelling out in rage at this latest revelation, proof if ever it was needed of my astonishing and idiotic naivety. But Trevor hadn't finished crowing: 'I even arrange a la diablesse attack on Cassidy! My Angela, she play de part! Oscar-winnin'! She even borrow a Carnival cow-hoof, boss. An' Cassidy, he roll right over! All I has to do is put him out wid chloroform!'

'*Jesucristo.*'

'After, we stick he fat ass in de picker bush.' Trevor fumbled in his pocket for a phone. 'Look, boss, I got great shot of Angela! She sexy la diablesse, no?' He held out the picture but Pablo's lack of interest was palpable even from where I lay. 'So, boss, I always sort out meh shit. I is reliable!'

Newton rose to his feet. 'All complete, boss. Twenty-six thousand dollar US.' 'Quite a hole in my bloody bank account,' I growled into my fist.

'*Bueno. Muy bueno.*' Pablo stood titanic, Trevor's neck still gripped like a chicken's in his enormous hand. Soft sounds of weeping came to me. 'Newton,' he snapped. 'Shut those fucking women up. They're irritatin' me.'

The stooge obeyed, moving heavily along the top of the dam. I saw him grab Churchill by the collar and plant him next to Yvette and Lily. The women stood holding each other, silent now, the family corralled like wayward cattle. Newton, taking up position nearby, wasn't alert enough to stop Yvette running forward and hurling herself at her brother. She knocked the phone out of his hand and belaboured him with her fists. With an audible sigh, Pablo let go of Trevor and cocked his gun. Yvette froze, her profile inches from her brother's.

'Boss,' babbled Trevor, his voice rasping with panic, 'dis my big plan: my hot sissy, she fetch you good price in Caracas.'

'You think?' With horrid deliberation, Pablo reached out a hand and actually cupped one of Yvette's breasts. He gave a bestial grunt of approval and, in a realisation atypical of a lifelong Christian, I knew at that moment that Pablo would have to die, even at my own hand if necessary. 'So, Trevor,' he drawled, 'you offer me your women as whores?'

'Yah man. Dat some nice tits an' bamsee.' Trevor then jerked his thumb at Lily. 'An' my mother, maybe she a fat ol' woman, but she highly profitable with certain client.'

'Oh-hoooh!' It was the stentorian voice of the Obeah woman: 'Yvette, darlin', come back here an' hol' my hand. Leave dat creature alone. He no son of mine, no longer you brother. Come!'

Yvette's jaw jutted. 'Burn in all de fires of hell, Trevor.'

Pablo seized Yvette by the hair and hauled her back. 'Quiet, all of you!' he roared. 'Newton, do your fucking job!' He flung Yvette towards his stooge who dragged her back to join Lily and Churchill before taking up sentry duty again behind them.

Pablo took a step towards Trevor. The cowardly weak creature's dreadlocks had tumbled out of the cloth and were partially covering his face. Pablo was purring: 'I will think about your kind offer... of quality female merchandise, Trevor, but it makes no difference to you now. You have fucked me over once too often.'

'Why, boss, please, I—'

'Cassidy was working for *me* in the U.K. and if he fails to deliver today, whose fault will it be, Trevor?'

'Mine?'

'*Si, pequeño.*' With one hand he rocked Trevor by the shoulder. With the other, he pressed the pistol to his forehead. 'So finally you understand.'

'Yeah, boss. Sorry, boss—'

'You agree now perhaps, when I say you are unreliable?'

'Yeah, boss.'

'*Adiós, amigo.*' Pablo pulled the trigger.

If the shot stunned me, it alarmed hidden squadrons of cocricos into a full surround-sound cacophony of distress and outrage. The women screamed and ran forward, pushing past Pablo to throw themselves upon Trevor's inert body. In the same instant I saw Churchill raise the cutlass blade and flick it across Newton's throat. Before I had time to think, before Pablo could make up his mind to murder the rest of the family, I was up and over a low wall and running along the concrete causeway which topped the dam. Hearing me pelting towards him, the monster turned to meet the full force of my left shoulder powering into his chest. Fury such as I had never known choked me as I grabbed his gun hand and forced it upwards. The man stood no chance: to win this final round, I would have ripped off face with my teeth. With both hands occupied keeping the muzzle of that pistol away from me I jammed a knee hard into his groin. He appeared not to notice. Our faces were inches apart.

He was breathing garlic at me. 'Feeling lucky, Cassidy?'

I nodded. 'Abso-fucking-lutely.'

He tried to headbutt me, but I was ready for him and ducked aside. I heaved with both legs but the colossus had gained a foothold against the wall on the reservoir side of the causeway. I might as well have tried to uproot a silk cotton tree barehanded. Pablo grinned down at me, his cruel face wreathed in triumphant malice in the golden light of a new day.

'So, this is *adiós* for you too, Meestah Cassidy. You left the contract somewhere at Shurland for me?'

'Yup, in an envelope with your name on it.'

'*Excelente.*'

His complacent self-assurance gave me the strength to haul down once more on his wrist. The gun fired again, this time into the water, the volley of noise sending clouds more birds squawking out of the trees. Pablo rumbled with amusement, knowing my strength would eventually fail. But in that moment of dread realisation for me, something butted into Pablo's haunches with the ferocity of Big Billy-goat Gruff dispatching the Troll.

Yvette.

Caught off-balance between us, Pablo was finally toppled. With a hoarse cry, I threw everything I had left at him and he flipped backwards over the wall. With a yell of fury, he rolled over and over down the slippery concrete slope and into the water.

But despite a soaking, the Venezuelan was not yet done. The brute emerged splashing from the lake and wrestled himself to his knees amidst a raft of floating bamboo stems. He pushed a hank of water-weed out of his eyes and shook water from his gun.

Churchill's voice: 'Get dong!'

We dropped behind the wall. Pablo fired time and again, bullets ricocheting, sending shards of concrete to sting the back of my legs. Then, without warning, an agonised scream, a series of splashes, and silence.

At a sign from Churchill, and with infinite caution, we raised our heads to peer over the parapet. Down the slope, at the reservoir's edge, we saw churning, roiling water, upended bamboo stalks and a glimpse of a hand lifted as if in silent salute to his vanquishers. In those few short seconds Pablo had been taken.

As the birds settled back into the treetops, I stared at dark curves wheeling in the water. Black-ridged shapes broke the surface before whatever it was dived out of sight to enjoy the spoils.

Churchill was the first to move. 'Eh-ehh, Mother Earth revenge.' The clang of a blood-stained cutlass on the wall beside me as he sat himself stiffly down and lit a cigarette. He was still reeking of rum. 'Caiman,' he said simply. 'They ent like to be disturb in nestin' season.'

26

A couple of minutes later I was walking slowly towards the centre of the dam. Before me, the pageant of another superlative Caribbean sunrise unfolded across billowing pink-edged clouds. To my right, a blue heron preened on a branch overhanging mirror-like water which gleamed silver-pink and orange in the early morning light. Beyond, as far as the eye could see, the jet black silhouette of pristine forest full of birdsong was daubed with emerald green.

I was still trembling from what I had just witnessed; how much I had changed in the past two weeks: from po-faced insurance broker and favoured Sunday speaker at the Lewisham Ecclesia to profanity-ridden participant in scenes of exorcism, kidnap and murder. I shook my head in an attempt to focus my thoughts. I should give the family a moment to grieve over Trevor's body but then it would be time to make ourselves scarce before the police and press arrived.

'The press!' I muttered to myself. 'Of *course*. That's the answer. I must call Max.'

I reached into my pocket only to remember my phone was stuffed down between the sofa cushions at Shurland. I had no means on me of contacting the outside world. One of the women might have a phone, I thought. I hurried back towards the family group but found my way partially blocked by Newton's corpse. Staring grimly at the dark red pool in which he lay, I was struck by another sobering realisation: that any on-screen imitations of blood-letting I'd witnessed from the comfort of my armchair paled utterly in comparison to the stomach-churning horror of grisly reality. To give him his due, Churchill could certainly wield a cutlass. I'd braced myself to step over the blood when I spotted the butt of Trevor's pistol protruding from Newton's pocket. Instinct told me not to leave it there. I had never touched a gun before and certainly had no idea whether it was loaded or not – or even whether the safety-catch was on or off – but, unobserved and with great care, I scooped it up and carried it over to my hold-all where I buried it deep amongst the packets of banknotes.

I approached the family. 'I'm so sorry to disturb you,' I began, 'but I need to make an urgent phone call if we're to have any chance at all of saving Shurland.' I tried to catch Lily's eye but she was looking away, a hand to her lips.

'Trevor de only phone here,' replied Yvette, her face streaked with tears. She held it up. 'But it need he thumb-print.'

'Let me,' I whispered, crouching beside her. Trevor's hand was still warm. I pressed the thumb against the haptic and the phone buzzed into life. He owed me this at least. 'Thanks,' I said to no one in particular.

Skirting Newton this time, I walked along the grassy bank to the far end of the causeway and leant against a large white sign declaring irrelevantly: *Restricted Area: No Bathing or Swimming. No Fishing. No Water Sports.* Over a crackly line, Max sounded grim when I told him what I wanted him to do. 'Alright, Ange,' he said at length, 'I'll give it a whirl, but I don't hold out much hope.'

'It's our only hope, mate. Everything is spinning out of control here and it's up to you and me to stop it.'

'No pressure, then.'

'Oh, and Max, before you go, there's another little job I need to run past you...'

By the time Max was up to speed, the first rays of sunshine were beginning to paint in molten gold the most idyllic and peaceful of tropical panoramas. Not a single man-made sound could I hear in this paradise. An osprey glided overhead on the hunt for a breakfast of fish, an anhinga stretched its snake-like neck and spread glossy black wings to dry, and something moved sluggishly near the caiman nests. I pulled Winston's business card out of my pocket, rang his number and asked him to bring the car to the foot of the dam.

'I see you already, Mr. Angel.' I spotted a vehicle moving between trees to the west. 'I freewheel all de way dong. Lily, she safe?'

'Everyone's fine, thank God.'

With Yvette supporting her mother down to the car, Churchill and I completed the unpleasant task of covering the two corpses as best we could with some plastic sheeting I found in the pumphouse. 'Let's hope the caiman don't find them before the authorities arrive,' I said. 'We're going to have enough trouble explaining this to Cleve as it is.'

Churchill nodded skywards. 'Corbeaux already circlin'.'

'Lot of it about,' I replied, picking up my bag of money. 'Don't forget Winston's cutlash, whatever you do. It'll be covered in your fingerprints.'

Churchill winked at me and with commendable athleticism, seized the weapon by its blade and sent it arcing towards the rising sun. It sliced into the reservoir some twenty yards out.

A car horn sounded. At the foot of the slope, Winston clambered out of what I could now see was an antediluvian green Toyota Corolla. 'Hey, Winston!' Churchill called, 'I owe you a cutlash. But how come you here?'

'I de getaway driver, bro!' He was waving to Lily. 'You wait right where you is, Obeah woman! I comin' help you dong.'

While Winston made heavy work of climbing the rough track, I remained at my post at the centre of the dam unable all of a sudden to take in a full breath; I must have been hyperventilating. I felt not only breathless but numb and sick. I leant forward onto my knees to try and draw in a decent lungful of forest air. And this ploy might have worked had I not been so aware that despite all that had occurred, I was still beset with the same problem I'd started out to resolve; relieved I might be that Trevor, Pablo and Newton were out of the equation, but the big guns of Janice and McClung would still be expecting me at Shurland in only a few hours' time. I looked up as a cormorant broke the glassy surface of the reservoir and flew off to the north. 'You're right, mate,' I thought, 'onwards and upwards.'

A hand on my shoulder. Yvette had materialised beside me. 'You okay, Gabriel?'

'I've felt better. Must be in shock.' I looked out over the water, blinking back the beginning of tears. 'Still, on the bright side, you and I are quits. I saved your life the other day and now you've saved mine.'

A welcome gust of cooling wind sent ripples fanning across the water whilst behind us the two old men were helping Lily into the back of the car. 'Eh, you comin'?' called Churchill. 'Leh we go before de authorities reach!'

'On our way,' I called, my voice cracking.

I picked up the hold-all and, with a final glance towards Pablo's watery grave, put an arm round Yvette's shoulder. Together we walked with uncertain steps down the grassy bank.

We drove down the valley in silence, passing unchallenged through an encampment of turquoise-painted Water And Sewage Authority buildings. This was just as well because I was in no state to face down questioning officialdom who would doubtless declare 'dat illegal' to wander without written permission from Head Office in their *Restricted Area* at six-thirty on the morning of Ash Wednesday. Even then, we were not in the clear because a mile later, the road curled directly into a quarry past mountains of graded road-stone and beneath a Meccano mayhem of rusting gantries, pipes, conveyor belts and workshops.

I leant forward: 'Winston?'

'Yes, young man?'

'Don't hang about.'

The old mechanic stamped his foot down and we scudded out of that place in a cloud of dust so thick it would obliterate any busy-body's view of our number plate.

I was squeezed into the back seat with Yvette, Lily – and the elephant in the car. 'Listen, Lily,' I said, 'I think I've pretty much worked out the part you played in the theft of my twenty thousand, but—'

'Mr. Gabriel, I—'

I held up a hand. 'But what I fail to understand is why you agreed to help Trevor in the first place. I thought you and I were... well, on the same side.' Lily was shaking her head, lips pursed. I wondered if she was going to burst into tears. 'Lily? Speak to me, my friend. I won't bite. I'm too fond of you – of you both – for that.'

Seeming to make up her mind, the deflated Obeah woman gave a little smile and reached across her daughter to squeeze my hand. 'Mr. Gabriel, what happen was... well, I become Trevor accomplice because he threaten to tell you what I done to you.'

'To me?'

'Yes. When you first arrive at Shurland.'

I stared at her. 'Go on.'

'Well, I add certain someting in de herbal tea you like so much.'

'Mother!' snapped Yvette. 'Explain!'

'Darlin' gyal, I done it to make Mr. Gabriel more... compliant, less effective wid de Cordner woman, you understan'? I mix in an ol' Obeah remedy. But I should never have tol' Trevor.'

I sighed. 'What remedy, Lily?'

She was twisting the fabric of her skirt like a naughty schoolgirl in the Head's office after Assembly. 'Angel Trumpet, Mr. Gabriel.'

Despite the loud stereo steups from the old men in the front seat, I was none the wiser but Yvette turned on her mother. 'What? You put brugmansia in Gabriel tea? That so dangerous, mother! People die of Angel Trumpet hallucination!'

'Eh-ehh, darlin'! I wouldn't let Mr. Gabriel die! Everytin' under control! Dat why I stop an' give him coffee instead. I simply tryin' to stop Mr. Neville evictin' us.'

Again, I was having difficulty filling my lungs. 'So, let me get this straight. All that time I thought I was suffering from some bloody 'flu bug! Now it turns out I was being poisoned by someone I thought was my friend offering me a nice cup of tea! What the *fuck*?' My hand was tingling to smack the bag of money I was cradling but, remembering the loaded gun nestling inside, I managed to control any violent urges. 'For God's sake, Lily!' I cried instead, glaring out of the window, 'I was freaked out for days!' Winston was watching me round-eyed in his rear-view mirror. He'd be dining out on this story for weeks.

Lily was sobbing. 'I doh know how to make it up to you, Mr. Gabriel. I so sorry.'

'And I suppose you were also involved somehow with setting up my uncle's carer to poison him in the same way.'

'What you sayin'?'

'Don't play the innocent with me, Lily. The woman's name is Mabel. She's a Trini – and presumably some Obeah disciple of yours. She was feeding Neville some potion or other – I saw her do it! It gave him hallucinations just like mine.'

Yvette touched my arm. 'You know, Mr. Gabriel, hallucination sometime occurrin' wid dementia.'

Lily met my gaze at last. Seeing her so contrite and sorrowful was enough. 'I doh know no Mabel, Mr. Gabriel,' she whimpered. 'Not in de U.K., I swear. How can you suspeck me of such ting?'

I did not answer but for a mile or two continued to brood, gazing out of the window at the view north-eastwards over the bays and crags of Tobago's wilder Atlantic coast. I spotted my first Yellow-headed Caracara on a wire – but was in no mood for ornithology. At the bottom of a steep hill we took a right onto the coast road and five minutes later passed a stall selling bamboo wind-chimes and hanging planters made from calabash shells. It was perched on a hairpin bend high on a cliff within sight of Scarborough. Next to it stood a wooden roti shack painted red, orange and blue. Perhaps it was the consoling waft of curry that brought me to my senses, or perhaps my unwillingness to appear unchristian in front of my friends, but I judged that I had let them stew long enough. I would give Lily the benefit of the doubt about Mabel, concluding how it must have been stress causing me to fall victim to my own conspiracy theories. On the matter of her poisoning me to delay the sale, there was little point in sulking any longer. As Lily herself might have said, 'it in de past'. I took a deep breath and turned to face them: 'Let's just forgive and forget, shall we?' I said. 'Besides, we'll be needing all our energies for this afternoon.'

Winston glanced over his shoulder. 'Spoken like a true Christian, Angel.'

27

'Not wishing to appear insensitive to your loss, Yvette,' I said an hour or so later, bringing in some late breakfast, 'but your family needs to decide when Trevor's absence can plausibly be reported without raising suspicion.'

'I go dongstairs an' discuss it right now, Gabriel.' She was frowning at me. 'You feelin' okay?'

'I'm aching in places I didn't know even existed, but I'll survive.'

I watched her out of sight and lowered myself stiffly into a dining chair. I was in fact feeling utterly sick with nerves at the thought of confronting Janice and McClung. I was also regretting the rather nasty-looking chicken-curry-and-avocado omelette I'd cobbled together from left-overs in the fridge, especially since Yvette had taken one look and declined a share of it.

Alone now, I checked my phone. There was nothing from Max as yet; only a terse message from Janice announcing their arrival at about five. The era of positive prevarication had finally run its course and I was grimly aware that it was up to me to prevail using whatever ammunition Max might supply – and my own wits, shot to pieces as they were.

Since there was nothing to do but wait in the heat of the day, I walked slowly to my room and lay down for a siesta with the air-conditioning cranked up to full blast. It seemed like only a second or two later when I was being roused by Yvette. 'Wake up,' she said, flinging open the curtains. 'You got work to do.'

I rubbed my eyes. 'What time is it?'

'Almost three. Get your shoes on!'

Ten minutes later, I was standing mystified and slightly irritated with Yvette in front of the old cocoa house. Since my last ill-fated visit, the Yale lock on the door had been removed and there was no sign of Trevor's stash. It looked as if someone had swept the place clean to remove any evidence. Archly, Yvette instructed me to pick up a pair of gardening gloves and an old spade of Churchill's then led the way up the track to the slave quarters. To my surprise, she didn't venture anywhere near where Lily had conducted the Obeah ceremony but pushed instead through thick undergrowth to the back of the ruin. Here she stopped, looking up at a rusty barred window.

'Yvette,' I said, leaning on the spade, 'would you mind telling me precisely what we're doing here? This place gives me the creeps and it's bloody hot. How long are you going to need me?'

'Ten minutes tops, Gabr—Angel. We here to break a curse.'

I couldn't believe she'd chosen now to start in with her Obeah nonsense. 'What the hell are you talking about?'

'Gabriel, please understan', my Grandma Marie laid a curse on your uncle.'

'You're joking.'

'Jesus, fella! No mo' talkin'!' Yvette actually stamped her foot. 'Normally, my mother would preside but she nuh feelin' well enough.'

I gritted my teeth. The girl was having a hard time of it too. 'All right, ten minutes, but that's your lot. What d'you want me to do?'

Yvette slapped at a mosquito on her arm. 'Mother say look for a flat slab under de window. It have a slave name carve on it to mark he grave.' I was minded to ask a question, but Yvette's raised eyebrow silenced me. 'It ent takin' long,' she pleaded, 'so dig!'

I dropped to my hands and knees in the earth, pulling away the vines and foliage which grew in profusion in this dank and sunless corner. An orangey-black land-crab scuttled sideways into the bushes. With my spade, I scraped away a mat of rotting grass and leaves until, to my surprise, I unearthed a rough pinkish stone about the size of a pillow. Further investigation with my fingertips confirmed the single word *Isaac* scratched crudely into it.

'Now,' Yvette said, 'it need liftin'.'

I dug around the stone until I could lever it up and lean it back against the brickwork. Directly beneath was what might have been a leather parcel flecked black and white with mould and bound with rotting string.

'Don' unwrap it, Angel. Jus' hand it to me.'

'I can't believe I'm even doing this.'

'Give it to me an' don' play de cynical Westerner.' She took the package and unfolded the cracked leather. Inside was a rusty tobacco tin. Producing a stubby screwdriver from her pocket, she prized off the lid and extracted a folded piece of mildewed paper. Despite continued misgivings, I felt my treacherous heart thumping as I watched her spread it out on her knee.

Written on it in faded ink were two words: *NEVILLE CASSIDY.*

'Good Lord,' I murmured.

'Mother say you now understan' why your uncle still alive when he brain is mush.'

'Yvette, I'm not really in the market for this hocus-pocus nonsense. Not today – of all days.'

The girl put a hand on my shoulder. 'Mother also say she callin' a family conference after McClung an' Baddis gone.'

'But I'm not family—'

'She request you presence in particular, Angel.'

'Well, jolly good, I look forward to it. But in the meantime, have we done here? Is this all your mother wants?'

'No, we mus' break de curse!'

'Are you telling me,' I snapped with increasing incredulity, 'that you seriously woke me up to bugger about in the undergrowth defusing some bloody Obeah spell?'

'Yes, Gabriel.'

I was powerless against the solemn fervour in those great blue eyes of hers. 'Then you'd better please explain.'

She smiled in triumph. 'So, if you need to *affeck* someone you write de offendin' person name on a paper an' bury it in a someone else's grave.'

'Ah.'

'An' our task today is to bring de curse on you uncle Neville to a termination.' Yvette pulled a matchbox from her shorts pocket and gave it to me. 'We need to burn de paper, Angel, but it goin' to be tricky because he damp. Light me one.' I struck a match and she held the paper to the flame. It took seven matches and an *ad hoc* funeral pyre of dried leaves and twigs on the pink stone to reduce the paper to ashes. 'There,' murmured my nutty young friend, stamping out the embers with her sandaled foot, 'we done. Now you believe in Obeah?'

I pushed poor Isaac's stone back into position and looked at her. 'You're really asking if I believe something's going to happen to my uncle as a result of this little charade?' I stood up and brushed off my knees. 'What should I expect? A miraculous recovery from dementia? The reversal of his prostate cancer and eternal life?'

'I tol' you already: don' be cynical. It doh suit you.'

'Alright, so tell me this: why did your grandma put a spell on Neville?'

'I don' know! Maybe mother explain later. Let's go.'

I grabbed the spade. 'If you wish to believe in the powers of Obeah,' I said, pulling back a vast fern frond to let Yvette pass, 'then that's fine by me, but you can't expect me to become a convert overnight.'

She turned and raised the eyebrow again, a shaft of sunlight illuminating her proud and beautiful face. 'But dese days,' she said, 'you mo' open to de idea, yes? Tobago changin' you mind about you own religion?'

'Maybe or maybe not.' I looked away. This wasn't the moment to engage with her on the merits or otherwise of Christian rituals. After all, what we'd just performed here in the forest was neither more nor less ludicrous than what we used to do every Sunday morning as we remembered Christ's sacrifice by consuming symbols of his body and blood. 'I'm just saying that an octogenarian developing a terminal illness is to be expected, but as a result of someone dispensing a curse...? Well, that's a whole different kettle of credulous fish.'

'Hmm,' she murmured, not looking at me. 'We talk about dat later. Right now, I mus' report back to de Obeah woman. An' after, if you is needin' me, I pickin' limes. Mother say to make fresh juice for your visitors. It so hot today.'

28

I had showered and changed when Max rang. He was serious and to-the-point and I listened to what he had so say without interrupting. 'I've done all I can,' he concluded. 'Good luck, Ange.'

'Thanks a million, Maximilian.' I hadn't said that since university. 'Fingers crossed.'

At just after four thirty, the sound of a car horn down the drive violated the late afternoon peace and sent a rush of adrenalin through me. Janice was early, meaning I had no time to search the gardens for Yvette and update her with Max's news. I had just slipped on my only jacket when a dusty maroon car pulled up at the bottom of the staircase. A skinny young chauffeur climbed out and stood to almost comical attention holding open the back door for his VIPs. He was wearing a limp black suit and an outsized peaked cap. Janice was giving him a hard time. 'Dwayne, go fill up with gas and hurry back! We don't want to be stuck here the whole night.'

I came slowly down the stairs, playing it cool and proprietorial, despite the heat and my beating heart.

Janice was wearing her most obsequious politician's smile and a tangerine orange-coloured trouser suit that hurt my eyes. 'Gabriel,' she purred, coming in for a kiss which I parried with an extended hand, 'such a pleasure. How was the U.K.?'

'Cold, wet and unpleasant, thanks for asking.'

'Wife well?'

'Blooming.'

'Allow me to introduce Mr. Bill McClung'

I had imagined him to be obese, but it was a wiry, bandy-legged little man who emerged from the car and gripped my hand, his ratty little eyes darting here and there. 'Call me Buck,' he said, laughing preposterously for reasons I couldn't fathom.

My father would have disapproved of Buck's sartorial choices: scuffed cowboy boots, spotless butterscotch trousers, pink shirt with white collar and one of those miniature bullhorn bootlace affectations round his neck. He had an overly tanned face dominated by greying handlebar moustaches and whiskers which melded seamlessly into a head of neatly coiffured, luxuriant, white curly hair. I suspected the hand of expensive outside interference in the creation of this caricature Texan, and when he had the nerve to top it all off with a white Stetson it was all I could do – despite my nerves – not to snigger. I wondered if Yvette or Lily had heard them arrive and found some vantage point from which to enjoy this charade of bonhomie.

The odious Buck was still pumping my hand. 'Pleasure to meet you, Gabe,' he drawled. 'Great location you gat here.'

'Absolutely.' Meeting his eye, though, I detected only the gaze of a dedicated demolition expert assessing the time/cost ratio of razing it all to the ground.

Dwayne backed the car away. My opponents were being abandoned here with no escape vehicle. Nonetheless, I played the cordial host and invited them up to the balcony. Janice spotted at once the bag of cash I'd left in pride of place on the coffee table. To give Baddis her due, she managed to refrain from actually drooling.

'So, Gabriel,' she said, eyes cold behind those tinted glasses. 'I was just telling Buck how you snuck back into Tobago early – and undetected. How clever of you.'

I slathered on a rictus of a grin to match hers. 'Spies let you down, did they, Assistant Secretary? But yes, I admit it, I've been back since Sunday night. I decided it would be absurd to miss Carnival by only a few hours so I hopped on an earlier flight to experience Tobago at its most ebullient and care-free.' Janice's face was a picture. 'Don't worry, I won't be asking you for the fee to change my booking.'

McClung was observing our mockingbirds at the fruit bowl. I hoped the irony of their presence would not escape him for long. He smirked at me: 'Only wish ah could'a done the same, Gabe, but urgent business kept me chained to mah desk.' He clapped me chummily on the shoulder and I wished I possessed a superpower to smack McClung so hard into the stratosphere that he wouldn't regain consciousness until he made landfall in Houston. 'Main thing is you're here today, bang on time and with – ah can't help but notice – the wherewithal for mah associate packed and packaged in readiness. You've met Janice a couple'a' times before, ah think?'

'Mm.'

'Beautiful old place, Gabe. So excited to be takin' it off your hands. Glad you and your uncle saw fit to humour me after those, ahm, initial delays. Ah run a tight ship and mah shareholders are the very devil to satisfy. Like so many o' mah women.' He winked at Janice and I bit my cheek. 'But, Gabe, you brought along the requisite paperwork?'

'Of course.' Swallowing down a bolus of nausea the size of a coconut, I reached behind the living-room door and picked up the well-travelled buff envelope. I pulled out the signed contract and handed it to him, glancing surreptitiously at my phone: four fifty-eight. 'I know the sun's not quite over the yard-arm,' I said, 'but while you're perusing that, what say you both to a glass of something cool and refreshing? Yvette would be only too happy to—ah! Here she is.'

A sound of glasses and Yvette, looking quite the part in one of her mother's floral aprons, swept in bearing aloft on one hand a tray of glasses and a jug. Her experience waiting at the Kariwak was standing her in good stead. 'Good day, Madam Assistant Secretary; Mr. McClung,' she said, all smiles. 'Might I tempt you to a glass of ice-col' lime juice? The fruit was still on the tree only a few minutes ago.' She was sharpening up her accent and delivery for their benefit. I hoped she wouldn't over-egg her performance.

McClung and Janice helped themselves from the tray. Yvette placed a glass for me on the balustrade. 'You like extra rum?'

Buck interrupted his mental undressing of the young woman. 'No thanks, honey. This'll do jus' fine. Mm, tasty.' He knocked his back. 'Most refreshin', with a kick like a young mule. Try some, Ms. Cordner. Put hairs on your chest – if you'll pardon the expression.'

Yvette withdrew to a respectful distance, a half-smile playing about her lips as she watched Janice drink.

McClung's eyes had reverted greedily to scanning the documentation for initials and signatures. Time froze as he passed the papers to Janice. Finally, they exchanged a nod.

'Excellent, Gabe,' said the Texan. 'Mission accomplished. Those lil' ol' Tropitel shareholders will be over the moon.' He pulled out a gold-plated fountain pen the size of Apollo 13. 'You know, this deal is gonna make your uncle a very rich man – an' a famous one too. Ah'm thrilled this has worked out so well for everyone. Janice, honey, you'll oblige me by witnessing?' I watched miserably as he signed with a flourish so exaggerated that it left a line of ink on the white paint of the balustrade.

'My pleasure, Buck.' Baddis licked her lips and rooted in her handbag for what was in comparison to his a pretty workaday ballpoint. With her phone grasped in her left hand, she bent forward. 'Now, where am I signing?' she asked.

I jumped as her phone jangled. I saw the caller ID before she did. A delicious moment of indecision before she put the pen down on the incomplete contract, put the phone to her ear and cleared her throat. 'Mr. Secretary? Good day!' She added an

'Excuse me' *sotto voce* to us and waddled to the far end of the balcony. There, having listened in some consternation without speaking, she seemed to realise her boss had rung off. 'Mr. McClung,' she called, a sickly grin on her face, 'might I have a word? In private? There've been, ehh, developments.'

The Texan snorted, 'Chrissakes! Now what?' and scuttled to her side. Animatedly, they whispered together, McClung glancing at me now and again, his face contorted with white-hot fury. My heart was going like a jackhammer.

'Well, well, Cassidy,' hissed the Texan, marching back towards me a moment later with his fists clenched. 'Your team has been busy.'

I breathed again. I could afford to enjoy this. 'My team, Mr. McClung? I have no team. You may yourself benefit from armies of legal beagles scattered across the globe but I have only the one lowly U.K. solicitor.'

'Whatever.' McClung cleared his throat noisily, red blotches erupting even through the fake tan on his cheeks. He seemed to be chewing on something. 'Now see here, ah flew all the way down to the Caribbean with the express intention of signing off on a deal to drag this godforsaken fleapit into the twenty-first century. Jeez, ah even brought along mah ceremonial silver spade to cut the first sod. It brings me luck. Used it all over the world.'

I smiled. 'I'm sure you have, Mr. McClung. I bet you were looking forward to bulldozing a mangrove swamp or two as well.'

He held my gaze, a hand to his throat. 'It's true, there ain't nothin' ah likes better than operating heavy earth-movin' machinery.' His eye fell on the contract. He picked up Janice's biro and with an odd screeching noise, snapped it in two and hurled the pieces into the bushes below. 'But there seems to have bin a change of plan. That not right, Ms. Cordner?' He coughed. 'You better do the explainin' in case ah'm overcome by an urge to kill someone. Besides, ah gat calls to make.' He pulled out his phone and strode away, coughing more insistently, struggling to clear his throat.

'Of course, sir, Mr. McClung, sir.' Janice's voice rang hollow with panic, her eyes darting between me and the bag containing her hoped-for windfall. 'Mr. Cassidy,' she grated at me, the effort of speaking causing her too to cough, 'perhaps you can guess who that was on the phone.'

'How nice for you to receive a call from your boss. Isn't he the Minister blokey responsible for – if I remember rightly – the "Tobago, Clean, Green, Safe and Serene" campaign? I looked him up only the other day. Sounds like an honourable sort of chap.'

She glared at me, emitted a more than usually revolting porcine snort and ingested about a litre of mucus. She was abominable. 'Yes,' she snarled, 'and he has just received a formal enquiry from an investigative journalist named Donna Gibson at *The New York Times*.'

'How serendipitous,' I remarked, feigning mystification.

'The Secretary tells me that the House of Assembly cannot be seen to be involved in bobol and, given certain allegations of violence, corruption and coercion cited by this journalist busybody, the Tropitel project in Tobago is dead in the water.'

'As dead as the coral reef at Buccoo would have been,' I said, my heart ready to burst.

'Buck has the final word, of course.' Janice gripped her throat, tried to swallow but only collapsed into a coughing fit again. I had no idea what the matter was with these two. Surely they couldn't both be allergic to lime juice?

At the other end of the balcony, McClung seemed to have decided to capitulate. He was yelling at some lawyer in Texas, his voice strangulated, eyes watering. He was also staring daggers at Janice. Finally, he flung his hat onto a sofa and squawked, 'Rudi, they're threatening a public fucking enquiry, so just pull the plug like ah said!' He pocketed the phone, leant over the balustrade and hawked into the bushes. 'Christ, whassa matter with me?'

He turned a face the colour of puréed plums towards me: 'Cassidy, d'you know why the press should have seized upon today of all days to upset mah investors? My market value is plummeting!'

I tried – and failed, I suspect – to suppress my tone of triumph. 'I really couldn't comment, Mr. McClung.'

Buck collapsed into a chair and closed his eyes. He seemed to be having difficulty in catching his breath. In the twilight I saw Yvette approach and offer him a bottle of water.

Janice whispered to me, 'You may have won this battle, Cassidy, but not the war.' Emitting a sucking, honking noise like a drain being rodded, she helped herself to two packets of cash from my hold-all and slipped them into her handbag. 'I'm sure you won't begrudge me some expenses.'

'Oh, be my guest, Janice.' I despised this woman. 'And by the way, couple of things I meant to ask: were you behind that revolting little souvenir I found impestilating my luggage in the U.K.?'

She lowered her eyelids and, with some effort, smirked. '"Give a dog a bone"? Isn't that one of your British sayings?' Baddis belched. 'I think one of Officer Cleve's subordinates at airport security came up with the idea.' She was wracked by a fit of coughing so ferocious I almost felt sorry for her.

'I see,' I said when she was once again in a position to listen. 'There's one more thing: the sultry Mabel, my uncle's nurse? I take it she's in your pay? Just nod or shake your head.' This time Janice looked at me as if I were mad and vigorously shook her head. 'My mistake,' I said, shrugging, Mabel's status as a product of my own paranoia confirmed. 'Must have been imagining things.'

McClung beckoned me over, still breathing with difficulty. He had loosened the bootlace thing at his collar and, with much grimacing, was undoing his top shirt button. 'So, Cassidy,' he spat, 'seems you outsmarted us this time.'

'Possibly, Mr. McClung, although Janice seems to think she hasn't finished with me yet.' I collected up the contract and ripped it into eight, allowing the pieces to flutter over the balcony. Something for Kenny to chew on later. 'I fear she's planning on sending one of her hired thugs to catch me off-guard one dark night but, you know, in order to save even the smallest piece of Tobago, I'm willing to take the risk.'

McClung seemed to reach a decision. He coughed again, beads of sweat bursting out on his furrowed brow. 'You know, Cassidy, ah'd be the last person to give in to press blackmail, but a compromise has occurred to me: mah shareholders would be just as pleased with an extension of Tropitel's ongoing developments in Barbados and Grenada – if ah couch the potential financial gain in the right terms.' The man had moved on; Shurland was already a footnote, a rare failure to be deposited deep in Tropitel's archives. 'Cassidy, ah'm aware you'd rather we pulled out for ecological reasons, but that ain't mah style.' His voice cracked as he made this declaration of U.S. Republican environmental unrepentance. He put a hand to his throat and, with a sound like the cry of a mating corncrake, gave in to another fit of hacking that made my eyes water. What was going on? I felt absolutely fine for once.

'Cordner, we're outta here,' McClung said, grabbing his hat and moving with difficulty to the top of the stairs.

I detected a heady mix of pure regret and panic in Janice's eyes. She was still eyeing the money. 'B-buck, the driver's not yet back with the car. I'm so sorry.'

'Fuck you, *Assistant* Secretary! This whole disaster is down to you and your shit staff-work.' The man took off his hat again and threw himself into a sofa. 'Call that bastard driver now!' His voice was almost gone.

A second or two later and Janice broke the early-evening birdsong with a sudden screech into her phone: 'No way! Make it three minutes max, asshole, or you're dead meat!' She wobbled towards me, tugging at her neck-scarf and levelling her most malign gaze upon me. I imagined she was missing Pablo. 'What in Jesus's name have you and your slut done to us, Cassidy?' She was struggling for breath like an asthmatic, hair undone, composure in tatters.

'You callin' me slut, Baddis?' Yvette had appeared at my side, all pretence at educated accent evaporated. 'Dat rich, comin' from a woman wid you reputation. What? You no answer meh? Frog in de throat?' Yvette was prodding Janice's shoulder with an index finger. 'You people allergic to lime juice? Or monkey don' see his tail draggin' in shit?' Acclimatising to these turns of phrase was going to take years. 'But doh worry about a ting. You soon feelin' better. Is a passin' *inconvenience.*'

With McClung and Janice out of action and at my mercy until their ride appeared, it seemed too good an opportunity to waste for a spot of sermonising. I glanced out at the majestic view fading in the evening light and said, 'So, Buck, shall we call this failure to broker a deal payback time for my bruises and humiliations –and what these good people have been through fearing they would lose their home?'

'Whaa?' gurgled McClung.

I stepped over and, while Janice was occupied with another coughing fit, rooted in her handbag to retrieve the money she had so recently stolen. I showed the wads to McClung before tossing them to Yvette. 'As far as I can see, you two are nothing more than a pair of morally corrupt corporate vandals.' The pair stared at me bulgy-eyed. Merciful headlights flickered through the trees down the drive. 'Listen, your lift is here so don't let me keep you. And Janice, I've just had a thought: if your boss is really opening an enquiry, it might be a good time to make yourself scarce. Texas is pleasant at this time of year, I hear. I'd start packing if I were you. That should keep you out of my hair.' If looks could kill. 'Shame: such a promising career in politics thwarted by dishonesty, greed and bobol.' She was making noises like chickpeas in a blender. I pressed home my advantage. 'And Buck, do have a safe trip home and, if I may say, look after Janice during her exile. Make sure she earns her keep. I know how you MAGAs love a refugee.'

A horn sounded and, spluttering in their impotence, McClung and Janice hauled themselves out of the sofa. They were in a sorry state, hawking and gagging, eyes running with silent tears. As they reached the bottom of the stairs, I called: 'Oh, by the way, Janice, whatever happened to good old Pablo? I've been expecting him to turn up unannounced all day. But, you know, I've been out and about so maybe he—' I couldn't resist it, '—just caiman went.'

With a final look of hatred, Baddis shoved aside the terrified chauffeur and squeezed her bulk into the car. A moment later, to the sound of yapping fury from Churchill's dogs, the vehicle was out of sight.

29

'You'll forgive my natural curiosity,' I said, rubbing in an offhand way at McClung's ink stain on the balustrade paintwork, 'but would someone please explain what just happened?'

Lily and Yvette had appeared arm in arm at the top of the stairs, their expressions a comedic picture of smug defiance. 'Oh, you understan', Mr. Gabriel,' giggled the mother, a little out of breath, 'as Obeah woman, I make meh own small contribution.'

I did the eyebrow thing these Pitt women favoured. 'Is that so? Do tell.'

'So,' she said, 'seein' de clientele, I decide to employ a traditional spell – always effective. Yvette, darlin', can you please locate our assistant?' I watched bemused as her daughter dropped to all fours to peer around her at floor level. 'You see him, gyal?'

'Cool your herbs, mother!' Yvette reached behind a large pot-plant near the stairs. 'Come on, Kenny... got you!' She lifted out a disconsolate-looking crapaud whose mouth had been clamped shut with a small yellow padlock I recognised.

'What have you done to the poor thing?' I cried. 'And that's mine! It's off my bag.'

Yvette produced the tiny key from her pocket and while Lily held the sulking amphibian still, unlocked the device. She then reached a little finger into his mouth and hooked out a slip of paper which she unfolded and showed me.

I read the two names on it. 'Don't say you wove a spell to silence my adversaries.'

Lily looked offended. 'Mr. Angel Gabriel, people in trouble always askin' me for help. Las' November I stop de mouth of a unsympathetic prosecution witness wid de same spell. It on de TV news. I is notorious.'

I folded my arms and sighed. 'No one's denying that, Lily, but what's not so plausible is the notion that you simply scribbled the names of that pair of corrupt hypocrites on a scrap of paper, folded it neatly and then padlocked it into a crapaud's mouth! And this, you want me to believe, caused the buggers' throats to close up so much they couldn't utter a coherent word for coughing and spluttering. That is some serious dark magic.'

Yvette took up the thread. 'Sure is, Angel! I knew you'd understand. On de day of de trial, I wen' dong early and put Kenny on de courthouse steps.'

'And, don't tell me, the witness named lost the power of speech?'

'Yip, an' today is de turn of Baddis an' McClung.'

'Right.' I was falling down an *Alice in Wonderland* rabbit hole, but it seemed not to matter any more. 'I suppose we're talking the same principle as burying my uncle's name in Isaac's grave.'

Yvette smiled. 'Truth,' she said, and reached for a large leaf-shaped moth minding its own business near a security lamp. This she gave to the crapaud. 'For your trouble, Kenny.' Then she carried the misused creature downstairs and released him under a bush, the wriggling moth still tight in his mouth.

I looked out to sea for a moment; perhaps a rational explanation for the bizarre silencing of our visitors would come to me. Drawing a blank, I braced myself for confrontation. 'Ladies,' I said, pursing my lips in the Tobagonian way, 'tell me the truth now: have you anything else to confess?'

For a moment neither spoke. Then, with Yvette grinning guiltily, Lily blew out her cheeks. 'Okay so, Mr. Angel, what also happen is I instruct Yvette to crush sap out of a dumb-cane leaf and stir it in de lime juice.'

'Ah.'

'As back-up in case Kenny fail, you understan'.' She indicated the pot-plant which had concealed the toad. 'Dieffenbachia. It cause temporary swellin' in de throat.'

I turned to Yvette. 'Which is why you so thoughtfully gave me my own glass.'

'Of course.'

I sighed. 'So although it's a win to the Obeah woman and her apprentice... you needn't have worried.' I reached behind me and produced Trevor's gun from under my jacket. 'I had the situation covered. Just as well it didn't come to a shoot-out, though, because I've no idea how to use the bloody thing.'

'Lors,' whispered Lily to her daughter, 'our retired insurance broker now a gangster.'

Holding the muzzle pointed towards the garden, I fiddled with the weapon in an attempt to disarm it. The clip however refused to come out.

'Jesus, man, give it here,' hissed Yvette, and with a deft twist and a click the vile thing was made safe. She shook out the bullets onto the coffee table.

My turn again to be astonished by these women. 'How on earth do you know how to do that?'

Lily nodded sagely. 'Wise gyal take no chances.'

I splayed my lips, pressed my tongue against my upper teeth and sucked. A strangely satisfactory noise like bathwater down a plughole issued from between my clamped jaws.

Lily let fly a noise like a parrot. 'You steups at meh? I never hear mo', boy!' Yvette laughed and squeezed my wrist. 'You a real Tobagonian now!'

'Mr. Angel Gabriel,' declared Lily when she had finished mocking my efforts, 'I goin' dongstairs order roti from Chanderpaul in de village.'

'Good idea,' I said. 'Supper on me. I'll put some beers in the freezer.'

With Lily and Yvette downstairs, I texted Max to thank him for his sterling work with his sister and pass on the good news about Shurland. I had just pressed "send" when an email from him pinged into my phone.

Dear Angel,

I am the bearer of sad news. Your uncle Neville died peacefully this afternoon at about three o'clock. I was with him only a couple of hours earlier having been summoned to amend his Will. I know you'll be feeling conflicted, but please accept my sincerest condolences.

Off the record, I can report that yesterday Neville asked the ever-obliging Mabel – the one you erroneously insist is a spy – to read and re-read him that Tobago environmentalist's article you left. During a whispered conversation in the driveway, Mabel told me your uncle had undergone a curious transformation, becoming almost contrite since your last visit. She put this down to a) a fear of meeting his maker and b) the contents of the newspaper article. This might have explained his desire that I redraft the Will. As you are one of the beneficiaries, I am attaching details.

I glanced through the bullet points and leant back in the sofa. A gecko cocked his head and peered at me expectantly from a curtain rail. I closed my eyes and waited for a surge of sadness that never came, proof if ever it were needed that I was indeed conflicted.

At seven-fifteen a motorbike puttered to a halt outside with a cardboard box containing our food. Lily, Yvette, Churchill and I sat at the table on the balcony to eat together for the first time.

While Yvette unpacked the roti, I described the role Max and his admirable sister had played in scuppering Tropitel's plans. 'It was a shame McClung didn't pull out for either honourable or ecological reasons,' I said. 'I suppose the threat of a scandal and its financial implications will have to suffice.'

My explanations over, Lily struggled to her feet. 'Today a sad one for a mother who lose a son, but a happy day for Shurland.' She raised her bottle. 'So, tank you, Mr. Angel, for all you done to protec' us from eviction. We all deep in yuh debt.'

I rose and embraced her. 'Tobago is where I belong now. I'm the one who should be thanking you.'

'We see about dat, Mr. Gabriel,' Lily said.

Yvette looked sharply at her mother. 'What do you mean?'

'I tell y'all after we eat.'

We ate in silence in an atmosphere laden with an unspoken something until, seeing we had more or less finished, Churchill declared, 'Eh-ehh, dat tasty an' nourishin'! Chanderpaul make de best roti on de island.' He reached once more into the box and lifted out a polystyrene container brimming with something bearing a strong resemblance to congealed Caribbean-coloured paint sprinkled with a darker blue powder to match. 'Dessert!' he crowed exultantly. 'Chanderpaul wife speciality!'

Melodramatically, I held up a hand to protect my eyes from the thing's unnatural glow. 'Unfortunately,' I said, 'I'm stuffed.'

'Maybe later, Mr. Gabriel?'

'Daddy,' said Lily, 'no one wan' dat sweet an' sickly stuff now. An' anyways, I have sometin' to say.' She seemed to have aged ten years in the two weeks I had known her. 'Yvette, Mr. Angel, prepare for a long story.'

'I too have announcements to make,' I said, thinking of Max's email, 'but you go first, Lily.'

'Yes, go on, mother.'

Lily paused for a moment, gazing out into the darkness. A moth fluttered about the single lampshade overhead. 'Well, y'all need to go back quite 1963.'

'Year of Hurricane Flora,' put in Churchill, spinning an empty beer bottle.

'You often tol' me about this, mother.'

'Yes, darlin', but I never tol' you of de double catastrophe to strike at de heart of Mr. Neville. At de time he jus' marry Miss Beryl, beautiful daughter of de High Commissioner—'

'My wife Marie mo' beautiful,' interrupted Churchill.

'Daddy! Who tellin' de story?'

The old man squeezed the bridge of his nose. 'You got any rum up here, Mr. Angel?'

'Well, actually yes—'

'No, he can do widout for once.' Lily patted my hand as Churchill subsided into his chair. 'So, you know, Mr. Angel, your uncle own Shurland – house, plantation an' forest – an' he employ Churchill and Marie as estate manager and housekeeper. Den October '63 come de hurricane. Plantation, it flatten. Poor Miss Beryl, she get kill by a sheet of galvanize.'

I was reminded of that horrible hallucination I'd had on this very spot so many lives ago. Yvette snorted with impatience. 'Mother, we know!'

Lily ignored her. 'Naturally, Mr. Neville, he devastated. He sack de workers, start to drink.'

'Let me tell it now, Lil,' said Churchill with a paternal gentleness I had not seen before. 'You go only upset yourself.' Lily nodded and closed her eyes. 'You see, Mr. Gabriel,' he went on, 'after de storm, only me and Marie kep' on as worker. An' maybe Mr. Neville, he grievin', or maybe he drunk, but on de very day he put Miss Beryl in de ground he went lookin' for my own wife, Marie. He foun' her busy tryin' to straighten out de cocoa house.' Churchill paused a moment, his eyes also drawn to the darkness of the sea. 'Marie never tol' me what happen exackly,' he said, 'but Lily was de outcome.'

Yvette stared. 'You never tol' me it Mr. Neville,' she whispered, slipping an arm round her mother's shoulders. 'I thought it some fly-by-night workin' on de banana boat.'

Lily was in tears. 'Now allyuh know de truth.'

Horror then shame had risen within me. 'Lily,' I murmured, my mouth dry, 'I'm appalled... so sorry, I... don't know what to say.'

'Not your fault, Mr. Angel.'

Churchill wandered stiffly to lean on the balustrade, a hand rubbing at his white whiskers. 'As y'all know,' he went on, 'Marie was Obeah woman. As soon as she find she wid child, up she went to de slave quarters and lay a curse on de Englishman.' He wagged a long finger at me. 'Dis why your uncle cyan' die': Marie curse scramblin' he brain.'

Lily put in, 'Maybe now de curse broken, ting changin'.'

My own somehow anticipated news would have to wait until this awful tale came to a close. 'Dementia is certainly a curse,' I added, lamely.

Lily looked at me, her face grim. 'My mother, she cussed Mr. Neville alright. Of course, he always deny responsibility so Marie and Churchill – Lord bless dem – bring me up as their own. Meanwhile dat man he carry on drinkin' an' whorin' in Scarborough, an' treatin' us as slave – an' never raisin' a finger to help wid my upbringin'. But dese blue eyes of mine, Mr. Angel, dey his.'

I had been staring at a heart-shaped stain on the sofa cushion. 'Which explains your blue eyes too, Yvette,' I said. 'But, I feel I must ask, who is – was – your father?'

'Oh, he a fisherman from Parlatuvier.' Did I detect a hint of uncertainty in her voice? 'But he drown when I was small. Everyone know dat.'

Lily drew in a long breath and pressed Yvette's hand to her breast. 'It true I fall in love wid a fisherman up de coast, name Anthony. He certainly Trevor father but he...' She stopped, eyes cast down. Churchill moved behind her, his hands on her shoulders.

'What, mother? Tell me.'

'Anthony ent your father.'

Yvette eyes opened wide. 'What? All dese years I livin' a lie? Who in Jesus name my real father?' She tried to get up, but Lily had her fast by the wrist.

'Be patient, gyal. Let me explain.' She took both her daughter's hands and kissed the fingertips. 'Mr. Neville eventually move to Trinidad and become teacher dong Pointe-à-Pierre.'

'June fifteenth, 1967,' muttered Churchill, scratching at his neck. 'A day for rejoicin' I no likely to forget. No more mistreatment, no more hollerin' and breakin' furniture. I fetch he to de ferry an' make certain he gone. An' he stay almost thirty years, tank de Lord, leavin' us alone to run Shurland as guesthouse an' bird sanctuary – an' payin' us a pittance. An' I tellin' you, Mr. Gabriel, when Marie drop dead of heart attack she still workin' as Shurland cook and Obeah woman.'

'So despite my uncle's utterly dreadful conduct, you continued to devote your lives to Shurland,' I said, my stomach trembling with emotion. 'Lily, please carry on.'

She sighed again. 'Just before Christmas 1998, Mr. Neville come back to Shurland for a las' weekend before retirin' to England. I was thirty-three an' establishin' myself as Obeah woman. Mr. Neville, he nearly sixty. But still *strong*.'

Some instinct made me rise to my feet, the white weatherboarding of the house swimming before my eyes. Yvette was looking stricken, eyes fixed upon her mother. I spoke: 'Please don't tell me my uncle was drunk again. Not that.'

'No, Mr. Gabriel, it worse: he stone-cold sober. At five o'clock, day before he flew out for de las' time, he send my dad out to buy supper.'

'Fresh fish.' Churchill's voice was almost inaudible. 'Mahi-mahi from Captain Stanley.'

Lily took Yvette's face in her hands. 'I still remember Mr. Neville words, what he tell me dat night. He say he want to experience de "magic of de ol' place one las' time".' I was staring at her, my ears whistling. 'I keepin' de secret so long... but, yes, my own father, he also father to my daughter.' She puckered her lips. 'So, Mr. Angel, because of Mr. Neville, we all family here.'

The shimmering silence that followed this second revelation was broken only by the buzz of cigalles. Without a word, Yvette rose and disappeared inside. I heard her crying in the kitchen.

I squeezed Lily's shoulder and went to stand at the far end of the balcony for a moment. The time was fast approaching when I would have to break the news to them that my uncle, in spite of his cavalier, racist past and appalling lack of care for others, had with his last breath tried to make amends.

'Mr. Angel,' called Churchill, 'I takin' Lily dongstairs now. We see you in de mornin'.'

'No, Churchill, wait,' I said. 'I've some things to say too. We just need Yvette.' But the girl was already standing at the sitting room door, head bowed. I walked over, took her hand and led her back to her mother.

'We all family now,' Lily was whispering through her tears. 'All family.'

I held both their hands. 'You and Churchill have known all along, Lily, but for Yvette and me, this shocking information comes as a bolt out of the blue.'

'I should've tol' you long ago, Mr. Angel – an' you, darlin' Yvette, but—'

'Lily, it really doesn't matter,' I said. 'The timing of such an announcement makes no difference now.' I forced a smile. 'But, you know... it's wonderful we're actually related, if not by blood. It sort of explains the bond I've always felt between us – an understanding.' Lily stood and I put my arms round them both. 'Churchill, come and join in.' The old man leant against Lily rather than embracing us wholeheartedly. What must it have been like for him to witness these revelations and reconciliations after half a century of unspoken resentment towards my uncle? Unable to trust my voice, I whispered, 'Everything seems to make sense now.'

Yvette let out a deep sigh. 'Today I thought losin' one family member was enough, but now I lost two. But I gained another, haven't I?' She looked up at me, her eyes full of tears. 'But I not your cousin. My mum, she your cousin. You an' me, Angel, we are firs' cousin *an'* firs' cousin-once-removed. I been makin' de calculation.'

I kissed her forehead. 'I'll take your word for it.'

'Now come sit down, fella,' Lily said, indicating the sofa. 'What you got to tell us? You ain't leavin'?'

'Not if I can help it, but I do have news.' I squeezed in between her and Yvette while Churchill shuffled to the top of the stairs ready to make a dash for his rum as soon the time was right. 'The first thing is that on the dam this morning I reached a decision and I set in motion divorce proceedings.' I pulled off my wedding ring and set it on the table.

Lily put a hand to her throat. 'Serious?'

'Yup. I shan't be seeing Sarah again. I now know for sure it's the right thing to do. Not that it'll be plain sailing: she'll threaten me with being "withdrawn from" and all that—'

Yvette looked up sharply. 'Meanin'?'

'Christadelphians don't believe in divorce, you see, so in the eyes of God Sarah and I remain forever married. This implies that my former friends, colleagues and family members will close ranks and I'll be sort of exiled from both their society and the Ecclesia. It's their way of protecting themselves.'

Lily put a hand on my arm. 'You okay wid dat?'

'I think I'll be able to cope, especially with the support of my new family and four and a half thousand miles of ocean between Sarah and me. I must take the view that it'd be a sorry excuse for a God who'd wish a life of inauthenticity and indolence upon any

281

of his flock.' I glanced around. 'Sarah's going to be devastated, I'm afraid, but I'm hoping she'll agree to my terms and won't cut up too rough.'

One of my cousins steupsed, but I couldn't tell which.

'Terms?' rumbled Churchill, leaning against the balustrade. 'What terms, boy?'

'Max is writing to inform her she's welcome to everything we jointly own in England—'

'But, Gabriel!' shrieked Yvette. 'You givin' away you share in de house an' ting?'

'Oh, Sarah can have the place with my blessing. I always hated it. Having sold my company I've more than enough to see me through, especially as we have no children. As for my belongings... well, it's only stuff. Sarah's welcome to it as a souvenir of twenty-five years of moribund arranged marriage. I have everything I need here, don't I? I suspect, though, that my worldly goods and chattels will be in bin bags and dumped at the charity shop before the week's out. Time to move on.' I put my arms round the women again and held them tight. 'I hope Sarah will find it in her heart to forgive me one day, but Tobago is where I belong now. With my own people.'

'You full of surprises, Mr. Gabriel,' continued Churchill. 'What de other news?'

'Well, it's about my uncle—'

'Mr. Neville?'

'Yes.' I was aware of muscles in my belly quivering with emotion. 'He died today.'

'Today?' Yvette was on her feet. 'What time, Gabriel?'

'Actually at about the time we burnt the paper with his name on.' Yvette sniffed and lowered her eyelids. 'And don't you look at me like that, young miss. I'm sure it was just a coincidence.'

'Like I tol' you, de curse released,' said Yvette. 'But all de same, dat man who was my father an' who I never goin' to meet now, he no longer sufferin'.' She burst into tears. 'May he rest in peace.'

'Amen,' responded Lily, dabbing at her eyes. 'Come here, darlin'.'

I bowed my head as the two consoled each other and after a long moment heavy with emotion, I cleared my throat. 'There has been, however, yet another development.' The eyes of my new family were upon me. 'An hour or two before he passed away, Neville amended his Will.'

Lily's voice was almost inaudible. 'Shurland yours?'

'As it happens, no.' I took a deep breath. 'I am fortunate enough to be inheriting his house in England but... well, the thing is, he left the Shurland estate to... to someone else... on the condition it not be sold.'

'Someone else?' murmured Lily.

'Until a few minutes ago I was at a loss to understand his reasoning, but now I get it. He did in fact leave it to a person named in the document as his granddaughter...' I glanced at my young cousin in momentary confusion. 'Presumably to stop tongues wagging.' I reached behind a cushion and handed over the envelope of property deeds I'd carted halfway across the planet. 'Shurland is yours, Yvette.'

30

Astonishment gave way gradually to a grim satisfaction at this turn of events. Lily spoke first: 'I has no desire to speak ill of de departed, but it seem to me like Mr. Neville tryin' las' minute for absolution.'

Churchill looked exhausted. 'I amazed Mr. Neville come good at de last but right now I needin' a drink an' a lie-down.' Solemnly shaking my hand, he made his way unsteadily to the staircase, patting Yvette's shoulder as he passed.

Shurland's new proprietor was silently leafing through the paperwork, shaking her head and blinking now and again as if to clear the mists of incredulity and incomprehension. Lily meanwhile had ceased her nervous plumping of the cushions and was starting to clear the table. I took her elbow. 'Lily, stop,' I said gently, taking the pile of plates from her. 'Sit yourself down for heaven's sake and let me do the chores for once. You've been through enough in the past thirty-six hours and there's no further need to play housekeeper. As you said, we're all family now.'

'No, Mr. Gabriel,' she retorted, 'you done all de important work, so you relax, fella! Plus an' too besides, I been providin' for people here for forty years an' shall continue so.'

I looked across at Yvette and sighed. 'Well, I've tried my best with her.'

'I know, Angel. Mother, she set in her ways.'

Lily was indeed unrepentant and soon reappeared with her apron full of ice-cold beer bottles. She lowered herself into a seat. 'I ent learnin' no new routines, Mr. Angel, nuh 'til after my Trevor lay to rest.'

Yvette said, 'On dat subjec', we surely expectin' a visit from Cleve?'

Lily jumped as if bitten by a soucouyant. 'I ent say?' she whooped. 'Cleve mother, she call meh earlier, she crying: her boy been retrenched from de police an' dem! He too often drunk an' now workin' by a security firm in Diego Martin in Trinidad. Dey offer Cleve post as Turtle Warden in Tobago but he say No. So Officer Cleve, he ent botherin' us no mo'.'

'I'll drink to that,' I said, opening a bottle of Carib for her. 'But listen, I've just had an idea: why don't you and Churchill come and live upstairs? There are, er, plenty bedrooms.'

Lily dismissed my plan with a wave of her hand. 'Oh, dat kind, Mr. Angel, but we happy dongstairs. It would feel wrong. Beside, de new owner, she might have other ideas.'

Yvette smiled and stuffed the deeds into their envelope. 'We jus' need to concentrate on creatin' a desirable ecolodge like Mr. Gabriel first suggested. Earn money from de birdin' community.'

I said, 'Might you need an extra pair of hands?'

Yvette grinned. 'All de help I can get. Mother, she sure to be retirin' soon.'

A steups from Lily. 'Oh-ho! You people too harden! I continue workin' 'til I drop dead like Marie my mother!' She reached over and pinched Yvette's chin. 'Besides, gyal, soon you an' me startin' you official Obeah trainin'.'

'Serious?' cried Yvette.

'Sure.'

She kissed her mother and turned to me, her face alight. 'So, Angel, you really in?'

'I'd be honoured.' The three of us clinked bottles. My phone rang. A local number. 'Excuse me, ladies,' I said. 'This better not be the police.'

Yvette frowned. 'Newspaper more like.'

In the style of Janice and McClung, I walked slowly along the balcony. 'Hello?'

'Gabriel?' came a familiar voice. 'Maisha here. You nuh dead?'

'Oh, good night, Maisha! No, still here by the skin of my teeth. I was going to call... there's plenty news.'

'What happenin'?'

'Long story.'

There was a silence. 'You got some explainin' to do, fella.'

'I agree. When do we meet?'

'Gabriel, it have Ash Wednesday beach lime at No Man's Land tonight.' This was where McClung had been planning to build his hotels. 'I been cookin' pelau chicken all day, an' Roots he bringin' de drink truck.'

'Am I invited?'

'What you tink? Allyuh welcome. Ten o'clock. Be there if you ent wan' see me vex.'

'Anything but that. You can rely on me.'

When I ended the call my cousins were looking at me with barely concealed suspicion. 'What?' I enquired, feeling my cheeks redden. 'It's only an invitation to a party at No Man's Land.'

Eyebrows were up. 'Who Maisha?' they asked in unison.

'Someone I met at Jouvert. Is that okay?' Neither responded so I added, 'You're both invited, of course.'

Lily said, 'Yvette, you go wid him. It hardly appropriate for meh to go limin' today.' She looked me full in the eye. 'You a dark horse, Mr. Angel. Wherever you go, one set of bacchanal will follow.' She finished her beer. 'Now you two go an' enjoy yourself. An' Yvette, give dis Maisha gyal – an' everyone on de beach – a message from me.'

'A message?'

'Make certain dey know it was yuh cousin – our very own Angel – who help safeguard Tobago for us all.'

I laughed. 'Oh, please, I—'

Yvette pressed a finger to my lips. 'Sshh, Angel! It all over de news tomorrow: termination of a drug cartel an' Tobago saved from catastrophe.'

I shook my head and with some success tried out an 'Eh-ehh, allyuh people too harden.'

Fifteen minutes later, Lily had kissed us both goodnight and retired downstairs. With an hour at least before we were due to leave for the beach, Yvette and I sat in companionable silence on Shurland's balcony. I gazed out mesmerised as a breathless moon stippled the surface of the sea with shards of diamond. Fireflies danced against the undergrowth whilst above us in the samaan tree, a jumbie bird piped its mournful song from its customary branch. Down the hill beyond the garden, the waves boomed their eternal refrain upon a deserted shore.

The familiar creak of a door downstairs; Churchill was emerging from his lair. I hauled myself out of my favourite chair and leaned over the balustrade. 'Goodnight, Churchill.'

'Goodnight,' he intoned, lifting his cutlass in salutation. 'Enjoy limin' tonight. An' take good care of my lil gyal.'

'I promise.'

'One ting mo', Mr. Angel.'

'Yes?'

'Welcome to Paradise.' Churchill gave a low whistle and, dogs at his heels, shambled off into the night.

The End

Acknowledgements, notes and discussion points for book clubs

Twenty years ago, my wife-to-be (herself born and brought up in Trinidad & Tobago) invited me to join her on a trip to experience her beloved homeland. Little did I suspect that during this first visit I was being auditioned as suitable husband material. However, I passed her test with at least a high Merit because, like my hero Gabriel, I immediately relished the islands' colours and contrasts, interacted with the inhabitants and developed a lasting obsession with photographing its extraordinary bird life. I am now irrevocably invested in the ecological wellbeing of Tobago and the welfare of its people – with some of whom I have forged lifelong friendships, and in whose company, like Gabriel, I feel completely at home. To my wife Julie Baker, then – for all the above, for her textual edits, for tolerating an ofttimes mutinous author/husband, and for cajoling me out of my own Eurocentric comfort zone – I am profoundly grateful.

With regard to Obeah traditions and Tobago folklore, I am indebted to Giselle Alleyne, Maisha Oben, Nicole Richards, Nikeisha Alfonso, Africka Alexander, Trevor McBarrow, Cheri-Ann Pascall, Wendy Mohammed, Shurland James, Randall

Dubery and, most of all, Regina Dumas and Desmond Wright at the Cuffie River ecolodge. Vivid first-hand reports of supernatural goings-on were my initial inspiration to begin writing, and these have – most of them – been included in this story. I am also grateful to Yvonne Ramsey-Asankuthus for plot inspiration derived from the blue of her eyes, and to Tele Cruz for allowing me to use both the name of his bar and that of the Fog Angels J'ouvert and Mas Band for the Carnival scenes.

I am particularly grateful to Matt and Jayne Mitchell, he for being the original adopted Ghanaian and his wife for countenancing the thought of her husband's story being fictionalised in the first place. Huge thanks too to Carol Kent and Trisha Baker for their work in checking the novel's religious content, and to Emma Lee-Potter, Andrew Eames, David Pick and Rachel Lee-Young who read drafts at various stages and made endlessly supportive and constructive comments. Special thanks though must go to Joanne Husain and Faraaz Abdool for their dedicated labour in narrative continuity and the wrangling of my dialogue into colloquial Trini.

However, the novel would never have reached fruition without the painstaking work of my editor and literary guru, KT Forster. She it was who withstood blasts of bad-temper and outraged ego from an author who on occasion (i.e. *usually*) needed a day or two to realise that the striking though of a word, sentence or entire paragraph was all to the good. I thank KT for her patience, advice, good humour and unstinting support.

* * * * *

For those tempted to visit Tobago – and I hope that will be many – all locations I describe first-hand and, as this book goes to print, remain as quaint or beautiful as Gabriel found them. There are photos of actual locations, inspirational faces and birds at the

Angel in Tobago website. The ruined hotel at Arnos Vale, for example, setting for Gabriel's kidnapping, still exists, albeit in an increasingly dilapidated state. It is my habit (when visiting the bay to snorkel) to trespass up the rickety outside staircase and inspect the fruit bats which inhabit its long abandoned and decaying bedrooms. Ironically, as I shall explain, the fate of the property now depends upon the arrival of an imaginative entrepreneur to save it from encroaching forest and the depredations of vandals.

Julie and I have stayed many times at Grafton, the former plantation house I call Shurland and have watched birds and sunrises from its magical balcony. Indeed, in 2008 we were married on Stonehaven Beach. We had planned to hold the ceremony at Rocky Point but were prevented from doing so by the fact that the beach had a few weeks before been washed away during a storm. I can report, though, that the sand has once more returned. During this first visit too, we encountered a family grieving for a lost son around a burnt-out car.

However, this is all by-the-by because, as Faraaz Abdool wrote in his foreword, in a stroke of supreme malignant serendipity, Rocky Point – the very location for my fictional Tropitel development – is now under threat from Superior Hotels Trinidad & Tobago Ltd who intend, with the blessing of the current government, to "develop" it in the teeth of environmental objections and despite the majority of hotel bedrooms on the island remaining empty. *Angel in Tobago* was completed just before this latest ecological horror story began to unfold. It remains to be seen whether any of Tobago's natural beauty, forest and wildlife will still exist in twenty years. My personal fear is that, as has happened in several other Caribbean territories, the island and its people will be sold out to the developers: truly a paradise in peril.

About the Author

Tim Bartholomew not only a tall novelist but also a reasonably wrinkly actor who is constitutionally unable to resist dragging up on occasion as Mimsey McWirter.

On TV recently, Tim has appeared on the BBC's *Doctors, Call the Midwife* and *Meet the Richardsons*, Warner Brothers' *Pennyworth* and Sky's *This England* (with Kenneth Branagh as Boris Johnson).

He filmed two movie roles in 2024: a country solicitor in *Christmas at Plumhill Manor* (starring Maria Menounos) and a comedy vicar for *Go Away!* with Hugh Bonneville.

In theatre he tends towards English gentlemen ranging from Captain Hook in *Peter Pan* to Andrew Wyke in *Sleuth*.

Tim has featured in about thirty TV commercials. Abroad he has appeared in ads for Twix and Richard Tea in Russia, Swiss wet-wipes, German yoghurt and both Austrian and Israeli chocolate brands. At Christmastime in the UK he has starred as Posh Santa for Marks and Spencer, a dotty Grandpa for ASDA and Scrooge for Curry's PC World.

Seasonally, he is to be found as Mad Santa in a grotto somewhere in Kent.

As a public speaker, he entertains large groups at gatherings of the University of the Third Age, Probus or Rotary Club, before or after dinner.

Tim is also a bird photographer. His pictures are on Instagram (@timbakerbartholomew).

His website is timbartholomew.co.uk.

Angel in Tobago is his fifth novel.

For background and inspirational material, and photos of people and real-life locations, please go to angelintobago.com

By the same author

Lessons in Humiliation – by Timothy Edward
Published by Matador Books

"The wit of the writing is absolutely sublime and made me continuously laugh out loud. Some writers just have a gift for seeing bizarre characters in an otherwise normal people and bringing them to life, and Edward has this gift. A novel based around the author's own experiences, it is heart-breakingly hilarious."

Goodreads

The Slave to Beauty Trilogy
Awarded a Readers' Favorite 5-Star Medal

Published by Deep Desires Press

I: Body Language

"If you're looking for a novel that's erotic, adventurous, and a true 'page turner' wrapped in language that fits perfectly in the literature box, Body Language would be your book of choice! Tim Bartholomew is highly skilled in the mechanics of story-telling."

II: Love Knot

"Tim Bartholomew ups the ante not only with the sex scenes, but also thrilling adventure. A wicked and totally unforeseen plot line clearly raises the bar. The characters are true to life and the eroticism exceptionally well described."

III: Casting Couch

"This trilogy is a must read for fans of eroticism, British humor, stories that don't belittle or demonize the myriad sexual relationships of humans, and more than enough thrills and mystery to keep the reader turning the pages."

LAS Reviews

Printed in Great Britain
by Amazon